The
SECRET

The
SECRET

ADRIAN MALONE
and STEVEN TALLEY
with Sharlene Belanger

Houghton Mifflin Company
Boston 1984

Library of Congress Cataloging in Publication Data

Malone, Adrian.
  The secret.

I. Talley, Steven. II. Belanger, Sharlene.
III. Title.
PS3563.A4322S4 1984 813'.54 84–3753
ISBN 0–395–35356–4

Printed in the United States of America

P 10 9 8 7 6 5 4 3 2 1

The words spoken by Jesus of Nazareth on page 88 and those
quoted by the Old One on page 88 are taken from *The Nag
Hammadi Library,* edited by James M. Robinson (New York:
Harper & Row, 1981), pp. 126 and 125 respectively.

To the children:
David, Sian, and James Malone
Jamie Holter and Michael Talley

Acknowledgments

Most people are all too familiar with the assorted collection of classical and contemporary books that have had a second life as a film and, more recently, as a television miniseries. Sometimes we even applaud the result. But how does one explain the genesis of a work that was first conceived as a television documentary on mythology, subsequently underwent a "sex change" into a dramatic miniseries for television, *in utero,* and finally emerged three years later as a novel? The answer: Mythology, Ltd. and Embassy Communications, Inc. A riddle? Not really. Mythology, Ltd. is a small group of private investors who chose to express their interest in mythology through financial support for the development of a television documentary. During this stage we decided to translate our research into a fictional drama. At that point Embassy Communications, Inc. stepped in as our second godfather, and the bible for a dramatic television miniseries was written. We then decided that, instead of submitting the bible to a network for consideration, we should send it to Houghton Mifflin. And therein lies the genesis of *The Secret.*

Behind each of the organizations that have supported this work are a number of individuals who took the time to criticize—in the best sense of the word: to advise, and to lend support. In particular I want to single out Dr. Stuart Brown of Mythology, Ltd.; Messrs. Norman Lear, Jerry Perenchio, Alan Horn, Robin French, Al Burton, Michael Weisbarth, and Ms. Kelly Smith at Embassy Communications, Inc.; and Austin Olney, Liz Duvall, and Helena Bentz at Houghton Mifflin Company. To all of them, a thank-you.

To one person who stands alone, Joseph Campbell, a very special debt of gratitude.

MICHAEL

ACTA GALACTICA

PLANETARY SYSTEM: G1 DWARF
SECTION: LIFE-SUPPORTING PLANETS
PLANET: 5–3–365

5–3–365 is one of two life-supporting planets in the G1 system. As on many other planets in many other systems in the Galaxy, conditions on 5–3–365 ultimately determined that a complex, technically intelligent, heterotrophic life form would predominate. And like similar forms in other systems, complex life on 5–3–365 successfully evolved a planetary civilization in the predictable phases: Crustal-Symbiotic, Invasive-Dependent, and, ultimately, Dominant-Free Will.

At the point, however, at which the final phase of planetary adaptation would normally have exhausted itself, and the life of 5–3–365 would have taken the routine step beyond the crude beginnings of mere planetary adaptation, it became apparent to the Galactic Consciousness that Planet 5–3–365 had become a highly dangerous anomaly in the galactic energy field. Something had gone wildly wrong with its evolutionary development. Only once or twice within multiple generations was its life form capable of producing even one individual with the genetic capacity to continue the successful course of its own evolution. (See this section, under Biographies: Jesus, Pythagoras, William Blake, and passim.) The overwhelming majority of the dominant species had mutated significantly and were rapidly heading down an evolutionary pathway that could bring the species only to stasis and extinction, and would in all probability pose a serious threat to the planet itself.

Worst of all, the interplanetary system of symbolic imprints, the umbilical cord of images through which the Galactic Consciousness links itself to developing life on all life-supporting planets (see, for example, the entry for 5–3–365 under Mythologies) and through which it guides that life through its early growth (as a parent guides a child's steps until the child can walk) had on 5–3–365 been all but extinguished by the epidemic of mutation. As a consequence, the Galaxy was no longer able to control the planet's evolution through normal means and bring it back on track. Faced with an emergency of unprecedented seriousness, the Galaxy decided to intervene.

I

The Giant

IN THE SPRING OF 1865 there was little enough to eat in the parish of St. Bran's, but no one thought to remark much on it, for not even the widow Corrigan, the oldest living human in the county (one hundred and two years old by parish records, one hundred and twenty years at least in the reckoning of those who knew better), could remember a year of plenty in St. Bran's. The parish, hidden in the mountains of the far southwest, was one of the poorest in all Ireland. The thin soil of those mountains lay over the bedrock like a threadbare blanket over a starving body. From the green patches where the earth's bones did not show through, the farmers coaxed crops of corn and wheat; but what little they grew their landlord took to sell in the markets of England, leaving his tenants only their own tiny plots of potatoes. At least in this year the potato crop, while small, had been healthy; the farmers had inspected the tubers, and finding them to be firm and white, had crossed themselves and given thanks to God. Everyone but the younger children remembered well the terrible year 1849, the last and worst year of the Famine, when there had been no potato crop at all in St. Bran's or anywhere else in Ireland. In that year the grinning dead lay unburied in their dozens along the parish roads, and the living walked through the fields in a hunger madness, clawing up the black, rotten potato roots, pulling at the very stones in search of a morsel. But rot and stones were all they had found in that cursed, infected soil, and many more had died — a full third of the parish in a single winter. After that, when the potatoes came up sound again, no one complained of a small harvest. But in the spring of 1865, while the horrors of the Famine were still vivid in their minds, a new calamity descended upon the people of St. Bran's.

Ever since the Famine, when Her Majesty's government had opened English ports to ships bearing American corn and wheat in order to bring more food into the country, the landlord of St. Bran's had been losing money on the grain his tenant farmers grew. To compensate for his losses he had raised the tenants' rents. But while the price of grain had been falling, the price of beef had been rising, and by 1865 it had at last become apparent to the landlord that he should long ago have converted his tenant farms into a single large pasturage for cattle. Conversion to pasturage meant that most of his tenants would have to be removed from their land, but there was no helping that. In any case, the majority of the tenants could no longer pay their rents and had become his charity cases, and charity, while undeniably a Christian virtue, was also an intolerable interference with the natural forces that governed a free market. His Honour the landlord believed strongly in natural forces. If they were allowed their normal course, the economy prospered. If men interfered with them out of misguided motives, the economy suffered. And, His Honour believed, in a prosperous economy a poor man who was willing to work would always find employment. But if, because of some natural disposition toward laziness (and so many of the poor had this disposition, which explained why they were fated to be poor), he was unwilling to work, then nothing could be done for him. Therefore, in the spring of 1865, just at planting time, His Honour ordered that the evictions begin.

Among the first to be evicted was one Padraic Devlin, whose farm was at the foot of the mountains on the parish's far western boundary. His Honour's men came early in the morning, when thick mists still lay on the mountains; they were almost at the Devlin cottage before Padraic, who was behind the house attempting to mend a broken plow, caught sight of them. There were four: His Honour's bailiff and three others, not of St. Bran's. If eviction was your business, you had to hire your help from the outside, for even during the Famine no man of St. Bran's could have been induced to do such work against his neighbors, for fear of his soul or of his life.

Padraic Devlin had striven faithfully to pay his rents, even hiring himself out on road gangs to bring in extra money. Only after the most recent rent raise had he fallen into arrears. When the evictions had begun he had not expected the bailiff. The shock of seeing him with his hired thugs drove Padraic to a double fury, an unthinking rage. He came at the four shouting curses, waving the wooden mallet he had been using on the plow. But the bailiff and his men rode their mounts around him until they had imprisoned him in a circle of horseflesh. Then the biggest of them grabbed Padraic's mallet arm, squeezing it white in his fist, and all four kicked their horses forward and marched Padraic backward to the cottage door. His wife had heard him shouting and was already there. Her baby, snatched up from the warm fireside and poorly clad against the mists, screeched to the heavens.

The bailiff and his men released Padraic and dismounted before the door. Over the baby's howls Padraic's wife began to plead with the bailiff, but he pushed her aside without a word and led his men into the cottage. By now Padraic had come to his senses and realized that against four he could do nothing. He brought his wife away from the door and stared hotly at the earth while the bailiff's men carried out his meager furniture and unceremoniously dumped it on the ground. When everything was out of the cottage one of the men brought out shovelfuls of burning peat from the hearth and threw them on the thatched roof. Burning the roof was an easy method for ensuring that an evicted tenant would not reoccupy his farm. The fire in the thatch would eventually ignite the large timbers underneath. When the timbers burned and the roof collapsed, the cottage would become uninhabitable, because it would be unrepairable. In the nearly treeless west of Ireland a poor squatter would be hard put to find timbers for a new roof.

The thatch was damp from the mists and smoldered for some time before it caught. The red glow through the mist attracted the attention of the Devlins' neighbors, who came running to fight the fire and then, seeing what it was all about, stood with Padraic and his family and shouted curses at the bailiff and his men. But curses did not mean much to those men, no more than a woman's pleading or a baby's cries; the men were paid well for their work, and they had come of age during the Famine, when more than one young man in Ireland had learned not to be too finicky about how he got a good day's pay. When at last the smoking thatch burst into flames they lingered only a moment, to make sure the fire had really caught, before starting for their horses. But then the bailiff, who had just taken hold of his brown mare's bridle, stopped.

"Hold," he said to his mates. "D'ye hear it?"

The men stopped and listened. Over the cacophony of cursing farmers, sobbing women, and howling babies, they heard it too — a new sound, coming out of the mist. The bailiff and his men exchanged a glance.

"From the high, sad sound of it," said one, "I'd say 'tis a farmer's dog, lost in the mists."

"It's not a high sound that I hear," said another, "but a low, deep one, a fine roaring like a great black bull that's been frightened by the fire."

" 'Tis the banshee," said the third, his eyes widening. "Someone here's t' die."

"Hush!" snapped the bailiff, annoyed at this superstition. "Can ye not hear that it's the voice of a man?" (But later, to the police, he avowed that no Christian man who had heard such an inhuman sound would ever want to hear it again.)

The bailiff walked forward, leading his mare by her bridle, staring at the gray wall of mist. He leaned his head forward, listening. It seemed to him that the weird sound was getting louder. It indeed began low, an angry roar, but it ended high, like a cry of pain. He was certain it was coming close, behind the wall of the mist. What sort of man-creature could make such a dreadful noise?

Suddenly the sun broke through the mist, dazzling the bailiff's eyes. The bridle jerked from his hand as his mare whinnied and reared. Thinking her panicked by the sudden burst of sunlight, the bailiff turned, a curse on his lips, to control her. But as he did he heard behind him the quick thudding of footsteps on the turf. He wheeled about and saw coming full tilt at him the largest human being he had ever seen, a giant who (as he later said) seemed to have burst from the rising sun.

The giant was a full seven feet tall (though the bailiff swore later that his height was at least ten feet), and except for an iron plate strapped to his breast, he was absolutely naked. His body was streaked with sweat and the black grime of mountain soil. His red hair, nearly the color of fire, flamed in tangles around his huge head. Behind him the sun rays diffracted through the mist into a kind of halo, a milky aura against which he stood out momentarily as a monstrous silhouette, black and faceless, charging straight at the bailiff. So fast had he run down the steep mountain slope that now the momentum of his great body was beyond his control and he waved his arms wildly, trying to keep his balance. From each of his wrists hung a heavy iron chain which swung behind his flailing arms.

The awful roaring came again from the giant's throat, and the bailiff's mare reared up and would have bolted had her master not gripped the reins with all his might. But the howling giant rushed past, oblivious of them. He ran straight to the burning cottage and somehow brought himself to a stumbling halt. Then he stood quite still, like a tree suddenly planted in the yard, and watched the cottage burn. The bailiff and his men also stood quite still, keeping a grip on their nervous horses and their eyes fixed on the giant. He was watching the burning cottage in an apparent state of deep emotion, his chest heaving, his huge hands opening and closing, his eyes wide and frightened like an animal's. It was now plain to see that his breastplate, which on his dirt-streaked naked body completed his resemblance to the painted warriors of the old Gaelic kings, was part of a crude harness. He must have stripped off his clothing for work. The heavy chains were the sort that oxen wore when they pulled plows through the fields. It occurred to the bailiff that Padraic Devlin must have sold his draft animals to pay his rents and acquired this monster to take their place.

Then one of the men, who had been looking closely at the giant's face, burst out: "By God, 'tis only a boy!"

The others looked again and saw that this was true. The giant's cheeks had never felt a razor. Probably he was no more than fifteen years old.

Padraic Devlin walked forward and laid his hand on the boy-giant's quivering arm. The great head inclined itself downward, the neck sinews swelling and rolling like ocean waves. Now that the giant was standing still, he carried out even this simplest motion with an exaggerated slowness, as though he had long since learned to make his slightest movement with extreme care, lest the force of his body accidentally destroy something nearby.

The giant looked at Padraic. The bailiff, watching, had wit

enough to detect in the boy's eyes what he alone had also detected in the roaring voice: an intelligence that lay hidden behind the ponderous, almost torpid movement of the massive body. Watching this enormous lad move, anyone could easily dismiss him as a moron, a monstrous mistake of nature. But he had the spark of a mind, and perhaps not a dull one, gleaming in his eye, and the bailiff saw it. And having seen it, the bailiff put his hand into the pocket of his coat and made sure that in all the commotion he had not lost his pistol.

Padraic spoke gently to the giant boy: "Be easy, Michael, be easy now." He kept his hand on his arm. The boy Michael opened his mouth to speak, but could not; some great mass of emotion seemed to be rising within him, too great to be forced through the narrow opening of his throat. Then the wind which had dispersed the mist grew stronger and shifted direction; it fanned the flames on the cottage roof and sent the smoke swirling downward, enveloping the people on the ground. Everyone looked up to see the roof timbers, cleaned of thatch by the fire, fall inward between the walls in a great shower of sparks. The bailiff's work was done: the Devlins were homeless.

The wind blew the sparks down and whirled them about the giant boy's head. The dancing sparks made his wild hair seem even more flamelike, as though it were a flickering wreath of fire woven of the sun. Again Michael slowly shifted his gaze from the burning cottage, but this time his eyes fell on the bailiff. The bailiff saw in them not the simple anger he had expected but a wild, helpless anguish, something powerful and inexpressible which Michael was nevertheless trying hard to express. The boy's eyes filled with tears; his body began to tremble. The great emotion inside seemed to be pushing itself out through every pore of him, like a mass of molten rock pushing its way out of the earth. The bailiff and his men stepped backward in alarm. Their horses edged away, prancing nervously as they might have done moments before an earthquake. Even Padraic moved away a little, still muttering, "Easy, lad, easy." But a moment later, with a great noise, Michael erupted. A deep animal cry of anguish and rage tore loose from his throat. His arms and trunk began to swing, slowly at first, then more violently, as his outpouring emotions overwhelmed him. It was not an attack on anyone, this flailing of arms, any more than the driving force of a steam engine's pistons is an attack; it was physical force moving physical mass. But when Michael's arms began to swing, the heavy iron plow chains began to swing with them, at the level of a man's head.

In an instant there was chaos around the burning cottage. Michael, roaring, staggered about, his great arms thrashing, the black chains flying behind. Padraic ran toward him, then quickly ran backward as a chain whistled near him. The bailiff and his men, their work finished, tried to mount their horses; but the horses, now thoroughly terrified, bucked and shrieked and would not be mounted. Obscuring all was the smoke of the fire, churned up into white billows by the wind. Through the smoke Padraic heard Michael bellowing and saw him reeling among the men and horses. He tried to keep him in sight, but the smoke stung his eyes and hid Michael from his view.

And then what Padraic had feared would happen, what he had run toward Michael to try to prevent, happened: one of the plow chains, swinging through the smoke, struck one of the bailiff's men on the side of his head. Without a cry the man dropped to the ground. Padraic ran to him and saw what he already knew, from the stonelike way the man had fallen: he was dead. Padraic stood looking down at him stupidly and wondering what to do, knowing full well that there was nothing to do, that all was lost. Then a frantic whinnying made him look up, and through the smoke he saw a horse collapse onto its side, crippled by the flying chains. The other horses had galloped off, there being no one to restrain them any longer. All three of the bailiff's men now lay dead on the ground, killed by the chains.

The bailiff was peering intently into the smoke, trying to get a clear view of Michael flailing about only a few yards away. He held his right arm straight out in front of him, and Padraic saw that the arm was bobbing up and down in time with Michael's violent movements, as though the bailiff were directing them or controlling them along an invisible wire. For a moment Padraic wondered why the bailiff was pointing so resolutely at Michael, until something glinted at the end of the pointing arm and Padraic saw that it was a pistol. With a shout he ran at the bailiff, but an instant later the pistol puffed and flashed and Padraic saw Michael jerk backward in midmotion and fall to the ground, the smoke of the fire curling over him like a shroud. The bailiff had fired pointblank into his chest. Padraic knew that Michael was dead. So he ran on at the bailiff, to kill him.

The bailiff was frantically ramming a new load into his pistol when Padraic came near him. With the ramrod still dangling from the barrel he pointed the pistol at Padraic's face and pulled the trigger, but the hammer lacked a fresh percussion cap and snapped harmlessly. In his fury Padraic hit the bailiff so hard that both men fell to the ground. The bailiff dropped the pistol; Padraic snatched it up by the barrel and brought it high over the bailiff's head, ready to crush his skull. But at that instant a voice cried, "Don't, Da!" and the sound of it broke through Padraic's frenzy so that he checked his arm and sat rigid, stunned, astride the whimpering bailiff. The voice was Michael's.

Padraic twisted around and saw Michael standing still in the smoke, panting and exhausted, as though some possessing demon had suddenly released him from its grasp and fled. Padraic stared at him in shock. Nowhere on his body was there any sign of a wound.

"Don't, Da," Michael repeated. Now that his raging fit had vanished the giant boy radiated a preternatural calmness, the sort of inhuman self-possession one senses in great stones or thousand-year-old trees. Padraic and the bailiff rose together, both staring at him. Padraic's wife and the neighbors fell silent and stared too. Everyone had seen Michael fall. The bailiff's shot could not possibly have missed. Could a bullet, fired pointblank, not penetrate his flesh? Or was it Michael's ghost that now spoke to them? Suddenly the bailiff felt disinclined to pursue the mystery further. With a hurried tracing of the cross on his chest and a whispered invocation of the protective powers of the Mother of God he was gone, tearing over the fields after his horse, without even glancing over his shoulder at the indestructible giant whose pursuing step he was sure he heard just behind him all the way to the road.

After the bailiff had run away Padraic walked over to Michael and touched his arm again, this time very carefully, as though he did not quite believe that his hand would not pass through a phantom. But the arm was real; Michael was alive. Padraic and his wife and the little crowd of their neighbors all knelt and crossed themselves. It did not occur to any of them (for the Irish are a superstitious lot) that the miracle of Michael's deliverance was attributable not to God but to the iron harness plate on Michael's chest, against which, in fact, the bailiff's bullet had shattered. But even if this had occurred to them, or been pointed out by some tough-minded realist in the group, all would have agreed that it was a miracle that God in his infinite foresight had so ordered destiny that Michael Devlin was fated to be wearing the plow harness that morning. And would they have been wrong?

For a moment the little group knelt silently around Michael, who stood staring uncomfortably at them, as bewildered as anyone else by his own survival. Then, looking up, Michael saw for the first time the sprawling bodies of three dead men and the crippled horse, lying on its side and breathing hard in its pain and fear. Without a word he walked to the horse and knelt. Slowly, gently, his huge hands lifted its trembling head, and softly he spoke into its ear. The Devlins and their neighbors could not hear his words, but they saw that as the animal heard them its trembling eased, its breathing slowed. It was something Padraic had witnessed dozens of times, this strange power his giant son had over animals, but it never had ceased to frighten him a little, and seeing it now he felt, as always the impulse to cross himself again, to ward off evil. Despite (or because of) his size, Michael had always been the gentlest of souls; but when his animal-power came over him his father had always caught a whiff of Satan's brimstone in the air.

Still cradling the horse's head, Michael brought his mouth away from its ear and looked into its eyes. The black pupils gazed back, impenetrable, solemn, inhumanly calm. The horse and Michael were now completely quiet. Padraic, edging nearer, saw that Michael's eyes and the horse's eyes had become the same, equally black, equally inhuman, as though Michael and the horse were not man and animal but brothers swearing some solemn vow. When he saw this, Padraic finally crossed himself.

For a long moment Michael held the horse's eyes with his. The animal gazed back, strong now, unafraid. With one fast blow of his fist Michael broke its neck.

With liturgical precision Monsignor Terence McLoughlin elevated three cupped handfuls of water from the basin to his cheeks, each time trying not to wince. This morning the washing water was icy cold, as it had been every morning at every one of his lodgings since he had left Cork. For a moment, as the first handful of water struck his face and he felt gooseflesh spread over his arms and shoulders, he succumbed to the temptation to wish himself done with this wretched tour of the west and back in Dublin. The iciness of washing water was not of itself enough to perturb the monsignor; he felt sure that he could have endured it with grace, in the ascetic tradition of the great spirituals of his faith, had his bedroom not also been so unseasonably, abominably cold. Nor would the breakfast which he knew from experience was about to be carried through the door behind him provide any warmth; the porridge was invariably tepid and gelatinous, the tea (as they called the black liquid served with the porridge) undrinkable.

Monsignor McLoughlin remained sulking in a lapse of zeal until he began the meditative ritual of shaving. Guiding the razor over his gleaming cheeks, he reminded himself that his mission to the west was an important one. In fact, he reminded himself more sternly, he had had to make a bit of an effort, thrust himself forward so to speak, to be selected for it. It was exactly the sort of assignment he wanted right now, because the archbishop was personally concerned with its success. If one of the archbishop's inner circle of ancients, monumentally secure in his position and power, were to accomplish it, the archbishop would be grateful; but if a younger man, relatively unknown in the archdiocesan hierarchy, were to succeed, the archbishop would take notice of him. So, he reminded himself even more forcefully, he had made good use of all the influence he had to ensure that Monsignor Terence McLoughlin had been chosen to carry out this important work of the church in the west. His success in it would answer once and for all the question (and he knew it was asked, and by whom) of whether the elevation of one as young as Terence McLoughlin to the rank of monsignor had been premature. And therefore, he told himself with Jehovan sternness, he *would* succeed.

By the time Monsignor McLoughlin had finished shaving, the forces of faith had rallied within him and dispelled the dark legions of doubt. He accepted cold porridge and undrinkable tea from his awestruck landlady with a dignified graciousness that bordered on the saintly. When breakfast was over he even made a point of gravely approving of the wholesome simplicity of her fare, a compliment that sent her into speechless rapture. Then he rose from table and punctually descended to the carriage waiting to convey him to his rendezvous with the squad of police hunting Michael Devlin.

But several hours later, as his carriage entered the village of Brandon, seat of St. Bran's parish, the monsignor was feeling out of sorts again. This was not from the jolting carriage ride (though it had been rough indeed), nor from fear for his own safety in a dangerous manhunt (for he was surrounded by twenty armed and mounted members of the Royal Irish Constabulary). At first the monsignor had asked himself whether the extreme poverty of St. Bran's parish was affecting him. On its way to Brandon the monsignor's detachment had passed through a landscape that was desolate indeed: treeless hills patched here and there with sparse plantings of wheat or a few scrawny sheep. What the local soil seemed to grow in abundance was stones. They were everywhere, an inedible bumper crop tumbled in piles. Here and there the piles were higher and covered with thatch, shaped by human design into squalid cottages. Occasionally, as his carriage passed one of these, the monsignor caught the watching gaze of a barefoot inhabitant, the meat of the eyeball a dazzling white against the black dirt on the face, the expression dull and dark, not the worshipful stare of landladies. But many more of the stone piles were uninhabited, abandoned by families evicted, or dead of the Famine, or fled to America. Sometimes there were whole villages of these roofless piles, returning slowly to the ground. The well-read monsignor had made the analogy to Sisyphus: purgatorial lives of labor spent piling up rocks that soon fell down again. But he had long ago accepted from Our Lord that the misery of the poor would always be with them; and poverty of the worst sort was to be expected in the west. It was something else that troubled Monsignor McLoughlin.

At some point early in his morning's journey a silly notion had begun to play persistently in his mind — the notion that he was no longer traveling in Ireland, a mere two hundred miles from his Dublin home, but had passed into some exotic, savage domain far beyond strange lands and seas. The monsignor had been annoyed with himself for thinking something so absurd, and he was even more annoyed when his mind, well trained in logic as it was, nevertheless continued to think it.

But not long thereafter he had encountered evidence that his fanciful intuitions were perhaps not entirely wrong. As his carriage bounced along the abysmal roads of St. Bran's parish his eye had been caught by something up ahead which he had assumed to be a milepost until, approaching it, he saw that it was an ancient standing stone monument of the heathen Celts, about eight feet in height. Carved into the top of this venerable stone, glaring down fiercely at all passersby, was a truly barbaric head, with baleful eyes staring wide and pupil-less and a fearfully scowling mouth. What had struck Monsignor McLoughlin about this heathen stone was not its antiquarian quaintness but the rather more startling fact that it had obviously been converted to Christianity — two stubby arms having been chiseled out of its middle to suggest a perfunctory cruciform shape. Now actively curious, the monsignor had asked the sergeant of constables to call a halt abreast of the stone so that he could examine it. Leaning from his carriage window, he had noticed further proof of the monument's Christian purpose: beneath the terrible head a rudimentary hand clutched a bishop's crozier. Monsignor McLoughlin decided that the head was a portrait of the parish patron, Saint Bran, clumsily rendered by some antique bumpkin who had lacked the talent or spirituality to portray the benign holiness radiating from the visage of one beloved of God. Suddenly it occurred to the monsignor that in all his years of ecclesiastical study he had never heard of Saint Bran. Who was he? A companion of the Blessed Patrick perhaps, one of the early faithful who had bravely stood by Patrick's side at Tara Hill on that Easter eve when he had silenced the howling Druids and converted great kings to the worship of Christ? Or a martyr of the monasteries, cut down untrembling in the serenity of prayer by a raiding Northman's sword?

The monsignor had been getting lost in such historical musings when he had noticed some of the dismounted constables sniggering and pointing to the bottom of the stone. Looking there himself, he had seen something that instantly quashed his curiosity about the identity of Saint Bran. The local attempt at hagiographic portraiture had extended to the saint's nether regions. The anonymous artist of old had piously endowed the blessed Bran with a gigantic phallus.

Monsignor McLoughlin had stared openmouthed at this obscenity for only the inevitable instant before yanking his head back inside the carriage like a frightened turtle retreating inside its shell. A moment later, to his vast relief, he had heard the sergeant silence the sniggering constables, remind them sharply in whose company they rode, and give them the order to mount. For the duration of the journey to Brandon the monsignor had glanced only rarely out the window of the carriage. Whenever he had, it had seemed to him that invariably he saw on the hillsides some other heathen stone, decorated with weird designs or hideously bare. But in his troubled mind he imagined that all of them glared down at him with the face of the monstrous Saint Bran, angrily wondering what outsider had dared to enter his domain.

And there *were* those on the hills who watched; but they did not wonder. From their fields and doorways the people of St. Bran's stared at the black carriage and its escort of mounted constables moving slowly along the roads. No one knew who was riding inside the carriage, though they guessed that he must be of the gentry, but everyone knew why the constabulary had come. In the two weeks that had passed since the burning of the Devlin cottage the police had already swept through St. Bran's twice in search of the murderer Michael Devlin. Each time they had failed to arrest him, for the simple reason that the giant boy had apparently vanished from the face of the earth. This at least was the sum of opinions the constables had obtained from everyone questioned, from the youngest children of the parish to Padraic Devlin himself.

But when the police had departed the people had switched from English back to their harsh native Gaelic and talked among themselves. There was no one in the parish who had not heard the story of the killings more than once, from a corps of "eyewitnesses" whose growing number threatened to match the total parish population. And there was little doubt in the minds of most that the story was absolutely true, because its details agreed so completely with certain things which, everyone now remembered, they had always suspected about the giant boy, Michael Devlin. For years it had been common talk throughout the parish that the Devlin lad was exceedingly strange. People whispered about his unnatural size, the odd, ponderous way he moved, the strange power he seemed to have over animals. But now the local gossips could also recollect with absolute certainty that long ago they had noticed some prodigious signs upon the boy. One swore that more than once she had seen on Michael Devlin not the usual ten fingers but fourteen, seven on each hand. Others agreed and quickly added that the toes on each of his feet also numbered seven. And in each of his eyes, if you looked when he was unaware of your looking, you could see the seven pupils, each set with seven brilliant gems. The signs were unmistakeable.

And now they were confirmed by the "eyewitnesses," who recalled the monstrous sight of the Devlin boy on the day of his fury. He had burst through the mists with streams of fire shooting forth from his head, which burned white with the heat of the very sun itself. So mighty had been his rage when he saw his home in flames that he had turned round and round inside his skin until his feet and his knees stuck out behind him instead of in front. From the top of his scalp a great shower of black blood had burst forth and confounded his enemies in a mist of gloom. And as he rampaged among them more signs had appeared. One of his eyes had hidden deep in its socket while the other protruded upon his cheek. And — most telling of all — at the moment of his triumph over the bailiff's men, his brow had blazed with the mystical sign of the hero's moon, a device of such fearful potency that it was dangerous even to describe it. So mighty had he been, so full of powers, that the heat of his body had melted the bailiff's bullet as it sped toward him. More than one of the "eyewitnesses" had actually seen the drops of cooled lead on the ground, before the constabulary took them away as evidence.

All of this was very wondrous, indeed miraculous, but not in the least surprising; for the people of St. Bran's knew very well whose signs had appeared upon the Devlin boy. "Cuchulainn" was the name they whispered to each other in the fields, by the hearth, at the pubs — Cuchulainn the Invincible, the Hound of the Forge, Son of the Sun, who as a beardless lad of fifteen had been the greatest warrior of Ireland in her ancient days of freedom, under the Gaelic high kings. For was it not Cuchulainn alone whose battle heat was such that he had caused three bathtubs of icy water to boil before his body cooled? And was it not Cuchulainn alone who even as a boy had entered battle in a frenzy so powerful that never did he return to himself until he had laid a hundred of his enemies lifeless around him on the ground? Cuchulainn it was, they all knew, who had tired at last of the suffering of his people of Ireland and had now come back to be their champion against the English and the landlords. It was he of the seven fingers and toes, of the seven pupils set with brilliant gems, who in his heroic heat — the heat of the sun itself — had slain the landlord's lackeys. And not until he had readied himself to come again to the aid of his people would the police know of his whereabouts, and then they would be very sorry that they did.

Throughout St. Bran's this was vehemently asserted to be the truth of it, and most vehemently asserted by those who knew the Devlins best and who had known the boy Michael since the day of his birth. There was much talk and much joy in the parish at Cuchulainn's return; some of the young men spoke of banding together as his companions in arms when next he appeared to strike a blow against the landlords. By their fires the grandparents heard this fine brave talk and nodded, their dim eyes smiling. But their thoughts were of an old, old law of the parish, older even than the time of Cuchulainn and the high kings — fairy law no doubt, the law of the trees and hills and stones: When life has been taken, a life must be given before things can again be set right.

It had been raining intermittently for several hours by the time the constables and the carriage halted in Brandon village. From the carriage window Monsignor McLoughlin saw shambling toward him, with umbrella aloft, the man he had expected to see: Father Francis Monagan, priest of St. Bran's parish. It pleased the monsignor to observe that Father Monagan exactly fitted his notion of a simple country cleric: short, aged, a crimson face knobbed like a harvest gourd, owl-tuft eyebrows of purest white, a small avalanche of snowy hair sliding wildly off one side of his head. *Probably spends a bit of time in his cups,* the monsignor thought, studying Monagan's alarming color. *Well, who wouldn't, out here.*

The carriage door opened. Monsignor McLoughlin assumed his

most dignified expression, the expression he adopted whenever he intended to overwhelm one of the lower ranks of Christ's service with the majesty of his office and the power of his person. Although the priest of St. Bran's was clearly some thirty years his senior, the monsignor was prepared for his hierarchical gravity to have its usual intimidating effect. Then Father Monagan poked his flaming face through the open carriage door.

"Well, well, Monsignor, welcome to St. Bran's! My goodness, such a long way for you to come and in such terrible weather. Come in, come in, and have a cup of tea."

Before he could pronounce his archdiocesan greeting, indeed before he could think of it, Monsignor McLoughlin found himself trotting through the rain, stooping awkwardly under the umbrella held by the much shorter Monagan, who hurried alongside, talking nonstop.

"Constables! Good to see you lads again. Cup of tea for you? No? Ah well, 'tis a miserable day to be about on the queen's business, or any other business, eh? Well, come round in a bit then, when Monsignor and I have had our chat, if you change your minds . . . Ah! Mind the step, Monsignor, watch now . . ."

Monsignor McLoughlin felt his elbow seized and lifted as Monagan hoisted him over an ancient stone threshold and plunged him into the absolute darkness beyond. Even the dim light of the rainy day was too bright to allow an easy adjustment to this abysmal gloom. The monsignor's shins banged against oddly protruding stones; his boots caught on the tilting edges of an uneven floor. Without Monagan's firm grip on his arm he would surely have sprawled on his face.

Then Monagan opened an inner door, and mercifully there was light in the pitch-black vestibule. The monsignor, his expression no longer very dignified, stepped into the pale twilight of the church of Saint Bran.

Father Monagan released his visitor's arm and shook the rain from his umbrella, continuing his pleasantries all the while. "I trust that His Grace the archbishop remains in good health. Though sure 'tis a grievous business that brings you here, 'tis an honor indeed that His Grace in his concern for us has sent such a distinguished —"

"Excuse me, Father Monagan." Monsignor McLoughlin was

pointing at the near corner of the gloomy nave. "What is that?"

Father Monagan turned to follow the monsignor's pointing finger. He saw that it was aimed at one of the stone corbels which bore the weight of the roof in the corner. On this ancient stone was chiseled a human likeness — human, that is, in its hairless head and ogling, popping eyes, its grotesque nose, and its crooked, maniacal smile. Its body too was human, except the legs, which tapered below the knees into the semblance of a broiled fowl's drumsticks. But Father Monagan guessed immediately that it was none of these anatomical features, unusual as they were, that had elicited the monsignor's urgent inquiry. It was rather the fact that beneath its wicked smile, between its drumstick legs, this female figure (for female it was) displayed the gaping hole of her sex, her hands pulling the lips of it wide apart, to maximum extension. Thus opened, she perched above the nave of a building consecrated to the worship of Jesus Christ, inviting, as it seemed, the entire congregation to enter her.

"Aha." Father Monagan cleared his throat. "Well, Monsignor, that is a little bit of a nothing that some in the parish like to call the Sheela — Sheela-na-gig, that's the whole of it. Ah . . . there's a little story told in these parts which relates how our own blessed Saint Bran met the Sheela of an Easter Day and resisted all her wiles before converting her to the ways of Our Lord . . ."

"Yes. Quite inspirational, I'm sure." The ferocious face of the phallic Saint Bran was glaring again inside the monsignor's mind. "Father Monagan, I believe we have important matters to discuss. The constables are waiting."

Father Monagan nodded gravely and led the way up the aisle of the nave to the altar, then right to the door in the transept that opened on his own rooms. The altar of St. Bran's was not the polished slab Monsignor McLoughlin expected to see but a great rough stone, crudely leveled, embedded not in the floor but in the earth itself. It gave the impression of having been in place for a million years before Saint Bran or any other human had arrived in the parish. From this rock a disturbing sacredness emanated — disturbing because it seemed to owe nothing to the Christian trappings that surrounded it. As he made the customary brief devotion the monsignor felt himself genuflecting to the rock and not to the rather obscure crucifix tacked up behind it. Remembering himself, the monsignor lifted his gaze to the cross, but he was immediately distracted again, for above the cross, dwarfing it, an enormous stone statue loomed at him out of the shadowy apse. Like the roadside monument, this statue was carved with barbaric crudeness from a single block; one noticed the stone itself, not the figure it purported to represent. But at its top, glaring down with its usual ferocity, was the frightening face of Saint Bran, with an arm beneath it angrily clutching a crozier. Monsignor McLoughlin noted with relief that in this conception of the saint the nether regions were entirely unrepresented. Nevertheless, a few minutes later, as he sat in Father Monagan's parlor watching the old priest pour his tea, he resolved that once the Michael Devlin business had been concluded he would initiate an inquiry into the purity of the Christian faith in rural western parishes.

"Well, now," said Monagan as he passed the monsignor's cup. "I presume from his letter that His Grace has taken a strong interest in our recent tragedy."

"Yes," said the monsignor, eager to get down to business. "And that is why I have come with the police, as his personal representative." (The monsignor wanted it understood from the start whose voice was speaking). "The constables have twice searched this parish unsuccessfully for the fugitive, Michael Devlin. On both occasions the local people refused to cooperate with them. His Grace has sent me to St. Bran's to convey his urgent wish that the people, and especially the clergy, of this parish render all possible assistance to the civil authorities pursuing Michael Devlin. It is His Grace's hope that the lad will soon be arrested and brought to justice."

At the word *justice* Father Monagan's smile widened imperceptibly. "Ah, Monsignor, it was indeed a terrible thing that happened here. I have known Michael Devlin since I christened him, and I always feared that his unnatural size would bring him to harm. Not that he ever had harmed a flea in his life before two weeks ago. But the poor lad was always a little odd, you know . . . queer notions always coming into his head. And now with all the sufferin' that we've seen out here, the Famine, and the people bein' turned out of their houses . . . But the truth of it is that when he saw the terrible thing he had done in his fit of madness,

Michael Devlin ran straight away from his family and fled along the roads without a word to anyone about where he was going. So you see, Monsignor, it's not really a matter of cooperatin' with the authorities. The people of St. Bran's are always respectful of His Grace's wishes. But there isn't a thing they can do."

Monsignor McLoughlin put down his cup. "Father Monagan," he said firmly, "let us review the facts of this matter. Two weeks ago a half-witted and probably deranged young man, a freak of unnatural size, murdered three men who were carrying out the right of eviction guaranteed a landowner under the law. Within twenty-four hours of this heinous deed the lad vanished. Now it is widely known that this giant boy is stupid and prone to hysterical fits of emotion. It is therefore highly unlikely that he is capable of forming a rational escape plan on his own. He has a family; he has friends. He has lived in this parish all of his life. He is a full seven feet tall and is therefore impossible to disguise. Now, Father Monagan — can anyone seriously expect His Grace to believe that in two weeks neither the boy's family nor anyone else in St. Bran's has seen him or helped him in any way?"

He waited for Monagan's answer, but the old priest only smiled, glowed crimson, and sipped his tea.

"Listen to me, Father Monagan." The monsignor's face had regained its look of dignified severity. "I don't think that the people of your parish understand the seriousness of this affair. Three hundred years ago the English queen, Elizabeth, sent her armies to Ireland with orders to treat the Irish people as they would so many savages, and in that time the land of Ireland ran red with the blood of her own. Two hundred years ago the English sent upon us the curse of Cromwell, a man so vilely wicked that he rejoiced to put the heads of our women and babes upon his sword in the name of his Protestant God. And one hundred years ago the English monarchy made the practice of our Catholic religion virtually a crime. Now — only just now — after these three hundred years of persecution, there are at last liberal forces in the English government which are prepared to consider what the English have ferociously denied since Queen Elizabeth: that we Irish are a civilized nation like any other and deserve to be treated as one. And now, just when the English are prepared to consider us as civilized as they are, to give us the rights of self-determination we have so long deserved, we in Dublin hear of landlords and their employees murdered in the west, of secret groups of hooligans training in arms by night, of emigrant armies in America awaiting a signal to invade! And worse, we hear these blasphemous, nonsensical rumors — yes, even in Dublin! — that the mighty, mythical Cuchulainn has appeared again as a giant boy in the far west to lead Ireland to victory against her oppressors! Now if there is to be some silly uprising of tenant farmers in this parish in the name of Cuchulainn, what, I wonder, will the English Parliament conclude from it?"

Monsignor McLoughlin felt himself heating up, and paused. "We know well," he said quietly, "what the poor of the western counties have suffered. His Grace has not been blind to the horrors of the Famine nor deaf to the cries of the wretched homeless. But the surest way, the *only* way, to relieve this misery is through the patient operation of civilized government. And we must first of all convince the English that we *are* civilized and can govern ourselves. So whatever he has suffered, however he has been wronged, the boy Michael Devlin must be delivered up to justice. Mark you, Father Monagan" — the monsignor rose from his seat and paced the floor in agitation — "Mark you, there can be no Cuchulainns appearing now in Ireland. We want no savages. If it's our savage past we show to England now, England will repay us with savagery tenfold, as she always has. Michael Devlin must be arrested. *Now, do you understand this?*"

For a few moments there was silence between the two priests. Monsignor McLoughlin stood looking down at Father Monagan. Father Monagan took a long, reflective drink of tea. The rain beat on the windows of his tiny sitting room. Through the windows the monsignor could see the constables huddled beneath a shed, awaiting him.

At length Father Monagan looked up and spoke. "Monsignor, when the people of St. Bran's parish look around them, it's not Ireland they see. They are simple. They see only the rocks and trees, the mountains and the springs. Maybe they believe a little too much in small blasphemies like the Sheela. But 'tis a harmless thing really, just a part of living near the soil. 'Twas never clearer seen than here in St. Bran's that the Lord God formed man of the dust of the earth. The high talk of governments means little to our people. They know what they have suffered and they know that they will suffer it again, without an end to it, as sure as the storms come every winter. And consequently it means much to them if a thing happens that gives them a little hope. What is proposed is that I ask them to betray their hope. If I asked it of them, they could not do it. And as I am one of them, and answerable to them as the shepherd of their souls, ask it I cannot."

There was another silence, a longer one. Father Monagan sat looking imperturbably at Monsignor McLoughlin. His face had deepened just one shade of crimson. Monsignor McLoughlin stood thinking. *But if some younger man, relatively unknown, were to succeed . . .* Finally he smiled a tight, grim little smile and asked: "And what shall I tell His Grace?"

Father Monagan caught the threat and rose from the table, smiling himself. "Pray tell His Grace," he answered pleasantly, "of the deep gratitude of our parish for his pastoral solicitude."

When Monsignor McLoughlin left the church he took the sergeant of constables aside and advised him to detail a few of his men to watch St. Bran's church day and night. "And if any difficulties should arise," he added (speaking on the archbishop's behalf), "you have our permission to arrest Father Monagan."

The day after the monsignor's visit Padraic Devlin went out into the mountains to fetch his son. After the murders Michael had hidden himself in a stone shepherd's hut tucked into the rocks of the mountain heights, too steep for horses and too remote for the eyes of strangers. Padraic found him where he knew he would, eating at a cairn a little down the mountain, where his family left him food. It was evening, rainless for once, the dying sun already down behind the mountains, the cold wind quickening in the pass. For the two weeks of his hiding Michael had done little but ask himself, over and over again, *How did it happen that I killed three men?* He had never intended to harm anyone when he saw his home on fire. He had only been dreadfully unhappy and had lost control of himself. The rest, he was sure, had been an accident; but he found it impossible to absolve himself of blame. His sensitive nature, which made his emotions so hard to contain, embraced all living things, the bailiff's men included. Although any of them would have slain Michael if he could and thought no more about it, Michael grieved without ceasing because he had caused their deaths. God's commandment not to kill had always seemed to him the greatest of all. It was hard for him even to help his father slaughter pigs (when they had had pigs), so deeply did he feel their suffering. And now he had violated God's greatest commandment and could not forget it. He felt fear as well, a terrible fear of the authorities, who would someday find his shepherd's hut and carry him off to their unforgiving justice. But why should they forgive him, when God surely would not? So he was thinking when Padraic found him. He looked at his father in silence, but with the still unanswered question in his eyes: *Dear Da, what shall I do?*

"Come on with me," Padraic said. "We've someplace to go."

The two of them walked down the mountain through the final melting of the daylight, avoiding the ridges that would show Michael's giant form against the sky. Then they kept on, now in the dark, across the valley bogs, which oozed rainwater like soaked sponges under their boots. Michael saw far to the east the few low lights of Brandon, the one light higher than the rest marking the tower of St. Bran's, where the patient constables waited to arrest him. "Where are we going?" he whispered to his father. But Padraic said nothing and kept squishing on through the bogs for what seemed to Michael another hour at least, until in the moonless night Michael had lost all sense of where they were. It was then that he saw an even darker patch against the dark, a shadow on the shadow of the night: a thick grove of trees against the horizon. There was no easy path through the denseness of this grove; Padraic and Michael ducked their heads and entered it with their arms up, pushing branches aside, protecting their eyes. But ahead of them a firelight was glowing, and as they got close to it Michael could see that it illuminated the faces of men he knew, men of St. Bran's. In their midst Michael saw Father Monagan. Then Padraic stopped abruptly and gave a sharp whistle. The men all looked in their direction, and one gave an answering whistle. Then Padraic and Michael stepped from the trees into the clearing around the fire.

As soon as he came into the clearing Michael understood that whatever was about to happen, he was to be the center of it. The men crowded around him in greeting, patting his shoulders, offering him pulls of whiskey from an earthenware jug. Michael noticed that most of them carried their scythes or pitchforks with them; a few had guns. He stood still in their midst, bewildered. Was there to be a fight? Suddenly these older men, these friends of his father's, seemed to be treating him as a hero or, worse, as a leader, for the simple reason that he had lost his senses and quite by accident bashed in the skulls of three men. He wanted only to be alone with Father Monagan, to do what he had most wanted to do since the day of the killings — to confess his awful sin and his terrible guilt to God.

Father Monagan saw the confusion in Michael's eyes and gently led him forward to the fire. The men arranged themselves in a circle around them. Then Father Monagan smiled up at him and spoke. "Don't be frightened, lad. A few of the men thought they'd best have their weapons about them in case the constables happened to drop by. We've all of us come here to help you in your terrible trouble."

At the sound of the old priest's kindly voice, the voice that all his life had calmed his fears, Michael's two weeks of brooding overcame him. "Oh, Father," he burst out, weeping, "I am so very sorry —"

"Hush, boy, hush." Father Monagan touched his arm. "In truth 'tis an awful thing to have the life of a man, even a wicked man, upon your conscience; for any life taken is a crime in the eyes of God and must be atoned for. So you must atone to God. And you must also keep free of the authorities who are hot in your pursuit. Therefore, I have decided to impose on you a penance of exile from St. Bran's parish, a penance that will cleanse your soul of its stain and keep your flesh safe from incarceration."

Michael stopped his tears and stood staring at the priest, his relief at the prospect of atonement mingling with his terror at leaving the only place on earth he had ever known. He opened his mouth to speak, but just then one of the men came forward with a ragged leather purse and placed it in his hands. Michael felt round lumps of coins inside.

"From your friends," Father Monagan said, smiling.

Now Padraic was coming forward with a bundle. Michael felt the fear growing inside him. Was he to leave this very night? Then he saw that Padraic's eyes were wet and shining, and he knew that he was. Padraic unwrapped his bundle and held up something round and metal that shone in the light in the fire. "Your inheritance," he said to Michael with a smile. In his hand was an enormous watch, a full three inches in diameter, its ancient surface tarnished to blackness. He must have dug it out from the ashes of their home.

"My father," said Padraic, "had this from his father, who had it from his. If it works I can't tell ye, for I've never used it for the time. But there's an odd device on it that they say has brought the Devlins what little luck they've had. Look here." Padraic scraped a little of the soot from the cover, and in the firelight Michael saw that there was indeed a very strange design engraved on it — a four-armed symbol not unlike the holy cross of Christ, but the four arms of the cross were broken and bent into right angles, so the cross gave the impression of whirling counterclockwise, like the pinwheel toys sold at country fairs.

"What is it?" Michael asked.

"I never did hear an explanation of exactly what it was," said Padraic. "But as I've nothin' else to give ye I want ye to take it along now, with whatever luck that's left in it." He wrapped up the watch again and thrust the bundle into his son's huge hands. Two tears were on his cheeks now, rolling down.

Michael experienced a sick feeling of everything moving much too fast, of his father, his life, everything he knew racing away from him in an instant of time. "Da," he said, but choking on the pain of it, he could say no more.

For a moment Padraic left his hands engulfed in Michael's; then he began to blink violently, and turning without a word, he walked quickly back to the group of men.

It seemed to Michael that if he began to cry he would never stop. With a grimace he bent his head to fight back the tears.

"Michael," the priest said gently, "you must go now, in the night, to avoid the police. Now listen carefully to me. There's never been a doubt in the minds of us that know you that you're a remarkable lad. You understand that 'tis more than your size and your strength that I'm speaking of. I'm saying that the odd way you have about you sometimes, with animals and such, is a sign of vocation, a sign that God has chosen you for something. And a sure proof of it was God delivering you from the bailiff's bullet. D'ye get my meaning?"

Michael nodded solemnly, trying hard to understand.

Father Monagan's face was glowing red as the fire, his wild white hair billowing up from it like a column of smoke. "Now in the old dark days of the heathen kings, before the blessed Saint Patrick brought our Christian faith to Ireland, there were idolatrous priests who knew how to bind even the strongest warrior — even a Cuchulainn — by a mighty oath, an unbreakable promise. There is a promise you must make to me now, Michael Devlin, one you must always keep, on peril of your soul. Promise me that you will find out what God intends for you to do. The exile I send you on tonight is not to be a mere wandering through the world. It is to be a search for God's purposes in creating you as he did."

Suddenly Michael was afraid again, but this time he was afraid of Father Monagan. The priest's gentleness had gone; he seemed to have become another man, a flashing dark thunderstorm of a man, as he spoke.

"Swear to me now, Michael Devlin, that from this night you will dedicate yourself to discovering God's plan for you. Swear to me that at every fork in your path, when you find a road that leads you closer to God, though it be the harder one — and I tell you it always will be, as it was for the prophets and the saints of old — on peril of your life, on peril of your very soul, you must always choose it. Swear it to me!"

"I swear it!" cried Michael, trembling at the force of the old man's words.

The promise given, Father Monagan grew gentle again. He smiled and muttered, "Good, lad, good," more to himself than to Michael. Then he abruptly turned away and called cheerfully to the group: "Gentlemen, we can't be sendin' this poor lad out into the wicked world without askin' a proper blessing for his journey!"

There was a murmur of agreement among the men, and then, pulling off their hats, they parted themselves into two neat ranks alongside the fire. Beyond the ranks Michael saw what the assembled men had blocked from his view. At the far end of the clearing, just at the boundary of firelight and darkness, a tall stone rose up, half-covered with slimy moss. Looking closer, Michael saw that the stone was a statue, the familiar image of a scowling man holding a crozier.

Father Monagan took note of Michael's stare. "Have ye never been into this grove before, lad? Well, 'tis not surprisin', really. Not many of the younger people know of it. But our older folk still remember that it's long been sacred to our own Saint Bran. And now that the constables are watching the church, we thought it best to bring you here to ask a blessing for you."

Michael nodded rather absently; all that seemed simple and clear. What was not so clear was why two of the older men had left the group and returned leading a fat old ram on a tether. Stranger still, when Father Monagan saw what they had done he nodded and asked everyone to kneel. Michael knelt with the rest to receive his blessing, still wondering about the ram, which stood placidly cropping grass by the fire, watching the humans begin their ritual.

Father Monagan took from Michael's hands the bundle containing the watch and, unwrapping it, held the watch aloft before the statue of Saint Bran. Michael heard him asking the saint to imbue the watch with his protective powers and to watch over its possessor and keep him from evil and harm. *When the blessing is over,* he thought, *I shall have to go.* In another moment he would be an exile, cut off forever from all he had ever known. What power in heaven or earth could keep him from harm? Father Monagan was droning on, asking Saint Bran to guide Michael Devlin always toward the fulfillment of God's inscrutable plan. For a moment Michael succumbed to a bitter resentment of the honor of his call. Inside the great body the not-so-stupid mind that the bailiff had noted was working its way methodically but persistently through the mystery of a divine vocation. Why would God have chosen Michael Devlin, a miserable sinner, a murderer, to carry out his plans? Surely God would not entrust the doing of good (for all his designs and wishes must be good) to a soul too weak to avoid evil? Since Michael had been a baby he had been told that it was the Devil who found sinful people useful. Then why had Father Monagan — but what were they doing now?

The old men who had brought forward the aged ram had kindled bundles of sticks in the fire and held them aloft, standing quite erect on either side of Father Monagan. Father Monagan was still praying to the statue of Saint Bran, but what he was now saying was quite unlike anything Michael had ever heard at Mass. "Life has been taken, life must be given. Accept our sacrifice of blood for blood, life for life. Let no unhappy spirit claim vengeance on this boy. Let the debt be paid; let the people be absolved."

Father Monagan gently touched the shoulders of the old farmers holding their torches at his side. Michael watched them leave their stations and carry before the saint's image a large wickerwork basket filled with straw and twigs. It was no longer fear and sadness that Michael felt; it was curiosity. He had already received his blessing. What was this? One of the men had untied the ram's tether and was leading it inside the wickerwork basket. He closed a door behind it, and Michael saw that the basket was in fact some sort of cage. Still holding their torches, the two men took up positions on either side of the cage. For a moment everyone was silent. The men knelt with heads bowed. Father Monagan stood still. The only noise in the grove was the crackling of fire in the wind. Michael, still on his knees, looked up at the old men's torches rippling in the breeze like fiery banners. He had just begun to think again of the burning thatched roof of his home when Father Monagan suddenly raised his arms high in supplication to Saint Bran, and the two farmers, in one solemn voice, called out: "Let the people be absolved!" Then Father Monagan lowered his arms, and on that signal the men dropped their torches into the wickerwork cage.

In a matter of seconds the straw inside the cage was blazing. The trapped ram bleated in terror and threw itself at the door until it scraped the flesh from its face; but then it too was all afire, and it collapsed into a jerking death agony. Father Monagan and the two old farmers piously crossed themselves and bowed to Saint Bran. Padraic and the younger men looked on uneasily, their hands fidgeting with their hats, as if they had known of such things but were actually seeing them for the very first time.

Michael was on his feet, staring with horror at the thrashing body of the ram burning alive. Then his animal-power came upon him, and his flesh became the ram's flesh, and he felt the flames burning into it. With a roar of pain he tore at his hair and clothes. In his agony he looked across the flames of the sacrifice, the ancient heathen sacrifice of blood for blood, and into the wide glaring eyes of the old stone god of heathen farmers, who demanded it.

For a moment — only a moment — he saw the statue's eyes blaze with fire. More than fire: they burned white-hot, hot as two suns, it seemed. Michael tried to look away from them but could not, and stood pierced by their horrible whiteness, which burned straight through him, into his very core, like the Devil's trident transfixing his soul.

Then he felt Father Monagan thrust the watch into his hands, and everything seemed to spin around in a whirlwind of smoke and fire. He thought he saw Father Monagan's face one last time, glowing red as Satan's in the flames of pagan sacrifice, and then he was alone in the dark, running as fast as he could down the old Cork highway, shivering with fear.

It seemed to Michael that for the next three days he ran without stopping. In fact, of course, he did not; he hid by day and walked fast by night, drinking stream water and eating wild berries, relying on his youth and his great strength to keep him going. But in his soul he ran. He was running away from what his simple Catholic faith could not absorb: the frightening thing he had seen in Saint Bran's grove, the inescapable knowledge that by his hand three men had died. In his deep confusion he clutched at one idea: he must fulfill his penance. But how? Father Monagan had made him swear to seek God's plan for him throughout the world. But the only "world" he knew was the one he had lived in; in all his fifteen years he had never once been outside St. Bran's parish. There was only one other place he had even heard of, and that was Cork, the great seaport that lay somewhere, he thought, to the east. To Cork, then, he would go. Whatever God wanted him to discover must be waiting for him there.

He hoped he had been following the roads correctly in the dark. At dawn of the fourth day he began to pass more and more houses and yawning, newly risen people — more, in fact, than he had ever seen together in one place. But he dared not ask anyone directions for fear of attracting attention to himself; his size alone had already been enough to make one or two people turn and stare. Finally he saw a stone milepost that read CORK. So he had succeeded in entering the "world." What now? Find a church and a priest to hear his confession. In the inviolable sanctuary of the confessional he could unburden himself to a learned man of God without fear of arrest. Perhaps the priest could even tell him what God wanted from him, so that he could get on with doing it and be absolved of his sin.

It occurred to Michael that it was as possible to hide oneself in a great crowd of people as in the lonely, empty hills, so he plunged into the human streams now swirling through the streets and let the torrent carry him onward, past buildings bigger than any he had ever seen and through streets full of houses stacked up on top of each other, three or four to a stack. Finally he saw what he knew must be a church, because it had a bell tower topped with a large cross, but in truth it looked more like His Honour the landlord's castle, being many times larger than Father Monagan's church and adorned with all manner of turrets and towers and great colored windows that sparkled in the sun. Nevertheless, Michael steered himself toward it until he was standing inside its cavernous interior, staring up openmouthed at a ceiling that seemed to him higher than the sky.

After an awestruck moment Michael recovered himself and looked around for a priest. He was relieved to see that the miles of pews before him were virtually deserted. There were only a few ancient widows busy at their devotions far at the front of the nave. One of these finished her prayers, left the pew and genuflected, and hobbled down the aisle. Michael stopped her as she passed. "Ma'am . . ." he began shyly.

The old woman, not much liking it, craned her neck to stare up at him. "What is it you want?"

"Ah . . . might there be confessions heard here today?"

The old woman shook her head. "There will not. Father hears confessions only once a day, before morning Mass, and that's been over with a good hour now. Come back tomorrow, if ye wish." She lowered her head and started on, but the look of deep despondency that had come over Michael's face at her answer made her stop and stare at him again with harsh curiosity. Just what sort of thing had this huge young man done that required immediate absolution?

The old woman's stare brought Michael to himself. "Thank ye," he muttered, and turned to leave the church. But as he turned Michael saw a priest enter the confessional. Or perhaps it was a monk of some sort; instead of a clerical suit he wore a long black robe with a hood that obscured his face. In any case he was a duly ordained cleric, qualified to hear confessions. Seizing his chance, Michael hurried into the confessional.

The dividing panel slid backward with a crack. Michael leaned forward toward the little ironwork grill. Suddenly he was afraid again, even in this sanctuary, of the enormity of his crime. At home, knowing that Father Monagan was listening, it had not been hard to unburden himself. But it was not so easy to walk off a city street and tell a stranger, even a priest, that he had murdered three men. Finally Michael swallowed hard and spoke. "Bless me, Father, for I have sinned. My last confession was two months ago. Since then I . . . I have taken the lives of fellow men." Michael stopped. In the ritual of confession it was now the confessor's privilege to ask more information of the penitent. But no voice came from the other side of the grill. For a few long moments there was silence, an absolute, unnerving silence, as if no one were there at all. Then Michael, not knowing what else to do, repeated himself, a bit more forcefully. "Bless me, Father, for I have sinned . . . I am a murderer."

This time a voice answered, but the sound of it nearly sent Michael out of his skin. It was not a human sound. There was scarcely a sound that it was like. It was the claw of a leopard in his eyes; it was the slash of a razor at his throat; it was a cup of acid thrown at his face.

Murderer! Your sin is pride, *my boy, not* murder. *Three insignificant people get their skulls broken because you can't control yourself and you beat your breast and call yourself a murderer. Well, you didn't kill those men. I did. You aren't of any use to me at home with Da.*

Silence again. Michael resisted with all his might the urge to run away. He was saved from slipping into absolute panic only by the fact that what was happening to him was unbelievable. The horrible voice, whatever it was, knew exactly what he had done. After a full minute of nerving himself he managed to speak. "F-father, who are you?"

The mocking voice lashed out at him again. *You're a good boy, aren't you, Michael? You want to do penance for your dreadful sin. Well, if you want to do what Father Monagan told you to do, listen to me. Every week a ship leaves Cork bound for America.*

*It sails today. Sail with it, or with the next one, or fly there on
the back of a bird. I don't care. Just go to America. And when
you get there, do not rest until you have found your Grandfathers.
Only they can tell you what to do.*

It was all so incredible that Michael had forgotten to be afraid.
"Who are you?" he whispered through the grill. "How do you
know me?" But the voice was silent. Michael whispered again:
"Father?" Nothing but silence.

Michael stepped quickly out of the confessional and stood before
the curtain on the confessor's side. Whoever this was, he had
only one way out. But no one came out. So Michael bit his lip
and did something he had been brought up never to do, on pain
of grievous punishment: he took hold of the confessor's curtain
and gingerly drew it aside. There was no one behind it.

Across the nave the old woman who had spoken with Michael
was lighting candle after candle before the image of the Virgin,
reflexively dipping and muttering in prayer, absolving herself once
again of all the spiteful thoughts that were her greatest pleasure.
Suddenly she looked up and saw to her great annoyance that
the same oafish young man who had earlier accosted her was
now standing between her and the Virgin.

"What do you want?" she snapped.

Michael's hat was knotted in his sweating hands. "Pardon me,
ma'am, for disturbin' you again . . . Did ye happen to see where
the priest went to after he left the confessional?"

The old woman's face wrinkled in anger. "D'ye not listen when
people talk to you, boy? I told you that Father hears confessions
only before morning Mass. I saw him leave the church a good
hour ago and he's not returned since. Now be off and don't be
troublin' me again."

For a moment Michael looked at her with the face of a man
who has suddenly stepped into icy water. Then he spun about
and almost crashed through the front doors of the church. The
old woman stood for a moment looking after him, shaking her
head. This young man was clearly burdened with either a very
great sin or a very small brain.

The panic that had sent Michael fleeing from the church did not
carry him any farther. Outside the church he simply stood still,

his mind numb. He was like a man who has just received a terrible wound but will feel no pain for several minutes, until the shock wears off. It was not yet possible for him to formulate a coherent thought about the unbelievable thing that had just happened to him.

After a while he began to walk, without any direction. He reentered the rushing torrent in the streets and allowed it to carry him along toward its common destination, the great docks that lined the river in the city's heart. On the docks he became vaguely aware that here were some astonishing things he had never seen before — ships. He had slowed down to examine one of them, marveling at the mystifying intricacies of its rigging, when a man's voice boomed in his ear: "Union Pacific Railroad! Strong men wanted, seeking adventure and good pay in America!"

The shout in his ear knocked Michael out of his stupor. He saw that he was next to a burly, bearded man who stood on a barrel, bawling his message over the din of the dockside crowds. Evidently he had made himself heard; a line of men stood by the barrel waiting to speak with his partner, who sat at a table with an open account book before him. Michael watched as the recruiter at the table handed each man a piece of paper, which the man signed. Then the recruiter entered something in his book, shook the man's hand, and sent him aboard the very ship Michael had been gazing at. She flew a stars-and-stripes flag and had the name *New York* painted on her stern. *Every week a ship leaves Cork bound for America* . . . Michael stood staring at the recruiters. Propped against the barrel was an elaborate sign. Michael read as much of it as he could. Apparently the Union Pacific Railroad Company wanted men to build a railroad that would go all the way across America. *Sail with it, or with the next one* . . . Michael was in the line; he was waiting his turn to speak to the recruiter. *Or fly there on the back of a bird. Just get to America* . . .

"Good God, look at the size of this one. What's your name, Goliath?"

"Ah . . . Michael Devlin, sir."

"So, Michael Devlin, it's work on the railroad you want? Well sure the railroad can use you. If all our crews were the size of you we'd be across the continent in a week's time, and probably

in China at that. Just a minute now . . . a few formalities . . ."
The recruiter was running his finger down a list. Michael read
its upside-down heading: FUGITIVES WHO MAY BE SEEKING EXIT
FROM THE UNITED KINGDOM. The recruiter's finger had stopped
next to a name. Michael saw that the name was his.

The recruiter looked down at the name on the list for what
seemed an eternity. Terrified as he was, Michael still had the wit
to see that the man was thinking something over. Finally he looked
up at Michael.

"Michael Devlin, can you read and write?"

This was not at all what Michael had expected him to ask. In
his confusion he stammered out the truth: "A-a little . . ."

"Are you *sure*, Michael Devlin, that you can read and write?"

The man's insistence so startled Michael that despite his fear
he suddenly stared him straight in the eye. The recruiter gave
him a very, very hard look. At last Michael understood what he
wanted him to say.

"No — I cannot."

"Ah. I thought not. Well, no matter — just make your mark."
The recruiter held up one of his papers that was covered with
small writing. In a space at the bottom Michael started to write
his name and then, catching himself, crossed it out and made an
X. The recruiter took the paper and made a new entry in his
ledger. Michael saw him carefully spell out the name "James
Walsh." When he had finished he held out his hand. "Good luck
to you, Michael Devlin. I'll tell you now that your crew boss
will be a happy man when he sees that big strong back of yours.
Off you go then, and get aboard. We sail with the tide."

In the evening, when the tide had risen, Michael stood at the
rail of the ship and watched the crew work her away from the
dock. Only now could he begin to reflect on what had happened
to him that day. A disembodied voice had spoken to him and
he had followed its command. He was going to America, to the
place where people went when their food or their luck ran out,
to find his grandfathers. But he knew where both of his grandfathers were; they were at home in St. Bran's, not in America. Then
who was he going to America to find? The ship was away from
the dock now, drifting into the river channel. Michael remembered

that the voice had come to him in a church confessional, and
had known who Father Monagan was and what he had said; it
must have been a good voice, perhaps an angel's voice bringing
guidance from God. But then why had it spoken in that frightening
way? Why had it mocked him so? And why in God's name would
an angel use him to commit murder? It was an impious thought
he was thinking, and he shied away from it; but it would not
disappear. The minions of Satan could seize his body and make
it kill three men; they could not speak to him inside the holy
sanctuary of a church. Therefore it was an angel of the Lord
who had boasted of his own . . . evil. But the sheer blasphemy
of this made Michael shudder, and he thought no more of it.

Some of the other men aboard had relatives and friends who
had come to see them off; a little knot of people stood on the
receding dock, waving, sobbing, shouting all manner of things.
Michael watched them for a moment and then suddenly burst
into tears. There was no one on the dock to see him off; his father
and mother didn't even know where he was. He was lost to them
forever, and they to him. Now, as the ship set her sails, his tears
flowed uncontrollably. Whatever he had known and loved — his
parents, his baby sister, the mountains of St. Bran's — lay behind
him, and ahead there was nothing but the grim ocean waves, dark
as the night, and unknown America beyond. For all of his great
strength he was suddenly a miserable, frightened, fifteen-year-old
boy, wanting more than anything to be back in the womb of his
childhood, before a charge of murder had thrust him into the
world of men. And it was just then, at the moment that his sadness
overwhelmed him, that he thought he saw someone he knew among
the crowd on the docks.

The man next to Michael at the rail was shouting a final cheery
good-bye to his mother when he felt a giant hand clamp his arm.
"What th — " he sputtered, but Michael cut him off.

"D'ye see him? There? On the dock?"

"Who? I see many people."

"Him! The priest!"

The man stared hard for a moment into the dimming light.
"Now look, lad," he said finally, "don't be daft. There isn't a
priest on the whole length of the dock. Now if you'll kindly let
go of my arm . . ."

Michael dropped the man's arm. A full minute passed before he could bring himself to glance again at the dock. But when he did look, he saw him again, plain as day, in the front of the crowd: a tall, faceless figure in a black hooded robe, come down to the docks to see Michael Devlin off to America.

2

The Shaman

AMERICA, THE UNKNOWN LAND beyond the waters, proved to be even more fantastic than Michael Devlin could have imagined it. New York was a city of vastly greater energies than Cork, a frenzied miracle of a place that seemed every morning to have doubled its size and pace overnight. After Michael had wandered its streets for a few days and had concluded that he could not be any more astonished by any other place as long as he lived, he and his fellow Irish were packed aboard trains and then riverboats and transported to the Union Pacific railhead at Omaha. From New York to Omaha was a journey of over one thousand miles. By the time Michael had completed it he had ceased to set any limits whatever to his astonishment.

Not even the ocean had awed him as much as the Great Plains. Michael stood at the edge of tiny Omaha and saw, stretching flat and level to infinity, enough land to swallow a hundred New Yorks, a thousand St. Bran's. But he was allowed only a moment of contemplation before the Union Pacific gave him a twenty-pound spike hammer and a berth in a monstrous triple-decker bunk car and sent him and his mates to build a railroad across infinity.

By the summer of 1866 the Union Pacific crew had laid nearly two hundred miles of track. Their work pace was already a legend. The Union Pacific bosses were the best engineers in America. Many of them had been officers in the armies of the Civil War, and they knew how to build a first-rate machine out of flesh and blood. They cut their hordes of Irish laborers into squads and drilled them relentlessly until they could lay two miles of track, on a good day five, from sunup to sundown. Light horse-drawn carts brought rails and spikes in quick relays from the supply trains to the head of the line, where ready teams of men rolled out the rails — five hundred pounds each — and ran forward to lay them on the ties. In an instant other men were kneeling between the unspiked rails with wooden gauges, spacing them exactly four feet, eight and one-half inches apart. When the gauge was fixed, the spike men swung their hammers — and the Union Pacific moved one rail-length closer to California. Before the spike men had finished another rail was in place ahead of them. Four rails a minute, four hundred rails to a mile, two miles a day, racing across the prairie to meet the Chinese gangs of the Central Pacific who were blasting a few inches a day eastward through the Sierras.

By the summer of 1866 Michael Devlin had become an efficient part of this most efficient machine, swinging his spike hammer with unerring precision, setting the rhythm of the work for the others. True to prediction, his foreman and his fellow workmen marveled at his size and his great strength. But at sundown, when the human machine dismantled itself into its weary parts, Michael's mates avoided him. Every night after supper Michael climbed alone to the roof of the gigantic bunk car, on which (following a common practice among the crews) he had pitched a tent for himself to escape the monumental heat and odor of the car's interior. Night after night the others saw the black mass of his body stretched out on the roof, gazing up at the clear starlight. In the dark the qualities that made him a marvel by day seemed suddenly sinister, unnatural. The tracklayers whispered among themselves. Had Michael Devlin not once been seen to take a single rail, all five hundred pounds of it, in one of his hands and bring it forward from the supply cart? Indeed he had. And had he not been seen more than once deep in conversation with the draft horses as they grazed alongside the train?

A certain faction within the crew — its rather more superstitious element — pointed to these facts as unimpeachable evidence that Michael Devlin was a demon giant, a fairy spirit who could summon dangerous powers at will and who kept animal familiars. But the majority of the tracklayers scoffed at such nonsense. They sided with the few of their number who had let it be known that they had heard of this giant lad back in Ireland. This group held that Michael Devlin was most certainly not a fairy spirit. Far from it — he was a dangerous criminal fleeing from the authorities. But this group's members had never succeeded in agreeing on exactly what crimes Michael Devlin had committed. At least a dozen offenses, from stealing a crucifix to mass rape, had been asserted, and the originator of each story was vehemently certain that his story was correct. But the debate continued unresolved, because resolving it would have required someone actually to ask Michael exactly what horrible thing he had done. And there was no one in the crew, including the foreman, who had the least inclination to do that. Everyone had seen what Michael had once accidentally done to a badly angled spike, a pound of solid iron, with a single blow of his hammer. They all agreed that the big lad seemed gentle enough; but perhaps some questions were better asked in whispers.

For his part, Michael was glad to be left alone. He had not fled from the home he loved for a tracklaying crew's companionship. He lay on the bunk-car roof and gazed into the American night sky, smeared with stars, and thought. For over a year he had been an exile. He had kept his promise to Father Monagan. He had followed the frightening voice that had spoken to him in Cork; he had come to America and was working his way from one end of it to the other. And for a year and more nothing whatsoever had been revealed to him. He had faithfully scrutinized his exile's life for some evidence of God's design, but he had seen only days of labor, nights of weary, deathlike sleep. He had waited for the mysterious Grandfathers to appear, but they had not appeared; nor had he received even a hint as to where he should go to find them. Since it had spoken to him in the Cork confessional the voice had been silent. Indeed, as time passed Michael had begun to doubt that he could ever really have heard anything so strange.

And yet there was something that did sometimes come to him, very faintly, as he pounded spikes by day and lay exhausted on the car at night. The others, abuzz with camaraderie, kept themselves from feeling it. It was the *indifference* of the American land, of land that had never been subdued. The railroad was about to transform America into what human beings were used to and took comfort in — land that served them, covered with towns and farms, cloaked in waves of nourishing wheat. But the tracklaying crew ruled an empire that was as yet only four feet, eight and one-half inches wide; the landscape around it, for thousands of miles, was entirely inhuman, with a face of its own. It was the awful outline of that face that sometimes came to Michael, and the profound indifference of its gaze frightened him and intrigued him and made him sure that someday he would learn in this country the things he had been exiled to learn. But when? And how?

So Michael was thinking, perhaps for the millionth time, as he lifted his hammer over a spike on a particularly hot late August day. But before he could swing, the hammer blow and his thoughts were arrested by a shout.

"Indians!"

In a matter of seconds the Union Pacific's railroad-building machine came completely apart. The parts reassembled into a little group of men that stood on the elevated roadbed and stared together into the oceanic prairie. Michael stared with the rest. Whoever had shouted had been right; riding at a trot toward the rail line was a party of mounted Indian braves. Someone was counting them: fourteen, fifteen, sixteen. There were over three hundred white men on the Union Pacific work train, and the train was liberally supplied with rifles. Nevertheless, as the Indians rode nearer, the tracklaying crew scarcely breathed. The Nebraska bands of the Sioux and Cheyenne were killers, and they hated whites. The winter before, the United States Army had paved the way for the railroad by attempting to exterminate them. Now the blood of their women and children was on the white man's hands, and the tracklayers knew it.

Most of the Irishmen in Michael's crew had never seen an Indian, but every day they imagined them lurking in vast hordes beyond the prairie horizon, waiting for revenge. It was the general belief among the crews that anyone who ventured alone out of sight of the work train was a dead man. The little parties of surveyors and roadbed graders who worked miles ahead of the train were heavily guarded by soldiers. Now sixteen warriors had suddenly appeared and were boldly advancing on the train. Unstated in the air among the railroaders watching them was a logical conclusion: if sixteen braves rode forward so boldly, there must be a thousand more behind them.

The crew stood paralyzed until an old plainsman who shot buffalo on contract for the railroad wandered up to have a look. He squinted at the oncoming Indians and then at the openmouthed, wide-eyed Irishmen, and began to laugh.

"Hell, boys," he said with a chuckle, "they ain't come to fight. They come calling on us. Looky there — Sioux don't fight in their fancy dress!"

And indeed the Indians were magnificently arrayed in smooth buckskins lined with porcupine quills and edged with dazzling patterns of brightly colored beads. They carried only bows and a few arrows and the short, decorated coupsticks with which they proved their bravery, by touching their enemies in battle. And braided into every man's long black hair, signifying a deed of exceptional courage, was the white-tipped feather of an eagle.

The Indians halted their ponies at a little distance from the rail line. Despite the hunter's reassurances, Michael and his mates continued silent and openmouthed, now from sheer wonderment at the sight of this splendid group. Then the old plainsman took the foreman firmly by the elbow and walked him down the roadbed and into the prairie. This was evidently what the Indians had been expecting. When they saw the two white men coming, two of them also came forward. Michael studied them. One, taller and even more splendidly garbed than the others, was clearly a chief. But when the two parties met in the prairie it was the other, apparently the chief's interpreter, who spoke.

Meanwhile, word of the Indians' arrival had passed down the line, and the head of construction, the General himself, had come up to take charge. The General had earned his rank on the front lines of the Civil War; he stood exactly five feet four inches tall and feared no man alive. The tracklaying crew parted ranks for him as he strode through to join the parley in progress. Once he arrived matters were quickly settled. The Sioux warriors and their chief were to be the honored guests of the Union Pacific for the day.

At a signal from the chief the Indians rode forward and dismounted. With the punctiliousness he usually reserved for visiting Union Pacific dignitaries, the General invited the chief to observe his tracklaying operation. Michael listened to the chief replying through his interpreter, speaking his unknown savage tongue. For a moment he thought of certain elders of St. Bran's whose English was so bad that they needed help from their grandchildren to speak with anyone ignorant of Gaelic.

As Michael listened he studied the chief's magnificent buckskin shirt. It was painted all over with rather gory battle scenes through which the chief rode, larger than life, lancing his enemies. Michael's eyes wandered over this curious garment, reading the record of the chief's mighty deeds, until they came to its right breast; there they suddenly stopped, and widened, as Michael fumbled in his pockets for his watch. On the right breast of the shirt was a very familiar design. Michael held up the ancient Devlin watch and saw that its cover design was exactly the same: the whirling cross, its four arms bent. He was stunned. How was it possible that this heathen savage could possess the Devlin family's own good-luck charm? But there it was, painted on the right breast of his shirt.

Michael decided to show the chief his watch and ask him if he knew what the strange design meant. But at that moment the interpreter finished conveying the chief's acceptance of the General's invitation. The foreman barked his orders, and Michael and his mates went back to work. They moved through their paces at a record clip to impress the visitors, but whenever he could, Michael kept his eye on the chief. There was now in Michael's mind a bond between himself and this utterly alien man — the bond of an astonishing mystery, the incredible possession of the same mysterious symbol by them both. In more than a year this was the closest Michael had come to recognizing a sign. But the chief was the General's guest, and Michael a common laborer. How was he going to speak to him?

When the tracklaying crew had spiked down a few rails the General led the chief and his braves on a tour of the work train. It had dawned on the General that the Indians' social call was not without its element of reconnaissance, so he made a special effort to show his guests what they had come to see: the racks of brand-new Spencer rifles lining the ceilings of the bunk car. The merest hint of shock flickered across the sixteen impassive faces when they saw the rifles, but the General noted it. He saw he had been right; the wily old chief had wanted to size up his enemy before he attacked. And the sight of the Spencers had accomplished just what the General knew it would; the attack was being reconsidered. But the General wanted to be absolutely sure that his guests appreciated his power. At the end of the work train were the four locomotives that pushed it westward. The General proposed that the Indians mount up and race the rearmost engine on their ponies.

A few minutes later the Indians were lined up abreast of the engine, chattering loudly to each other, giving out little whoops of excitement, holding back their restless mounts. The engine had been uncoupled from the train and sat placidly exuding steam. The tracklaying crews, all three hundred men, had dropped their work and stood in great bunches waiting for the race to start. Michael's eyes were still on the chief, who was riding toward the General to declare his braves' readiness to race. Michael had made up his mind that somehow, before the old Indian left, he would speak with him and show him the watch. A moment later he saw his chance. As the chief rode up, something like a wink or a nod passed between the General and the engineer. The engineer touched a valve inside the cab, and suddenly an enormous burst of hissing steam shot from the locomotive into the chief's path. His horse bucked in terror and nearly threw him. The braves' ponies caught its fear and reared wildly, dancing in circles. The Indians were wonderful horsemen and did their best to quiet their mounts, but the horses had never encountered a hissing locomotive and were truly panicked, as in fact were their riders, who had no notion whatever of an inanimate thing and believed the engine to be some sort of a great demon enslaved by the white man's power. The watching whites burst into laughter.

Just when it seemed that the Indians were to be unhorsed and humiliated, Michael ran forward from the laughing crowd and faced the chief's rearing horse. Its hoofs flailed wildly a few inches from his chest, but Michael put out one of his great hands and touched the animal's neck. The horse reared again and tried to move away, its hoofs again coming dangerously near, but Michael simply moved with it, keeping his hand in place on its neck, gazing calmly into its eyes. The horse did not rear a third time. It stood quietly and met Michael's gaze. Michael came closer and stroked its neck. He whispered into its ear. In another moment the horse was completely calm, and the braves' ponies, taking the cue, settled down as well. The white men stopped laughing and whispered to one another.

Michael stepped back and smiled at the chief. The chief looked at him in complete astonishment. A moment later he came to himself and beckoned for his interpreter. The two men spoke in Sioux and then the interpreter turned to Michael and said, "Kills Four thanks you."

Behind him Kills Four, the chief, nodded from his horse.

Michael replied, "Kills Four is welcome," and reached into his pocket for the watch. But at that moment the General came striding up, the model of dignified apology, and asked the chief to accept the honor of riding with him in the engine cab during the race. Kills Four had apparently had enough of the white man's demon; he refused to go near it again. The General, who wanted the race to go on and who was now regretting his little joke, insisted on doing him the honor of riding in the cab.

Michael stood to one side, apparently forgotten by everyone, his chance to speak with Kills Four fading. Then Kills Four pointed at him and spoke to his interpreter. Looking at Michael, the interpreter said to the General, "Kills Four will ride if this one, the giant one, rides with him. This giant one has power over four-leggeds. He can keep the iron devil from harming us."

The General saw no reason not to agree to this. Michael mounted the cab with him and Kills Four. In another moment the Indians had reformed their line and the rowdy whites were silent. The General pulled out his pistol and fired it into the air. The braves let out a whoop and shot forward on their ponies. The engineer put his throttle into reverse (the engine was facing the work train and could not be turned around), and the great machine started.

At first there seemed to be no race at all. The Sioux ponies easily outran the sluggish locomotive. In the cab Kills Four laughed with joy and beamed triumphantly at the whites, but as he did he felt the locomotive pick up speed. A minute later it was running at fifteen miles per hour, gaining fast on the Sioux. The braves kicked their ponies to their utmost speed, but the outcome was already clear. In another minute the locomotive shot past and left them in its smoke. Having made his point, the General could not resist one final joke, and as the engine passed the Indians he gave the whistle cord a yank. The white man's demon let out a fearful wail, and the frightened Sioux instinctively swung behind their ponies to protect themselves. Seeing their terror, the General and the engineer forgot themselves and burst out laughing.

Michael did not laugh. In St. Bran's he had learned the other side of humiliation, and he thought it a shame that anyone, even a savage, should be treated so. Because Michael did not laugh, Kills Four turned to look at him, sadness and shame in his eyes. When Michael saw that he had the chief's attention, he reached into his pocket and held up the watch. He opened his mouth to speak to Kills Four; but then he stopped. Something very peculiar was happening. It was high noon on the Nebraska prairie, but the engine cab had suddenly begun to grow quite dark.

For a moment Michael thought clouds were covering the sun, but there was not a cloud in the sky that day, and he knew it. The cab was almost lightless now, dark as deep twilight. Michael's hand, holding up the watch, began to shake. He realized with a shock that he no longer heard the deafening roar of the speeding locomotive. Had the train's boiler exploded? Was he dead? But he could still see the faintest outline of Kills Four's face gazing at him. He must not be dead; he must only be fainting. Everything was dark; everything was absolutely silent. Then, to his horror, Michael saw that Kills Four's eyes had begun to glow.

In another instant they flashed white-hot across the gloom of the cab, dazzling his vision, burning into his eyes. Michael gasped and nearly gave way to complete panic before he suddenly remembered whose eyes these were. They were Saint Bran's eyes. And no sooner had he realized this than a voice he knew knifed into him: *Clod! You have wasted your time and mine. Go with the Indians. Only they can help you. Only they will understand.*

The voice said nothing more, but the white-hot eyes burned even brighter, until they seemed to sear the back of Michael's skull. Michael cried out in pain and shut his eyes. The instant his eyes closed he heard the roar of the train again, and, startled, he opened them.

It was as though he had opened a door in Time. Everything was exactly the way it had been a moment before. The train was still running ahead of the Indians. The General and the engineer were still laughing. Michael was still holding up his watch. No one seemed to have noticed anything unusual at all. Only Kills Four was different. He was no longer sad and silent; he was talking excitedly with his interpreter, pointing at the watch. Stunned as he was, Michael hoped that Kills Four might be about to reveal something about the design on the watch. But when the interpreter spoke, he said, "Kills Four accepts your gift and thanks you."

"Oh — no, no," said Michael. "Please tell Kills Four that I don't intend to give him my watch. My da gave it me to keep, and I must keep it for a son of my own. I want to show him something — "

But Kills Four had understood the refusal and was speaking angrily to the interpreter. The interpreter said, "Kills Four says that you offer him a gift. You cannot now refuse it."

The General beckoned to Michael. Michael leaned his seven feet down to the General's five. Over the roar of the train the General spoke in his ear. "Look here, Devlin, give the old boy the watch. Make him happy. I'll send to Omaha for a brand-new one for you to give your son. That old clunker probably don't even keep time."

Michael straightened up to seven feet again. "No sir," he said quietly. "I cannot."

The General looked up over the two-foot difference and frowned. "Son," he said, "that's an order."

Michael saw himself blackballed from the railroad, jobless and destitute in Omaha. Then he saw his father in Saint Bran's grove, unwrapping the watch, his eyes wet and shining. He looked down at the floor of the cab. "I'm sorry, sir. But I can't be obeyin' your order."

For a long moment the General glared furiously up at Michael. But he was a practical man, an engineer, and he came to the practical conclusion: his best spike man was too valuable to lose over a gift to some savage. But then Kills Four would be left unsatisfied, and while he could not attack the train, he might still make trouble for the surveyors if by his code of hospitality he felt himself wronged. Someone had to give.

"All right then, dammit." The General ripped his own gleaming timepiece from his vest pocket and shoved it into Kills Four's hand. "Tell the chief," he said to the interpreter, "that the white chief is insulted that he accepts a gift from one whose rank is low. Tell him that the giant one's gift has no medicine. My gift is a chief's gift. It has big medicine. It is a gift from one great chief to another." But Kills Four was already turning the watch over and over, his hard, dirt-lined hands moving in wonder over its polished, spotless brass.

At the end of the day Michael watched with the others as the Sioux rode off into the prairie. At supper that night his mates, who had seen him calm Kills Four's horse with a touch of his hand, gave him an unusually wide berth. Michael said nothing to anyone. As soon as he could he climbed to the bunk-car roof to think. At last the sign he had waited for for so long had come, but now that it had he was terrified, not relieved. He now knew that the burning eyes of Saint Bran and the frightening voice of Cork, the voice of the hooded priest, were one and the same. Father Monagan's prayer, it seemed, had been answered. The saint, or whatever power it was that demanded blood for blood and that murdered and exiled men to achieve its ends, was indeed guiding him as he wandered in the world. And now, having killed three men, having torn Michael forever from his family, having driven him from green Ireland across the sea to the desert land of America, that power had spoken again. It had commanded Michael to leave his own race behind and dwell with savages.

For the rest of the night Michael lay awake on the roof, listening to the chorus of snores in the car below him and thinking everything over. It seemed impossible to him that a white man could live among Indians, whose ways were dark and unknown, who killed whites whenever they could and were killed in return. But there was no mistaking the voice's command, nor the burning power of the eyes, and there was no forgetting a promise made to Father Monagan — a promise always to choose the right path, the saint's path, the lonely, dreadful path to God. Whether the voice and the eyes that haunted him belonged to God or the Devil he did not know. Or perhaps he feared to admit what he thought, which was that only Satan could do such things as he had seen done. But God's voice or Devil's voice, God's eyes or Devil's eyes, Michael knew now, though he wanted so much *not* to know, that he must follow them. Toward the end of the night he climbed quietly down from the roof of the car. As the first line of light appeared on the rim of the prairie, he picked up the trail of the Sioux ponies through the grass and followed it.

*

Why are they coming back so soon? Kills Four asked himself. It was always at this time of the year, in the Moon of Black Cherries, that the buffalo herds began to move. It was time to be watching for them. When the Moon of Black Cherries came, Kills Four had moved his band to its annual rendezvous with the other Sioux bands along the Platte, where there was water for many. The scouts had gone out searching for the herds. The hunters had prepared their weapons; their wives had collected food and extra moccasins, and cut poles for the pony-drags from the cottonwoods along the river. The assembled Sioux, some two hundred of them, sat taut as new bowstrings waiting for the hunt to begin.

But when the scouts returned after a week they had seen nothing. The Moon of Black Cherries was now nearly past, and still no buffalo had come. Kills Four and the chiefs of the other bands had met in council to discuss the situation. They had agreed that the white man's road of iron was to blame, so Kills Four had taken his bravest warriors and ridden out to see the road of iron, to find out whether it could be destroyed. He had returned with the bad news that on the road of iron there were great wagons filled with white men and with guns that talked fast, as many of them as raindrops in a storm. And the white man kept a great demon on his iron road to work for him, an iron demon that ate fire and talked fire and was bigger than three buffalos and faster than the fastest pony. The council of chiefs heard this and sadly agreed that the iron road could not be attacked. That had been yesterday; this morning the scouts had gone out again. They had planned to ride even farther, to stay out longer in search of the buffalo herds; but now Kills Four saw them far in the distance, coming back to the camp.

"Why are they returning so soon?" he repeated, this time aloud, to his wife, White Horse Woman. She stopped work on the moccasins she was making and squinted into the distance. White Horse Woman was Kills Four's second wife, the younger sister of the previous one, who had died in childbirth; she was only fourteen, and her eyes were young.

"They have captured a buffalo calf," she said, "and they have taught it to walk on two legs, as I taught my dog."

"A buffalo?" Kills Four stood up and looked again. The four scouts had indeed captured something, which they had tethered behind their ponies on four ropes. Whatever it was, the creature *was* as big as a young buffalo, and it walked on two legs. For a moment Kills Four was completely baffled. Then he understood, and laughed out loud.

"It is not a buffalo," he said to White Horse Woman. "How can it be that they have caught the giant white man?"

It took less than an hour for the herald to make his rounds of the Sioux encampments, announcing that a captured white man, a giant, was in the camp of Kills Four, and that Kills Four had requested a council of the chiefs. By the time the tribal heads met outside Kills Four's tepee they were surrounded by virtually everyone in their four congregated bands. In the center of the crowded circle sat Michael Devlin.

"Tell him to stand up," Kills Four said to Yellow Bear, the interpreter, "so the people may see how tall he is."

Michael stood up on command. The rim of the surrounding circle gave forth a sound in unison, a gasp and a shout, a mingled drawing in and exhalation of breath. There was only one thought in Michael's mind, shouting itself to every muscle in his body: *Don't show them your fear.*

"We found him," said Yellow Bear, "walking alone in the prairie, just as he is. Little Knife and the others wanted to kill him right there with their arrows. But when we came close he called to us that he had a gift for Kills Four. I remembered that he had used his animal-power to help us, and that he did not laugh when the white man's iron demon was faster than our horses. So I told the others not to kill him. Now we have brought him to give his gift to Kills Four."

When he heard this Little Knife scowled. He rubbed the long scars on his right arm, the mark of a cavalry saber. "Yellow Bear is a woman," he snarled. "The giant one is a white man. Let us kill him now. When has a white man's gift brought good to anyone?"

"A moment," said Kills Four. He smiled at Michael. "You helped me, Giant One, and I thanked you. Now you have risked your life to bring me a gift. Again I thank you. What is your gift?"

When he heard the translation of this Michael fished in his pocket and brought out the watch. "This is my gift," he said, holding it up. "I'm ashamed that I'd not give it to ye before."

He had gambled that Kills Four would not be angry with him. Kills Four laughed and he felt a huge relief. But then Kills Four held up the General's watch.

"You know that your chief has already given me a fine golden jewel," he said through Yellow Bear. "Yours is black and dull. Your chief's shines like the sun. What shall I do with yours?"

The night before, on the bunk-car roof, Michael had worked out his answer. "Tell Kills Four," he said to Yellow Bear, "that my jewel does not shine, but sure it has great medicine in it, even greater power than my chief's, which shines so bright. Kills Four knows the sign of this power. It is painted on his best buckskin shirt. Tell him to look for himself and see if 'tain't also been carved into my jewel!"

Michael came forward and gave the watch to Kills Four. This was a greater gamble: that the odd design of the broken cross was more than just a decoration to the Sioux. Again he let go an imperceptible sigh of relief when Kills Four saw the broken-armed cross and looked up at him in pleased surprise.

"I have never seen this on anything a white man owns," he said. "I believe you. Your jewel must have great power, and I thank you for it. But you are a white man, and no white man ever gave me anything without wanting something for himself. What do you want of me, Giant One?"

Even now Michael hesitated before he spoke. This was the greatest gamble of all: that the Sioux would understand why he had come. *Go with the Indians. Only they can help you.* Michael took a deep breath and spoke.

"What I want is the honor of dwellin' in peace amongst your people. Yesterday in the locomotive I heard a voice tellin' me that the Sioux were people of great wisdom. The voice told me that from the Sioux I could learn things that even my own white people could not teach me. In return for my gift I wish to learn the wisdom of the Sioux."

As soon as Yellow Bear had translated this an uproar broke out among the Indians. Michael listened uneasily. A heated debate seemed to be going on. From the tone of voice Michael tried to get a feel for what was being said. No one sounded very pleased with his request, least of all the brave with the scars on his arm.

"As we all know, to our sorrow," Little Knife was saying, "the white man's treachery has no end. This is only another of his tricks. Leave this Giant One to me. I will fill him with my arrows and leave his body for vultures. This is all any white man deserves."

"Little Knife is right," said Walks At Dawn. This was bad for Michael; Walks At Dawn was one of the four chiefs in council and widely respected for his judgment. "A white man came to us and asked for our land; now it is his, not ours. A white man came and asked us for our buffalo; now it seems they are his, not ours. And today a white man comes to ask for our holy wisdom, for the traditions of our fathers, which have kept us always walking the good red road. If we teach him these sacred things, then they too will belong to a white man. And white men do not share; they only take. He will take away the sacred power of our traditions for himself, as his brothers have taken our land and our buffalo. And then we will no longer walk the good red road; we will walk the black road of sickness and death. Give the Giant One to Little Knife."

When Walks At Dawn finished there was a murmur of agreement from the younger men clustered around Little Knife. Counting coup on the body of an enemy so large would bring much glory to a warrior.

"But this Giant One is not like other white men," said Yellow Bear. "The eyes of white men are always shifting. They are the eyes of madmen. This one's eyes are quiet and deep. His body is calm, not restless like other whites'. And he has a mighty power over four-leggeds. He calmed Kills Four's pony with a touch of his hand and a look of his eye. I myself saw him do this at the white man's iron road. I think that his heart is sound, not like his brothers, who live only in their heads. I think he has the mountains and the sky in his heart, as we do, not the poison that his brothers have. I think he will not harm us. And perhaps his power can help us hunt the buffalo."

"His power is bad power!" Walks At Dawn shot back. "If what you say is true, he is an evil spirit. He is too big to be a human being; he is a demon, a monster. The buffalo are afraid of him and will not come to us as long as he is near. Kill him now and the buffalo will come!"

There was another, louder cheer of agreement. Kills Four sat silent, wondering what to do. He did not want to give in to Little

Knife and Walks At Dawn for the simple reason that he did not want the Giant One's ghost pursuing him. Who knew what other powers it might have? In fact, he was half-convinced that Yellow Bear was right. But the majority of the warriors seemed to be siding with Little Knife and Walks At Dawn; if he opposed them, the braves might simply override his authority, kill the Giant One, and leave his band. He could lose his power and acquire in return only a vengeful spirit. There was but one solution: the Giant One must go away. So he said, "Your gift is a fine gift, Giant One, but what you ask in return I cannot give. Go back to your own people. The white man and the Sioux cannot dwell as brothers. Go back to the iron road and leave us in peace."

This was exactly what Michael wanted most to do. Surrounded by angry Indians, he was suddenly sure that it *was* Satan who was behind all this. Satan had tempted him, as he tempted all fools, and led him into mortal peril. He would be fooled no more; he would go back to the railroad, and everything would be all right. But then he remembered the eyes in the engine cab; it seemed that they were looking at him now, burning his brain. He heard words come out of his mouth.

"Tell Kills Four that I'll not be goin'. A voice, a voice from God I believe, has brought me to the Sioux, and with the Sioux I will stay!"

When Yellow Bear translated this the warriors around Little Knife howled with rage. Michael heard Kills Four speak sharply to them, but he saw that they did not grow quiet. A violent argument broke out between Little Knife and Yellow Bear. Michael did not understand a word of what they were saying, but he understood very, very well what was being so hotly debated: his life. And he saw that on the side of the scarred warrior, the man who had wanted to kill him on the prairie, there were many, and on the side of the interpreter, the man who had saved him, there were none.

The braves had stood up now and were brandishing their bows. Their anger had spread to the crowd, which yelled along with them, drowning Yellow Bear's voice. Michael saw that the scarred warrior had an arrow in his hand and was looking hard at the chiefs. He seemed to be waiting for the signal to shoot. It suddenly came to Michael with perfect clarity, as though he had burst through clouds into sunlight, that he was about to die. For some reason this revelation was not in the least terrifying. It was calming; in fact it was almost soothing, and for a moment Michael took comfort in it, like a frightened child who has found its mother's arms. If God had led him here to die, then so be it. If it had been Satan, then death was his punishment for following. He had only one reflexive urge, the urge to cross himself and commend his soul to God, but even now, when it no longer seemed to matter, something in him said, *Keep still.* Then one of the chiefs who so far had said nothing rose and spoke, in a voice that was not loud but very firm. Even Michael felt the weight of its authority. When this man began to speak everyone, even the warriors, instantly fell silent.

The chief spoke very briefly. Michael could not understand a word of what he said, but the man's voice compelled him. It was the voice of a man you listened to in any language. Michael saw that something he said made the scarred warrior start with anger, but for some reason the scarred warrior was now keeping his anger under control. When the chief had finished he sat down.

Kills Four spoke through Yellow Bear to Michael: "Wolf Eye wishes to adopt you."

Michael's jaw dropped. *Adopt me?*

Yellow Bear was continuing to translate for Kills Four. "Wolf Eye," he said, pointing to the chief who had spoken, "has no wife. His wife has gone to the tepee of another. He needs a strong boy to do the woman's work in the buffalo hunt. So he wishes to adopt you. This is your choice, Giant One. If Wolf Eye adopts you, you may dwell with us. If you refuse, you must go."

Michael gave a long, long sigh.

"Please tell Wolf Eye," he said, "that I'd be pleased to be adopted." He looked directly at Wolf Eye and smiled, to show his gratitude. Wolf Eye looked back at him, and suddenly Michael found it hard to maintain his smile. In his benefactor's eyes was a look of pure hate.

The day after the excitement of the giant white man's arrival the scouts went out again, and this time they found the buffalo. Even after the white man's depredations the herds were still vast. Michael saw the golden prairie turn black as the bison covered it. For a week the Sioux hunted every day. Most of the men left the main encampment to stalk the herds and do the dangerous work of killing. The women followed them with their butchering tools, inspecting the arrows in the dead animals for their husbands' marks. When a woman found her husband's arrows in a kill she set to work.

Michael worked with the women, doing the chores abandoned by Wolf Eye's unfaithful wife. The Sioux thought this demeaning work for a man, even a white man. On the first day of the hunt Wolf Eye merely pointed to where the women were gathering and rode away after the herd, leaving Michael on his own to puzzle out the use of the elk-horn hide scrapers and the bone butchering tools. After he found a kill with Wolf Eye's arrows in it, he first spent a little time watching the women around him. They skinned off the hide, scraped it clean, and cut the exposed meat into portable chunks. Then they dug out the brains to rub on the hides to soften them and took out the savory liver to eat raw as a treat. Except for handling the great woolly hide, the process did not seem very different from the butchering Michael had done at home, and to his relief the buffalo was already dead and he did not feel its suffering. Michael set to work with his bone tools on Wolf Eye's buffalo and by the day's end had managed to reduce it to the very few of its bones considered useless by the Sioux. When Wolf Eye rode up he had packed everything neatly on his pony-drag, as he had seen the others do, and stood smiling, holding the pony's rope. Wolf Eye hit him as hard as he could across the face with his bow.

Michael gasped with pain and shock. Wolf Eye circled him once on his horse. He was shaking with anger. He lifted his bow again, and Michael brought up his arm to ward off the blow, but Wolf Eye did not strike him; he pointed the bow out across the prairie. Michael looked and saw among the white bone piles three black lumps — unbutchered kills. Wolf Eye was a very great hunter, utterly fearless, a dead shot with bow and arrow from the back of a galloping horse. He had killed four buffalo that day. His wife could have butchered that many kills in as many hours. Michael had been slow and left three in the sun. The day had been hot; the evening breeze already carried on it the stink of rotting meat. Wolf Eye sniffed the stink on the air, smelling his losses. Then he hit Michael again with the flat of his bow and galloped back to the camp.

Kills Four had also slain many buffalo that day; he had worn the Devlin watch during the hunt and was pleased with the power it gave his arrows. His heart softened toward the Giant One. The next day he told Yellow Bear not to hunt and sent him with White Horse Woman to help Michael. White Horse Woman showed Michael the things Sioux women learned from their mothers that made butchering faster. Yellow Bear told him about Wolf Eye.

"His name," said Yellow Bear, "is a name he gave himself, after a vision he had when he was a boy. No one knows what name his parents gave him. White men who traded with the Sioux killed his mother and father. He saw them die. He was a little boy then, not more than seven summers, so I am told. This was near the Greasy Grass. Lakotas found him wandering on the prairie. For all of one moon he did not speak. Then one day he said, 'My name is Wolf Eye.' But he didn't say anything else. There was an old holy man who was living with those people. One night he looked at Wolf Eye for a long time and said, 'You have had a vision.' 'Yes,' Wolf Eye said. 'You must perform your vision for the people,' said the old holy man, for this is what we Sioux do when one of us has had a vision — he shares it with the people, so everyone can benefit from God's words to him. But Wolf Eye said, 'No, I won't.' And he has never told anyone his vision."

"And why did his wife go and leave him?" Michael asked.

"Wolf Eye is a brave warrior," said Yellow Bear. "In battle he has never shown fear. I think there is no man braver among the Sioux. He is also, as you see, a mighty hunter. He could feed many wives if they would stay with him. But his woman could not live with him. He is a great chief, but he acts like a sick boy. He goes away by himself and lives many days away from his tepee. Once he spoke to no one for the days of one moon. His wife was eating well, but she was always afraid. Finally she left."

"Why does he hate me?"

Yellow Bear shrugged. "You are a white man. When Wolf Eye stood up in the council and said he wanted to adopt you, we did not believe him. No one among the Sioux hates the white man more than Wolf Eye."

Michael wiped buffalo brains off his hands onto the prairie grass. "But where I come from, if you hate a man, you don't adopt him."

Yellow Bear shrugged again. "Little Knife thinks that after the hunt is over, when he has used your great strength to do his woman's work, Wolf Eye will kill you. Little Knife says this because he wants to kill you himself. But Wolf Eye has adopted you. Little Knife cannot kill you now because you are Wolf Eye's family."

Yellow Bear was silent for a time, while Michael and White Horse Woman packed meat on the pony-drag. Then Yellow Bear said, "Giant One, Little Knife may be right. You may wish that you had walked away from our council and returned to the prairie. Little Knife would have followed you and killed you quickly with an arrow. Wolf Eye is a *wichasha wakan,* a great holy man, a shaman. He has traveled the spirit road many times; he speaks to the thunder-beings of the sky as I speak to you. He has strange powers that no one understands. When he has an enemy, that man does not know how he will die."

The Moon of Black Cherries waned; the Moon When Calves Grow Hair rose in the sky. The hunt was over. The Sioux had killed many buffalo; they would have much meat during the bitter winter to come. As usual, Wolf Eye had slain more than most, and Michael was busy from dawn to dusk. He sliced meat into strips and hung it on racks to dry in the sun; he stretched hides and tanned them; he gathered wood and fetched water and boiled meat in the kettle for Wolf Eye's supper. When Kills Four could spare her, he sent White Horse Woman to teach Michael how to dry the meat and prepare the hides. Wolf Eye never spoke to Michael, but if some drying meat was sliced too thick, or a hide was ruined because the blood had not been cleaned from it in time, or boiled meat was not ready when he wanted it, Michael felt the flat of his bow.

Little Knife began to tell people that the Giant One was losing his strength, that doing woman's work would soon make him weak as a woman. Was he not larger by half than Wolf Eye, but when Wolf Eye struck him did he not stand silent like a frightened girl? When Little Knife spoke thus Yellow Bear told him angrily to hold his tongue. If Wolf Eye struck *him,* would *he* have the courage to strike Wolf Eye back? But the Moon When Calves Grow Hair became the Moon of Falling Leaves, and Michael continued to endure Wolf Eye's anger. Yellow Bear, who came every day to teach him Sioux, explained to him that under Sioux custom he could simply leave, as Wolf Eye's wife had, and join the family of Kills Four. Michael nodded and thanked him and returned to Wolf Eye's tepee. Even Yellow Bear began to despair of the Giant One's courage.

But it was not cowardice that kept Michael in Wolf Eye's family. Wolf Eye's blows hurt him and angered him, but he had resolved to endure them. He had made up his mind to wait. When he had come to the Sioux, only Wolf Eye's intervention had saved his life. And Wolf Eye was a man who, like Michael, had visions, visions so dark that he never spoke of them. Michael was beginning to understand a little more about the business of following a divine vocation. He was beginning to detect the pattern in seemingly random events. He was learning to anticipate. From Ireland to America; from the railroad to the Sioux; from the Sioux to Wolf Eye, the man who had visions. The next sign would come from Wolf Eye. Whatever happened, with Wolf Eye he would stay.

One day, when the Moon of Falling Leaves was new, Michael was lugging water up from the Platte when he heard an unfamiliar sound coming from Wolf Eye's tepee. As was his custom, Wolf Eye was living a little apart from the main encampment of his band. Normally there was no sound at all around his tepee as he sat brooding inside. The sound Michael heard was high and chirpy at a distance, like little birds calling; he had no idea what it could be. But as he walked a little nearer he heard it again, coming in bursts from behind the tepee. It was children's laughter. Michael rounded the tepee and nearly spilled his water in surprise. Wolf Eye was sitting on the ground in his best clothes, at the head of a circle of little boys and girls. In front of every child he had placed a bowl full of the finest delicacies: raw buffalo liver, blackberry pemmican. The children were happily stuffing themselves, and Wolf Eye, the dreaded warrior who rarely spoke to anyone, was chattering gaily with his guests like a young woman with her mother. When Michael discovered them he had just begun to lead everyone in a merry song.

No one noticed the astonished Michael watching. Yellow Bear had told him about this. From time to time a mood came over Wolf Eye, and for a day he changed into a different man — a generous, jovial, utterly sociable man. On these days he delighted little children and dragged the people he usually ignored into his tepee for a feast. But the next day he was his usual self again, and no one dared to remind him of the day before. When he had heard this Michael had felt sorry for Wolf Eye, in spite of everything; suddenly he had seen that the man was lonely, that he suffered from some invisible wound which crippled his feelings the way a withered leg would have crippled his running. But in his moods, when he craved companionship as a man who has not drunk for days craves water, he seemed to be temporarily healed, and Michael had waited for a mood to come to approach him in friendship. Here at last was the chance.

The song was over; everyone was laughing. It was all so happily incongruous that Michael burst out laughing too. Wolf Eye looked up and saw him. He did nothing to acknowledge Michael's presence, but a few minutes later he loaded the children up with presents and sent them off to play. They ran away laughing and singing and waving good-bye to him, and Wolf Eye laughed and smiled and waved back. When the children had gone he turned to Michael. Michael laughed again and said in his awkward Sioux, "My heart is glad, Wolf Eye, to see you happy today." Wolf Eye stared at him for a moment, then vanished into his tepee. He came out a moment later with his war club in his hand.

Michael had not expected this. Perhaps Little Knife was right; perhaps Wolf Eye was going to kill him now. Why? A moment before, Wolf Eye had been happy. It was wrong, it was an affront to God, that a man should hate this deeply. Michael decided then and there that whatever the consequences he would not lose his life to a blindly vicious man. When Wolf Eye raised his club to strike, Michael reached out one huge hand and easily stopped the blow. Wolf Eye glared at him, his eyes full of hatred. Michael saw that if he released the club Wolf Eye would simply swing it again and again, until he struck. So he raised his other fist high in the air to break Wolf Eye's neck. But an instant later Wolf Eye had disappeared and Michael was lying flat on his back.

He struggled to his feet. It was not only Wolf Eye that had vanished; the tepee and even the main encampment were gone.

A great wind was blowing over the prairie, so hard that Michael found it difficult to stand. The earth and the sky looked the same as they had a moment before, except that they seemed to glow a little, as though they had haloes. And circling around Michael, its eyes glittering, its teeth bared, was a gigantic wolf.

Michael did not wait for the wolf to attack. He ran toward it to grab its jaws and pull them apart until they split in two. But after the first step he realized that he could not feel his feet hit the ground. After the second step he fell forward on his chin. The great wolf came closer and bent its face to Michael's. Michael tried to move his body, but he could not even feel it; his eyes and mind seemed to be suspended in air. He looked up at the wolf's wet teeth, its speckled red gums. Its lips flexed back into a grin, and a low rasping noise came from its throat. Growing delirious, Michael fixed his mind on this noise. It sounded to him like somebody laughing. Then suddenly everything was white; there was no more wind blowing, there was no more prairie, no more sky, no more wolf. Michael screamed in terror but there was no scream. And then there was no whiteness; there was nothing. Michael was dead. He was not even that; he was not. And then he was again, but where he was and when he was he could not say.

His first thought was that he had somehow returned to New York. He was on a street lined with tall, beautiful buildings topped with elegant round windows and fanciful cupolas. In the streets a mob of people rushed to and fro, along with . . . but Michael had no word to describe the other things that jammed the streets by the dozens. They looked like little wagons, but they acted like animals; they roared loudly and ran forward on their own, very fast, without any horses pulling them. They were impossible to classify. They bunched up together and pushed each other forward, braying loudly like cattle; but they had four wheels and carried several people each, like wagons. But wagons did not bear children, and these creatures had many; their little ones had grown only two of their wheels and raced madly in between their parents with people on their backs clutching their horns, hanging on for dear life.

And as if these unbelievable things were not strange enough, the people riding on them were like no people Michael had ever seen. Some of the men had almost no hair at all; others had hair as long as women's hair, or the hair of Sioux warriors, which they certainly were not. The women were all very thin and to Michael's great embarrassment many of them wore no skirts at all. When two of them brushed by him on the street Michael turned his face away. He caught sight of his reflection in a shop window. To his amazement he saw that he too had almost no hair and was dressed as these strange men dressed, in a matching jacket and pants made of some very fine, soft, bright blue material, a white shirt that was even finer and softer, and a dark blue necktie that hung like a rope almost to his waist. Even in New York no one looked like this. Where was he?

Michael took a few hesitant steps along the street, looking for some clue. The relentless crowds hemmed him in and he dared not step into the street, where the monstrous little animal-wagons ran by faster than racehorses. At last he reached the corner and saw a blue sign on the building above him. He spelled out its letters: M-O-N-T-P-A-R-N-A-S-S-E. What did that mean? The letters were English, but the word was nonsense. Michael looked around. A little hut next to him had a sign on it: T-A-B-A-C. More nonsense. But inside this little hut there were pages on display that looked like newspapers, and Michael bent down to look at one. At the top of the page he spelled out L-E M-O-N-D-E, and underneath it, to the right, P-A-R-I-S 24 A-V-R-I-L 1968. This was no help at all. Michael stood up and looked impatiently around the intersection, trying to find something that he could recognize. And he did. Gliding toward him through the crowds, apparently unseen by anyone but him, was the black-robed priest of Cork.

Michael stood in shock as the priest came nearer. The great black cowl obscured his face; Michael could see only a shadowy hole in its middle. Now the priest stood before him face to face. The seven-foot Michael rarely stood face to face with anyone, but somehow this priest matched his height. Michael felt a moment of sheer terror. Even now, when it was only inches away, he could see no features inside the blackness of the hood.

On a panicky impulse Michael grabbed the folds of the hood and opened them wide. The priest did not move. Michael peered inside the hood, but what he saw only increased his terror. The priest had no face. Instead Michael saw another world inside the hood, a flat plain like the Nebraska prairie, stretching to infinity.

A bowl of blue sky encircled this land, and in the center of it pulsed a shimmering white sun, unbearably hot, parching the cracked earth. Michael's eyes looked into the sun. It beat silently in the sky like a heart, and with each beat it grew larger and brighter, filling the blue sky, blasting the shadows from the earth. Then there was no more sky, only sun, only incredible heat, and the dry grass covering the land burst into flames. Michael's eyes burned; he felt his own face blistering, but he could not look away. There was no more city around him, there was no more priest, no more hood; rocks on the ground beneath him were melting, he was engulfed in fire. He knew only his own terror. From the depths of him, already disintegrating, came a rending scream . . .

"Sit up! Sit up!"

The voice was speaking Sioux. Michael was sitting upright, shaking, drenched in sweat. Every muscle in his body was locked.

"Breathe!"

Michael tried to breathe and could not; his diaphragm was rigid. He tried again, and this time, with a croaking, gasping sound, he succeeded. His muscles unlocked and he felt an unbelievable weariness. He slumped backward onto something thick and scratchy — a buffalo robe. Then a man bent over him, gently daubing his face with water. The man was Wolf Eye.

"Lie still, Giant One," he said quietly. There was not a trace of hatred in his face. Michael stared at him.

"Lie still, Giant One," Wolf Eye repeated. "The return is always the hardest." Michael's eyes widened. Return from where?

"Do you know where you have been?" Wolf Eye asked.

Michael shook his head, and managed to croak, "Do you?"

"No," said Wolf Eye, "but I saw you go. When you raised your hand to strike me I became a wolf. The wolf is my friend. His spirit is my protector. In my first great vision, when I was a little boy, the wolf came to me. Since then I have been a wolf as well as a man. When I live in my tepee I am a man, and I see with a man's eyes, but when I ride into battle or to the hunt, or when I am alone on the prairie, I am a wolf. I run with the wolves and speak their language, and I see with their eyes. And when I see with the eyes of the wolf I see many things that men cannot see. Today, when you lay before me vanquished by my power, I saw your spirit leave your body and fly into the sky. I saw you travel on the spirit road, as I have many times. Then I knew that you spoke the truth to Kills Four the day you came to us: you are a man who follows a voice from God, a man who sees what other men do not see — a man like me."

Michael was so tired that he could scarcely move his lips, but he fought to concentrate, to say the right thing.

"Wolf Eye . . . you are the man I have been sent to find. I have killed men, I have left my beloved family, I have crossed a great water. I have traveled many miles to find you. I have had visions, but I do not know what they mean, or who sends them to me, or whether they are evil or good. Wolf Eye, your wisdom is great. What shall I do?"

Wolf Eye was silent for a little while. Michael fought to stay awake. Wolf Eye seemed to be overcoming some final hesitation. At last he said, "You must go to ask the Grandfathers."

Michael heaved himself upright at the word.

3

The Vision

WHEN MICHAEL HEARD Wolf Eye speak of Grandfathers he forgot how tired he was and begged Wolf Eye to tell him who the Grandfathers were and how he could find them. Wolf Eye told him to go to sleep, and left the tepee. Within a minute Michael's exhausted body overpowered his mind, and he slumbered deeply, as deep as death, for the length of a night and a day.

When he awoke it was evening again. He saw Wolf Eye and Yellow Bear sitting near him in the tepee, eating supper. Michael smelled the meat and began to shake with hunger. He opened his mouth to ask for some, but only a croak came out; his throat was completely dry. But the Sioux heard the croak, and Yellow Bear brought him water and meat.

Michael ate for half an hour without stopping. Yellow Bear had to make several trips outside to the drying racks to fetch more.

When at last Michael had eaten enough and felt strong again, Wolf Eye spoke to him. "I asked Yellow Bear to eat with me tonight because he talks with your tongue. You have spoken of seeing many visions. Tell me what you have seen."

With Yellow Bear's help, Michael told Wolf Eye everything that had happened to him since the day of the murders in Ireland. He had never told these things to anyone, and even now, telling them at Wolf Eye's sympathetic invitation, it was hard for him to believe that they were real. But he left nothing out, from the night in Saint Bran's grove to the strange city and the terrifying conflagration of his last vision.

Wolf Eye did not interrupt him once, and even after Michael had finished it was a little while before he spoke. Finally he said, "Beyond everything that we see, beyond the earth and all its creatures, the wingeds which fly in the air and the four-leggeds and two-leggeds which walk the earth, beyond the sky and the stars in the sky, there is one Power, Wakan-Tanka, the Great Mystery. Wakan-Tanka is the Father of everything that exists; he dwells in the birds and the buffaloes and the blades of prairie grass, in the rocks of the earth, in all people. So he is many things, as many things as there are in heaven and earth. Yet he also exists beyond everything that exists; he existed before existence, and will exist after it. He lives beyond. He is One, unknown and indescribable."

"Who are the Grandfathers?" Michael asked. "The voice never mentioned Wakan-Tanka."

Wolf Eye ignored the question. "The voice you have heard, the voice of the thunderstorm, comes from Wakan-Tanka. The eyes that burn you are filled with his pure light. They are the eyes of the soul, the eyes that see what the eyes of flesh do not. I think the holy man of your village was right — Wakan-Tanka must want you to do something important. Otherwise he would not have spoken to you in the white man's world, where his voice is not heard. You are the only white man I have known who has heard it. And Wakan-Tanka has brought you to this people because this people knows him and walks in a sacred manner before him, ever mindful of his greatness beyond all visible things, which are only a pale reflection of him."

"What must I do now?"

"You must humble yourself before Wakan-Tanka. You must send your voice to him in a sacred way, as we do when we are seeking power and wisdom. It is *hanblecheyapi,* the rite of crying for a vision; and you must perform it day and night, without ceasing, until Wakan-Tanka sends you the vision that will give you the answer you seek."

"You said I'm to ask the Grandfathers," Michael said impatiently. "The voice told me to ask the Grandfathers. Please tell me who they are."

Wolf Eye frowned. "Be patient! *Hanblecheyapi* must be performed in absolute humility. A man is nothing before the greatness of Wakan-Tanka. It is when he knows this and becomes nothing that Wakan-Tanka hears his prayer. When you cry for a vision you offer your body for the hope of your soul: you hunger, you thirst, you are cold in the night and hot in the day. You live naked and alone, far from your friends, unprotected from wild animals and enemies, and all the time, day and night, you must never cease asking Wakan-Tanka for a vision. If you can endure all this with patience and humility in your heart, Wakan-Tanka will hear your prayer and bring your spirit to the Grandfathers. They are great spirits who live in heaven; they know the secrets of all things. Wakan-Tanka is the Grandfather of all the universe. Now, tell me: are you willing to cry for a vision, to suffer everything until the vision is granted?"

"I am indeed," Michael declared. "When shall I begin?"

Wolf Eye continued to frown. He looked hard at Michael. For a moment Michael saw the wolf's eye gleam in the twilight.

"Giant One," said Wolf Eye, "tonight your belly is full. You have slept for many hours. On the second night of *hanblecheyapi* your belly will cry for food, your eyes will cry for rest. You will hear a wolf howling for your blood and you will shake with fear. Be sure that you are ready, or in your pain you will curse Wakan-Tanka and bring his anger upon us both."

Michael looked back at him. "Did I not have strength and patience to endure *your* anger, Wolf Eye?"

Wolf Eye's frown gave way to a smile. Something like a laugh escaped from him. "In three days," he said, "we shall begin."

On the promised day Wolf Eye woke Michael long before dawn. Michael came outside the tepee and saw Yellow Bear holding horses.

"Where are we going?" he asked.

"To the Tall One," Wolf Eye said as he mounted up.

"Tall One? Who's he?"

Wolf Eye smiled. "In three days we shall see him."

"Three days?"

"Keep silent. Wakan-Tanka already watches you. Prepare yourself to speak to him."

The three rode through the day in silence. That day, and the next, they saw nothing but the prairie, but on the third day, at evening, Wolf Eye pointed to the horizon.

"Look," he said to Michael.

On the edge of the horizon mountains rose — a wall of them, at the limit of the prairie. The setting sun was behind them and made them black silhouettes, their ridgetops fringed with its glow. One of the ridges was higher than the rest, the highest mountain Michael had ever seen. Wolf Eye pointed at it.

"Behold. The Tall One."

Another day's ride and they were in the mountains. After nearly a year and a half on the prairie, Michael, a child of mountains, was enchanted by what he saw. In St. Bran's, and on the prairie, there had been trees only in little clusters along the rivers; here there were great forests, deep ranks of pine stretching into the sky. All around him rose peculiar formations of rock: turrets and battlements of it, like great castles; great waves and tumbling falls of it, like water arrested in motion. The rock was somehow vital here, imbued with life. As they climbed over the first ridge Michael felt himself passing through a barrier to another world, and when at last they halted in the shadow of the Tall One, which rose before them in a single mass above the trees, he was not in the least surprised to hear Wolf Eye say, "Here is the center. Here, in this place, the sky meets the earth. Here you will cry for a vision."

Wolf Eye pointed to a nearby hilltop whose crown was clear of trees. Yellow Bear got off his horse and without a word disappeared into the forest, heading up the hill.

"Where's he going?" Michael asked.

"To prepare the circle," Wolf Eye answered. "One must cry for a vision in a circle with a center and four directions. The circle is holy because it is the image of the universe. When Yellow Bear comes to the top of the hill he will make a hole in the ground in a level place." Wolf Eye picked up a stick and illustrated this by making a hole in the ground where they stood. "And then he will cut a long pole and place it in the hole. This pole is very sacred. It marks the center of the circle, the holy spot, just as the Tall One is the holiest spot, the center of the universe. Then Yellow Bear will pace out ten strides from the center pole in each of the four directions."

Wolf Eye expanded his diagram on the ground to show this. "He will place a pole at each of the four directions: north, south, east, west. He will make a bed of sage for you at the center pole, for if you fall asleep you must rest your head in a sacred position, because even asleep you must keep asking Wakan-Tanka for a vision. And then he will return to us, for the circle will be complete."

Wolf Eye completed his drawing. "Behold," he said quietly, "a circle and a cross: the image of all that is."

Michael studied the drawing. He seemed to see something else in it. In a moment he knew what it was. He bent down to the ground and with careful hands smoothed dirt back over parts of the circle until he had altered it into a slightly different design:

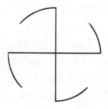

It was the design on the Devlin watch, on Kills Four's shirt. Michael stood up and looked at Wolf Eye. Wolf Eye nodded.

"It is the symbol of good fortune," he said, "of a universe in harmony. In the middle the center, the four quarters unified around it, and then the whirling boundary of existence. Beyond that there is only the Great Mystery, there is Wakan-Tanka. And for Wakan-Tanka there can be no image."

They heard movement in the trees and looked up. Yellow Bear was coming back.

"Good," said Wolf Eye. "The circle is prepared. Tonight we will purify your body, and tomorrow morning you will begin your prayer."

Wolf Eye and Yellow Bear cut branches in the woods and built a tiny hut. As night fell they kindled a fire inside the hut and placed rocks in it. The three men sat naked around the fire. When the heated rocks glowed red Yellow Bear sprinkled water on them with a whisk of sage, and in an instant the hut was filled with a fragrant steam. Michael breathed it in and felt it scorch his lungs, his eyelids, his throat. His body glowed; soon it was dripping wet. The air in the hut became unbearably hot. Michael could only breathe in gasps. In the dim light of the fire he saw Wolf Eye hold a black stone pipe over the smoking rocks. Then Wolf Eye held the pipe aloft. He closed his eyes and rocked from side to side, then began to sing, his voice low and harsh.

> "O Wakan-Tanka, our Father and Grandfather,
>   first and eternal One!
> A young man is here: Behold him!
> Behold a young man whose mind is troubled!
> Behold a young man whose heart is sore!
> He wishes to travel upon your sacred path:
>   He offers this pipe to you.
>   He offers his body to you.
>   Be merciful to him!"

Steam-seared as they were, Michael's eyes filled with tears.

The next morning was cool and clear, bearing the first snap of winter soon to come.

"Take off your clothes," Wolf Eye said to Michael, "even your moccasins. Before Wakan-Tanka a man goes naked."

Michael did as commanded. Yellow Bear gave him a buffalo robe for the cold of the night, and Wolf Eye gave him instructions on how to pray. Then Wolf Eye turned to the west and held the sacred pipe up to the heavens. Yellow Bear and Michael raised their right hands and Wolf Eye called up into the sky:

> "Hee-ay-hay-ee-ee!
> Powers of the world!
> Peoples of the heavens and the stars!
> All creatures that move in the universe!
> All the waters! All the trees! All the stones!
> All the sacred things that be!
> Hear me!
> Today this young man will send his voice to Wakan-Tanka!

He offers the pipe, he offers himself, he holds
  nothing back.
He asks to live in a sacred relationship with you!
May he have your blessing!"

Wolf Eye lowered the pipe and placed it in Michael's hands. It was time to begin. Holding the pipe in front of him, offering it to the sky, Michael walked slowly toward the hilltop. As he walked he began to chant, over and over again as Wolf Eye had instructed him, "O Wakan-Tanka, have pity on me."

Again his eyes filled with tears. This, too, was proper ritual, the display of complete humility before God. But Michael's tears were not ritual ones; nor was his prayer. If Wakan-Tanka did not hear his plea, if his wandering went on and its purpose was never revealed, if visions and voices came and went without a reason, he knew he would go mad.

When he reached the hilltop Michael found the circle prepared exactly as Wolf Eye had described it. Never lowering the offered pipe, never ceasing his prayer for Wakan-Tanka's mercy, he walked directly to the central pole. He began to pray as Wolf Eye had told him to. Facing west, he walked very slowly from the center to the pole at the western edge, all the while offering the pipe to the sky with both his hands. When he reached the western pole, he halted and called again as loudly as he could, to the forests and the mountains beyond, "O Wakan-Tanka, have pity on me!"

It seemed to him that his words came back to him, echoing off the face of the Tall One. But Wolf Eye had told him never to think, only to pray. Michael walked back to the center and then out again, to the northern pole; then back to the center and out to the east; then back to the center and out to the south; then back to the center and out to the west again. At each pole he sent his prayer to Wakan-Tanka.

The sacred circle was not twenty feet in diameter, but Michael took nearly one hour to make his first circuit of it, so slowly had Wolf Eye instructed him to move. And so he would go on moving, traveling with agonizing slowness from the center of his universe to its edges and back again, not eating, not drinking, not sleeping, and not thinking, only praying without ceasing to the Great Mystery until a sign was granted him.

Michael walked and prayed continuously for a day and a night. Toward the morning, returning to the center pole, he collapsed, still visionless, onto the bed of sage. He was sleeping when the first light of the rising sun struck the hilltop, illuminating the sacred circle while the forests below were still in shadow. The sudden bright light opened his eyes. They opened on the sky; directly above them, hovering in the silent dawn, was an eagle. Michael struggled to his feet. Wolf Eye had warned him to watch for an animal, even a tiny ant, who would bring him the first sign. Here it was. The eagle was a messenger that revealed by its silent presence that Wakan-Tanka had heard Michael's prayer. His heart leaping, Michael raised the pipe aloft in his aching arms and resumed his prayer, whispering it now through cracked lips. A few moments later the eagle wheeled about and flew soundlessly into the rising sun.

The next sign came at noon. Since he had seen the eagle at dawn Michael had pushed himself to keep praying. But his hunger and thirst and weariness, and the sheer monotony of the ritual walk, were breaking down the remnants of his will and his great strength. At midday, as he shuffled out for the uncounted time to the western pole, he stopped. His great body, its last energy spent, began to crumble toward the earth. Michael pressed his knees together and drew in his elbows to his chest and struggled to stay on his feet; one more time, as he teetered over the ground, his lips moved in prayer. Then he dropped to his knees and began to cry. In another moment he was weeping hysterically, his body heaving and gasping. But even now his fingers tightened around the stem of the pipe and kept it pointed toward the sky.

For a moment Michael heard nothing but his own sobs, absorbed into the dead silence of the wilderness around him. Then he heard something else, a low rumbling roar — the sound of distant thunder. Looking up, his raw eyes blinking through their tears, Michael saw his sign: a line of dark thunderclouds descending from the peak called the Tall One, drawing like a black curtain across the cloudless noon sky.

Michael gazed in bleary astonishment. Before he had time to be afraid the storm was upon him. Lightning flashed from the big black clouds and a crack of thunder boomed over his head. The sun was gone. Everywhere it was suddenly night. For a moment Michael could see nothing. A current of panic passed through him. Then the lightning flashed again, and he gasped. He saw that the eagle was hovering overhead, bobbing in the tempest, and he heard its voice speaking to him, inside his mind.

It is time, said the voice. *It is time. They are calling you.*

Three bursts of thunder exploded like bombs around the hilltop. The lightning flashed and flashed again, in clusters; it was light, then dark, then light again, then dark. Michael's eyes were dazzled by this rapid change. He became disoriented and thought he saw, when the lightning flashed, the peak of the Tall One moving closer to him. Or was he moving closer to it? The lightning flashed again. Michael saw the Tall One towering in the sky right over him, an infinite cliff, its peak lost in blackness. Then the light-dark-light-dark flashing grew very dim, the thunder grew quiet, and Michael looked down and cried aloud in terror and wonder. Beneath him, miles beneath him it seemed, he saw his own body sprawled in the circle on the hilltop, apparently lifeless. He thought to raise a hand to look at it. There was no hand; he had left his flesh below him on the earth. He was only some kind of spirit now, some kind of perceiving energy, drifting upward in darkness, miles above the muttering thunder and the lightning flashes, miles above the Tall One's peak.

I am dead, he thought. *I am a soul on its way to hell.* A new wave of panic overwhelmed him at the thought of eternal damnation. But then in an instant the darkness changed to light, and he saw the eagle again.

It was sitting on an outcropping of what appeared to be a mountain peak. Michael found himself standing on treeless, naked bedrock that seemed suspended in an infinity of sky. No land, nothing but pure blue, was visible below. To his even greater wonder, Michael discovered that he had reentered his body. He looked at the eagle again, hoping it would tell him where he was, but when he looked he saw that its eyes were the eyes of Saint Bran.

In another instant the white glow of those burning eyes expanded into an enormous aura, a blinding circle of pure light that enveloped the eagle. A second later the eagle was gone and the light had transformed itself into the faceless priest of Cork in his long black robe. Inside the shadows of the cowl the eyes of Bran were glowing, watching Michael.

"Who are you?" Michael whispered.

I am the Old One.

It was the voice from the confessional, no longer mocking but still very frightening — a voice that was no human voice but closer to the noise that great rocks might make, grinding each other under incredible pressure at the center of the earth. In spite of his fear, Michael had heard the voice and seen the eyes enough times to be a little bolder now. He had more questions to ask of the power that was driving his life.

"How old *are* you?"

Older than everything. Older than the earth. Older than the sky. Older than the universe. Older than Time.

Michael swallowed hard. "Are you Saint Bran?"

The eyes glowed; the voice said nothing.

"Are you Wakan-Tanka?"

The voice said nothing. An awful thought occurred to Michael. "Are you Satan?"

Michael had the feeling that at this last question something faceless inside the hood had smiled. The voice replied: *All of these are parts of me. They are names that men have called me.*

Michael was suddenly afraid again, afraid to anger this power with impertinent questions. Then he remembered that he was seeking an answer to the meaning of his life, and that without it he would surely go insane, so he asked again, *"Who are you?"*

The eyes flared up hotter, and Michael stepped back in alarm, his fear rising. He had pushed too hard. Wolf Eye had said: Approach in complete humility. He was about to beg forgiveness when he saw that the scene before his eyes had begun to change. The Old One's black robe had lost its depth. It seemed to be no longer a physical object but simply the color black, an abstraction of the mind which was now melding itself with the whiteness and blueness around it, entering into a flux of raw energy without form. The Old One, the mountain, and the sky lost their distinct shapes and disappeared into this vortex, leaving Michael staring in panic, wondering if he was about to dissolve too. Then something like a pattern of fire took shape in the flux, and leaped and sparked in lines and shapes; and at the same time, in rhythm with its movements, Michael heard the Old One's voice:

I am the part of everything that does not change or die. I am Spirit. I exist in everything — in animals, in birds, in fishes, trees, plants, a stone, a speck of dust, the universe.

As the Old One spoke the energy flux transformed and retransformed itself into configurations of nature. Michael saw a buffalo sprout into a tree, the tree shrink into a fish, and the fish explode into a galaxy of stars, like the expansions and contractions of a kaleidoscope. None of this made him feel any less afraid.

"What is this place you have brought me to?" he whispered.

The voice replied:

I have brought you beyond the center of the universe, beyond the meeting of heaven and earth. This place is anyplace; it is everyplace; it is noplace. You are outside of Time.

This was more than Michael could comprehend. Outside of *Time*? But the voice went on, while the scene changed and changed again.

Outside of Time all beings are one being. Outside of Time there is neither death nor life. Outside of Time Spirit is not trapped in Matter. I have given you a body, and confined myself in one as well, to shield your mind from what I really am, and where we really are, and what this really is, because your mind is a human mind, shackled in the bonds of Matter, and would not survive the revelation of their removal.

Michael understood absolutely none of this, but indeed it already seemed that in this incredible place his mind *was* reaching its limit. He anchored himself to one idea, to one unraveling thread: keep asking questions . . .

"Why have you brought me here? What do you want with me, Old One?"

Again there was that feeling of a smile.

Yes, Michael Devlin, I want something from you. I have brought you here because I have a little story to tell you — a parable, a myth. This myth is true; but it is not the Truth. I cannot tell you the Truth because the Truth cannot be told in words, and to you I must speak in words. If I were to take away the words I speak and these forms I inhabit and the human body I have given you, you would see all of me, everything that was, is, and shall be, and you would know the Truth; but your mind could not stand to know it and would disintegrate. And then you would be of no use to me.

Michael's fear rose, but so did his curiosity. For a long year and more he had asked himself one question, day after day, and now it would be answered. The voice went on.

The myth I will tell you is the myth of the Fall of Man. You have already heard it many times. Father Monagan told it to you. The Lord made the man, Adam, and the woman, Eve, and they dwelt happily in paradise until the Serpent brought them to Original Sin. But Michael, Father Monagan never knew the whole of the story. It is not a story of a man and a woman. It is the story of the Mind. For it is in the Mind, Michael Devlin, that humanity fell. It fell into Time. When humanity evolved, its Mind was the highest refinement of animal life, life suffused with an intelligence that at last knew itself and was conscious of Spirit. But the true meaning of the conspiracy of the Serpent and the woman Eve is this: the animal in the man, his older, darker self, conspired with his body to overwhelm the Spirit and plunge it into an abyss of darkness. The Mind forgot that it was Spirit. It perceived only what the senses perceived and confused Matter with Reality; and at that moment it fell into Matter, which is the prison house of Time. This was humanity's Original Sin. And since then the Spirit has lain hidden from a Mind that looks only outward, through the senses, and sees only Matter. Because the Mind, like the moon, has a dark side, where light, the foundation of Matter, does not shine; and in there, in your own darkness, where you fear to look, am I, the Spirit that you were evolving toward before you fell. In that dark half where I dwell there are no iron laws of Matter, and Time cannot rule; it is a small eternity, outside of Time, as we are now. And it is in that small eternity that every one of you is linked to me; I am in you, and you are in me. But since humanity fell, most humans have lived all their lives within the prison of Matter. Only rarely does someone catch a glimpse of me. It comes in the strange, half-understood, half-remembered hieroglyphs of a dream, or in the anguished echoes of an ancient myth, the myth of a fall from union with God into a timebound, deathbound world. In the night sometimes humanity cries for me. It yearns to regain its wholeness. It aches to be free of its prison, to be evolving once again toward its destiny, toward me. But Michael, in every generation evolution produces a few mutations, and these few have the capacity to leave their prison, if only for a little while. They can travel to the dark half of themselves and see with the eye that needs no light; they can leave Time and Matter behind and join themselves to me. They are the great holy ones, the great shamans.

They are the Grandfathers. They know the secret of who they are, and who I am. They are the ones I brought you to America, and beyond Time, to find. And now at last you shall see them.

Something very strange was happening to Michael. He had understood very little of what the Old One said, but when he learned that he was about to meet the Grandfathers thoughts came into his head, crystal-clear and cool: *I am excited. I am afraid.*

What was strange was that they were only thoughts. He *felt* neither excitement nor fear. An instant later he understood why: his body had disappeared. Emotions like fear and excitement required flesh to exist, and Michael was no longer flesh: he was his own spiritual consciousness, liberated from Matter, a wave in the ever-changing field around him. *I am terrified,* he thought, and felt absolutely nothing; and then he perceived that the flux surrounding him had grown solid again. He looked down and saw his body standing on earth. Confused as he was by the Old One's utterances, Michael understood this much: the Old One had brought him back into Time.

But *where* in Time was another matter. Looking around him, Michael saw an unfamiliar place. He was in a valley between low sand hills on which not a speck of vegetation grew. Above him burned a deep blue sky, cloudless, moistureless. Every drop of water in this land was concentrated in one place: a thin ribbon of river which trickled between thick bunches of trees and grass that clung desperately to its edges. And there, by the river, Michael saw a busy scene taking place.

Naked in the burning heat, gangs of men, their gleaming heads shaven clean of hair, were chopping a diversion channel out of the riverbank. They worked in two neat lines, swinging their digging-sticks in unison to their overseer's chant. Others scooped up the rich river mud in woven baskets and carried the baskets on their heads to a place where women molded it into bricks, which soon baked hard in the sun. Other men plastered the dried bricks together with mud. They were building a wall. Behind them rose walls already completed, and roofs, and a great tower made of stone, and before them, nourished by water already diverted from the river, grew fields of wheat in the parched desert.

Michael watched the laboring men and saw that their work had a rhythm to it, the machinelike quality that revealed planning and organization. It reminded him of his tracklaying days on the Union Pacific. The chanting overseer, naked too except for a white garment around his waist, was no taller than the Union Pacific's diminutive General, and he kept the human machine going as the General had, pacing to and fro, keeping his eye on everyone at once, interrupting his chant to yell and direct. But then Michael saw the difference: the man carried a long whip in his hand, and he used it with a will. On the stone tower stood larger men with stone axes — soldiers, ready to back him up. Then in his mind Michael heard the Old One speak to him:

Behold Cain, the Artificer . . . son of Adam and Eve, the first great revolutionary in history. Cain has invented the two pillars of all civilization: agriculture and the city. Nearly ten thousand years will pass between this moment and your time on earth, Michael Devlin, and in those ten thousand years Cain's revolution — civilization — will succeed beyond his wildest dreams. But his brilliant triumphs — his fertile fields, his surplus of food, his prosperous city — are founded on his hideous crime.

There was a stir among the men working at the river. Michael saw the overseer, Cain, stop his chant and peer at the hills on the horizon. Something was coming over the hills and onto the desert plain made fertile by Cain's efforts. It was an immense herd of animals — sheep, goats, and camels — and in another moment it had covered the plain, flooding over it randomly like a sheet of water. In the midst of this herd, not driving it but moving with it wherever it went, was a tall man clad in skins, with long graying hair and a flowing, untrimmed beard. Then the Old One spoke again:

Behold Abel, the Breath of the Desert . . . brother of Cain. He is a man of no substance, in his brother's eyes. He goes where his herd leads him. His eyes look inward; his mind is full of the knowledge of God.

Michael watched as Abel's herd overran Cain's operation. The animals browsed among the tidy fields, uprooting crops; they left their hoofprints in squashed mudbricks; they pushed Cain's workers aside as they moved, placidly, inexorably, toward the river to drink.

Cain was livid. He ran at the animals, shouting, cracking his whip, punching them with his fists, all to no avail: there were hundreds of them. Finally he stood before his brother, quivering, red-faced. Abel looked at him with a gaze of complete serenity, as though he was unaware that his herd had damaged anything of significance. Michael heard the Old One say: *You have heard the story of these two . . .*

Suddenly it seemed that time had passed. The city had grown bigger, more imposing. Michael was standing inside its walls, on a kind of plaza before the great stone tower. All around him the city's populace stood in ranks, looking up at the tower. Michael guessed that they were waiting for someone. A moment later Cain appeared at the top of the tower. Behind him stood Abel. Abel's look of serenity was gone; his calm face was sad and dull, as though he had been infected by some wasting disease. Michael saw that two of Cain's soldiers held his arms. Then Cain held something aloft for the crowd to see. It was a knife, its wicked blade chipped from obsidian, black and sharp as glass. The raising of the knife was a signal to the soldiers, who spread Abel's arms apart and braced his body with their own. Abel turned and looked at his brother's flushed, remorseless face and at the knife held high in his hand. He opened his mouth to speak; he seemed to understand. Then Cain drove the knife as hard as he could into Abel's heart.

Abel's body jerked forward at the blow; he was dead. The final spasm sent him over the tower's edge and he fell, turning end over end, to the plaza below. The black knife left his body in midair and shattered when it hit the ground. Abel landed on his neck, which snapped with a loud crack at the moment of impact. His body sprawled out behind his head, which tilted crazily, the eyeballs staring upward, the tongue lolling out. For a moment the crowd looked at him in silence; then they raised their eyes to the tower top, to Cain. Cain threw his hands aloft in triumph. His brother's blood stained them. The crowd below sent up a long, howling cheer. Michael turned away in disgust, but as he did he heard the Old One whisper:

The founding of civilization! Abel was the first Grandfather. He was a nomad, a wanderer, a man like your friends the Sioux, who live in harmony with heaven and earth and are bound only by the seasonal rhythms of the herds, because they know that in Spirit they are related to all things. Abel knew this; and because he did,

Cain murdered him. Cain murdered Abel to destroy the knowledge of Spirit, for no one who knows it can make war, as Cain did, against heaven and earth. And when Abel died the Fall was complete. The children of Cain saw only an alien planet of inert materials, of soils and minerals and metals, to be possessed and exploited. They knew only of distant, fearful gods, perpetually angry with them for their sins, placated endlessly by their priests. They knew no more of Spirit. When Cain murdered Abel he murdered one half of their minds — the loving, creative, mystical half, in which they knew themselves to be at one with all. Since the crime of Cain his children have known only the intellect, cold logic, which divides itself from the universe and then drives to conquer it. They have lived ever since estranged from Spirit, in terror of time and death. That is their inheritance from Cain; and they have not squandered it. They have gained dominion over the earth. But in every sad generation, a few of them hear someone calling in their dreams, and they yearn for the murdered Abel within them, and the secret that he knew.

Michael did not know how to respond to this, but he never had to; the scene before him was already beginning to break down. In another instant all was flux again, a field of energy without permanent form. Then the voice of the Old One spoke again:

The search for Abel's secret has been the search of all the shamans — the poets, the artists, the musicians, the prophets — all who hear his voice calling beyond the boundary of their senses. The shaman seeks to resurrect humanity from its Fall. But no one yet has succeeded, and the children of Cain, unbalanced by their estrangement from Abel, commit greater and greater crimes in their war against nature and each other. And here is the strangest thing of all, Michael Devlin: the children of Cain, because they are his children, fear Abel as desperately as they yearn for him. When any one of them comes too close to resurrecting Abel, to healing the Spirit they profess to hate, they kill him. Behold the second Grandfather!

The flux of energy solidified. Michael was back in Time. When he saw where he was and who was there with him, he dropped to his knees in awe. His fingers traced the cross upon his breast.

He was in Jerusalem, on the hill of Golgotha; above him were three crosses, and on them three bodies hung. Under the central cross a little group of mourners stood, carefully watched by Roman soldiers. Of all the moments of history, this was the one Michael knew best: the Passion of his Lord and Savior, Jesus Christ. And just then, even as he suffered on the cross, the Lord appeared before him. He looked just as Michael had always seen him in pictures and statuary: tall and lean, with long brown hair and beard, clad in a spotless white robe.

"Lord," Michael whispered, "is it your face I see before me?"

He had expected Christ to smile beatifically, as he did in so many of his portraits. Michael was rather taken aback when instead the Son of God gave him a look of pure annoyance.

"Do you think you know my face?" he said. "You do not. You know only this one face, a face given me by the men who built their empire in my name." He paused, and then he did smile at Michael, but his smile was not beatific. "I will show you," he said, "the true number of my faces." And suddenly the scene behind him was no longer the hill of Golgotha.

Once again Michael did not know where he was. He seemed to have been transported to the gleaming marble courtyard of some large and ancient building. But somehow the cross on which the suffering Jesus hung had been transported too, for it was still before him, or so it seemed. Then Michael saw that what stood before him was not exactly the cross; it was a pine tree, its branches pruned but still intact and swathed in wreaths of violets. And tied to the trunk was what made the tree resemble a crucifix: the stuffed straw effigy of a young man, spattered with caked blood, head drooping as in death. As Michael contemplated what appeared to be a bizarre parody of his faith, he heard someone softly call his name. He turned and saw that Jesus stood next to him. Immediately he dropped again to his knees and clasped his hands in reverence, eyes fixed on the ground, as he had been taught to worship. But after a moment, when nothing seemed to be happening, he timidly raised his glance a little to meet his Savior's, and then his head snapped erect in shock.

The Son of God had transformed himself into a woman. His beard had fallen out, his long hair was hidden inside an elaborate veil, and his robe had changed into a sleeveless pleated dress that fell to his feet. On his breast hung the golden image of a woman on a throne.

"L-Lord." Michael gasped. "You are a . . . a . . . ?"

The transformed Jesus laughed. "Not a woman . . . but not a man either. My real nature is neither male nor female, but divine. I am a god — surely you remember that? And there I am, you see, enduring my Passion, giving my life for the world." He pointed to the gore-stained dummy hanging on the tree.

"B-but . . ."

"My worshipers, however, do not call me Jesus, or the Christ. They *do* call me the Good Shepherd, or, more accurately, the Handsome One. For I am Attis, the beautiful boy of Phrygia, darling of the great goddess Cybele, her lover and, many say, her son. You and I are standing in the city of Rome, in the reign of the emperor Claudius. The man known as Jesus of Nazareth was crucified not twenty years ago. His followers are a tiny fringe sect of Judaism, despised by the empire. But Claudius has just incorporated the rites of Attis into the official religion of the state, and those rites are already ten thousand years old, and more . . ."

Michael stood up and seized the simpering, smooth-cheeked creature beside him by the shoulder. Under the woman's clothing he could feel the bony hardness of a man.

"I don't care who ye are," he said angrily, "I'll not hear such things about my Lord and Savior Jesus Christ."

The creature did not move; he only smiled. But Michael felt a searing pain shoot up his arm. He fell to his knees again. Attis looked down at him, still smiling.

"But Michael, I *am* your Lord. You have worshiped me every year of your life, for my rites have always been a part of your religion."

With his good hand Michael kneaded his aching arm. He dared say nothing more, but he gave Attis a miserable, puzzled look. Attis smiled a pitying smile and went on.

"I was born of a virgin, sired miraculously by the divine father of all things: the almond seed. The Great Goddess saw me and loved me, and the wide earth prospered. She made me her priest and swore me to a vow of chastity, but I was unfaithful to my vow, and in her fury she struck me mad. I wandered in delirium to the foot of a great pine tree and there, addled beyond hope, I unmanned myself and bled to death. The goddess mourned me; the plants and crops withered; the earth was sterile and barren.

But then, a miracle! I returned from death and with me came the fertility of the earth. The land gave forth a bounty of crops and vegetation, and life was renewed. Since then, every year I die again and the world mourns, and every year I am resurrected and the world rejoices, for I bring it the hope of salvation from death. Now does any of this sound familiar to you?"

Michael said nothing. He did not know what to think.

Attis continued. "Indeed, you may find it not entirely surprising that the festival of my death and resurrection here in Rome begins every year on the twenty-second of March, the day of the sun's rebirth from its wintry grave. Do you know of any other annual festival of death and resurrection that dates its celebration from March twenty-second?"

Michael knew. "E-Easter . . ."

"Exactly so. Today is March twenty-fourth, the day of my death, the Day of Blood. You would call it Good Friday. Today I hang on the tree, and my worshipers mourn me. See how my Passion moves them!"

Michael saw that the courtyard had filled with a crowd of people. A great many of these people seemed to be ordinary citizens, but in their center a group of women — no, men in women's clothing, judging by the muscles of their bared arms — danced, brandishing knives in their hands. They danced in a whirling frenzy, their arms aloft, their eyes closed, their heads tossing to and fro, lost in the mystery of the suffering god. Other priests played for them, a weird cacophony of whining flutes, crashing cymbals, pounding drums. As Michael watched the flutes whined higher, the cymbals crashed louder, the drums pounded faster, and the dancers sped round and round, their heads thrown back, their mouths open, the strings of their long hair whirling out behind.

Michael stared. "What is this, Lord?" he whispered.

The crowd was affected now; it swayed with the music and dance. The music played ever faster. The dancers flew about the courtyard, around the tree, and then all at once they began to slash their arms open with their knives.

Michael gasped. "Lord —"

"Hush," said Attis. "Watch."

Streams of blood were flying outward from the dancing, whirling circle, spattering the crowds and the god's image on the tree. But the priests, far from weakened by their wounds, danced all the faster. Their humanity was extinguished now, they were with the god, they knew his agony, they were dying as he died. And many in the crowd now also seemed to be entering the passion, their eyes wide, their bodies jerking with the rhythm of the music.

Michael heard a cry and saw a young man leap from the crowd into the center of the dance, where he moved crazily, heaving and shaking, frantically tearing off his clothes. In a moment he was completely naked. He ran to the tree and grabbed a long sword that leaned against the trunk. When the crowd saw him do this, it shrieked with excitement. Michael wondered whether the crazed young man was going to slash his arms as the dancers had. But then he saw him thrust the sword blade between his legs and straddle it. With his other hand he reached down and pulled out his scrotum; then he yanked the sword blade forward, and his testicles came away in his hand.

A great cheer arose from the crowd. The young man, his face a blind mask of ecstasy, waved his bloody genitalia aloft for all to see. Then he dashed through the courtyard and into the streets, his blood running down his legs, and the crowd and the priests danced after him.

Michael watched them go. He was fighting the urge to be sick. Behind him he heard the crooning voice of Attis.

"He will run through the streets until he stops before a house, any house, and then he will fling his manhood through its open door. Whoever lives there must furnish him with a set of woman's clothes. He will put them on and enter the priesthood of the goddess, and live out his life in a pious imitation of mine. Tonight, weeping with joy, he will join his brethren for the vigil at my tomb, for now they will bring my body down from the tree, tenderly, with tears, and dress it and anoint it and lay it in the grave. All will fast; all will mourn; all will tremble at the triumph of death. But lo, at midnight a light will shine; the tomb will be opened, and the high priest will pass among the mourners, whispering the glad tidings: *He is risen.* And tears of sorrow will become tears of joy. They will sing hymns and break their fast, and in the morning all of Rome will riot in a great carnival, the Festival of Joy." The god smiled a self-satisfied smile. "And why not?

Once again they know that thanks to me, they shall all rise triumphant from the grave."

Michael did not know what to say. He lowered his head in defiant confusion. All of this was the most shameful blasphemy. He could not accept it — but how could he not accept it? To deny it would be to deny everything the Old One had revealed to him, and to do that would be to deny the meaning — indeed, almost the reality — of his own existence.

The eunuch god behind him seemed to know his thoughts, for Michael heard him say gently, "It is true, Michael Devlin. My worship was celebrated throughout the empire, in Rome, in Syria, and even near Jerusalem, at a place called Bethlehem, where there is a grove of trees sacred to me. In a grotto beneath those trees Jesus Christ is said to have been born."

Michael opened his mouth to speak but quickly bit his lip. Tears welled up in his eyes.

"But this Jesus," Attis went on, "the one you know, is not the Jesus who really lived. He is a political concoction, a mosaic of every god worshiped within the vast boundaries of Rome. Part of his myth, as you see, derives from me; part of him is Mithras, the Persian savior who was born of the virgin Earth while shepherds watched, on the day of the winter solstice, December twenty-fifth. And another Persian savior, the Zoroastrian Saoshyant, was born of a virgin and will come at the end of time to judge the living and the dead. The Persians explained him to their subjects, the Jews, who called him the Messiah, the Anointed One. Later the Jews explained him to their new masters, the Greeks and the Romans, who translated "Anointed One" as Christ. Oh, Michael — these are only three of your Lord's faces; he has more. In Egypt, in Alexandria, people followed the cult of Osiris, the Judge of the Dead, also a murdered and resurrected god. By the time of Jesus, Osiris had been giving salvation to worshipers for thousands of years. His rebirth was celebrated on January 6, when the Nile flooded and resurrected the land and the star called the Maiden appeared in the sky. The Maiden was Isis, Osiris's wife, who gave birth to her murdered spouse; her star was the sign that the god was reborn. And so it was said for three centuries that the Magi, guided by the star, traveled to Bethlehem on January 6 to see the newborn Jesus. Jesus even has a Roman face — the face of Romulus, mythical founder of the city, who was said to have ascended into heaven while the world grew dark at noon and who then reappeared a few days later, declaring that he was a god. No, Michael, the Jesus you have worshiped was the son not of God but of Rome, and he resurrected not himself but the Roman Empire, unifying its disparate loyalties into one religion, re-creating its tottering structure as his powerful church. His creation was indeed a stroke of genius, but it was genius worthy of a Cain."

Michael heard all this with patience, but he had not quite resigned himself to losing his faith. "Well then," he asked, "who might the real Jesus be?" *I will show you,* said smiling Attis, whose voice was suddenly the Old One's voice. As he spoke he began to disintegrate before Michael's eyes, and then Michael was no longer standing in the courtyard of the temple but was back on the hill of Golgotha, watching a man die on the cross.

This man was absolutely unremarkable to look at. He had very dark hair and a dark beard, like a Jew, but they were cropped and curly in the Greek manner, a sign that he fancied himself a philosopher. If he was one, he was soon to be a dead philosopher, for the slow asphyxiation of crucifixion had begun. He breathed in rapid, shallow gasps, and his head rolled from side to side.

Beneath his cross were Roman soldiers, a token few detailed to oversee the execution, and an audience of one: a middle-aged man who also sported a philosopher's beard. Michael found it strange that this man did not weep to see his friend in agony; in fact he sat quite peacefully on the ground in a most peculiar manner, his legs crossed and his feet, soles upturned, on top of his bended knees. Michael thought this position must be impossibly painful, but the man seemed not to be in the slightest pain. His spine was erect and his hands rested peacefully in his lap, the thumbs touching each other. He did not even look at his dying friend; his eyes were half-shut, staring at some point on the ground.

Michael thought such behavior at the death of a friend more than a little distasteful. But since there was no one else to ask and he was afraid to ask the soldiers, Michael bent down and said to him, "That man on the cross. Might he be Jesus of Nazareth, called the Christ?"

The man did not reply; he did not even turn his head. Evidently

Michael was once again invisible. But the man on the cross suddenly opened his eyes wide, glared at Michael, and fiercely spoke to him: "Split a piece of wood, and I am there. Lift up a stone, and you will find me there."

The man on the cross stopped speaking and slumped forward, exhausted by his effort. He breathed in sobs, pulling in the air with all his might; death was coming. His friend below continued to sit quietly in his odd position as though nothing were happening. Michael stood pondering what he had heard. Whoever he was, this crucified philosopher could not be Jesus, because Jesus had never said anything like this. But then in his mind he heard the voice of the Old One:

Behold, Michael Devlin, the real Jesus of Nazareth, a man who was crucified because he had learned Abel's secret. He learned it from the East. Shakyamuni Buddha had preceded him on earth by some five hundred years. Buddhist missionaries followed caravan routes from India to Antioch, Alexandria, and Greece, and Greeks and other westerners followed the same routes eastward, searching in the wisdom of India for the voice of Abel.

The man who sits beside you is Thomas, the disciple of doubting fame. Doubting Thomas saw beyond the political amalgamation of his master with other gods. He wrote a gospel of his own, a book that has long lain buried in the desert of Egypt, suppressed by the Roman church. In this gospel Jesus speaks as the Buddha did, of a blessed kingdom that is not in heaven but in the Mind, in a stick, in a stone, in a blade of grass, waiting for those who discover it. And he says, "There is light within a man of light, and it lights up the darkness . . . If he is undivided, he will be filled with light, but if he is divided, he will be filled with darkness." Do you see, Michael Devlin? The man Jesus was a great shaman, a Grandfather. He knew the secret of Abel. He had rediscovered Spirit, in himself, in the stick, in the stone. He knew that he was the kingdom, that everyone is the kingdom, that the kingdom is waiting for those who can cleanse and unify their minds, as Buddha did, and see again with Abel's inward eye. And because he knew that secret, and for no other reason, he was murdered by the frightened children of Cain.

The scene before Michael was breaking down; in another instant he was again outside of Time. In the flux before him he saw the dim outlines of faces of men and women peering at him for moments, then dissolving again into pure energy and re-forming as someone else. Michael recognized none of these faces; they seemed to belong to many moments inside Time. Then he heard the Old One say:

After the murder of Jesus there was new division among the children of Cain. Something of what the real Jesus said had not been covered up. People began to push at the boundaries of Cain's world, the world of church and empire, in search of Abel. Some of them were mystics, as Abel had been, but others were a new kind of mystic, the scientist. All of them were shamans. They knew, as Abel and Jesus knew, that God and Truth are accessible to the Mind. They abandoned the mythology of the church, Cain's myth of the subordination of nature to man and to a distant God, and turned again to their own minds. But when they did they confronted, alone, the conflict of Cain and Abel in themselves, and even then the outcome did not change. Cain still feared his brother and still slew him . . .

The vague sea of faces before Michael's eyes had now composed itself into a single face, that of a rather prim-looking man well on in years and wearing an outlandish ringleted wig. Moving from the face outward, the white energy flux began to change to black. Another moment of Time composed itself. Michael stood in a very dark room with only one light, a dull yellowish glow emanating from a small brick furnace. The glow illuminated the face of the bewigged old man, who stood before the fire clad in a long black coat covered with stains and smears of various bright colors. Beside him stood another man, much younger and much better dressed, in a natty brown suit and silk knee stockings, with an elegant wig on his head. Michael was not yet certain where he was in Time. These men in wigs and silk stockings reminded him of the pictures of lords and ladies in a history book he had pored over during his three years of schooling. He expected the Old One to enlighten him momentarily, and an instant later the terrible voice came again into his mind.

The elder of these men is one of the greatest scientific geniuses your species has evolved: Isaac Newton, discoverer of the laws of gravity, the spectrum of light, and the mathematics of calculus. Newton's incredible powers of calculation have given humanity the theory of a universe neatly contained in absolute space and time, an infinite clockwork of interlocking perfection designed and set in motion by the master clockmaker, God. Newton's universe would have delighted Cain. It has no messy ambiguities, no question marks. But Isaac Newton is not satisfied with it. He is angry that physics has fallen under the sway of irresponsible French speculators such as René Descartes, who taught that the universe is a wholly material affair. Newton has now devoted himself to proving what he knows: that Descartes' materialism was wrong. But he cannot tell his colleagues at the Royal Society very much about this remarkable work of his. To pursue it he has become a member of a clandestine society of men sworn to absolute secrecy: the society of alchemists. The art of alchemy has been practiced since the time of Jesus, but Newton believes that it is the original true science of humanity, hidden since the beginning in a bizarre mythological language to keep it from the fallen minds of sinful human beings. In a way he is right, for the secret work of alchemy — the work that Isaac Newton has undertaken — is the discovery and the liberation of the principle of Spirit, the life-principle trapped in Matter. It is the search for the secret of Abel, and for many years now it has obsessed Newton. And it may be that because of this obsession, Newton has found another one: young Monsieur Fatio de Duillier, aged twenty-five, late of Geneva, Switzerland, the most promising young scientist of his day. Newton has known Fatio for three years now; only daily duties keep them apart. Newton worries a bit that Fatio's enthusiasm for alchemy is at times more mystical than scientific, but for reasons he does not understand he cannot bring himself to condemn it. The reason, Michael Devlin, is this: Fatio's passion makes Isaac Newton a whole man. Charming, warm Fatio has melted cold, distant Newton and drawn from him another man, a man truly alive, whom Newton's few friends have been astonished to discover. And Newton has become even more brilliant in deciphering the mythological view of alchemy. Every day he seems closer to revealing again the original wisdom of humanity. Newton plus Fatio creates a hermaphrodite, the reunion of two principles long opposed — the reunion of Cain and Abel.

The scene in the laboratory changed. Isaac Newton was alone now, reading a letter. As he read he grew angrier and angrier, until finally he hurled the letter onto a table and charged out of the room. Michael heard the Old One say:

But, alas, an explosion occurred between Isaac Newton and Fatio. Fatio allied himself with a "friend" in London, a physician and dabbler in chemistry, and applied his alchemical knowledge to the mass production of a miracle medicine which would make him a fortune. Newton was furious. The secrets of alchemy, the original wisdom, were never to be revealed to the wicked world for mere gain. Fatio's project was sacrilege, and Newton headed for London to put a stop to it. Over the next few days no one knew of his whereabouts; indeed, he did not even know himself, for in that time Isaac Newton was not quite of sound mind. He dashed off wild letters to his oldest friends, accusing them of vile schemes involving money and women and wishing them dead. When he returned to himself he begged forgiveness of his friends, but his friendship with Fatio was over.

Suddenly Michael was out of doors, surrounded by a crowd of noisy and rather smelly people. This crowd was giving its undivided attention to a group of men and women who sat just above their heads on a raised platform. Michael noticed that the seats were very odd: they had bars across them which confined the sitters' hands and feet, and locks upon the bars. Whoever these people were, they were being forced to sit in public and endure the abuse of the crowd below. And abuse there was: the crowd laughed and yelled curses, and a few followed up their verbal taunts by hurling tomatoes and eggs. One particularly large and overripe tomato landed squarely in the face of a distinguished-looking elderly gentleman. His hands were locked under a bar, so he had to shake his head to rid his face of the rotten tomato pulp. Then he glared fiercely down at the raucous crowd. Michael could see that there was something in his stare that was not quite normal. The man screamed at the crowd: "Upon mine enemies shall I call forth my terrible judgments! My terrible judgments! *Samanatha abralatha xathetos!*" At his final string of nonsense the crowd hooted with glee and loosed another volley of tomatoes. The man sitting next to the one who raved about his terrible judgments got three of them spattered on his elegant brown suit. With a shock Michael saw that the man was Fatio. At the same moment the Old One spoke:

Fatio's alchemical money-making schemes came to nothing, but after his break with Newton his mystical side suddenly ran rampant and unchecked. He abandoned science altogether and fell in with a notorious sect of Frenchmen called the Prophets. For three years he ran with them through the streets of London, crying of visions and speaking in tongues. He huddled with them in darkened rooms and took down every word of their scandalous ravings, and when the London authorities finally condemned the Prophets to the humiliation of the public stocks, Fatio voluntarily went with them. Isaac Newton, now Sir Isaac Newton, the highly paid master of the Royal Mint and president of the Royal Society, lifted not a finger to help him. He had eliminated Fatio, and alchemy, from his life. Fatio's indiscretion was only an excuse. Newton felt he had come too close, and he drew back. He feared the Abel emerging within him, and murdered him. In the end, the genius who might have started humanity back from its Fall proved himself a true child of Cain.

The city square, the pitiful lunatics in the stocks, the malodorous crowd began to disintegrate into pure color and shape. In a moment Michael was outside of Time again, in the endless waves of energy without form. The Old One's voice was still speaking to him.

Isaac Newton's mathematical universe, with its certainties of absolute time and absolute space, cause and effect, led the children of Cain into your own time, Michael — a time so completely unaware of Abel that the victory of Cain seems finally assured. In your time the most intelligent people believe that their logical, rational minds can comprehend and conquer every mystery of existence. They are simply waiting for the next Isaac Newton to come along and put the final pieces of a completely knowable and manageable universe into place. The human conquest of nature, the dream of Cain ten thousand years ago, will be complete. But, Michael, when the next Newton comes along — and he is coming soon — he will shatter Newton's universe and Cain's dream. Cain and Abel will war in him, as they do in all people. But early on in his life Abel will win, if only for a moment . . .

"Einstein!"

Michael saw a tall, very lean man striding forward through a group of teenaged boys. The man was well along in years but he moved fast, his gray hair sweeping to the rear of his head. His agility was even more impressive considering where he was walking: on the very steep slope of a treeless mountain higher than any mountain in St. Bran's, higher even than the Tall One — the highest mountain Michael had ever seen.

The boy named Einstein turned when he heard the old man call him. What Michael noticed right away, and what his gaze kept returning to, was Einstein's eyes, which were enormous, and colored the softest brown imaginable. Michael guessed that Einstein was about his own age; on his upper lip the first adolescent attempt at a moustache had appeared.

"Now, Einstein," said the elderly man as he reached him, "I see a fine example of the problem we were discussing last week." The other boys gathered round. "Look there," continued the man, who was obviously their teacher. He pointed off the mountainside with his walking stick. Michael could see a valley beneath them, at the bottom of a sheer drop of perhaps several thousand feet; on the other side of this valley a mountain reared into the sky. The teacher was pointing at its massive face.

"There," said the teacher, "is a beautifully exposed stratigraphic sequence. Its earliest layer is probably Ordovician. Einstein, remember what we discussed last week? Are these strata older at the bottom, or have they been inverted by the forces of nature and so are older at the top?"

The brown eyes gave the mountain only a perfunctory glance before they rested on the teacher. "Sir," said the boy, "I don't know whether they're older at the top or at the bottom. It's all the same to me."

There was nothing rude or sarcastic in this answer; it was stated as a simple matter of fact. The brown eyes gazed softly at the teacher. Michael bit his lip in anticipation of an immediate thrashing for young Einstein. But the teacher threw back his lean old head and laughed.

"Well! In response we are given example for example — another example of Herr Einstein's refreshing honesty. Off you go, then, Herr Einstein." The old man looked around the group. "Gentlemen, who among you has a burning desire to explain to me the direction of these strata?"

Michael. Above you.

Michael looked up. Not far above him the mountain slope passed into a wall of cloud. Just below the clouds, gliding through slow, lazy circles, was a great blue-black raven. The voice Michael heard in his mind was the Old One's, but it seemed to be coming to him from the raven hovering above.

This young man, Albert Einstein, is an honest boy indeed. In Munich, before he dropped out of school, his classmates nicknamed him "Honest John." His teachers hated him. He had no interest whatever in their classes, and he told them so — not with malice, but to be honest about it. But honesty of this sort has never been highly valued in the schools of Germany, so a year ago, just before they threw him out, young Einstein left. He was fifteen years old. School was not all he left; he repudiated his German citizenship and his Jewish faith, and he told his father that he had no intention of fulfilling his desire that his son become an engineer. And then, school-less, nationless, and godless, young Einstein left home. For a year he wandered through the thoroughly un-German world of northern Italy, reveling in sunshine, art, and freedom. Now his worried parents have placed him in a very liberal school high in the Swiss Alps. The old man is his teacher, Winteler. Einstein loves him, but he is nonetheless bored with geology. Earth is too gross and clumsy a substance to interest young Albert. There is only one thing that really interests him, and he thinks of little else, day after day. Einstein wants to travel on a beam of light. And now I am going to grant him his dearest wish. Watch!

A moment later Michael saw the raven end its lazy circling and dive straight at Einstein's head.

The boy had been hiking dangerously close to the mountain's edge; when he lurched to avoid the raven he slipped over it. The student nearest him gave a shout. Everyone ran to the precipice and saw Einstein clinging precariously to the final outcropping before the mountain became sheer and there were no more handholds for a thousand feet. Luckily, the nearest boy carried a good stout walking stick; he held it out to Einstein, who grabbed it and hung on desperately while his classmates hauled him to safety. The whole incident lasted less than a minute, but in that minute Michael had seen something that no one else had seen. He had seen the raven carry Einstein's spirit away into the sky.

The raven and Einstein passed into the wall of cloud which hid the summit of the mountain. Then they burst through the clouds into light, nothing but light. They were in a land of ice, of pure, clear crystal that splintered beams of sunlight into banded spectra shooting through the air — the bands of the spectrum, red to blue, that human senses can perceive, but a million other colors too, colors impossible for eyes to detect, unnameable, indescribable. The raven looked at Einstein, and its eyes gleamed.

Is this what you were dreaming of, Albert, through all those grim lessons in botany and Greek? Is this what you gave up school and citizenship and religion to find? There are none of those things here to encumber you; there is nothing at all here except light.

The raven flew faster, and faster still, along the splintered bands of the spectra, until all of them merged into one infinite whiteness. The future lay behind them, the past ahead. They were outside of Time, then they were outside even that; they were at the Boundary, and the soul of Einstein saw.

"Herr Einstein!"

Again Michael became aware of the group on the mountain.

"Are you all right? Yes? Good! Perhaps now it will mean more to you whether our strata here run up or down, eh?" The old man, Winteler, threw back his head and laughed, and everyone, even Einstein, laughed with him in relief. Michael studied Einstein. The great brown eyes shone with excitement, but it was only the excitement of a schoolboy who had had a great fright and now, having survived it, was thrilled with his adventure. For an instant he had seen beyond anything imaginable, yet he seemed not the slightest bit aware of it. His kindly old teacher clapped him on the back and strode away up the mountainside, the class of strapping teenagers hurrying to keep up with him. Michael was puzzled. How could this boy, who so obviously had failed to grasp his incredible vision, become the next Grandfather, the keeper of Abel's secret? Then he saw that the raven, the Old One, was circling overhead again, and the raven called to him:

You are wrong. The boy Einstein will become a great shaman, as he was meant to be. For the rest of his life he will be haunted by an intuition, buried deep in the dark half of his mind, of a moment of perfect vision, a ride on a beam of light. He will spend his life trying to regain it. He will push his incredible mathematical talent to the limits trying to describe what he saw, and still sees, in the dark side where Abel lies entombed. The mathematics he creates will prove that Newton, who clung to certainty, had failed reality; nothing in the universe is absolute. Einstein will know that everything that exists, even knowledge, is related to everything else. Do you hear, Michael, the first echo of Abel's voice crying to Cain's world? But it will be only an echo, for even Grandfather Einstein will fail. He will sign his name to a paper that gives the power of his vision to the children of Cain, and from it they will make a weapon so terrible that he who possesses it not only can conquer the earth but can destroy it. Young Albert will become the most talented of all the children of Cain, but never again will he break free of civilization and the flesh as he did when I carried him to light. The time is not yet when a child of Cain, though he be the greatest of shamans, can be a child of Abel.

It seemed that the raven's wings began to grow longer and longer, wider and wider. Its body began to grow too, until it joined with the wings and there was no more raven, only blackness enveloping the sky. Soon the mountains and even the ground beneath Michael had changed into black; everything was black, but more than black as the absence of light — it was Nothing. Michael heard the Old One's voice:

Your journey is finished now. You have met the Grandfathers. They are not the only shamans. There are hundreds more, women like Joan of Arc, men like William Blake, whoever has even for a moment freed his mind from the shackles of Matter and heard the whisper of Abel, the hint of the greater reality of Spirit that is beyond Cain's prison of Matter and Time. But it is enough now that you know Abel's secret, because now you will serve me as I intend you to. There is one more Grandfather you must meet!

In the midst of Nothing, something pale and white was taking shape. It was too vague a form for Michael to identify, but it seemed to resemble an infant, like his little sister on the day she was born.

There is a being, said the Old One, *who will not enter Time while you still live in it. But when he does he will at last cleanse humanity of the crime of Cain and restore Abel and his secret to life. He will do this because he will be your descendant. In service to me you shall prepare his way.*

Michael's stunned mind managed to formulate the frantic question "How?" but he never asked it, for in that instant Michael Devlin awoke inside the sacred circle on the hilltop. He sat up and looked around him. Just beyond the circle's edge stood Wolf Eye and Yellow Bear, waiting, it seemed, for his soul to return.

4

Abel

AFTER A FEW MINUTES, when Michael felt he could stand, Wolf Eye and Yellow Bear hoisted his enormous bulk and helped him down the hill. They had built a tepee in the forest below; they brought Michael into it, and asked him if he wanted to sleep. Michael told them, quite truthfully, that he felt fine.

"Very well," said Wolf Eye. "We shall conclude the rite of *hanblecheyapi.*" He picked up the sacred stone pipe, which he had pried loose from Michael's fingers on the hill, and broke the tallow seal that covered its bowl. A fire was smoldering in the middle of the tepee floor, and Wolf Eye put a coal from it into the bowl of the pipe to light the tobacco. When the bowl was glowing Wolf Eye smoked for a little while, then held the pipe aloft and circled its stem once in the air, crooning softly to Wakan-Tanka. When Yellow Bear had smoked too and Michael had touched the pipestem with his lips, as the ritual required, Wolf Eye said, "Giant One, for two days you have walked within the sacred circle, crying for a vision. Tell us, who have guided you, what you have seen!"

Michael opened his mouth to reply. He could not remember. For a full minute he sat silent, desperately thinking, his anguish growing. He remembered praying, struggling to stay on his feet, and then . . . but the rest was lost. The next thing he could remember was waking up. Suddenly he was overcome with panic, and a deep exhaustion that made him feel sick. He had come so far for this — and now it had all been in vain. How could he not remember? He hung his great head and softly wept. The two Indians waited in silence.

Finally Wolf Eye touched him on the shoulder and quietly said, "Giant One, while you were crying for your vision on the mountain I had a dream. Perhaps my dream can help you." And he told Michael what he had dreamt.

"In my dream I saw you, Giant One, fly into the sky on the back of an eagle. The eagle carried you along a long, holy road, the Road of the Sun. When you came to the sun the eagle swooped up high and dropped you, and you fell from its back into the sun.

"Inside the sun was a land where night never came. In this land everything was white. Even the earth was white, and soft, like water; and underneath it were some beautiful, holy people, who were singing songs in a holy language that I did not know. I saw you look down through the clear white earth and watch the holy people singing and dancing under the ground. A great voice, deep as thunder, powerful as the sun, cried out that whoever understood their song would become a great healer, a holy man who would help his people. And then a mighty tree with many great branches rose up from the white earth and grew tall as the sky."

Michael still could not remember having any vision in the circle, but Wolf Eye's dream fascinated him.

"What does it mean?" he asked.

Wolf Eye shook his head. "For the length of a day, since I dreamed this dream, I have asked myself its meaning. There is an old story among the people who follow the buffalo, which I think of now. A long time ago a brave young warrior rode far to the east, farther than anyone had ever ridden before, looking for buffalo. One day he saw a white man, and the towns that white men come from. He was the first of the people to see that. He rode back to his tepee and said to his wife, 'Where the sun gets up there are people with sun-colored skin and flame-colored hair. I think these people will do us harm someday.' So he and his wife and his family left their village to get away before the white people came. They traveled west for a very long time, longer than anyone had ever traveled before — they were so afraid of what would happen when the white people came. Finally they came to the biggest lake they had ever seen; it was so big that they could see only a little bit of its shoreline from where they stood. And this lake was very, very deep and blue, and there were big rough storms blowing over it all the time. The brave and his family just stopped and looked at it; they didn't know what to do. But one day as they sat by the lake they saw a spirit coming up from under the waves. The spirit called to them, 'Follow me!' and they did. They followed the spirit under the water. And they lived under the water for the rest of their days, and their grandchildren live there still."

Wolf Eye sat still for a moment, then continued. "I met a hunter once, a Cheyenne, who told me that when he was a boy he and his friends traveled west to hunt and camped on the shore of the big lake. That night, when all was quiet, they heard the under-water people singing and dancing in the lake. They wanted to go visit them, but of course they could not, because only the most powerful magic in the world would have kept them from drowning. When they came home they told the story of the underwater people who sing and dance in happiness because the white man cannot come to take their underwater land."

Wolf Eye was silent for a moment. Then he went on. "I know that the tree you saw in my dream is the Tree of Life, which grows at the center of the world. At the Tree of Life the whole universe is in harmony, as it truly is. All living things, the four-leggeds and two-leggeds and the wingeds and the plants and the stones, live around it as brothers and sisters, and all walk in a sacred manner before Wakan-Tanka. If anyone can find the Tree and dwell at the center, he also shall live in a sacred way with all things."

Michael thought he was beginning to understand what Wolf Eye was thinking. "Am I then to find the underwater people? Will they show me the Tree?"

Wolf Eye nodded. "I think that the holy people of my dream may be the underwater people. Giant One, there is something I must tell you. When Yellow Bear and I came up the hill after two days we found you lying as one who is dead. Your heart did not beat; your mouth did not breathe; your eyes were open, but they did not move. For a long time you lay on the ground in this manner. Yellow Bear and I left the mountain and built a burial platform for your body in the trees. We came back to bring your body down to bury it, but then you sat up and looked at us. You, who were dead, had returned to life. You are a very *wakan* man, a *wichasha wakan,* full of holy power. With this power you may go beneath the big lake to the underwater people, and come back. Maybe they know what you saw on the mountain. Maybe they do not know. But to those people, I think, you must go."

"Well then," said Michael, recovering his hopes, "wherever they are, whoever they are, to them I shall go."

A few weeks later, when the Sioux bands moved near the territory of the whites, Michael rode east with Wolf Eye and Yellow Bear. He feared to return to the railroad, which might arrest him for breaking his labor contract; so his friends took him many days' ride to the banks of the great river, the Missouri. Michael could follow it south until he returned to the white man's world.

On the last morning before they parted Wolf Eye gave Michael a small hide bundle. Michael unwrapped it and gasped with surprise. Inside was his watch.

Wolf Eye smiled. "Before we left I gambled Kills Four for it. He lost, as he always does." Then he mounted his pony and rode away without another word.

Yellow Bear lingered a moment to pronounce his favorite English valediction, the one he had learned from missionaries: "Go with God."

"Go with God, and thank you," said Michael. "And next time Wolf Eye wakes up in one of his happy moods, tell him for me that he is a very great and holy man."

Yellow Bear nodded. Michael handed him his horse's tether. Yellow Bear raised a hand in farewell; then he wheeled the horses about and galloped after Wolf Eye.

Michael watched the Indians ride away. Wolf Eye never once looked back. Michael remembered why the man was great: because the wound in him would not allow him to be anything else.

Michael walked south along the riverbank. Wolf Eye and Yellow Bear had given him some dried meat, which he rationed so carefully that it lasted until he struck the first dismal settlements of whites. The rough inhabitants stared at the enormous boy who had appeared out of nowhere, in Sioux buckskins and with flaming red hair tangled like a tumbleweed, and did not know what to think. They gave him food in exchange for his labor. Michael looked at them with equal incredulity. It was now almost the Moon of Popping Trees — December, by his own calendar — and the snow was falling, falling quietly every day over the grim little cabins of the whites. Four months ago these had been his own people, and the Indians savages; now they seemed like people from the moon. Michael felt no kinship with them or with their land-bound, farmers' ways, or with anything or anyone on the wide bleak prairie that was filling up with snow. He wanted only to keep moving, to recover his vision if he could. The story of the underwater people was his only clue, and it meant one thing: go to the big water, go to the sea. So he struck out again in the cold and made it to Omaha, where he caught a steamboat going downriver, the last one of the season before the river froze. The boat took him to St. Joseph, Missouri, where he passed the winter.

In the spring he saw great companies of freight wagons forming up for the journey to California. It was easy enough for him to hire on as a mule skinner and go west, until at last San Francisco lay beneath him, and beyond it the sea. It was all a dream now, the city-world that had once so astonished him. Michael passed through San Francisco as though it were a mirage, heading for the docks to find a ship that might take him back to reality, to the vision he had lost. He signed on with the first one he saw, the brig *Mary Beth,* already a year out of New Bedford, Massachusetts, bound for the Arctic Ocean to hunt bowhead whales.

As usual, Michael's size got him his berth. He knew nothing at all about whaling, but the mate, looking at his arms and back, decided he would make a first-class oarsman. So while the *Mary Beth* sailed north Michael sat in a whaleboat on deck and drilled at rowing, and waited for the burning eyes, the frightening, awesome voice to come to him again.

Weeks went by. Michael got the hang of boat rowing many times over, and still no eyes, no voice. The *Mary Beth* was in the Arctic now, working her way through chunk ice in the northern Bering Strait, searching for the bowhead. Michael had no desire to kill whales, and as the *Mary Beth* sailed closer to the hunting grounds he regretted not taking the time to sign on with a merchantman. But the days dragged on, and every day he stared out at the icy, blue-black ocean, and no helping spirit rose from its depths to meet him. On the day when the lookouts first saw whales he was glad, if only for the diversion.

The cry of "She blows!" electrified the *Mary Beth*. In the twinkling of an eye Michael saw six whaleboats hit the water and their crews leap into them. "Devlin! Move!" roared the mate behind him, and Michael leapt too, landing in the boat with a great thud and scrambling to his bench. Before he had time to think he was pulling his oar with all his might, watching the *Mary Beth* recede, hearing the mate at the tiller cursing and pleading for more speed. And then over the yells of the mate and the crash of the boat through the waves he heard another sound, the strangest sound he thought he had ever heard.

Magoowoo! Magoowoo!

It was coming from over his shoulder, in the bow of the boat. Michael eased up his pace just enough to turn his head around and see that the harpooner, an Eskimo named Asetcak, was singing. Asetcak had come aboard only a week ago, when the *Mary Beth* had put in for water near his village. He was neither a very big man nor a very young one; in the whaleboat he was not much taller standing than Michael was sitting, and the bristly stiff hairs that stuck out from his chin like wires were mostly white. But on every voyage the captain of the *Mary Beth* brought Asetcak aboard to throw the harpoon from his fastest boat, for all along the Arctic coast Eskimos and Americans alike knew him to be a mighty *nawligax,* a killer of whales.

So much Michael had heard from the mate when Asetcak had come aboard. It seemed unbelievable. The Sioux, tall and lean on their ponies, would have laughed at the notion that this tiny, grizzled old man stuffed into layers of skins could kill a creature that was bigger than several buffaloes. So it was with mixed fascination and skepticism that Michael now watched Asetcak prepare for the hunt.

The old man was moaning softly to himself, muttering odd sounds whose chanted connection with one another was barely discernible. While he moaned he unwrapped a dirty rag and pulled from it the dried-out paw of a wolf. This he hung around his harpoon; he then dug a little deeper into the rag, this time bringing out a miniature whale carved of ivory, slung on a leather thong.

The moaning got lower and murkier as Asetcak leaned over the plunging bow and fastened the little ivory whale to it. Then he raised his harpoon, on which the wolf's paw danced, and sang to it:

> *"Magoowoo, Magoowoowoo . . .*
> *alivakviminilyu, u, u,*
> *sanivakviminilyu,*
> *ya, ya, ya . . ."*

"Devlin!"

Michael snapped his head sternward to face the mate. At the same moment he realized that he had stopped pulling his oar.

"Well, *row,* dammit!" shrieked the mate. Michael bent his back and pulled with all his might. Behind him the mighty *nawligax* chanted on: *"Ya, ya, ya . . ."*

Asetcak's weird songs hurt the ear and his hunting charms were small, but their power was great; that day Michael's boat killed a huge bull whale. By the time they towed it back to the *Mary Beth* even Michael's arms shook with pain at every stroke. After the carcass had been tied at last to the hull of the ship, Michael discovered that he was not even then to rest; the mate gave him a flensing knife, a twenty-foot pole with a razor-sharp iron blade for a head, and ordered him onto some flimsy boards that hung out from the hull over the whale.

"Get out there," said the mate, "and cut his head off. Only way you'll ever learn."

Michael looked doubtfully at the work platform. The boards were scarcely wider than the length of his feet, and they rolled and pitched with the motion of the ship. Clutching the long, spearlike flenser, he took one careful step out; then he looked down at the dead whale and paused. Beneath him little Asetcak was nimbly clambering over the carcass, heading toward the snout.

"What's he doing there?" Michael asked the mate.

The mate leaned over the side and saw Asetcak. "Oh hell," he grunted. "That heathen runt. Says he always has t' do this when he kills a whale. Well, let him finish. Captain's order. Give a holler when he's done and I'll give ye a lesson in cutting in . . ." The mate hurried forward to yell at the capstan crew, which was winching another boat's kill alongside.

When the mate had gone Michael dropped back to the deck

and leaned over the ship's side to watch Asetcak. The odd little man was now standing on the whale's snout. In his hand was a wooden water flask. Michael saw him kneel on the rolling snout and heard him moan another of his strange songs, and then he saw him empty his flask over the whale. When the flask was empty Asetcak stood up again and made a funny little bow to the whale. Then he turned, saw Michael watching him, and smiled.

"Good evening to ye," said Michael.

Asetcak chuckled and nodded.

"Me Asetcak," he said, nodding again. "Plenty big *nawligax,* kill 'em big whale for 'merican man."

"Yes," Michael agreed, nodding back. "Kill big whale. Now why do ye pour your water on a whale that's dead?"

Asetcak looked surprised at the question. "Give whale big drink," he said.

"Drink? Why?"

"Whale plenty big guest Asetcak. Asetcak thank him. Asetcak sing him. He come boat."

It took Michael a moment to decipher this. "D'ye mean," he said finally, "that the whale *allowed* you to harpoon him?"

Asetcak nodded again.

"But Asetcak, I was in your boat today. I saw the whale swim from us as fast as he could when we came near. He didn't look very happy to see us. And now he is dead."

But Asetcak shook his head. "Whale not dead. Soul not dead. Soul never die. Whale hear my good songs. He like my good songs plenty much. Like my charms plenty much. Songs, charms make 'em feel good, big man whale. Whale feel good, feel big, give Asetcak his coat."

"His *coat?*"

Asetcak bent down and patted the carcass. "His coat," he said. "You my friend, you like my coat, I give you coat. Whale my friend, I like coat, I sing plenty good song, whale give me coat."

The image of a whale taking off his coat made Michael laugh. Asetcak was not in the least offended; he laughed too.

"Well, what then does the whale do for a coat?" asked Michael. "Sure 'tis mighty cold in that ocean."

"Whale soul go find new coat. Sedna give him."

"Sedna? Who's he?"

Asetcak smiled at such innocence. "Sedna not man. Sedna old lady, plenty big spirit. Sedna love all animals plenty much. Give 'em new coats. Make sure *nawligax* give whale big drink, or plenty angry."

This last assertion baffled Michael. "Ye mean that Sedna is watching you right now?"

Asetcak nodded. "Sedna see all. Whale see all. See Eskimo hunter man all time, now. See 'merican hunter man, big captain, all time. Whale see with eyes, no, no; whale see with soul. Hunter man think good thoughts, is good man, whale see. Whale is hunter man's friend, give him coat. Hunter man think bad thoughts, is bad man, whale see also, plenty good. Whale angry at bad hunter man. Keep his coat. Fight 'em, mebbe kill 'em." And with that Asetcak gave another little nod, smiled, and clambered up the side of the ship. Michael watched him stroll bandy-legged down the deck to help at the capstan. He remembered that he was to call for the mate, but for some reason he did not call. He leaned on the rail and gazed out into the night.

It was an arctic summer night, not a darkness but only an eerie twilight, a mere darkening of day. Over the drifting ice, over the bleak cliffs of Alaska bare as ice, the sun hung eternally in the sky, a great red ball. Michael stared. It began to entrance him, this subtle arctic night of everlasting light, this arctic space uncluttered, elemental, as it was in the beginning . . .

He looked down at the dead whale riding lazily by the ship, so huge, so profoundly mysterious, so unlike any animal or fish or any other thing he had ever seen. Was its soul watching him now, on his tiny ship bobbing in the vastness of the ocean, floating in the blazing whiteness of the night? Could Michael call to it now, as Asetcak could?

In his mind he saw huge herds of whales silently gliding miles below him, rolling like great gods over the prairies of the deep, gazing serenely into the dark, unseen, unknowable depths of the planet . . . He seemed to be there too now, in the ocean depths or in his own depths, or in both . . . Whales in the ocean, or in his mind, were singing to him, not in words as humans would sing but in a music of notes and sighs, of clicks and yawks and grunts. The wordless histories of unseen worlds, of joys and sorrows of universes inconceivable to humans, glided out to him through the trembling waters . . . *Whale see with eyes, no, no; whale see with soul* . . . There were other voices now, mingling in the depths . . . *He goes where his herd leads him; his eyes look inward, his mind is full of the knowledge of God* . . . Whose mind? Michael's mind: it rang with the songs of whales.

He lifted his eyes again to the infinite whiteness of the night. The red ball of the sun thundered through it, over the waters, and then, in the ghostly twilight, it began to melt. It poured down like a red liquid through the heavens, blending with sky-white and dawn-blue, swirling into shades of subtlest lavender and pink. It flowed into the black waters and streaked across them in spidery fingers to the side of the ship. It coated the icebergs with a roseate glow, shimmering indecipherably within them: light, pure light, refined to unimaginable subtlety . . . *There is Light within a man of Light, and it shines in the darkness* . . . Then something gave way in Michael's mind like a breaking dam, like an opening door, like a mudbrick wall crumbling at last after ten thousand years. *And if he is undivided, he will be filled with Light* . . . And the light was free in him, racing through his mind, penetrating his every cell, blinding his inward eye. It shot out from him in great beams that met and mingled with the sun. And his light-dazzled mind, dancing with the sun, singing with the sea, comprehended at last the wordless thoughts of whales, knew at once of all mysteries indescribable, indecipherable, inexplicable, knew Spirit.

Michael is the Light above them all. Michael is All. From Michael did All come forth, and to Michael does All extend. Split a piece of wood, and Michael is there. Lift a stone, and you will find Michael there.

Was it Jesus now, or the Old One, who spoke in him? There were no more burning gazes, no more frightening visions; there was only one final door to open, and now, very quietly, it opened. And Michael's mind opened to receive what it had longed for, what the world had longed for for so many, many days in darkness. Tears of joy, radiant joy beyond any happiness known, burst from his eyes and poured down his shuddering face, and the voice spoke again in him.

Leave the land, the old sad land, that groans under the yoke of Cain. Wander the water, the unconquerable element, the flowing realm of no-Time, of mystery, of unfathomed depths. On the water your mind will lose its fear; it will open itself to its own oceanic depths and the harmony it knew before Cain. And in those depths within you and around you, you will meet an unknown race. They are the brethren of Abel. If you are worthy, they will sing to you. When they sing to you Abel's secret will live in you, and you will know what to say to the one who follows you.

It was what he had known in the dark half of his mind since the vision in the circle on the hill; it was what he had searched for ever since. And now he would never lose it, for it lived in the marrow of his bones. His wandering would last all the days of his life, but his exile was over, his penance fulfilled. He was worthy; he was Abel.

The men of the *Mary Beth* needed six days of round-the-clock shifts to reduce their two whales to casks of oil and stacks of baleen. Michael toiled hour after hour on the bloody decks, silently, efficiently, with a peaceful smile on his face. His weary shipmates marveled at his cheerfulness and whispered that perhaps he got enjoyment from butchery and blood. Not a man among them could have guessed the reason for his smile.

On the seventh day, a beautiful day of sixty-degree weather, the *Mary Beth* rested not, but sailed on; and at midday she came upon an unexpected prize. A huge ice floe spanning half the strait was speckled all over with dark blubbery shapes — walruses, an enormous herd of them, placidly asleep in the warm sun. The whalers gave a cheer and readied their boats. The captain issued rifles to all hands. A cask of walrus oil sold for almost as much as a cask of whale oil, and a walrus was much easier than a whale to kill.

The six boats rowed quietly out to the ice and the men got out, moving forward silently with their rifles until they were among the sleeping herd. When the shooting began the walruses reared awake and tried to flee, but they were fat and torpid with slumber and made easy targets, waddling on the ice. Soon the whalers' boots were sticky with their blood.

Michael fired his gun into the ice. In the excitement of the slaughter no one saw him do it.

Asetcak killed five bulls with five efficient shots. Michael watched him kneel by the head of each and scrape up a handful of ice chips, which he put into his mouth and chewed until they were water. Then he opened the jaws of each of his kills and spat a stream of water down its throat. The great *nawligax* had five honored guests today. But then Asetcak stood up and looked about him at the dozens of dead walruses on the ice and the jubilant whalers killing more. His eyes met Michael's, and he did not smile.

" 'Merican man kill 'em, bang-bang, too much. Bad men, very, very."

Asetcak paced back and forth a little, muttering to himself. Then he ran over to the mate, who was just taking aim at a mother walrus protecting her pups, and yanked down the muzzle of his gun.

"What the hell!" the mate exploded. "Asetcak! You little heathen sonofabitch! Are you crazy?"

Asetcak gestured angrily at the slaughter around them. "Listen, matey man, listen Asetcak good," he cried. "Too much dead walrus. Too much kill. Sedna see bad thing 'merican man do. Sedna very angry. One year, by and by, 'merican man go home, take walrus; Eskimo man stay hunt walrus, find 'em no, nothing. Sedna keep 'em home, punish bad men. Eskimo man, Eskimo woman hungry, mebbe die."

By now Michael and some of the other whalers had seen the argument starting and had gathered around. Asetcak was very angry. His gun shook in his hands. The mate, with the *noblesse oblige* of the Anglo-Saxon race, attempted to explain grown-up economics to this child of nature.

"Lookee here, Asetcak," he said, waving his hands in support of his pidgin. " 'Merican man, 'merican captain, gottum big, big captain at home, biggest captain of all. Big captain say, 'Go north, where Eskimo live, killum whales, killum walrus, makum oil, plenty much oil!' We bring plenty much oil home, biggest captain happy, we eat much. We bring home no oil, maybe little oil, biggest captain angry, *we* go hungry, *plenty* hungry. Understand?"

Asetcak's face was set like a rock. "Too much kill," he repeated. "Sedna see, Sedna angry. Whale see, whale angry bad 'merican man. No give 'merican man his coat long time — you see!"

The mate spat onto the bloody ice. "Well, my heathen friend," he said contemptuously, "I guess I'll just hope and pray that old Sedna and the whales are takin' their naps right now. Sedna angry, me no scared; big boss captain angry, me plenty scared. You savvy?" The other whites laughed and nodded in agreement. The mate turned away and sighted his gun at the mother walrus again.

"Too much kill!" screamed Asetcak. The mate looked back and saw the Eskimo pointing a gun at him.

"Why, you little bastard," the mate snarled. Then he shot the mother walrus dead.

An instant later Asetcak shot the mate exactly where he had intended to, in the arm.

The mate fell to the ice, groaning and clutching his arm. The other whalers, who until a moment ago had thought the whole situation quite funny, stared openmouthed. But only for an instant. An instant later five guns were trained on Asetcak. For a few seconds the only audible sound was the mate's groaning. No one knew what to do next.

Finally one of the whalers said, rather uncertainly, "Asetcak. You under arrest. Give me gun." He started forward to take it.

"I'll get the gun," cried Michael, who started forward too.

But Asetcak jumped back from them both with a defiant shriek. This panicked the whalers, and five bullets entered Asetcak's brain.

When the boats brought Asetcak's body back to the *Mary Beth* the captain was angry at the loss of his best harpooner, but when he saw the wounded mate and heard what had happened, he agreed that the Eskimo had gone quite crazy and that shooting him had been unavoidable. He ordered the mate below for doctoring and threw Asetcak's body into the sea. Michael watched the mighty *nawligax* roll his bullet-mangled face under water, as if ashamed of it, and drift away. Then Michael went below to Asetcak's bunk and found the rag bundle of little whaling charms. He brought it up on deck and threw it after the sinking body. He had learned from the Sioux that when a great hunter passes to the Spirit world he takes his charms along, for the herds of the Spirit are vast and the hunting there is good.

Michael watched the little bundle float until it grew waterlogged and sank. Then he went below again and lay in his hammock and wondered when Asetcak and the walrus would be avenged.

The next day the *Mary Beth*'s lookouts shouted in virtual unison: an entire herd of bowheads was dead ahead of the ship. Again the lightning drill of the crew had the boats in the water in a breath. The tough old mate, his wounded arm pinned to his shirt, came roaring on deck and insisted on steering his boat with his good arm. Among the men in the boats a thrill ran like a current. This was what they had come to this godforsaken place of ice for, what the big boss captain wanted — plenty big whale, plenty oil. Plenty oil, big boss captain happy, whale man eat plenty good.

As the boats neared the herd a huge bull broke water directly in front of them. The mates and harpooners gasped; this monster by himself would render enough oil to fill the hold, bring the *Mary Beth* home early, and make her owners a fortune. The three lead boats, one of which was Michael's, came sharply about and took off after the bull as he swam away from the herd. A little breeze came up, as if a benevolent Yankee Providence had decided to aid the hard-working elect, and the boats raised sail and were soon closing in on the whale. The harpooners stood and shouldered their irons, ready to throw; but just as they closed with their quarry the enormous creature suddenly sounded. At the same moment, as if God were disappointed and were giving up the chase, the wind died. The boats struck sail and hovered over the whale's sounding spot, where a string of bubbles broke the surface.

"Damn," said the mate. "He's gone turtle. One the size of him'll have air in his lungs for an hour on the bottom. Well, boys, rest your arms; we'll wait. When a big one goes turtle he comes up tired. We'll get him when he breaches."

So the men shipped oars, and the boats drifted together in the dead calm over the whale hiding on the ocean bottom. No one spoke; they were listening for the whale's rise. Michael hunched over his oar, thinking of Asetcak's soul swimming beneath him, hunting spirit whales.

Five minutes went by. Ten minutes. The whale did not rise. The water was flat, dead calm; there was nothing on the air but silence. In this nearly absolute silence Michael's mind heard again, only faintly, the thought of a whale. Again it came wordlessly, an intuition like a musical note he had heard drifting by him and thought beautiful but whose meaning he could not explain. It sounded in his mind, this wordless whale-thought, once, twice, and a third time, and suddenly he grasped what it meant. He jumped up at his place, nearly capsizing the boat, and stood trembling all over, just as he had on the day His Honour's men had come to burn his family's home. His startled shipmates stared at him and cursed in whispers.

"Devlin! What the hell are you doing?" hissed the mate. "D'ye want him to know we're still here?"

Michael tried to speak to the mate, but again, as before His Honour's bailiff, he could not. A choking sound came from his throat.

The mate peered at him, puzzled. "What ails ye, Devlin?" he asked. But a moment later he forgot all about Michael Devlin. In front of the boat the whale exploded from the ocean depths.

Its huge bulk shot straight into the air and hung there for an awful moment over the openmouthed whalers; and then it fell, like a building, on one of the boats. The enormous wave of the splash knocked Michael flat on his face and washed his boat some distance away. Michael pulled himself up on the gunwale and looked back. His mates looked too, in silence. The whale had sounded and was gone, and where there had been two other whale-boats there was now only one. Its crew seemed to be sitting in a stupor, staring at a few splinters of wood that floated nearby in a little slick of red.

"Pick up survivors!" yelled the mate to the other boat. A man overboard in the Arctic Ocean was dead from the cold in minutes.

From the other boat a queer strained voice called back, "There ain't no survivors."

"What?" roared the mate, and he gave the order to row. When his boat drew near to the spot, the whalers saw to their horror that it was true. The whale had fallen on the third boat's crew and taken them with him into the depths.

"*Damn* him!" cried the mate, who looked wildly about for some sign of the whale's position. At that moment it broke water again and swam head-on at the other boat. "Kill the bastard!" shouted the mate across the water, and the crew shouted with him, except for Michael, who sat silent, trembling, the whale's wordless thoughts sounding in his mind.

In the other boat the harpooner lifted his iron. When the charging whale came close he threw it deep into its flank, just behind the head — a good hit. The stricken whale sounded, and the whalers cheered.

Michael's animal-power was coming over him. In his breast a terrible pain, the pain of the iron harpoon in the wounded whale, was throbbing. But no one noticed as his trembling increased and his breath came in sobs; all eyes were on the dead-calm water, watching for the whale's breach.

In the other boat the harpooner readied his long lance to finish the monster off. But suddenly he heard the water boil behind him, and turning, he saw the gigantic flukes of the tail towering over his boat.

"Jump!" screamed the harpooner, and a few men who moved fast did; then the great flukes stuck downward and crushed the boat. They reared up and struck again, and again, and again, beating the water in a rage, trying to kill the terrified whalers thrashing about in the sea. Then the flukes disappeared under water, and again there was silence. Michael's boat rowed toward the bodies, to see if any could be saved. But the water boiled again, and the whale was upon them.

He was bleeding badly from the harpoon in his side, but he was still full of fight. He came fast, charging straight at the boat. The oarsmen dropped their oars and turned to watch him come. The harpooner stood up and braced himself to throw, his teeth set, his fingers drumming on his weapon's haft. On the thwarts behind him Michael shook more and more violently, his spasms coming now like a woman's labor, tearing him apart. The pain in his breast was an agony. He felt the iron head grinding on his bones, cutting his flesh, as it twisted in the swimming whale. He stood up, gasping for breath. The boat rocked from side to side and the harpooner lost his balance.

"DEVLIN! SIT DOWN!" the mate screamed, but Michael was already clambering over thwarts and bodies toward the bow of the boat. The harpooner, one eye on the charging whale, tried to push him back.

"Are you crazy?" he cried.

Michael hit him once as hard as he could. The man dropped senseless to the bottom of the boat. Standing in the bow, heaving and shivering, Michael braced himself on the gunwale and stared at the oncoming whale. The great bull was now so close that Michael could see its wise little eye, a tiny window opening on unfathomable mysteries. Michael stared into it. The whale, very close now, stared back.

It was the whale that had brought Michael to his feet and forward to the bow, and made him strike down the harpooner; and now the whale's mind was his mind, and its thoughts were his thoughts, and its will was his will. It was the whale now that bade him lift the harpoon, and trembling, gasping, Michael obeyed. The whale came on; in another few moments it would strike the boat. Michael gazed into its eye, and the eye gazed back. Michael knew the whale's will and surrendered himself to it. He who was worthy would throw the harpoon. In the air he heard the words honoring the whale, sung by no one:

> *Alivakviminilyu,*
> *sanivakviminilyu,*
> *ya, ya, ya . . .*

The harpoon was shaking at his shoulder; it was flashing aloft in his hand, a smile of sunlight on its evil face.

Very faintly, a thousand miles away, a voice yelled at him, the voice of the mate: "Throw it, man! For God's sake, *Throw!*"

The whale was a boat-length away. Behind Michael men leaped to the gunwales, ready to jump. Michael looked once more into the eye, and the eye looked back with the calm compassion of a god who offers himself, in unimaginable love, for the sins of men. And then it seemed to say, inside Michael's mind, *Now.* And Michael obeyed. His arm moved; the harpoon flashed in the air; it struck. Michael's roar of agony split the sky.

The mortally wounded whale dove under the boat, nearly swamping it. The wash knocked Michael backward onto the shoulders of his mates, who pushed him upright. In the bow he turned and stared back at them, his body convulsed, his face twisted, his eyes wide and crazed. Ten thousand miles away some tiny men were cheering him.

Michael Devlin spent most of his life as Abel's child. He wandered the world on whaling ships, following the whales, as the Sioux had wandered the prairies following the buffalo herds. He rose from seaman to harpooner, from harpooner to mate, and from mate to captain, and when he killed, he killed with reverence, as Asetcak had, and he took no more than a few.

On one of his layovers in New Bedford he met a woman, Ann Delaney, whom he liked, and who liked him. When he had put by enough money from his captain's share of profits he asked her father for her hand. He built a big white house for his bride on a plot of land overlooking the sea, and then he was gone again, to the Pacific. Ann bore him a son, whom Michael first saw when the boy was two years old. Ann had given him the name she knew Michael wanted: Patrick, after Michael's dear father, so long left behind in Ireland. Michael beamed with pride and kissed his son and wife and sailed away for another two years.

But always he returned, and always he loved them, and they him; and finally, when he was fifty-four and had saved enough money, he came home to stay. As he brought his ship into New Bedford for the last time he saw the landmark he had always used to steer himself home by: the giant oak tree at the center of his land, its great branches sheltering the garden where his little son had played. His wife and neighbors thought it an impressive tree, but perhaps a bit overgrown, crowding the house. Michael had forbidden them to prune any of its branches, for he had made his home and settled his family around that tree, that harmonious center, and had carried it in his heart for all his years of wandering. Now Abel's weary child would return to the center and wander no more, and would live with his beloved son and beloved wife, with the memories of Wolf Eye and Yellow Bear and Asetcak, and the stars of the prairie sky, and a bailiff's bullet that killed him not, and Father Monagan praying in the grove. He would dwell at the center, in harmony with all, his journey ended, his goal attained, his visions fulfilled.

Abel's child came home to the twentieth century, in the year 1904. His son, Patrick, was a grown man, married during his father's previous time home to a local girl, Kathleen O'Donnell, and working on his father-in-law's fishing boat. Michael was delighted to discover that Kathleen was expecting a child. In the spring of 1905 she gave birth to a boy.

Michael was outside on the porch with Patrick when he heard the newborn's cries from the bedroom. He kept himself back just long enough to let Patrick hold his son, then burst into the house and scooped up the swaddled baby in his enormous arms. The midwife clucked and scolded and told him to be careful, but Michael laughed and bore the tiny bundle outside to see for the first time the earth and the sea, the sky and the sun. On the porch the baby squirmed in the cooler air and began to cry. Michael heard the midwife coming after him, so to quiet his grandson he pulled his watch from his pocket and dangled it in front of the baby, crooning and humming and bouncing him up and down. Immediately the crying stopped. Michael thought it odd that a newborn should be so instantly pacified. He took a good look at the wrinkly little creature cradled in his huge hand. The baby's eyes were following the swinging watch, almost the first thing they had seen, with a peculiar recognition. They gazed intently at the bent cross, the ancient symbol of universal harmony and order, as if they already knew it and always had. A stray fragment of thought came to consciousness in Michael's mind, an old thought welling up from the dark immensity below: *The one who follows you . . .*

The porch door opened and slammed; two soft, chubby hands darted between Michael's and seized the little bundle, and the midwife bore his grandson back into the warmth of the bedroom, loudly proclaiming the stupidity of men. Michael chuckled and stayed on the porch, out of her way. He was alone now in the evening light, with the earth and the sea and the sky. For all of his long, strange life, it seemed, he had been alone with them. He had lived his life in exile, in obedience to a promise made; the earth and the sea were his cousins now, the sky and the stars his friends. But the purpose of his life, he knew now, had been to wander, and to learn the things that wanderers knew. Those who wander — the Sioux and the Eskimo, the buffalo and the whales — know that the planet, the beautiful, powerful, frightening planet, is the home of all, and they love her, as Michael did now. He lifted his eyes in love once more to gaze at the vastness of the sea, and in his mind he heard the wordless songs of whales. And then that odd fragmentary thought that had come to him came again, but this time it came whole; and Michael Devlin heard for one last time in his life the voice of the Old One, the dark and mighty power that had forged him like a useful tool upon an anvil of suffering and search.

In those depths within you and around you, you will meet an unknown race, the brethren of Abel. If you are worthy, they will sing to you; and when they sing to you, Abel's secret will live in you; and you will know what to say to the one who follows you.

JOHN

ACTA GALACTICA

PLANETARY SYSTEM: G1 DWARF
SECTION: LIFE-SUPPORTING PLANETS
PLANET: 5–3–365

Having made the rare decision to intervene directly in the evolution of one of its planets, the Galactic Consciousness found the situation on 5–3–365 far worse than had been initially apparent. The maladaptive refusal over many generations to evolve beyond the final Dominant-Free Will phase of planetary civilization had resulted in a sort of evolutionary quagmire on 5–3–365, a perpetual floundering of its life in the primitive consciousness characteristic of that infantile stage. This consciousness is always limited to (and by) the division of time into past, present, future, the misperception of time as linear and absolute and of matter as the only reality, and a belief in verbal language as an accurate medium of description and communication. Instead of leaving behind these narrow, comforting crib walls and moving into the higher stages of Galactic and Polygalactic Adaptation, life on 5–3–365 was reproducing its cancerous mutant systems (see under Politics, Religions, Wars) in successively more grotesque forms. Each new generation of this repeated error brought an exponential increase in the probability of 5–3–365's extinction, as knowledge of the galactic evolutionary goals, formerly mediated by the now extinguished symbolic imprints, was lost.

Foreseeing in its omniscience the inevitable end of such a course, the Galactic Consciousness determined that in the case of Planet 5–3–365, measures even more drastic than direct intervention would be necessary. Moreover, new instruments would have to be found for the implementation of these measures, since the number of nonmutated individuals on 5–3–365 (whom the Galaxy would normally have used to bring an erring planet into line) was so low in proportion to the mutated population as to be negligible. To arrest the planet's headlong descent toward extinction, the Galaxy concluded that its future evolution would have to be rooted in the strongest possible foundation.

On the planet 5–3–365 the strongest single structure, the irreducible, indestructible unit, was the equilateral three-sided polygon, △; and this abstract figure lent its strength to life through an organic equivalent unique to 5–3–365: the *family*, a bond of father, mother, and their offspring. This constituted the base unit of planetary adaptation on 5–3–365 and harnessed the opposing energies of its life forms into evolutionary drive. The Galaxy determined that if life on 5–3–365 was going to survive, then it would have to make use of one of these families to save it.

I

The Tree

THE VERY FIRST THING that John Devlin could remember knowing was that there were two very big things in the world: Grandfather and the Tree. He remembered looking up from the dust of the garden and seeing the two of them towering over him side by side, like twins, identical giants rising out of the earth. And so they seemed to him in his earliest years — brothers, of one species and one ancient, gnarled flesh, their great shaggy heads together blotting out the sun and sky.

His second memory: after supper on long summer evenings he played in the garden and listened to the leaves of the Tree rustling in the ocean winds. Sometimes he thought the rustling leaves were a voice, the secret voice of the Tree whispering to him in a secret tree-language, and sometimes he really seemed to hear a voice calling to him through the leaves. And then the flesh of his neck would rise and tingle, and he would sit enthralled and quiet in the garden dust, suddenly feeling the mute plants around him throbbing with silent life as he gazed at the evening light dappling their shadowy stalks. In those moments he would rise and climb into the Tree and lie cradled in its huge oaken arms, feeling the mystery of its flesh next to his own and listening to its whispers and trying to imagine what they meant. When it grew dark he would climb down and run to Grandfather, rocking on the porch, and tell him about the Tree. And Grandfather, who knew the language of trees and could speak to them, would cradle him in his great thick arms, neither smaller nor less ancient than the branches of the Tree, and rock him and tell him in his quiet, lilting voice — the voice of faraway Ireland — what the Tree had said.

Grandfather and the Tree knew so many things that no one else knew. Both of them had been alive for hundreds of years. Grandfather said that he told stories to the Tree and the Tree told him stories, and between them they knew everything and everyone in the world. Grandfather told John that the Tree had seen the sunlight glinting on Captain Miles Standish's helmet on the morning he came gliding up the Achushnet River in his squat little ship to buy land from the dark Indian sachem Massasoit, and build Bedford Village. It had seen the tomahawk raised high in the bloody hand of Philip, Massasoit's murderous son, who had come by night to take back his father's land. It had seen the red-coated soldiers smiling at the pretty Quaker girls when the British marched out to burn the long city wharves and keep John Paul Jones from New Bedford supplies.

And Grandfather himself had been everywhere on earth in his hundreds of years. He had feasted with the savages of New Caledonia, who ate bats and beetles and other people, and worshiped rocks; he had hunted buffalo with real Indians far in the West; he had visited all of the savage tribes of the earth, the Oglala and the Kwakiutl, the Inuit and the Kanakas. In the warm summer dark on the porch he overflowed with tales of all the places he had been and all the strange peoples he had met. The boy in his lap listened spellbound as long as he could, until sleep overcame him; and then he slept peacefully in the dark, enfolded in the giant arms, riding tranquilly in the rocker like a boat riding quietly at anchor in a safe encircling bay. And anchored he was, happily and safely, to the twin giant pillars of his life: Grandfather and the Tree, who had been alive forever and would be alive forever more.

He lived with Grandfather and Father and Mother in the big white house on Grandfather's land, beyond the town, where the coast turned south in a long finger pointing into Buzzards Bay. It was a long walk to school and back, but he had never known a shorter one. In the winter he jumped on the ice ruts in the road and tried to crack them — without much success, for although he was a big enough lad, he was no giant like Grandfather. In the spring he stomped through the dust and sent clouds of it into the air. The sun turned the road dust into spinning flecks of gold, and looking at them sometimes made him feel the way he felt in the garden, when the Tree spoke to him. He would slow his pace, forget everything around him, and find his house from blind routine, like an animal who knows the path to the barn. He had moods, Mother always said, moods like Grandfather's, which he had inherited from him along with his flaming hair and his crystal-blue eyes. He was a good boy, smart, her darling, she said, but he had moods.

He was deep in a mood one warm April day not long after his tenth birthday, when he turned instinctively up from the main road toward his house and saw something so unexpected that he stopped walking altogether and stood for a few moments pondering it. An automobile, a brand-new Ford coupe, was parked in front of his house. Next to it a horse, hitched to a battered old buggy, browsed patiently in the grass around the porch.

John recognized the buggy immediately as his Uncle Matthew's. But why was Uncle Matthew here? When he came visiting with Aunt Margaret it was always on Sundays. Every other day they were down at their store from dawn until night. He hurried past the buggy and the mysterious Ford into the kitchen, calling for his mother, who always met him there when he came home from school and gave him something to eat.

But this afternoon the kitchen was empty. John burst through the door and found no Mother and no snack, only a few potatoes half-peeled in the sink. Again the strangeness of it brought him to a halt. Mother was *always* here when he came home . . . He selected an apple from the fruit bowl on the big table and, munching it thoughtfully, made an investigative circuit of the kitchen. On the counter next to the potato-filled sink the peeling knife had strips of dry potato skin clinging to it. A sure sign, thought John, that Mother, who would never have left a dirty knife lying on the counter, had suddenly abandoned her task. To greet Uncle Matthew and Aunt Margaret at the door? But then they would have come back into the kitchen, and talked while Mother peeled. There must have been someone else, in the mysterious Ford . . . Were they in the parlor? John took one last crackling bite of his apple and, chewing as quietly as he could, tiptoed very carefully into the front hall. He hid behind the big staircase that led up to the bedrooms and listened hard for voices coming from the parlor beyond it. And he did hear something, a low, muffled sound — a voice, from its rising and falling modulation. Someone was singing in the parlor, behind closed doors.

Instantly John hurried around the corner of the staircase and made a beeline for the front door. Mother was always dragging him to boring recitals, to ennoble his soul, as she said. He glanced over his shoulder at the parlor doors. They were open, not closed as he had assumed. He tiptoed back a few steps and peered cautiously into the parlor. It was empty. He could still hear the muffled voice. Where was it coming from, if not . . . ? Bewildered, he started back toward the kitchen. As he passed the staircase the sound grew noticeably louder. He turned and looked upstairs, and listened. Somewhere upstairs, in the bedrooms . . .

John ran up the stairs and stopped. At the end of the hallway Grandfather's door was open and the voice was coming through it, clear and recognizable now. It was Father O'Reilly, majestically intoning Latin.

Why was Father O'Reilly here? Hurrying more out of curiosity than foreboding, John came into the room. A wall of backs, all of them recognizable as his relatives', blocked his view of the chanting priest and the room beyond. John went to the back that he recognized as his mother's and tugged at her sleeve. When Mother saw him she dropped to her knees and took him in her arms. Her cheeks and chin were wet with tears.

"Oh, Johnny," she whispered, "I am so very sorry. He said after you'd gone to school that he'd just lie down again for a bit, and when I came in later . . ." But John was staring past his mother at the scene taking place in the bedroom. Grandfather lay quite still, his mountainous body filling the bed. Father O'Reilly moved gracefully toward him, chanting his sonorous, rhythmic Latin, bearing with a dancer's ease a small phial and a towel. John watched him bend over Grandfather's forehead and dip his finger into the phial. His fingertip came out glistening with oil. Breaking into a new measure of incomprehensible Latin, the priest traced his finger over Grandfather's forehead, leaving the oily outline of a cross on the flesh.

John's first thought was, *Why is Father O'Reilly being so nice today?* It was strange because Father O'Reilly had never liked Grandfather very much, and lately had liked him even less. About a month ago Grandfather had nodded off during Father O'Reilly's sermon — a minor offense, considering his age and the fact that more than one member of the priest's flock was routinely guilty of it. But whatever a man of Grandfather's size did in public was bound to be noticed; and to make matters worse, Grandfather's dozing had concluded in a most embarrassing way. He had not, to his family's vast relief, snored at all during the sermon, but when it was over and the choir led the congregation into a hymn, he had half-awakened and begun to sing too. He had sung with firm voice and deep enthusiasm, as he always did. Unfortunately, he had not sung the hymn.

In his mind, still half-dreaming, Grandfather had been a young man again, among the savage Indians, for what had come forth from his mouth had been the oddest conglomeration of syllables his grandson had ever heard. John had stopped singing and listened in fascination to the barbaric, monotonous sounds of the savage tongue, which had been quite audible over the Catholic hymn, much to his mother and father's chagrin. He had caught one strange phrase that Grandfather repeated over and over again: Wakan-Tanka. Then he had realized that everyone else in the church had stopped singing. The hymn had dissolved into shocked whispers and titters. Over John's head his father and mother were furtively shaking Grandfather awake. But Grandfather was not about to awaken; he sang louder and louder, filling the now-silent church with his odd chant. At last John had seen Father O'Reilly scowling from the pulpit and understood that Grandfather had better wake up. He had started shaking him too, and the extra push had finally roused him.

For a moment Grandfather had looked around the church, smiling at the staring congregation, and then he had rested his eyes on the pulpit and broadened his smile. John saw that he was meeting the angry gaze of Father O'Reilly. The priest stared at Grandfather in frigid silence for several long moments before he signaled the choir to begin the hymn again. And after Mass there had been an argument between Father O'Reilly and Father and Mother outside the church. Under Mother's orders John had gone off to keep an eye on Grandfather, who often wandered down the street after Mass, toward the wharves where the wooden ships of the disbanded whaling fleet lay crumbling. As he ran after Grandfather he heard Father O'Reilly raise his voice and say, very angrily, that Grandfather was a heathen.

John hadn't known what a heathen was. When he asked his father that night, Father explained that it was someone who didn't believe in God. It struck John as quite unfair that anyone should accuse Grandfather, who was always talking about God, of not believing in him. And there didn't seem to be anything wrong with singing an unknown song in church; after all, Father O'Reilly always sang in Latin, and almost no one in St. Lawrence's congregation understood him. But if John was his grandfather's staunch supporter, he was also a devout Catholic — rather more devout than other boys his age — and for the last month it had bothered him, even slightly frightened him, that Grandfather might have heathen tendencies.

John came back to himself in the bedroom. Mother was still holding him; Father and Aunt Margaret and Uncle Matthew had come to his side. Father O'Reilly was speaking English now.

"Let us pray." The solemn priest motioned for everyone to kneel. Father put his red, sea-hardened hands on John's shoulders and gently pushed him down as he knelt. Father O'Reilly began the rosary.

John knew the responses by heart; he intoned them without thinking, his mind and his eyes on Grandfather. From his kneeling position he could see only Grandfather's head rising over the edge of the bed, floating in space without a body. The stillness of it was not that of a living thing. Bolstered a little by the soothing ritual of group prayer and response, John allowed himself to think at last the unthinkable thought: *Grandfather is dead.* But having thought it, he did not feel it immediately; it was incomprehensible. Grandfather was asleep. But his sleep, which had lasted undisturbed through chanting and anointing and now praying, seemed indeed to be a permanent one. Stealing glances at his family, John saw that Aunt Margaret was weeping as Mother wept, and Father and Uncle Matthew were blinking their eyes and biting their lips.

Grandfather is dead. How could it be? A peculiar feeling arose inside him, a terrible tight sick feeling, creeping from the center of him out to chest and limbs and head. *Grandfather is dead.*

He felt dizzy. It was hard to breathe. The stuffy bedroom, full of bodies, seemed devoid of air.

Grandfather is dead. The rosary ended. Everyone stood. He stood with them, quivering. *Grandfather is dead.* Father O'Reilly was coming over to him, his hands thrust out in benediction. Father was gently pushing John forward, toward the priest's embrace. The benedictory hands lowered smoothly over his shoulders, the glistening fingertips passed his face. *Grandfather is dead.* The hands on his shoulders drew him into the priestly garments, folds of blackness. *Grandfather is dead.* All was blackness. He could not see; he could not breathe. *Grandfather is dead.* He tore himself from O'Reilly's oily hands, and before Father could stop him he had fled.

He ran down the hallway, down the stairs, out the front door. Uncle Matthew's horse shied away from him as he stumbled down the porch steps into the yard. He didn't know yet where to go. Whenever he was upset about anything he always ran to Grandfather. *Grandfather is dead.* The relentless thought pounded him again, and he felt something like an abyss open inside him, where there had always been a warm feeling of security . . . He was running into the garden, to the Tree. They would come after him in a moment, to comfort him. He wanted no one's comfort from that room of death. He wanted the Tree.

About a year before, Grandfather had helped him build a treehouse in its topmost branches. It wasn't really a house, only a simple open platform like the crow's-nest of a ship; but to John it was a sanctuary. He climbed quickly to it now, finding some relief in the effort of climbing. In the treehouse, as always, he felt better. Walking slowly, he made one complete circle around the platform. To the east he saw the blue, mysterious ocean, where Grandfather had spent so many years, stretching to infinity; to the west the river, the Achushnet, snaking inland, surrounded by the town of New Bedford, whose rooftops sprawled to the north. To the south the ocean reappeared beyond the curving coastline. Whenever he faced south from the treehouse he always paused, and he did so even now, troubled as he was, for to the south lay the island, an uninhabited rock with fringes of green about its cliffs rising from the sea.

To John the island was Eldorado, the unknown continent.

Mother had declared it too far a sea voyage for her boy, despite all his protestations of maturity, but Grandfather (who had been there as he had been everywhere else) told him stories about it. He said that a fearful monster lived there, a beast part lion, part crocodile, and part hippopotamus, that had birds' wings and claws and an old lady's head at one end and a snake's at the other, so no one could sneak up on it . . .

Grandfather is dead. He sighed miserably, his eyes on the sea. It was so hard to understand. Grandfather's body was still here, asleep in his bed, but he was gone. Gone to heaven. But what was it that went, if his body was still here? His soul. But what was a soul? Was it another body inside his body? Did it look just like Grandfather? And if it *wasn't* a body, then what was it? John's lower lip began to tremble. He bit it and swore he would not cry. Abruptly he turned away from the ocean and gazed inland, his eyes resting on the tiny stream that trickled from the woods behind the house and flowed past the garden. A rickety footbridge spanned the stream. With bitter satisfaction John exercised his imaginative power to confer immortality. He stared at the footbridge and summoned from his memory a complete moment in time.

It had been a hot Saturday afternoon of the summer before. John could re-create it in his mind down to its last detail: the heat of the sun on his back through his shirt, the feel of rough splintery boards on the backs of his knees, the green water crawling beneath his dangling toes. He was sitting on the bridge holding a fishing pole, watching the cork float on his line bobbing lazily in the current. And there next to him was Grandfather, his own pole ludicrously small in his huge hands, his battered old captain's hat pushed back on his forehead, his sleeves rolled up, the great sinews of his arms still firm under the leathery skin. Grandfather was telling one his wonderful stories that had no end: *"Well, Jonah was a man of the Hebrews, livin' in God's land of Israel, peacefully goin' about his business, just like you and me. But one day when Jonah was out diggin' in his garden a little cloud floated over his head, and he looked up happily, hopin' it was goin' to rain on his thirsty plants. But instead of rain God's voice came down from the cloud, booming like a clap o' thunder. It flattened all of poor Jonah's plants and knocked the hoe right out of his hands. And God said, 'Jonah! I've a little job for you . . .' "*

"John! Johnny! Come on down now, it's nearly suppertime!"

He looked down from the treehouse and saw his mother standing on the porch, wearing her apron, shielding her eyes to see him in the angled afternoon light.

"I'm coming," he called down.

Uncle Matthew's buggy and Father O'Reilly's Ford were gone. How long had he been up in the Tree? It *was* evening now, he realized; he had been up in the Tree for several hours. How was it that your mind could make time disappear sometimes, when other times (for example, in the last period of school on a beautiful day) time hung like an axe over your head and seemed realer than anything else in the world? Another mystery. When he came into the house he forgot about time and remembered Grandfather.

"Wash yourself," Mother said gently, reaching out to touch him, but John was already halfway up the stairs. He hurried along the upstairs hall again, Grandfather at the bridge still vivid in his mind. Father O'Reilly and the others were no longer there. He could be alone with Grandfather, not knowing what that would mean or accomplish, only wanting it, wanting things to be as they always had been for the two of them. He came to the end of the hall and pushed open the door. The bed was empty. Grandfather was gone.

For a moment John stood still in complete bewilderment. Then he heard the door behind him creak open. He turned and saw someone standing over him, a ghostly outline in the growing dark, the face barely visible in the shadows. Black, faceless, it seemed for a moment to some deep and unknown part of John's mind to be a visitation of Death, as if the unseen fact now charging the black air of Grandfather's darkening room had suddenly materialized before him. A spasm of fear passed through him and he shuddered. The black figure put out its hand immediately and touched his shoulder. At its touch he knew it was Mother's hand, and his shuddering stopped. Mother knelt and put her hand behind his neck.

"They've taken him to dress for burial," she said quietly. "Come down and sit with me while I'm cookin'."

"I will." Mother seemed to know that he wanted another moment alone. She nodded and stood, then went downstairs. John turned around again to face the room.

The daylight was making its final effort. Everything was only just illuminated now, a pale gray, but it was still visible. John could still see Grandfather's giant bed, neatly made by Mother for the last time; he could still see the comb and razor and washbowl laid out carefully, ready at their stations, on the mirrored dresser; he could still see the shelves of Grandfather's mysterious books on the far wall; and on the open closet door he could still see Grandfather's hat and coat hanging. Yesterday he had watched Grandfather hang the hat and the coat on the door. He had watched him shave and comb his hair and lay everything out neatly on the dresser top; he had watched him take down a book and heard him read from it, in his awkward, self-educated way, of things wonderful and incomprehensible. Again the sense of a mystery came over him. Everything in Grandfather's room was just the way it had always been. Yesterday Grandfather had been sleeping in his bed, reading his books, combing his hair, wearing his clothes, and planning to do it all again tomorrow. The room still reverberated with his presence; his bed and his books, his comb and razor and hat and coat all awaited him. Nothing had changed — except that Grandfather had gone forever and would never be here again.

From the window the final gray of twilight filtered through the curtains; it fell upon the objects in the room and faded away. And in that moment everything faded away with it, dissolving before John's eyes into pure blackness, into night. As John's eyes lost their sight in the blackness he saw in his mind the image of a great wing, a black, evil wing unfolding itself over all creation. The wing was night, and the wing was death, and it had come for Grandfather and borne him away, and now it enfolded everything, the living earth and the warm sun, in its terrible span. Alone in the blackness, John began to shudder again, uncontrollably; and then, at last, he burst into tears.

In the middle of the night John woke up. The branches of the Tree were slamming rhythmically against his window. From his bed he could hear the wind howling and rain drumming on the window glass. Now and then his bedroom lit up as lightning flashed and a wave of roaring thunder rolled over the house. John sat up in bed and watched in astonishment. The evening had been warm and crystal-clear, with no hint of such a terrible storm on

the way. Then the lightning flashed again and the thunder roared
and he grew frightened, as he always did during thunderstorms.
Half-asleep, instinctively, he ran to Grandfather's room, where
he had always run, to get into the giant bed with Grandfather
and be comforted. But the bed was empty, and John, standing
alone in the dark room and fully awake now, remembered his
misery. It overwhelmed him again, and again the tears welled
up in his eyes.

But just then, when the dark world seemed an abyss of night
and the shadow of the black wing hung over him, he heard somewhere, through the howling of the storm,

> "Tim Finnegan lived in Walkin' Street,
> A gentle Irishman, mighty odd . . ."

Finnegan's Wake. It was Grandfather's song.

It was coming from outside the house. He turned to the window;
the lightning flashed again, and in the flash he saw him standing
in the treehouse, his huge old head thrown back, belting his song
into the fury of the storm.

"Grandfather!"

John fairly screamed in his delight. *How could it be?* Without
another thought he was down the stairs and out of the house,
running through the wind and rain in his nightshirt, pushing his
way through the garden plants, heading for the Tree, then climbing,
the wind and the branches slashing at his face, pushing him back.
The cold rain drove into his face and eyes, soaked his nightshirt,
chilled his flesh. But blinded by rain and leaves he could still
hear above him, through the wind:

> "Tim revives, see how he rises,
> Timothy risin' from th' bed . . ."

Was it a miracle? He was halfway up when the wind blew a
branch right into his face. The blow almost knocked him off the
Tree, but he grabbed another branch and hung on — barely. He
felt something warm run down his cold forehead. When he had
pulled himself back to the trunk he put his free hand to his face.
It came away smeared with watery blood, and he felt a pain above
his eyes. But he managed to heave himself up one more branch,
and then he felt an enormous hand seize his shoulder and lift.

Suddenly he was standing in the treehouse, in Grandfather's arms, shivering from the cold and from sheer happiness.

"Grandfather," he cried, "you came back!"

Grandfather looked down at him with his glittering old eyes. "Well now, Johnny, lad," he said. "Did ye think I would go to the Spirit and not say good-bye to ye?"

"Well, no, but . . ."

"But what?" Grandfather seemed to glare at him. "Do ye doubt me, lad? Am I not standin' right here before ye?"

"Oh, yes, yes, you are . . . it's wonderful . . ." John was afraid Grandfather was angry with him.

But Grandfather's frown melted into a smile, and he spoke gently: "That's a nasty cut on your forehead, Johnny. Are ye all right?"

John wiped his face again and nodded.

It was a miracle. An inexpressible ecstasy glowed inside him and filled the hole of his pain. "Oh, Grandfather, Grandfather," he cried, "please don't ever leave —"

"Look here, now." His voice still kindly, Grandfather cut him off. He reached down and plucked one of the new spring leaves from the creaking oak. "Have a look at the leaf now, Johnny." He held it up between them.

John looked, feeling suddenly perplexed and disturbed. Why had Grandfather cut him off like that when he was so happy? It wasn't like him. There was some sort of funny change in him . . .

"D'ye see the patterns in the leaf?" Grandfather asked.

The lightning flashed and John saw that the surface of the leaf was an intricate web of hundreds of tiny veins, running from the spine of the stem out to invisible endings at the points, all of them connected to one another.

"Yes, I do," he cried impatiently, over the storm winds. "Grandfather, please tell me, how did you —"

"Good," said Grandfather. "Now listen well. There's some things that I'm goin' to tell ye now that ye must remember all your life. Number one: the day will come — standing out of Time I have seen it — when ye'll be a man of high position amongst the nations of the world."

He looked meaningfully at John, and John simply looked back, struck silent by the incredible thought.

"And when that day comes," Grandfather said, "remember this: everything ye do, no matter how insignificant it might seem to yourself, passes through all infinity." He held the leaf closer to John's face. "Remember the pattern of the leaf. D'ye see how every little vein is joined to every other one? That's what infinity's like. Everything connects to everything. If ye walk in a field and pick a pretty flower, someday, maybe in a thousand years, a terrible war may start, or a great invention will be perfected, because of it. Promise me ye'll remember that."

John nodded solemnly. He did not understand.

"Number two," said Grandfather. "From time to time a few special people on this earth catch a tiny little glimpse of infinity while they're still living, before they go to heaven. Remember old Jonah? He was one such. When th' Lord God called to him, he had a glimpse of infinity. Now remember this, all your life: you will be another one."

John's eyes widened.

"Aye," said Grandfather, studying him. "You're frightened to hear it. And well ye should be, for 'tis not an easy thing to bear while ye dwell in flesh and blood. And in truth, dear Johnny, I cannot help but feel sorry for you, for 'tis a fearful, fearful thing to be chosen by God."

"What?" cried John, suddenly truly frightened.

But Grandfather only replied, "There are two more things ye must promise me, Johnny. Swear them on your very soul. Promise me that whenever ye get such a look into the infinity of things, no matter how frightening it is, you'll not tell a livin' soul, not even your mama or your da, what ye have seen. Promise!"

"I promise!"

"Good. Now promise me too that whatever ye see when infinity comes into your mind, believe in it and follow it always, no matter what may happen to ye. Because ye cannot run away from such things, no matter how desperately much ye may want to. Remember Jonah!"

In the morning when John awoke the sky was cloudless and a brilliant blue. He was in his bed, in his nightshirt — quite dry — and from his window he could see the Tree and the garden basking in new sunshine, apparently none the worse for their buffeting by the storm. *The storm* . . . He remembered Grandfather's visit, at first with an ecstatic happiness. But on the ground below his window he saw only a film of spring dew. He felt his dry nightshirt and saw the stalks of the garden still neatly erect in their rows. He grew puzzled and a little uneasy. Had there been a storm at all? Perhaps Grandfather's visit had only been a dream. His eyes traveled over the familiar scene of his bedroom: the plain white walls, the tiny chest of drawers, the lace window curtains blowing gently in the morning breeze, the half-finished model of a clipper ship spread out over the varnished maple desk. *The world,* he thought. *What I see every day with my eyes. What Mother sees, what Father sees, what Grandfather saw . . . In a dream,* he thought, *when my eyes are closed, it would all look just the same.* A chill of fear crept over him. Was he awake now, or dreaming? He shut his eyes and his bedroom disappeared. He imagined it and it reappeared inside his head, just as Grandfather had reappeared yesterday, fishing from the footbridge. And last night . . . With a panicky start he opened his eyes and gripped the bedside table. This *is the world,* he thought emphatically, squeezing the table hard in his hand, shivering a little from his fear. *This is real. This I can see and smell and touch.* Grandfather's visit had been only a dream. There had been no real storm. But it was a dream that even now seemed so very real . . . He remembered a little more of what Grandfather had said to him, and the promises he had forced him to make; and then he wished very much that it all *had* been only a dream, and a very unreal dream indeed.

Then he heard Mother calling him to breakfast. He threw on his clothes and ran downstairs.

"John," said Mother as she set his breakfast before him, "how did you get such a terrible scratch on your forehead?"

2

The Ship

A WEEK AFTER GRANDFATHER'S FUNERAL Father went out fishing to bring in some money before the undertaker's bill came due. At the end of another week he returned home, his boat laden with fish. After a good catch he usually took a few days off to be with his family. After this one he was especially eager to do so. Early on Saturday morning he woke John and told him to dress warmly, for the sea.

"Where are we going?" mumbled John, not at all sure he wanted to trade his warm bed for the windy deck of Father's boat.

"Look," said Father. He held up a picture carefully torn from a newspaper. It was a picture of an enormous ship, an ocean liner, beautiful and sleek, racing through the water, its four great funnels tilting backward as if blown back by its speed.

"Fastest ship in th' world," said Father. "She passes Nantucket Lightship today, bound for Liverpool. Would you like to see her?"

John was out of bed in an instant and pulling on his warmest clothes.

In the wheelhouse, on the long trip out to the Nantucket lightship, Father told John more about the beautiful ship.

"She's British," he said, steadying the wheel with one practiced knee while he lit his pipe. "Owned by Cunard Lines. That's the big one. And she's their number-one ship. Number-one ship of the number-one line, how about that?"

John grinned happily up at him. Father grinned back and put his hands on the wheel.

"And she's not just big, she's fast, too," he went on, puffing on the lit pipe until the bowl glowed red. "Fastest ship afloat, I believe. She can make Liverpool from New York in seven days. Think of that, Johnny! Three thousand miles in seven days — with a thousand people on board her, too."

Again John grinned happily. Father was glad to see him so excited. That had been the whole purpose of this trip: to cheer him up, to get his mind off his grandfather's death. Father had known for years that when Michael died the boy would take it hard. For himself, grieved though he was, there was something very normal about Michael's departure from the earth. The son of a whaler grows up accustomed to an absent father. It seemed to Patrick that Michael had simply gone on yet another voyage, the ultimate one. But little Johnny had never known a morning of his life when the old giant had not been there to awaken him, or an evening when he had not tucked him into bed. For years Patrick had wondered what could possibly bring the boy through the grief of the inevitable day, and known only that no words could. Seeing the New York papers when he had, with the Cunard advertisements in them, had seemed almost providential.

"Want to spell me on th' wheel for a while?" he asked casually, knowing full well what the answer would be.

John's face lit up with excitement. "Can I really?"

"Sure you can!" said Father with a wink, and moved back for his son to take the wheel. John took it and steered to the compass, feeling the big boat respond to him. He was thrilled. He loved his father's boat, with its oily, rusty mysteries of machinery; he loved the sea, and the great adventure of sailing it; and so very few times had Mother allowed him to go out of sight of land that a trip to the Nantucket lightship was beyond all expectations. Feeling Father's strong, reassuring presence just behind him, he forgot his sorrow and his fear over what had happened. In his boy's mind it was not a fishing boat but a great British liner he was steering with expert hand — the fastest ship in the world.

Father had read in the New Bedford papers that the giant liner would pass by the Nantucket lightship at about three in the afternoon. By three o'clock the fishing boat was in position off the lightship. Father cut the engine and let the boat drift gently through the long ocean swells. John scanned the horizon with field glasses.

But three o'clock passed, then three-fifteen, and then three-thirty, and still no liner appeared.

"She must've had delays leavin' New York," Father said. "Happens all th' time, with those big liners. Some rich old swell can't get his two hundred suitcases packed in time and pulls strings to hold up the sailing." Father smiled at John, but John did not smile back. From the look on his face it was clear that he had already given up believing that the liner would appear. So Father decided not to wait until they returned to New Bedford to do what he had been planning to do that day. He went below into the cabin for a moment and returned with a present for John. It was Grandfather's watch.

"In his will," Father said shyly, "he passed it on to me, but I think that in truth it belongs to you. You were closer to him than anyone else was."

John took the watch and turned it over in his hands. The dull, smooth, worn feel of the cover with the odd old symbol engraved on it was so familiar to him, and so inseparably associated with Grandfather, that it seemed as if Father had just brought Grandfather back to life right there in the boat.

"Thank you, Pa," he said. Father saw that his eyes were shining.

"It belongs to you," he repeated, smiling and stroking his son's hair. "Let's not give up yet," he added, scanning the horizon again for the liner. "She's bound to come along sooner or later. The shippin' lanes will take her right past us."

So they waited, Father keeping watch through his field glasses, John passing the time examining the watch. Once he had asked Grandfather about the broken-armed cross engraved on its cover. "It's to bring good luck to th' Devlin family," Grandfather had said, and after a moment's hesitation he had added: "And it brings some other things as well. Presently I'll tell ye." But he never had. *And now,* thought John, *I shall never know . . .*

"Here she comes!"

John leaped up and followed Father's pointing finger with his eyes. There was a black smudge on the horizon. Underneath it something gleamed in the afternoon light.

"Here, look." Father gave him the field glasses.

John focused on the black smudge and suddenly it jumped closer.

"Ain't she grand!" whispered Father by his side. And indeed

she was, with her four towering funnels pouring smoke into the air, the blinding whiteness of her upper decks, the knife-edge of the black bow shearing the waves at eighteen knots, coming toward them so fast that in a very few minutes the field glasses were no longer necessary. Then the great liner swept past the tiny fishing boat like a passing mountain. John was overwhelmed. She was so close that he could hear the huge engines rumbling deep inside her, the hiss of water rushing past her hull. He craned his neck back as far as he could and saw tiny knots of people standing at the rail in the gleaming whiteness far above him. Other people were lined up in ranks on the deck. John heard a faint whistle and saw them file into one of the small white boats that hung over the side.

"Lifeboat drill," said Father, looking through the glasses. "Hard to believe a ship that size could sink. But it was just around this time three years ago that th' *Titanic* went down . . ."

He turned to offer the field glasses to his son, but John did not take them. Instead he stared straight ahead at the ocean between himself and the liner. He was pondering an object that was racing toward the liner underwater, leaving a track behind it in the sea that was absolutely straight.

"Pa," he said, pointing, "is that a dolphin?"

Whatever Father said in reply, John did not hear it. At that moment the straight-and-narrow track in the water intersected with the bow of the liner, and the liner blew up. John saw a tremendous flash and a column of flame shoot up from her waterline. The great ship seemed to shudder from bow to stern. Almost immediately her fast pace slowed. She pitched to one side and began to tip; her bow tilted under the water and her funnels lurched downward, pumping smoke and cinders over the sea. And then the screaming began. For some reason John could hear it very clearly, as loudly as if he were on board the sinking ship. It was a horrible noise, not the theatrical screaming of heroines in matinee melodramas but the shrieks of people who knew beyond any doubt that they were about to die — men, women, little children, clawing at the doors of staterooms filling up with water, slipping and falling in passageways that were rapidly tilting up on edge, forcing them to their deaths. The screaming grew louder, until John could stand it no longer and clutched his head. Then he saw the liner standing almost on end in the ocean, its huge propellers still revolving, flailing grotesquely in the air. It paused, almost for effect, it seemed, like a dancer or a diver; then one by one its four great funnels followed one another into the sea.

Not until the Union Jack at the stern had disappeared did the awful screaming cease, and then, mercifully, it stopped sharply, like a song when you lifted the needle from a Victrola. But now the fishing boat was floating in a silent sea of bodies, wave after wave of the newly dead bumping up against her hull. John stared down at them, hundreds of them littering the sea, the handsome young men and the beautiful girls, the parents and their children, the rich and the poor, and the white-jacketed crewmen; in all of their wide-open eyes he saw one last frozen look of the most profound terror. Then a great big man drifted by, with his eyes peacefully shut. John looked at him. It was Grandfather. Far, far away, in the broken hull of the liner gliding silently downward in the sea, living people were still drowning, still screaming; and now someone was calling his name.

"John! Wave your hands!"

Wave your hands? John saw Father smiling and swinging an arm vigorously over his head.

"Look, John, they're waving to us! Wave back!"

Waving to us? John lifted his eyes from the silent, body-strewn sea. The fishing boat was bouncing in heavy waves made by the wake of the huge liner that had just passed it. From the curved stern some people were waving gaily at them.

"Bon voyage!" Father shouted, as loudly as he could.

John looked around. There were no bodies in the sea; the great liner had not blown up and sunk. She was just now passing the lightship and beginning a majestic turn toward the open sea. And Father was looking at him strangely. Suddenly he felt very, very cold.

"John? What's wrong? Are you all right, lad?"

He was shivering, on the verge of losing control. Father was holding him by the shoulders. He could feel clammy sweat collecting over his upper lip. Then everything seemed to grow dark; he was crumpled up in Father's arms, being carried to the cabin below, and then he was in a bunk, smothered in blankets and sweaters, and he could hear Father above him pleading with the boat engine for more speed.

When they got home Mother put John to bed and kept him

there. Doctor Ferguson was summoned. He listened carefully to
Father's description of what had happened, thumped John's chest,
looked into his eyes, ears, and nose, stuck a wooden stick down
his throat, and asked him how he felt. John said he felt fine.
The doctor agreed that he seemed to be fine and asked him to
describe what had happened out on the boat. John looked at him,
and at Mother and Father standing behind him, and told the
first deliberate lie of his life: "I don't remember." Doctor Ferguson
shrugged, and told Mother and Father to keep him in bed for
another day or two — it might only have been the excitement
of seeing such an enormous ship so close.

When the doctor had gone Mother and Father left the room.
John could hear their muffled voices arguing outside. Mother,
he guessed, was setting back by years the date when her baby
could next sail far out to sea with his father, and Father was
resisting this decree, but not convincingly, since the fact of the
matter was that at sea John had become violently and inexplicably
ill.

He lay back in the bed and tried not to be afraid. He thought
hard. The ship had blown up and sunk; he had seen it and heard
it. But the ship had *not* sunk; he had seen that too. Father had
not seen the ship sink. The ship therefore must not really have
sunk. He must only have imagined it. But that was impossible,
because anything he had ever imagined he had always been able
to *stop* imagining, whenever it had become boring or too frightening, and what he had seen out by the Nantucket lightship had
been as grimly inescapable as any real event. There could be only
one conclusion, the one that had already occurred to him under
the pile of blankets and sweaters in Father's boat and the one
he now came to again: the ship had not blown up and sunk the
day before, at the lightship, but someday soon it *would*. He had
seen into the future. Having concluded this he immediately denied
it, for the obvious reason that it was impossible to see into the
future. But why not the future, if he could make the past a living
present in his memory? He remembered his "dream" of Grandfather, the treehouse, and the storm. Grandfather had warned him
about glimpses of infinity. Had the sinking of the liner been one
of these glimpses? And what in the world had Grandfather been
doing floating among the bodies of the drowned? Grandfather
was somehow wrapped up in all of this . . .

John made another mighty effort to think. If he really had seen into the future, then it was his urgent duty to warn the Cunard Line that its flagship was about to sink, so it could radio the captain and tell him to turn back. But as soon as he resolved to do this two things occurred to him. The first was that if what he had seen had really been one of the glimpses Grandfather had warned him about (and even in a dream he trusted Grandfather), then he had promised Grandfather not to tell anyone about it, no matter what. The second was a much more difficult and very frightening thought: if this terrible thing really *was* going to happen and all those people were about to drown, then how could anyone prevent it, even if they did know about it?

Suddenly John felt himself teetering on the edge of an abyss. Here, opening up the ground beneath his feet, was a mystery to beat them all. A group of people board an ocean liner; the liner sets sail; it blows up and sinks, and most of the people drown. Why those particular people? How did God pick them? Why would God pick anyone to send to a certain death? But *was* it certain? How did God choose the survivors? Could God change his mind if he wanted to? Why would he sink an ocean liner full of innocent people? Should John telephone the Cunard Line, or should he keep his promise to Grandfather and tell no one? *Could somebody who knew the future change the future, which God had ordained?*

So he thought over and over again for the two days he was kept in bed, until finally, in tears, he gave up trying to decide what to do and tried instead to forget that anything had ever happened.

A week of May passed, one week after the awful day at sea. It was perfect spring weather, blue, green, and gold, and it filled John Devlin's senses and pushed all his confusion to the back of his mind. Once again he was a carefree little boy of ten.

On a warm Saturday morning he was playing in his treehouse, rearranging his treasures and surveying the world beneath him, when he saw a shiny black buggy approaching his house. It pulled up before the front porch and a small man dressed in black got out. This man behaved in a very peculiar manner. He did not proceed directly to the Devlins' front door; instead he made several slow circles around his buggy, hat in hand, talking aloud and nervously waving his hands, as though he were rehearsing a speech and trying it out on his horse. John watched him from the tree-house. He was too far away to hear what the man was saying, but he was close enough to realize that this funny old man was vaguely familiar. Where had he seen him before? The little man made his final circle. He paused and tilted back his head, as if bracing himself with a deep breath, then marched up the porch steps to the front door. At that moment John remembered where he had seen him. The memory sent him scurrying down the Tree and into the kitchen to see what was up. The man's name was Mr. Watkins, and John had seen him at Grandfather's funeral. Mr. Watkins was the caretaker of the New Bedford cemetery.

By the time John ran through the kitchen and into the front hall Mother and Father were already talking to Mr. Watkins in the parlor. John peeped in from the hall. Mr. Watkins close up more than confirmed the impression made by Mr. Watkins far away; he was a very nervous man.

"You see, Mr. Devlin, Mrs. Devlin," he was saying, staring very hard at the black brim of his derby as it revolved rapidly between his fingers, "I've been short-handed recently over at the cemetery, and I haven't been able to stay much in the afternoons, on account of my wife, you know, she's been mighty ill these past two weeks."

"I'm so sorry," said Mother, and Father nodded.

"Thank you, ma'am," said Mr. Watkins. "Don't know what it is as yet, but she coughs all day and whoops all night to beat the band . . . Anyway, I was saying that I've not been around much in the afternoon, on account of my wife, and . . ."

Father and Mother nodded patiently. From long experience John knew this to be a sign that they were growing very impatient.

Apparently Mr. Watkins's diligent preparation of his speech had been to no avail. He was having great difficulty going on. "You see . . . well, the fact is that two weeks ago . . . Just the day after you'd buried your poor departed father, Mr. Devlin, may he rest in . . . in . . . ." For some strange reason Mr. Watkins could not bring himself to say *peace.* "Ah . . . some men came to the cemetery to pick up a body to be transported home . . . A Mr. McDougal, from Scotland . . ."

"Yes?" said Mother, not unkindly, but in that tone that said, *What do we care about Mr. McDougal?*

"Yes, Scotland . . . umm . . . You see, Mr. McDougal died very suddenly, same day as your father did, in fact, and since he had no relatives here, you see, the city just buried him here, not knowin' what else to do . . . But they did send a telegram to his family in Scotland. And the family wired back to dig him up and ship him home, for a proper burial . . ."

Mother and Father nodded vigorously. Their patience was ending, and Mr. Watkins seemed to sense it. The realization was like a kick from behind that sent him suddenly stumbling forward into what he had been trying to avoid saying.

"I was in a hurry, you see, to get home to my wife, and they asked me where the McDougal grave was, and I just pointed at it, from a distance like, and left . . . and they dug up your father by mistake!"

"They *what?*" cried Mother and Father in unison.

Now that the cat was at last out of the bag, Mr. Watkins was visibly trembling, and staring very hard into the boards of the floor. "Please accept my deepest apologies."

"My father was sent to Scotland?" Father sounded more incredulous than angry. Mr. Watkins took courage and lifted his eyes from the floor. Then he remembered what the answer to Father's question was, and quickly lowered them again.

"Well . . . no, Mr. Devlin, in fact he wasn't. Might I sit down?"

Mother took Mr. Watkins's hat and hung it out in the hall. The three adults sat in the parlor. John crept up close to the parlor doors and listened.

"Ah . . . you see, what happened was this," Mr. Watkins was saying. "Mr. McDougal was supposed to be shipped home from New York on a British ship, the *Cameronia*. So naturally the men who came for him sent your father's body to that ship. But just as she was about to sail, with your father on board, the British Navy requisitioned her for duty, you see, in the war over in Europe . . . So what happened was that your father was taken off the *Cameronia* and put on another ship." Again Mr. Watkins stopped speaking.

"And what ship was that?" Father finally asked.

"Ah . . ." Again there was something Mr. Watkins very much did not want to say. "Ah . . . it was the *Lusitania,* as a matter of fact."

Behind the door John pricked up his ears. *Lusitania.* That was the big ship, the fast one, the one they had gone out in the boat to see.

"Well then," said Father, "we'll have the Cunard Line send him back."

But instead of affirming the sensible suggestion, Mr. Watkins simply looked at Father and Mother in surprise. "Have you not seen this morning's *Standard?*" he asked.

"No," said Father. "Why?"

Mr. Watkins took a very large gulp of air. He held it in for a moment, as if hoping for a last-minute reprieve from what he had to explain next. Then he blurted out, all at once: "The Germans sank the *Lusitania* yesterday morning off the coast of Ireland. It was a submarine, a torpedo. She blew up and went down in fifteen minutes. It was horrible. A thousand people died, almost everyone on board. Americans, too."

Outside the doors John stood up; then he sat down again on the stairs and stared straight ahead at nothing.

In the parlor Mr. Watkins was still stammering on. "And the Cunard Line wired me that the coffin was not recovered. Ah, I fear, Mr. Devlin, that your father's body is . . . ah . . . lost . . ."

It had all really happened. Everything he had seen had come to pass. His eyes had seen the present; his mind had seen the future. John began to tremble. *I could have saved them,* he thought, *I could have saved them, why didn't I save them?*

Mr. Watkins and his parents were still talking. What were they saying? Why did Mr. Watkins have that funny accent? He hadn't had it before . . . But it was not Mr. Watkins speaking; it was a priest. Where was he?

The parlor and the hallway had disappeared. He was in a field. Behind him was a town, in front the sea. All around him were rows of coffins, hundreds of them. There was a hole too, an enormous hole in the ground, freshly dug. A priest was intoning something. People were swinging censers over the coffins. Some men, soldiers or policemen, were opening the coffins and looking inside. John could see inside, could see the faces from the water, the blue-white faces of the drowned. Someone had closed their terrified eyes. The men opened another coffin. Grandfather was inside.

"John!" It was Mother speaking. She held Mr. Watkins's hat in her hands.

"I don't know where your manners are. You didn't even say good-bye to Mr. Watkins when he left. Anyway, here's his hat. The poor man was so upset at th' news he brought us, more upset than we were, I think, that he ran out of here and clean forgot it. He hasn't gone far — that's his buggy down the road. Run and give him his hat!"

John took the hat and raced after the black buggy, shouting Mr. Watkins's name. The running kept him from shaking. He dared not think.

Ahead of him the buggy stopped. He caught up with it.

"Mr. Watkins, you forgot your hat," he gasped, and thrust the hat into the hand that reached down for it. Fingers touched his. They were cold as ice. It was not Mr. Watkins's hand.

John looked up. The icy hand disappeared into a black sleeve — not the sleeve of Mr. Watkins's suit but a rough woolen one, the sleeve of a robe. And above the sleeve, under the buggy's canopy, was a black hood. And inside the black hood, where a man's face should have been, was absolutely nothing.

John let out a breath of air that was almost a shriek. An instant later two eyes peered at him from inside the hood. He could scarcely bear to look at them, they were so unnaturally bright, so inhumanly fierce; he looked because he felt compelled to, as though they had locked his gaze with theirs. Then from inside the hood came a voice, a voice so frightening that when it spoke John's skin crawled:

> Little John Devlin had a scare.
> His grandpa served me well.
> Now I've sent Grandpa home to rest
> And a thousand down to hell.
>
> Little John Devlin saw me do it
> Before 'twas even done;
> Now little John must take Grandpa's place,
> But see how he will run!

The carriage drove on. John stood trembling in the dusty street, his guts churning, a thousand questions buzzing in his head.

Grandfather . . .

Grandfather was gone now; he couldn't answer the questions. Someone had to answer them. But John had promised; he could tell no one. And if he broke his promise and told, who would believe him?

Our Father, who art in heaven . . .

First the dream, then the ship; now this. An invisible weight dropped like an iron cloak on John Devlin's little shoulders — the weight of a secret, a dark, unbelievable secret, that was his to bear alone.

Hallowed be thy name . . .

Standing in the dust, too frightened even to cry, the boy shuddered and prayed to his God.

3

The Girl

AS TIME PASSED it seemed that the Lord had heard John Devlin's prayer. After the strange spring of his tenth year his life
returned to normal. A year after Grandfather's death he sailed
at last to the forbidden island and discovered no monsters there,
only a boy's paradise of tide pools and rocks and seagulls. By
the time he entered high school the old man and his stories had
grown remote in his memory; he went into the garden only to
help Mother, and he stopped climbing up to the treehouse altogether. He had no time for solitude now; he had friends, and
sports, and homework, and a sudden new interest in girls. And
that summer he began to crew for his father on the boat, living
out on the open sea for a week at a time.

The sea brought him to manhood. He worked from dawn to
dusk under the blistering summer sun and shivered through the
nights in its chilling fogs. The harshness of it tempered him like
steel. His boy's body grew hard and tough and his hands grew
calloused and capable, replicas of Father's. Toiling day after day
on the rolling deck next to that quiet man, and lying with him
night after night in the little cabin, he learned the unspoken lessons
of the sea: you kept your feet braced on the deck and your hands
pulling hard on the net and your eye on the weather, and your
fears to yourself, and your thoughts on your work and on getting
home alive. He was grateful to learn. He felt himself calmed and
strengthened by the body's work. On the boat there was neither
need nor time to dream about reality — reality was the shifting

deck beneath you, the sudden squall that threatened to sink you, the agony in your arms as you hauled in a net full of cod. And there was no one to talk about strange things with, either; Father, who had lived all his life simply pitting his strength and his will against the elements, and who knew no other life, could not have understood. At the end of a day's fishing on his boat they had time for a can of beans and a quiet pipe, and then instant, exhausted, deathlike sleep. John slept soundly, gratefully. The terrors of his tenth year vanished, and even his moods came over him less and less frequently, until at last they were nothing more than the remembered relics of a dreamy childhood. On the sea there were no dreamers. At sea a dreamer was soon swallowed up.

But still John dreamed. On calm nights he was sometimes awakened by a foghorn's dolorous moan, and through the little porthole near his head he heard the rumble of some great ship churning by in the dark, filled with a cargo of God knows what, bound for God knows where. And he dreamed. Beyond his home, beyond the quiet town where he had always lived and which he had never left, beyond the small part of the vast ocean he traversed with Father, lay the world, the great labyrinth of terrors and wonders hinted at so magically by his long-dead grandfather. He lay in his cramped bunk and listened to the laboring sound of ships' engines growing fainter and fainter in the night, and dreamed of the world. In Grandfather's day he could simply have walked from his home to the docks and signed on for a two-year whaling voyage around the globe. But it was the twentieth century, and in New Bedford whaling was a dead industry. The fishing fleet, John knew from his many trips with Father, went nowhere but the fishing grounds, year after year. As his high-school graduation approached and he found himself about to become a fisherman like his father, trapped forever in the round of New Bedford life, he began thinking hard about escape.

At first it seemed impossible. Expectations were against it. In John Devlin's world sons finished high school and joined their fathers in the fishing fleet, daughters finished high school and married. That was it. Every few years an exceptionally good student (as John was) might hope to be recommended to the seminary and priesthood — a prospect that John equated with being hurled from purgatory into deepest hell. There had to be another way. He briefly considered joining the Army or the Navy, and rejected both. The service seemed to him little better than the priesthood; you were told what to do and what to think and what to wear and where to go. The life of a New Bedford fisherman was freer than that.

Signing on with a merchant freighter seemed a better solution, and he made up his mind to do that, until one day, walking along the waterfront and picking his way through the bums and derelicts who frequented it, he realized that if he went off to a life at sea, he might easily wind up a derelict too, used up and discarded by an industry that changed with changing times. It was a significant insight. All the way home that day he brooded about the derelicts on the wharves. At last he understood: they were men without power. They had drifted through the world without ever acquiring the skills or the means to move freely in it and command its respect. For all of their adventurous lives they had been slaves too, as much as priests and servicemen — slaves to their own ignorance. *He* would not be a slave, he vowed, and immediately he felt closer than ever to defeat. How would a poor boy like him see the great world, except by trading his life away?

For the next few days he was gloomy indeed, and felt all was hopeless. But the very depth of his despair seemed to tilt his sights upward and reveal to him a solution he might otherwise never have dared to see. When he had seen it, he felt at once a soaring elation and a deepened fear. Of all the plans he had considered, this one would be the hardest to lay before his parents, still blissfully unaware of their only child's intention to abandon fishing and leave home forever. But he knew it was the right plan, the solution he had hunted for for so long, so he girded himself for their anger and told them.

"Mother, Pa . . . Aunt Margaret, Uncle Matthew," he said rather quietly toward the end of a Sunday dinner. "I've decided to go to college."

To his great surprise, then vast relief, then growing consternation, no one said anything. The four adults at the table put down their forks and looked at him and then at one another. It was an unheard-of idea. No one in the Devlin family had ever even seen a university campus. It was 1922. College was for the rich.

Growing increasingly uneasy in the silence, John finally broke it himself. "Well, what do you think?"

Aunt Margaret burst out laughing. "Bless me, Johnny Devlin," she said with a chuckle, "if you aren't the biggest tease of a boy, scaring us with your jokes so straight-faced like that . . ."

John swallowed hard and corrected her. "Oh no, Aunt Margaret, I'm not joking. My teacher says I've got the grades for it." He turned quickly to Father. "Now don't worry, Pa, it wouldn't be a burden on you. I've already applied for a scholarship —"

"Scholarship?" Aunt Margaret had stopped laughing. "To where?"

"To Harvard," said John, without looking at her. He was looking at Father, waiting for a reaction.

"*Harvard!*" Aunt Margaret snorted. "You can't be serious."

At last Father spoke. "No, Margaret," he said, "I think he *is* serious." Then he rose and left the table.

John lay awake in his bed well into the night. Although his parents' bedroom was at the far end of the hall, the boards of the old floor were loose and he could hear them creak. He knew Father was pacing up and down, sleepless, wondering what to make of it. Mother was awake too, he knew; they were talking it over. Once he heard them angrily raise their voices, though the sound was muffled by walls and closed doors. He felt bad, but he could do nothing else. He was sure of it. He turned on his side and stared out the window at the moonlit tree and the treehouse, so long neglected. *No matter what they say,* he thought, very calmly, *no matter how angry they are, I'm going.* A little while later the voices down the hall grew quiet, and a little after that he slept.

In the morning when he came down to breakfast Father asked him, "What about the fishing?"

He was too quick to answer. "Oh, don't worry, Pa. I'd come home every summer and help you. You wouldn't have to hire anyone." As he babbled on he could see in Father's eyes that Father knew he was lying and that he needn't have bothered, because Father didn't care about hiring someone. He was asking his son the essential question, the one that he couldn't really answer: how could he abandon everything and step off into the unknown?

"John." Father broke into his torrent of assurances. "Your mother and I talked it over last night and we're agreed."

John looked nervously from one parent to the other. "Agreed?"

Father looked at Mother. "Yes, we are," she said, coming over from the stove. She looked at John for a long moment and said nothing. John had the impression that despite what she had just said she was working hard to silence doubt. At last she spoke. "We're agreed that if your grades in school are up to it, and if you can get a scholarship, and if you really want to . . . then you should go."

"I can?"

"You can," said Father. And he smiled and added the all-important thing: "With our blessing."

And that was that. In the months that followed Father and Mother stuck by their decision. When Aunt Margaret declared that her only nephew would come to a bad end in the fleshpots of Boston, having first lost his faith by consorting with the morally lax (Protestants, or worse), and when Father O'Reilly opined that if the boy was stubborn about holding to his prideful course, he ought at least to be sent to a Catholic college where a wholesome spiritual discipline prevailed, Patrick and Kathleen Devlin thanked them both politely for their opinions and ignored them. John was allowed to carry out his own plan. Even in the spring, when Harvard granted him his scholarship and the possibility of his leaving home became a certainty, Mother and Father never wavered.

It seemed a miracle, John thought, and all through his final summer of fishing with Father he lived with the fear that a miracle could never really happen. But it did happen. John Devlin became a college man.

As his train pulled into the unfamiliar hugeness of Boston and the reality of what he was doing finally hit home, his boy's confidence crumbled and he felt plain scared, more scared than if he had been cast adrift at sea. But a vivid memory of his childhood arose in his mind against his fear — the memory of riding the stubby bowsprit of Father's boat on his very first fishing trip, plunging down and leaping up with it like a bareback rider, freed from the land and his mother's fears, shaking with the thrill of freedom and the open sea. In the first days at Harvard, amid the chaos of the new term, the countless new faces, the strangeness of the city around him, he saw in his mind again and again that boundless sea stretching out before him, and felt that he was once more surging forward into freedom, into a larger, unknown sphere of life. His courage returned. Life was just a series of circles, he thought, which people drew around you to contain you. First they drew a very small one, and when you got old enough and jumped over it they quickly drew a bigger one, and when you jumped over that one they drew another, bigger one, and so on. Each time they tried to hold you back, and each time you had to jump. His childhood friends back in New Bedford, the future fishermen and fishermen's wives, had not jumped; but he had. And now, thought John, they can draw a million circles if they like; I can jump a million times.

He had jumped — but would he land on his feet? He arrived at Harvard full of apprehension about being a poor boy on scholarship among the whelps of the great, and his first days there more than confirmed his fears. The other freshmen he met seemed to have known each other already for years, at one of a few schools everyone seemed to have gone to, whose exotic names he heard over and over again: Exeter, Andover, Choate. He had had no idea that these places, which everyone else knew intimately, even existed, and when he ventured to say so he endured looks of such derisive disbelief that he never made that mistake again. His first weeks were filled with similar small disasters. His clothes were all wrong; his speech was all wrong: his roommates wore tweeds and talked through their noses. And almost everything they talked about or did together was an absolute mystery to John. He tried to hold his own in conversations about tennis and trips to Europe by telling anecdotes from his own boyhood, and he encountered, at best, discreet amusement.

Through September he was miserable but determined. He would stay, he would succeed.

Football was his first success. The coaches had picked out his sturdy frame right away and recruited him for the freshman squad. He played well, backing up muscle and speed with brains. He immediately discovered that at Harvard, talent on the playing field compensated for a myriad of social sins. By the middle of a good football season his popularity was secure, and John had enough native shrewdness to take advantage of his new stature on campus. Now that he had an audience he improved his stories of fishing and the sea — not for nothing had he sat for years at Grandfather's knee — adding a few more adventures here and there (things that truly *might* have happened, even if in fact they actually hadn't), putting a bit more Irish lilt and timber in his voice, getting just a suggestion of a glint into his blue Irish eyes as he stared out past his listeners and conjured with his expressive hands the wild sea, the endless sky. And it worked. Within weeks of his arrival at Harvard the snobs who had laughed at him began to envy his adventurous boyhood, and to respect him. John smiled inwardly and marked the lesson well. He had discovered in himself a power to compel others. His many friendships were also trophies of a conquest, the bending of an alien world to his will.

From the beginning he worked hard and earned good grades and the respect of his professors. He found that he excelled in history, and when he had to declare his major at the end of his sophomore year he chose that as his field of study. By that time his classmates had given him a nickname of their own: "Pope John," for his pontificating tendencies in classrooms full of less able minds, and for his habit of faithfully attending Mass every Sunday, as he had promised his parents that he would. Pope John accepted his new name with good grace. In fact it pleased him mightily. However innocently it had been bestowed on him, the exotic Catholic, by his Protestant blue-blood friends, he heard in it a backhanded acknowledgment of powers that made him their equal and often their superior.

By the fall of his junior year Pope John's powers had blossomed. On his rare visits to New Bedford (true to prediction, he had eased himself out of summer fishing duties in favor of working as a researcher for his professors) his parents marveled at him; Father O'Reilly saw him at Mass and frowned; Aunt Margaret, he suspected, prayed for his soul. A dean's list student, star of the football team, he had long since acquired the right tweeds, the right pipe (an outdoorsman's rough-hewn one, in keeping with his Rudyard Kipling image), a taste for art (Italian Renaissance, Rembrandt) and music (Beethoven, Bach), and an expert ability to modulate his voice somewhere between an Irish lilt and the prep-school nasalization which was *de rigueur.* His popularity, aided by his tall, muscular build and his striking blue eyes, had long since expanded beyond his original circle of friends to embrace the affections of several young ladies from the Boston social scene.

Pope John enjoyed these liaisons as he enjoyed his male friend-

ships — warmly, generously, but with a certain ultimate reservation. Even now he discovered in himself an urge to stay aloof,
which puzzled him. His pat answer was that loneliness had been
bred into him by his summers at sea, but he was too smart to
accept this cliché as a true explanation, and the fact that he did
accept it was evidence of other reasons that he preferred to keep
unknown, even to himself. And he often feared his loneliness as
much as he desired it. From time to time — for instance, if he
happened to hear a certain sententious sort of music, Wagner or
Strauss — a vague feeling of fear arose out of nowhere and gripped
him for no apparent reason, sometimes for as long as a day. When
this happened he avoided Wagner and buried himself in the company of friends until the fear passed. With characteristic pluck
he made a virtue of this, telling himself that he had handled his
fears as well as he handled everything else, that he had beaten
them, and all by himself too, without the necessity of confiding
embarrassing secrets to others . . . But at this point he usually
felt the fear rising again, and quickly thought of something else.

Even his closest friends soon learned, if they were perceptive
enough, to keep their own slight distance from him. Perhaps because he was so different from them, and thus carried the magical
power of the stranger, even his intimates felt as if something quite
frightening might be lurking somewhere in him, behind the genial
mask. The poets of his group likened him to the sea he came
from, compelling and threatening at once: he attracted people with
a beautiful wild quality he had and others lacked, but when you
were with him you felt a little uneasy about that same quality,
which might suddenly turn on you.

In the fall of his junior year, it did turn. During the Yale game,
the last of the season, a particularly troublesome defensive halfback
needed blocking. John and a teammate hit him with a classic
double-team block: John dove low, driving into the belly, while
his teammate hit high, at the chest. It worked like a charm. The
Yale man went down with John and his teammate on top of him.
John remembered dropping low and plunging his shoulder into
the Yalie's gut . . . and then his teammates were pulling him
off the man, and the referee was bawling at him, and the Yalie
was screaming in pain.

The Yale doctor arrived. Three of the Yalie's ribs were broken.

His angry teammates shouted at the referee that they had seen John smash his ribcage with an elbow after tackling him, and no one on the Harvard team disagreed. Enraged Yalies surrounded John, shouting about sportsmanship and raising their fists. His teammates hustled him back to the Harvard bench.

To everyone John maintained that he had no idea what had happened. He was lying about this, but as much to himself as to others. He was genuinely confused about what *had* happened, except for a vague feeling that he had in fact done something very wrong. Only days later did a clear memory take form in John's mind, and he saw himself, as clearly as in the present, quite deliberately driving his elbow into the Yalie's ribcage. He remembered thinking nothing at the time, nothing at all, just *doing* it. It shocked him — not because of what he had done, for he could see the point of that, getting Yale's best defensive man out of the game, and feel only moderately sorry for the damage done accomplishing it. Football was a risky sport. What shocked him was that he could have done so violent and illegal a thing without first *deciding* to do it. Over three years he had made a life and a name for himself at Harvard, against the odds, by hard, self-conscious effort. He had no business losing control like that. If it had happened freshman year . . . But it had not, and his well-established stature among his classmates survived it, although not without some curious looks from his friends and a few anonymous mutterings about who was a gentleman and who was not.

During the winter he applied himself even harder to the study of history. That semester Pope John's grades were better than ever, and some of his professors began to speak of him as the logical recipient of one of the undergraduate prizes upon his graduation next year. And so he glided happily through the days of spring, once again supremely confident, until . . .

One very pretty morning he allowed extra time on his way to "The Rise of Prussia," his favorite class that term, to stop by a small campus gallery set up by some of his wealthier and more modern-minded classmates for exhibiting the sort of contemporary art to which the Fogg Museum, that dormitory of eternally athletic Greeks and pensive madonnas, would have barricaded its doors. Normally John found these exhibitions pleasant diversions, but on this day, once he managed to get inside the tiny gallery thronged with curious students and had a look at one of the paintings on display, he wasn't sure that he wouldn't have helped bar the way had anyone dared to bring such work up the Fogg's hallowed steps. What he was looking at scarcely seemed to be a painting at all, in any acceptable sense; it was more like a photograph of a dream (if such a thing were possible), or a madman's vision. From its title he knew that it was supposed to be a picture of a village, and sure enough, he could make out a few wooden buildings that looked vaguely Russian, far up in the right corner. Beneath the buildings was a bearded, booted farmer carrying a scythe, and next to him his dancing, kerchiefed wife, both properly rendered — except that they were floating in midair, and the wife was dancing upside down, her nose approaching her husband's feet. On the left side, about halfway down, was another recognizable rural detail, a woman milking a cow — but woman, cow, and milking stool floated over the enormous face of a horse, which stared with great soulful eyes at the nose and lips of a dark man whose angled profile was just barely in view across the canvas. Horse and man blended at points into a common background of pure abstract shape, like raw matter without a form. And in a limbo at the very bottom of the canvas, unrelated to anything else, a little tree bloomed, laden with flowers and fruit.

John stared helplessly at the small title card tacked up on the wall, in search of some clue to what this bizarre creation might mean. But under the title there was only the artist's name: Marc Chagall. Whoever this Chagall is, John thought in disgust, he's a loony, not a painter. John walked away; but at the next painting he stopped and stared again. This one was even more impossible: it had no people in it at all, not even upside-down ones, nor any trees or anything else even vaguely recognizable. The canvas was covered with a riot of weird shapes, boxlike, circular, serpentine, indescribable, parading across a background of an empty room. Here and there John saw one that resembled a starfish or a sea urchin — or a creature that he had never seen before, or even imagined — wafting gently through the air or strolling peacefully along the canvas bottom. Again there was no help for John in his perplexity, only the title with the artist's name: Joan Miró.

It was curious that despite his initial bewilderment over and even displeasure with the paintings, John Devlin did not hurry on but found himself intently studying every one of the canvases on display, endangering his prompt attendance at "The Rise of Prussia." By the time he had worked his way down one side of the gallery his displeasure had more or less disappeared, but his bewilderment had not. In fact it had grown; it had a personal dimension now. John was as much perplexed by why these apparently ridiculous paintings so compelled him as he was by the paintings themselves. He was standing in front of something entitled *Still Life,* a picture of a violin that was anything but still — the instrument looked like it had been dynamited or run over by a truck — when he finally achieved a few coherent thoughts about what was disturbing him. The violin was really dozens of violins — no, it was one violin, but seen from a dozen different angles. That was it: he was looking at one violin from a dozen different viewpoints, in a dozen different times and places, in one picture, that is, all at once. What surprised John was how restless and upset he suddenly became.

Somewhere outside the gallery an electric bell rang. John remembered "The Rise of Prussia." He spun around to go, turning his back on the maddening violin and colliding with someone standing directly behind him. Mumbling apologies, he stepped back before going around, but instead, for one long moment, he forgot himself and simply stared.

The person he had bumped into was without question the most beautiful girl John Devlin had ever seen. She looked at him with enormous eyes, incredible eyes black as coal, and smiled.

"Please excuse me," she said, very politely.

John said nothing; he could scarcely breathe.

The girl's English was clipped, immaculate, of British inflection but deliciously honeyed by her voice, which was closer to music or the song of a bird than human speech. Her skin was very dark, like pure chocolate. In the exact center of her forehead was a black dot.

"Aruna! Come on — we'll be late!"

She turned, waved to her friend, and was gone. The gallery was now twice as crowded, as people rushing out to their next class tried to get past people viewing paintings. John craned his neck and caught sight of the girl walking rapidly through the crowd, chattering gaily with another girl, the one who had called to her. They were heading out the door; he would never see her again. He looked at his watch, at his books, and then back at her, just in time to see her smile at her friend as they went through the door. Had he not seen her smile, he might have forced himself to go on to his class, but having seen it twice, he was lost. As fast as he could move through the crowd he made his way to the door and through it, following her. Today Prussia would have to continue its inexorable rise without him.

Outside he saw her walking with her friend toward Memorial Hall, a venerable red-brick edifice on the edge of campus which contained enormous, amphitheatrical lecture rooms. Who was she? The dot on her forehead meant she was Indian — a Brahmin, of the highest caste. She was wearing an exquisite gray suit of obviously European cut, which meant, of course, that it was unbelievably expensive. Her friend, he noticed now, was very pretty too, and also well dressed; she was dark-haired as well, but fair-skinned and obviously American — probably Jewish. That made sense, he thought. At Radcliffe foreigners and Jews soon found each other. The two girls were entering Memorial Hall; he quickened his pace, and in another few moments he entered too.

Sanders Theater in Memorial Hall was a cavern, its upper rafters lost in gloom, its highest seats so far from the lecturer that students saw him as if through the wrong end of a telescope. But when John arrived there were very few empty seats left. He was lucky enough to find one just above and to the side of the exquisite Aruna — a perfect vantage point for studying her while appearing to be absorbed in the lecture, whatever it was.

John tore his eyes away from the girl long enough to glance around the packed room, and was amazed to discover that in the immense crowd he recognized almost no one. The one or two faces he knew were those of physicists. Returning to reality for a moment, John groaned. What had he done? Skipped an installment of Prussia's rise for the most impenetrable and stupefying of all subjects taught at Harvard? But behind him the doors were closing; the crowd was quieting down. It was too late. A professor on the podium was already introducing a guest speaker whose name sounded vaguely familiar even to John: Dr. Karl Werner, Chair of Theoretical Physics, University of Göttingen, Germany. *Well,* thought John ruefully, *I have found Prussia today after all.* The professor was announcing the topic of Dr. Werner's lecture: the implications of something called relativity for research into atoms, whatever they were. John groaned again. He was not going to understand a word of this. But before he went back to gazing at Aruna he amused himself by trying to guess which of the gentlemen seated behind the professor at the podium was the distinguished Herr Doktor Werner. Apparently Dr. Werner was late, for the three men on the lecture platform who appeared properly professional in age and bearing were all Harvard physicists whom John had seen around campus, and the fourth man was obviously a graduate student, an assistant to one of the other three; he was in his late twenties, very blond and lean, and clad in a simple, cheap suit. John was just about to look at Aruna again when he saw the graduate assistant rise to his feet and, to deafening applause, advance to the podium to speak.

It so surprised John that a man who was clearly not more than ten years older than himself could be an internationally known scientist that he actually forgot all about Aruna for a moment and tried to follow Dr. Werner's lecture. But it was just as he had feared: Dr. Werner spoke in an impenetrable tangle of mathematical arcana, linked somehow to a series of indecipherable hieroglyphics he scribbled on a blackboard. Most of his audience — including Aruna, John noted — seemed absorbed in everything he was saying, whatever it was. Aruna in particular was diligently taking notes. *Perhaps she would be kind enough to explain all this to me,* John thought, remembering his reason for trapping himself in this incomprehensible lecture.

Smiling, he resumed his study of the Indian girl. It was interesting, he thought, that unlike most people, this young woman seemed more and more extraordinary every time he looked at her. Familiarity only deepened his first impression. The serious expression now on her face, the look of concentration in her dazzling eyes, brought her features into a sharp focus, like those of a finely worked sculpture, and made her all the more beautiful. During his many infatuations John had never felt anything like what he felt gazing at this exquisite Hindu girl. She was *not* a girl, he thought suddenly, or not only that; she was . . . *more;* that was the only word he had for it, the only thought.

Around him there was a general shuffling of papers and shifting of bodies in seats. John looked hopefully down at the podium. Was the lecture over? It was not, but Dr. Werner was now saying things John could understand. Apparently he had just completed the main body of his talk and was making some concluding remarks. Relieved to hear something intelligible, John listened for a moment, and his interest perked: Dr. Werner was no longer talking physics, he was talking John's own subject, history.

"I would like," he said in precise, chiseled English, "on this occasion, my first public lecture in America, to state my feelings of admiration for Christopher Columbus, a man who had the courage to launch himself into the unknown. Columbus sailed his ships right to the edge of his maps, and then over the edge, into a realm charted only in fantastic myths, full of impossible terrors and impossible paradises — who knew? But Columbus sailed until his provisions ran out. All he knew with certainty was that if he gave up and turned back, he and his men would starve. So he kept going, and found a new world. And Europe was not the same again."

Werner's voice had become passionate. He leaned over the podium and looked intently at his listeners.

"Imagine," he said softly, "what it meant. Here was a vast new part of the planet, long dreamed of but now suddenly real, proven beyond doubt to exist. Think of what went through the minds of Europe when Columbus came home. Perhaps in the New World Europeans would discover things that would throw everything they knew, or thought they knew, into question. America was a watershed, a great turning point, in the history of our civilization.

"Today western civilization is coming to its next great watershed. There is no single Columbus bringing it there, but rather a group within the generation now coming of age. They have no ships but are explorers nonetheless. They are pushing forward into the dark of another unknown world, also long imagined and now on the verge of being discovered — the world of the atom, the invisible foundation of the universe, ultimate reality itself."

John glanced at Aruna. The look on her face as she listened to Dr. Werner was one he had seen rarely in a classroom but often at Mass.

"Let us review," said Werner, "what little we do know about this new world of ours." He began to pace back and forth across the platform. "We start with Einstein's assertion that energy and matter, so long thought to be separate, are in fact interchangeable

— that solid matter is a kind of 'frozen' energy. And now Lord Rutherford in England has succeeded in transforming the atoms of nitrogen with tiny particles."

Werner stopped pacing and faced forward. "So it seems that the ancient dream of the medieval alchemists, the dream of the transmutation of matter, has at last become a reality. Beyond this . . . beyond this we are exactly in the position of Columbus setting sail from Spain in 1492. We have our maps, our charts, the brilliant work of preceding generations of scientists, but we know that very soon we shall sail off the edge of our maps into something completely unknown. We know this because already we have had to tear up several of our most reliable charts. For example, Einstein's theory of relativity has completely overturned our old conception of the physical universe, which was based on the absolute space and time of Isaac Newton. Thanks to Einstein and others, we now understand that absolute space and time, if indeed they do exist, might just as well not, since we can never know anything absolutely. In the aftermath of Einstein, Newton's absoluteness appears to be merely a limitation of the human intellect, an arbitrary structure that the intellect imposes on reality in order to comprehend it."

John was shifting uncomfortably in his seat. He felt restless. Werner was boring him with this esoteric talk of things relative and absolute. No, that was not it. He was not bored; for some reason he felt afraid, just as he had among the paintings . . .

Werner walked thoughtfully back to his podium and leaned on it. "So," he continued, "here we are in a pretty fix. We are sailing forward into an unknown new world with maps that we may never decipher! But indeed this is our situation . . . It may be that the ultimate goal of rational, scientific inquiry since the Renaissance — the absolute, final knowledge of everything in the universe and of every law that governs it — is unreachable, because the human rational faculty is incapable of attaining such knowledge. So the dream that western man has dreamed for hundreds of years, the dream of eventual mastery over the world, may really be only that: a dream. If this is true, then our civilization really has only two choices: it can disintegrate, or it can evolve."

A thought leaped into John's mind: *Why is he looking at me like that?*

It was an absurd thought. There were hundreds of people in

the audience, and Werner was looking at all of them. But Werner seemed less a scientist now than a prophet; you could see it in his eyes as he spoke of civilization's choices. John realized that the man was really quite handsome in a lean, pale, holy sort of way — the way the medieval Germans had depicted their saints, with flesh reduced to the minimum necessary to sustain a spiritual fire. He looked over at Aruna, who continued to listen with devotional attention, and he read on her face the same conclusions about Dr. Werner's Teutonic good looks. John hated the German.

"If we do succeed in evolving, it may be into a world utterly different from the present one, in which every scientific, social, and moral truth we now cling to has been smashed and replaced. Such a prospect, of course, makes progress a very frightening — or perhaps a very wonderful — possibility. But whatever it brings, progress will mean letting go of our absolute faith in our reason, our certainty about the evidence of our senses, and accepting, or perhaps reviving, a sense of uncertainty and wonder more characteristic of ancient religious man than modern scientific man. Whether we can live with uncertainty or will deliberately violate truth to retain our illusion of mastery over all things remains to be seen.

"Right now we are like Columbus's crew — as we sail inexorably forward we can only imagine what will happen to us. We see ourselves devoured by the demons of hell, falling off the edge of the world into nothingness, or perhaps sailing into heaven and frolicking forever with the angels. Any of these might happen. All that is certain is that the provisions are gone and the maps no longer useful. We have sailed too far. If we turn back, we will perish. If we sail on — who knows? But sail we must. We have reached the watershed, and therein lies our terror and our hope."

The lecture was over. Thunderous applause. In John's mind two thoughts battled for attention. One was a jealous impulse to give this Werner, this boy wonder whom Aruna found so attractive, his comeuppance (preferably in front of Aruna) — a history lesson, a warning to an amateur not to stray publicly into John Devlin's field. The other thought was the same damned stupid, persistent one that came out of nowhere: *Why is he looking at me?*

John stood up. Below him physics students surged in waves

toward the platform, pushing for a chance to speak to their idol. Aruna was already in the front rank. John had not the slightest doubt that if she wanted to, she could part any crowd, or the Red Sea, with her eyes. At the sight of her one of his two battling thoughts vanquished the other. She was standing just in front of Werner now, ready to address him. This was his chance. He clambered down the aisle until he came to the first row of seats. Instead of plunging into the mass in front of him he climbed onto a seat and, standing like an orator above the noisy crowd, boomed out his challenge.

"Doctor Werner!"

The pale, lean head, its cheeks almost sunken, turned toward him. So, he noted with satisfaction, did Aruna.

"Doctor Werner," he repeated, sophomorically pompous, "isn't it true that the research and experiments you've described are the obsessions of only a few European intellectuals? You speak of their changing civilization. But how can practical life, the governing of men and nations, possibly be affected by such" — he savored the damning word — "esoterica?"

He had finished; he stood on the seat, smiling arrogantly, awaiting the answer. An instant later he got one, but it was not at all the answer he expected.

Suddenly there was deep twilight in the great lecture hall. John could still see Dr. Werner and all the others in front of him, but for some reason their movements had become extremely slow, as if they moved through glue. An eclipse? Dr. Werner's eyes, hidden deep in their sockets, met his. *Why is he looking at me like that?* Then John lost all power to think. He saw that Dr. Werner's face was no longer there. In its place over the shoulders was a kind of black hole, absolutely empty. Eyes were glowing in it — not Werner's eyes, but someone else's eyes, eyes that shot into John's brain like two arrows and fixed themselves there, riveting him . . . There was no sound, absolutely no sound at all, anywhere in the room. *What's happening to me?* An instant later a voice spoke, the voice of the eyes, and it sent a shudder through John.

> Children grow up fast,
> The sun falls to earth;

Do you want to live?
Catch it if you can!

The eyes were gone; it was Dr. Werner who was staring at him now. But on his face was a twisted, tragic expression, as though he were in the act of witnessing some unspeakable horror. John stared back in a horror of his own.

"Sir!"

It was Werner's voice. The room was light; Dr. Werner's face had reappeared; and suddenly John's horror became embarrassment. Everyone was staring at *him*. He felt drenched in sweat.

"Sir! Didn't you hear me?" Werner asked mildly.

"Uh . . . uh . . ."

Werner smiled patiently. "I shall repeat. In answer to your question, many eminent physicists say that atomic research will never have any practical applications. I reserve judgment. But I find myself thinking often of a warning that one of my predecessors in physics, an alchemist, wrote: 'Deny the powerful and their warriors entry into your workshops. For such people misuse the holy mysteries in the service of power!'"

"Th-thank you, sir . . ."

Dr. Werner smiled again and nodded, then turned to another questioner. John got down from the seat and fled from Memorial Hall. He dared not even look at Aruna.

John cut all of his classes that day. From Memorial Hall he ran across the Yard and down through the streets of Cambridge until he came to the bank of the Charles, where he finally brought himself to a halt and stood panting, staring into the green river flowing by. After a while he began to walk along the bank, and he kept walking, upstream and downstream, for the rest of the day. What he thought for most of that time was *Damn, damn, damn*. After the first shock had worn off it had not taken him long to remember Mr. Watkins's hat and the first time he had seen those eyes, heard that voice, and then he remembered, in a sickening rush of thoughts, the *Lusitania* and Grandfather in the Tree. As if nothing had changed in eleven long years. *Damn, damn, damn.*

He realized that he could barely see the path in front of him, and panicked. Was it coming over him again? No: it was getting dark because it was nearly night. He laughed, and instantly felt pleased and relieved that he could laugh. It was over. He was all right. All he needed now was an explanation of what had happened. Unfortunately he had none. He had had none eleven years ago . . . But now he was sure that in time, when he had calmed down and thought sufficiently about it, he would find the explanation and get things under control, as he always did. He was very sure of it.

His stomach made a loud noise. Suddenly he realized that a day of frantic walking had made him ravenous. He looked about him and saw the lights of Cambridge just winking on in the twilight. As he watched this pretty sight the burden of his thoughts seemed to slip from him, and he set off at a lope toward town, thinking only of getting something to eat. He was heading for the college dining hall, but his way led him past O'Brien's, already packed with Harvard students, and the smell of food brought him to a halt. He stared through the window, fumbling in his pockets to see if he had enough money to eat right then and there. But before he had determined exactly how much money he did have he was through the doors and threading his way across the crowded coffee shop. Aruna was sitting at the back of O'Brien's, sipping a soda.

He crossed the room toward her very much in spite of himself. As he approached her table he was mostly conscious of what a fool he had made of himself in front of her that morning. She was sitting with her friend, the pretty Jewish one from the lecture; she had not yet noticed him. He could walk past her table and sit somewhere else. That was exactly the right thing to do, given his asinine performance at the lecture — but while he was wholeheartedly thinking this he arrived at her table and stopped.

"Good evening." *Why are you doing this, you jerk?*

Aruna looked up. She smiled at him. He had the feeling that whatever stupid thing he had done this morning did not matter to her. Even if it did, he could not possibly leave while she smiled.

"Ah — sorry I ran into you this morning. Are you all right?"

"Oh, yes, I am, thank you very much."

Her peculiar Indian voice speaking its singsong English really was entrancing.

"Oh, good. I assure you it won't happen again." He laughed weakly. *Don't make stupid jokes, idiot.*

Aruna nodded. There was a moment of awkward silence. Pope John had never been tongue-tied by a girl before. Pretty girls normally had the opposite effect on him. And he had always been very good at picking up silent cues from people about what they were thinking and what they wanted him to do, but he had absolutely no idea what Aruna was thinking. For a panicky moment he looked around the room, trying to think of something to say.

"Well . . . ah, there don't seem to be any empty tables. Do you mind if I join you?"

"There's an empty stool at the counter." Aruna's friend spoke in a distinctly unfriendly manner, not looking at him, her mouth full of hamburger. John turned around and looked. There was indeed an empty stool at the counter.

"Oh. Um, I think that someone's saving it for a friend," he lied.

"Please, sit." Aruna gestured toward the empty chair at their table. Even this simple movement had an exquisite grace. John had never seen anybody move an arm like that. Aruna's friend shot her a very annoyed glance. John smiled at Aruna and sat down.

"Thanks." He held out his hand. "My name's John Devlin."

Aruna took his hand. At the touch of her he would have closed his eyes and sighed, had he not made a conscious effort to control himself.

"Dev-leen." Aruna withdrew her hand. "My name is Aruna. Aruna Rajputani."

"Raj-pu-tan-i." John struggled to get it right.

Aruna laughed, another indescribable sound she made, too sublime to be human.

John held out his hand to Aruna's friend. "John Devlin," he said, turning on her his blue eyes and his most charming Irish smile.

But the girl merely grabbed his hand and wrung it once, with obvious reluctance. "Ruth Daniels." She did not smile. In fact, there was no mistaking the look on her face, which was aggressively hostile.

"Uh, nice to meet you," John said lamely, withdrawing the smile and turning his eyes back to Aruna. He opened his mouth to speak to her, but Ruth Daniels was faster.

"Now Aruna, as I was saying before we were interrupted, the problem with an idea like that is —"

"What did you think of the paintings?" John tried the smile on Aruna. If Ruth Daniels could cut people off, so could he.

"Oh, they were fascinating." Aruna seemed quite willing to let Ruth be interrupted. "It was so very interesting to learn that there are now painters in Europe who are seeing with the inner eye. Don't you think?"

"Uh . . . yes." John's smile froze on his face. He did *not* want to talk about the "inner eye." The phrase threw him back into his childhood, to the morning, to the lecture hall. He headed for safe ground, where he felt secure, where he could impress her. "They pose a tremendously interesting question, don't you think, about the society that produced them. You see, I have a theory." He bore down on her with the blue Devlin eyes, which in combination with his theories had always proven irresistible. "A theory that all human societies pass through predictable stages of growth and decline, stages that we may even predict —"

"Oh, yeah. Spengler." Ruth Daniels had interrupted him again.

"I beg your pardon?"

"*Spengler,*" Ruth repeated impatiently. "I hate to disillusion you, friend, but you're a little late with your theory of stages in civilization. They've already thought of it in Germany. Spengler did. Oswald Spengler. *Der Untergang des Abendlandes.*"

"What?"

"*Der Untergang* — you don't read German?"

"Ah, well, I'm not *fluent.*"

"Oh well. *Tant pis.*" Ruth smiled sweetly. "If you have to, you can read it in English. It's just coming out now, *The Decline of the West.*"

"I'll certainly look for it," John said glumly. Oswald Spengler? None of his professors had ever mentioned him . . .

"Yeah. I suggest you do before you give yourself credit for his theories."

"You seemed to be very interested in what Doctor Werner said this morning." Again Aruna smiled as she spoke; again the bombs went off. John flushed a truly Harvardian crimson. Her smile was devastating, but it was impossible to guess why she smiled. Was she mocking his foolishness at the lecture? Feeling a little desperate, he played his only other card.

"Yes, I was," he said quickly, moving the conversation on. "International points of view interest me. When I graduate I'm going into the State Department."

"Yes? Why?"

"Because" — he was sure he would impress her now — "I have decided to devote my life to making the world a better place. What happened in 1914 must not happen again, and I intend to do my part to see that it doesn't." Whenever he made this little speech to a girl he warmed to it quickly and assumed a lecturer's tone. "What I want to do is help create a world system that works as well as the American system, sort of an international government modeled on our Constitution, that would link nations together in legal and mutually beneficial ways, with checks and balances, you see. In such a system no one nation would be allowed to dominate the world, just as no one state or party dominates America. When we achieve a world like that, I'm sure we can eliminate wars."

"Question, friend." Ruth Daniels had once again interrupted him, but this time in a thoughtful sort of voice, as though she were very interested in what he was saying. He turned the smile on her again. Perhaps they had finally found common ground. "Yes?"

She smiled sweetly at him. "Have you read much history?"

Have I read much history? The question so stunned John Devlin that he lost his self-control. "I'll have you know," he snapped at Ruth, "that I have the highest average in the history department."

This revelation of his genius did not silence Ruth, as it was supposed to. "Oh-*ho.*" She smirked. "I see we have a man here who knows his history. All right then — question for the top history student. When has *anyone* preaching peace and brotherhood ever made the world a better place?"

The question seemed so absurdly easy that John almost laughed. "When Roman civilization declined," he said, leaning over the table and grinning nastily at Ruth, "and the Dark Ages began, the Catholic Church, under the enlightened guidance of Saints

Benedict and Gregory the Great, preached peace and Christian virtues and did a great deal to curb the endless fighting of half-civilized warlords. The world has been improving ever since, because of that."

He sat back, once again expecting Ruth to be silenced. Once again, however, she was not. In fact she laughed.

"Boy, they don't call you Pope John for nothing."

He was stunned. "How did you know that?"

"So the Catholic Church preached love and peace and saved everybody's neck?" She went on, viciously pleasant, ignoring his question. "Tell me, how many Jewish necks would you guess it saved?"

"Jewish?" This was an aspect of history not much taught at Harvard. "Well, uh . . ."

"Precisely." The sweet smile was back on Ruth's face. Annoyed as he was, John could not help noting that it really *was* a sweet smile. Such good looks wasted, he thought, on such a bitch.

"The Catholic Church doesn't save Jews," Ruth went on. "It burns them."

"Well, sure, but —"

"But what? They don't count? Or maybe it just never bothered you, Pope John. Did the Christ-killers get what they deserved, hmm?"

"No, of *course* not." John glared at her. "If you'll let me finish my sentence, I was going to say that I acknowledge the historical tragedy of the Jews and the church's despicable role in it, and I understand how you must feel — "

"*Please* don't presume to know how I feel. I can tell already you're mistaken. I'm not holding up my Chosen People as anything special. Being slaughtered over and over again doesn't mean you're any good. It just means you're weak. If history had been any different we'd have done it to you." Ruth took another bite of hamburger. "I brought up my ancestors," she continued, not very daintily, through a full mouth, "only to counter your absurd idealism." She chewed and swallowed while the barb sunk in. "The point is," she said finally, "that every time this lovely world of yours has gotten 'better,' Pope John, it's gotten better for one group of people and a whole lot worse for another."

"I take it you also study history?" John asked haughtily.

Ruth took another huge bite of hamburger and shook her head. "Anthropology," she mumbled through her food. "Intellectually, I surround you. I study all those dark nasty tribes that muster around the fringes of your glorious western civilization! From my point of view, sainthood is a late and not very typical bit of human behavior. I prefer the savage to the saint. I think in him you get a clearer view of the deeper human verities. And just to show you I'm not prejudiced, I offer you my own tribe as an example."

"Your tribe?"

"My tribe: the Hebrews. One group of savages who made it into the Civilization Club. Does your encyclopaedic knowledge of human affairs include the word *holocaust?*"

John had to admit that it did not.

"I didn't expect it would," Ruth said. "You Christians have always blamed us for the wrong crime, you know. You wail and moan because our leaders once quite sensibly executed a trouble-maker to avoid a hopeless insurrection against the might of Rome. But then you open your Bible and read Joshua with such pious approval! Anyway, a holocaust was a special kind of Hebrew sacrifice to God, a burnt offering that had to be completely consumed so God got everything and nothing was left over for Man."

"So?"

"So the holocaust turned out to be an extremely useful bit of ritual when the Hebrews decided to improve their economic lot in the world. When they left Egypt and set their sights on the fertile land of Canaan they were, of course, faced with the awkward fact that their Promised Land was already occupied by a lot of people who liked it very much and didn't want to move. But did they opt for the John Devlin plan? Did they sit down with the Canaanites and work out some nice checks and balances?" Ruth's voice was getting louder. "Not on your life! Not when a far more practical and *pious* solution was at hand. The Hebrews simply dedicated their Canaanite neighbors to God. This made them worthy kindling for a proper holocaust, and whoosh! All their cities were sacked and torched, along with everything and everyone in them, man, woman, child. Because after all, it would have been sinful to leave anything unburned, right? So the Hebrews took the best farmland between the Nile and the Euphrates and made points with their God for grabbing it! And the Canaanites just got burned. Pretty slick, if you ask me."

There was a moment of silence at the table. Ruth's white skin was flushed. John could see real bitterness in her pretty face.

"For a Jew," he said quietly, "you don't think very much of your religion."

Ruth glared at him. "I'm not a Jew," she snapped. "I'm an intellectual. I assure you that I have repudiated all of my inherited connections with an irrational superstition."

"Oh come on now, you've been talking about three thousand years ago —"

"Or about August 1914, or today, or tomorrow." Ruth's voice was very loud indeed. She jabbed a finger at John. "Wake up, Pope John. Mankind doesn't change, not even for a pair of pretty blue eyes. I don't care what the great Herr Doktor Werner said this morning, as I was just explaining to Aruna when you intruded with your do-gooder Catholic mush. Maybe physics evolves, but people only *re*volve, through the same invariable, inescapable behavior. All of your modern enlightened peace-loving nations are nothing but great big tribes. And every tribe that's ever existed has had its God, and its own selfish interests, and a myth of God's will in history to sanctify its selfishness. Today as much as yesterday, underneath all the fine rhetoric, every nation still defines a better world the way it's always been defined: whatever *I* want, and too bad for *you*. And that, my dreaming friend, is the way the world has been, is, and ever shall be, a-*men!*"

Ruth slammed her hand down on the table. Toward the end of her tirade she had come close to shouting. One or two people nearby were looking at them.

John was speechless. He was saved from having to admit this fact by the arrival of a waitress, who hustled up with pad at the ready and asked him, "Watcha havin', hon? We're closin' soon."

"Uh . . . a hamburger, please."

"Everything?"

"Ah, yeah — no, hold the onions."

"Suit yourself, sweetie. Don't get nervous, it's only a hamburger." The waitress popped her gum and departed.

Ruth and Aruna stood up. John gave Aruna a crestfallen look. "You're not going?"

Again the smile, the entrancing voice. "Yes indeed, I'm afraid we must. It is so late, and I have a test tomorrow."

"Is it late?" John got out his watch. It was Grandfather's watch, the ancient pocket one. In Cambridge he had found an expert jeweler who had given it new insides, and for the first time in generations it kept time.

"Oh my! How very interesting!"

Aruna was staring at the watch. "May I see, please?"

John gave it to her. She closed the cover and inspected it closely.

"How is it that you have a swastika engraved on your watch?"

"A what?"

"A swastika." Aruna was pointing at the broken-armed cross on the watch's cover. "*Swastika* means 'it is well.' In India this is a very ancient symbol of good fortune."

"It is? But my grandfather brought this watch from Ireland, and he told me that it means good luck there too." John gave Aruna a baffled look.

And the mysterious Aruna for once betrayed her thoughts; she looked right at him, just long enough to show that she was frankly curious about the watch, and moreover (was he imagining it?) about him.

"Ahem." Ruth had gathered up her books. "I hate to break up this discussion, but it *is* getting late. Nice to meet you, Pope John Devlin, historian and dreamer. No hard feelings, I hope. We intellectuals can't afford them. Let me know what you think of Spengler. Are you ready, Aruna?"

"Ready." Aruna turned to Ruth, then looked once more at John. "It is very nice to meet you. My test tomorrow will be over at noon. If you have time, meet me at the John Harvard statue. We must speak more of your extraordinary watch."

"Sure — I'll meet you there. Ah, goodnight."

But they were already at the door. John stood looking after them, still stunned by Aruna, still reeling from Ruth. His remarkable intellect could muster only a single thought: *I think I've just been double-teamed.*

4

The Warrior

April 12, 1936
Berlin

Today I am thirty-one years old. That in itself is not worthy of record. But my family, having for the previous week feigned complete indifference to the approaching milestone, surprised me this morning in the most charming way. Quite unintentionally I slept late (Ruth must have turned off the alarm) and awakened only when I felt a very firm tug at my pajama sleeve. The tugger turned out to be Steven, advance party and official herald of this and every other Devlin family event. True to form, he proceeded to deliver a birthday eulogy of his own composition, entitled "My Dad," in which he catalogued all my fatherly virtues with Homeric skill and concluded by placing me higher than President Roosevelt and second only to Lou Gehrig (even great dads have their limits) in his personal pantheon.

No sooner had he departed, after accepting my handshake of gratitude (now that he is seven he refuses male hugs), than into the room, as if on cue, came David, staggering under the weight of a breakfast tray fully laden with coffee, juice, and toast. When I relieved him of his burden by placing it on my lap he solemnly informed me that because it was my birthday he had prepared everything himself, from start to finish (except that Mom had to light the stove for him), and that he hoped I would enjoy my breakfast. Well, how could I not? The toast was carbonized and nine-tenths of what was in the coffee cup was sugar, but David's little face watching me so seriously as I ate was more than full recompense. When I had thanked him and hugged him (at four he still accepts hugs) I marveled aloud at how he had managed it all by himself, and he then explained to me, with equal solemnity, every step of his carefully planned preparation of my breakfast, which I must say showed some real independence and original thought, given his age.

My two sons never cease to astonish me. There is already so much of Grandfather showing in Steven; surely his lips touched the Blarney Stone before they found his mother's breast. And at four David shows that other Devlin streak, as Father does: somber, quiet, locked in silent thoughts of his own, and good with things — *the side of us that grew, I have always imagined, from the root of Grandfather's great competent hands, the knowing hands of the farmer, the builder of railroads, the captain of ships. Perhaps in David this side of us will flower.*

At any rate, David insisted on lugging the tray away all by himself, and no sooner had he disappeared than Ruth appeared, stifling her smiles until the boys were back in their own room. Then we laughed together and she slipped under the covers with kisses and hugs and two presents — the first an exquisite pair of gold cufflinks (with instructions that they be worn at next week's embassy reception) and the second (I don't know where she found it) an autographed German first edition of The Decline of the West. *At my look of surprise she assumed her best Ruthish manner, eyebrows arched, smile acidic, and cooed ever so sweetly that she trusted my German was* at last *up to Spengler. For a moment I was transported, laughing, back to that awful evening when she and I first locked horns. And then, all acerbity gone, she kissed me again, and we settled under the covers. I would gladly have discussed Spengler, or anything else, or nothing at all, with her for the rest of the day, had my telephone not rung and my secretary not gently reminded me that the ambassador was expecting me at ten. Ah, well. How can I complain? Nine years of rapid advancement in the Foreign Service, a beautiful and brilliant wife, and two of the finest little sons a father could wish for. What more could I ask? There are far worse ways to round the turn into the third lap. There are far unluckier men than John Devlin.*

April 13, 1936
Berlin

A very interesting day today, for two reasons.
First: Went to dinner tonight at the British Embassy. That in itself is not remarkable, since our mother country is always hospitable. Nor was the talk anything new. The topic, of course, was Hitler's occupation of the Rhineland last month, and what it forebodes. Opinions were divided along predictable lines. The Englishman Jenkins maintained, as he always does, that Germany is simply going through the birth pangs of its new order. The Nazis have already avenged themselves on all their other ene-

mies, real and imagined — on the Communists, the Jews, and even their own Brownshirts — and now they are avenging themselves on the French, who after all so ruthlessly occupied the Ruhr in the twenties. The demons of Versailles will now be exorcised, and by this summer's Berlin Olympics, Nazi Germany, eager to impress the watching world, will have settled down. Look at the signs, says Jenkins: soft-pedaling of draconian anti-Semitic laws, the return of German Jews who fled in 1933, etc. Jenkins is an economist; he sees it all in terms of the great interlocking international forces that keep dictators in hand. He speaks of Germany's need for foreign capital to rebuild its economy, a need that will muzzle Hitler until prosperity returns. When that happens, says Jenkins, Germans will forgive the Jews and the French, who supposedly caused all their problems, and return to their normal business of producing great scientists and musicians. But as Jenkins talked, Stepanski, the Pole, as always grew first very quiet and then very passionate, insisting that the Germans are not ruled by economics; that national socialism is fundamentally a spiritual phenomenon, a kind of German national dream come true; that Germany will someday soon sweep aside (as dreamers do) any consideration of life's "hard facts" in pursuit of its own terrible vision.

Having heard this debate at least half a dozen times a year and being still unconvinced that either of my colleagues is wholly right, I mingled after dinner in the hope of breaking some new conversational ground. And indeed I did. Spotting a German naval uniform across the room and deciding to practice my German a little, I introduced myself to a very sociable captain who, when he learned I was an American, told me a fascinating story. As a young officer in the World War he had served in naval intelligence and had been assigned to investigate certain matters during the international uproar that followed the sinking of the Lusitania. It seems that the U-20, the submarine that did the sinking, wasn't supposed to be where it was on the day it sighted the Lusitania. It had orders to sail up to the channel near Liverpool to hunt for British troop transports, but at the last minute the U-20's captain turned around and sailed in precisely the opposite direction, back toward Germany, because the weather suddenly became very foggy. For two days he couldn't see a thing through the periscope. On the third day, just before noon, the fog suddenly disappeared and the weather was beautiful, unusually beautiful for the Irish coast. An hour later the Lusitania steamed into the U-20's sights, about fifty miles off its own course and traveling well below top speed, without even bothering about precautionary antisubmarine maneuvers — in the midst of a war! So, my German friend concluded, Fate had to go quite a bit out of its way to sink the Lusitania and set in motion the events that eventually brought America into the war.

On my way home I meditated on the apparent truth of this, and as I did there suddenly sprang into my mind a little scrap of doggerel from that very strange time right after my grandfather's death — something that that old monk who somehow had dispossessed poor Mr. Watkins of his buggy hissed at me when I ran up with Mr. Watkins's hat:

> Now I've sent Grandpa home to rest
> And a thousand down to hell.

Meaning, of course, the thousand who died on the Lusitania. At the time of this strange occurrence, in my pious Catholic boyhood, I attributed the frightening things I sometimes saw and heard to Satan, and asked God for help. As an adult who no longer has the advantage of belief in these two great external powers I have long since decided that whatever odd sorts of dreams and hallucinations I have had (and fortunately, since my twenty-first year I have had none) came wholly from within my own young mind, which must have suffered from an occasional excess of imagination — not a rare phenomenon, I dare to hope, in intelligent people during their formative years. In fact, I am now certain that I "foresaw" the fate of the Lusitania because of an alchemy of dazzling sunlight and the effects of pitching through the waves in a small boat, combined with my own vivid imagination and unconscious memories of forgotten newspaper articles discussing the German warnings to the Cunard Line, which supplied me with the raw material to concoct a possible disaster for the liner I was watching sail out to sea. That my imagination coincided with reality is really not surprising — after all, there was a war on, and the Lusitania sailed right into the thick of it. So I need hardly believe anymore my boyhood fancy that I saw the future.

But coming home last night it struck me as very odd indeed that a German officer (not as a rule an inordinately imaginative group, German officers) would speak of Fate arranging the sinking of the Lusitania. So, it would seem, did my old monk, who claimed to have sent a thousand innocent people to their deaths just to bring Grandfather's body home to Ireland for burial. Now how could even my vivid imagination come up with that? For a few moments I became very interested in the possibility that the German's story in some way confirmed my own hallucinations. Which would mean, if true, that there might be some objective reality . . . Well, it's an interesting hypothesis, but I'm far too tired to pursue it tonight. Nevertheless, it was amusing for a moment to wonder if God and the Devil aren't still lurking somewhere in the wings.

I said there was a second reason why today was so interesting. Ruth received a letter from Delhi, the first in many years. Aruna is coming to Berlin. Apparently her old hero Dr. Werner, who is now in Berlin with *the Kaiser Wilhelm Society, has called for her mathematical talents. She arrives next week, just in time for our embassy reception. I've put her, and the Kaiser Wilhelm people, on the invitation list. What fun for Ruth to see her old friend after so many years.*

"How long has it been since you've seen Aruna?" John asked.

"Ten years," said Ruth. She was sitting at her dressing table preparing for the embassy reception, only an hour away. "When I spent a summer on an excavation in the Indus Valley. At the end of the summer I went over to Delhi to visit her before I came home." Ruth lifted a pearl necklace around her neck. In the act of fastening its clasp she paused and added, with just a hint of playful malice, "I'm surprised you don't remember."

Facing away from her, into the mirror over the bathroom sink, John gave the white wings of his bow tie a final pull. "Well, you know — at thirty-one the memory starts to go. You'll find out next year." He heard Ruth chuckle and he smiled himself, but he smiled into the mirror, deliberately not looking at her. In his eyes Ruth could have seen in an instant that she was right; his casual little question had been quite unnecessary.

The bow tie did not satisfy him and he pulled it apart. As he began wrestling with it all over again he knew that he had tied the damned thing perfectly well the first time. It was all an excuse to spend a little more time facing the mirror, avoiding Ruth, until his thoughts had run their course. He remembered very well the last time Ruth had seen Aruna. He remembered with painful clarity, the way he would have remembered a knife stab, Ruth walking with him across Cambridge Common in the fall of their senior year, telling him about her summer and her visit to India. About how interesting Aruna's family was; she had three brothers, one in medicine, another in law, the third in the army. About Aruna's Oxford-educated father, who was such an Anglophile that he wore tweeds even in the Delhi summers . . . and about how radiantly beautiful Aruna had looked on the day of her marriage. That had been the actual moment of the knife, the moment when it had cut through him and he could no longer deny the fact. It had happened. It was fact. Aruna Rajputani was lost to him . . .

Once again John tugged the bow tie into shape — not so well this time, but it would do. Ruth was still struggling with her clasp. "Help me, would you?" she asked him. He came away from the mirror and moved behind her, taking the ends of the necklace from her hands. She dropped her arms and watched the mirror as he took up the struggle with the clasp. Standing next to her, he forgot Aruna. Ruth had piled up her black hair for the evening, and below his hands her pale, bare neck and shoulders curved down and out like the unfolding wings of a swan. Their pure whiteness was framed by her black hair and the line of her black gown. Again he felt that a man could not be more fortunate than he. He hooked the clasp at last and lingered for a moment behind his wife, running his hands over her shoulders, along her neck, tracing with a finger the delicate ridge of vertebrae, the shoulders' flesh that still was so perfectly, girlishly ripe, neither bony nor plump.

"Mmmmm." Ruth sighed with pleasure at his touch, then patted his hand and stood up. "Come along, my wild Irish rose. Fraulein Schutze informs me that tonight's baby sitter is new. I must go over everything with her before we depart. What's the time?"

John glanced at his wristwatch. "Seven forty-five," he said. "You're right — let's go."

John put on his tails, pulled down his shirtsleeves (on which his new gold cufflinks shone), and helped Ruth with her wrap. He was glad to be behind her again, once more avoiding her eyes, because glancing at the beautiful gold wristwatch she had given him for his thirtieth birthday had reminded him of the ancient pocket watch, which was now relegated to a drawer of his bedside table. An American diplomat, especially an American diplomat in Nazi Germany, could hardly go about his business consulting an enormous antique pocket watch engraved with a swastika.

Thinking of the pocket watch had made him think again of Aruna, of their first date by the John Harvard statue and all the other dates that spring. He remembered learning, to his dismay, that she was a mathematics major (he was absolutely hopeless at math) and, worse, a senior (which meant that she would graduate in June and leave him behind). Nevertheless, he had pursued her all that spring with a hopeless ardor that she had neither discouraged nor encouraged but simply accepted, in an unnervingly calm way that had paradoxically fanned his passion instead of cooling it. In desperation, as graduation neared, he had determined to make her his. It had seemed perfectly simple to him. After her graduation Aruna could work in Cambridge for a year, probably as a teacher, while he finished his senior year and applied to the Foreign Service; after he was accepted they could marry and see the world. He remembered announcing this plan (which had, of course, really been a proposal) to her, with what now seemed to him to be wondrous boldness, in late May. And he remembered her answer, given gently, not without affection but also with that damnable calmness of hers that left him utterly clueless as to what she was feeling. *I am so very sorry, John, but I must tell you that I am already engaged to be married.* After that he had lain in his bed for two days and two nights in a state approaching catatonia, cutting classes, skipping meals, filling up ashtrays. And then he had written her a very nasty letter — a stupid, spiteful, peevish letter full of wild accusations of betrayal — and mailed it and immediately regretted doing so. Even now, ten years later, he cringed inwardly when he remembered his own foolishness, really almost his madness, over a campus romance. Somehow Aruna had really knocked him for a loop, back then . . . At any rate, after his silly letter there had been nothing more. Aruna had graduated and gone off to India to be married, and John had heard nothing more of her until he had run into Ruth in the fall.

"I wonder how Chandor will look," mused Ruth. They were entering the embassy ballroom. "Aruna didn't say anything about him in her letter. He really was handsome when I first met him, on the day he married Aruna. Very charming young man. Lucky for her — if I remember correctly, they hadn't met before the wedding day. Hmmm! What a gamble *that* was — marriage Monte Carlo. Good thing I had a look at you first. If we'd been Indians I would have insisted on it." She smiled her Ruthish smile at him.

"If you were an Indian, my dear, India would be a *very* different place." John smiled back. They were advancing toward the ambassador. In another moment they would cease to be private persons and become diplomat and diplomat's wife for the remainder of the night.

"Well," said Ruth with a sigh, "I'll be curious to see him." Again the smile. "As will you, I'm sure."

"Good evening, Ambassador," said John.

Because the ambassador had for years objected to waste and luxury among the mostly privileged members of the American diplomatic corps, the Berlin embassy had rarely entertained on the grand scale since John's arrival three years ago. But tonight's reception was very much the exception to that rule. John made the rounds of the ballroom and found himself chatting with representatives of virtually every embassy in Berlin. Scores of very important Germans were also present — industrialists, generals, diplomats, done out in full evening dress and all manner of dazzling Nazi finery. Everyone who could possibly be here, thought John, was here — except Aruna. Where was she? He made his way back to Ruth, who was still engaged in chat with the ambassador and his wife.

"In her letter," said Ruth, "Aruna said she was arriving on an evening train. She's barely had time to change. Patience, my dear, patience."

Ruth's little jibes were starting to annoy John. He opened his mouth to retort but said nothing, for just then there was a sudden drop in the level of conversation throughout the enormous ballroom, an almost palpable change of atmosphere, as though the barometric pressure had dramatically changed. John looked away from Ruth in surprise and saw immediately why the talk had hushed. One other guest beside Aruna was late, and now he had arrived.

If the new arrival brought a change in the weather, it resembled an electrical storm. Through the crowds of black-suited diplomats, who had been pleasantly imbibing liquor, their professional charm flowing forth, he swept sternly in a light-colored dress uniform, with a similarly garbed phalanx of high-ranking attendants in clipped step behind. The effect, John thought, was of a bolt of white lightning shooting through billowy black clouds. His next thought was that he understood why the conversation even of very worldly men and women trailed off at this man's entrance; no matter how sophisticated and cynical you thought you were, no matter how many times you had seen the pictures or heard the voice, when you actually saw him (and foreign diplomats rarely did) *you had to have a look at him*. There was a fascination about him, born perhaps of the fantastic paradox that he represented:

a genuine nonentity, an underdog who appeared so frequently weak (and *visibly* weak, when one finally saw close up the watery eyes, the ridiculous ears, the droopy, jowly face), had steadily acquired and finally possessed ultimate power over a great European nation. All of the important men and women around him in the room were powerful because of their educations or unusual talents or privileged positions in life, but he, the most powerful among them, was like a bumblebee flying through the air; there seemed to be no rational explanation for how such an ungainly creature could have accomplished such a feat, but it had.

John turned to Ruth to whisper a remark, but she was no longer at his side. Where had she gone, at such an important moment? He saw her standing next to the ambassador, who was beckoning to him to join them. He was forming up an impromptu line to receive the new guest. As fast as decorum permitted, John came forward.

"Good evening, Reichschancellor," he heard the ambassador say. "I'm happy you could join us tonight. I think you know my wife —"

"Who is that?"

The Reichschancellor was staring past the receiving line, behind it. The ambassador followed his gaze.

"I don't know who it is," the ambassador said.

"Aruna!" cried Ruth.

John turned and saw her coming toward them across the ballroom, wearing a stunning Indian sari of the deepest blood-red and surrounded by an entourage of her own: five of the great names in modern German physics. Her arm lay on the arm of the greatest, Karl Werner, who looked leaner and more spiritual than ever (quite emaciated in fact, as though he had just been seriously ill). John's heart leapt. Ten years had produced not the slightest flaw in Aruna's beauty. John looked for the dark man among the entourage of Teutonic blonds, the one who must be Chandor, her husband; but he saw none.

Ruth left the receiving line and started forward to greet her friend, but instantly she was swept aside by the chancellor of the Reich and the phalanx at his heels. The two groups — Hitler's light-uniformed one, and Aruna's dark one in evening dress — came together at the center of the room. Hitler said nothing; he simply stared at Aruna. John noted that among his silent attendants, questioning eyes were exchanging puzzled looks. He also noted that Aruna, who had just stepped off a train and found herself confronted by the most controversial person in Europe, was not in the least disconcerted. In fact, he had the distinct impression that Aruna had actually drawn Hitler to her by a sort of magnetic inevitability, an irresistible physical law. Hitler gazed at her, and she met his gaze. For a long moment John could feel a weird crackling energy in the air, as if great currents had suddenly leaped the gap between Hitler's dark eyes and Aruna's darker ones. *Look at them,* he thought. *I know who he is; I know who she is. But who else are they?*

"Reichschancellor, may I present Mrs. Aruna Jahan. Mrs. Jahan, Reichschancellor Adolf Hitler." Karl Werner's tone was quite correct, but it failed to hide his contempt for the man he was addressing.

I know who they are. Caesar and Cleopatra. The male power of the state meets the eastern queen, who has no army but wields power with her glance.

Introductions had broken the spell. Hitler smiled distantly at Aruna, conveyed a few pleasantries, and passed on. John, Ruth, and the ambassador were left staring at the stiff backs of the men following the chancellor.

"Caesar and Cleopatra . . ." John heard himself murmur.

"What?" said Ruth. She rushed to Aruna.

"You know," said the ambassador, "that's very odd, Hitler drawn to a dark woman like that. He only likes big blondes, you know. Valkyries."

John woke up late the next morning with a splitting headache. Hardly a surprise, he told himself, considering the amount of champagne he had consumed the night before . . . Ruth was already up, humming cheerfully behind the door of the bathroom.

After the strange meeting of Hitler and Aruna nothing unexpected had happened at the reception. John had, of course, spent a great deal of time talking to Aruna, who told him that she had come to Berlin for three months at Dr. Werner's suggestion, to participate in a series of Kaiser Wilhelm Society seminars that Dr. Werner, with whom she had corresponded for years, thought would interest her. What were the seminars about? He couldn't remember. Yes, he could — he remembered asking her, and her laughing and telling him very affectionately that even a very brilliant historian would not understand what they were about. She seemed to have forgotten his nasty letter. And she told him also that her husband, whose family owned several huge farms near Delhi, had not been able to spare time to accompany her. What else? He remembered chatting with Werner, who had been quite pleasant. John had mentioned attending his Harvard lecture, hoping that Werner would not remember their embarrassing encounter afterward. What else had they talked about? Not much of substance that he could recall; this morning his mind seemed to be made of mud. Of course, Germans were all so circumspect these days, especially when Der Führer was in the room . . . What else? There had been several young men, Werner's protégés; they were friendly, but he could not remember more about them. Did Aruna have children? She did, two, a boy and a girl.

"Good morning, dearest." Ruth, who never drank, emerged from the bathroom ready for the day. "I hope you feel better than you look. There's a new bottle of aspirin in the medicine cabinet if you want it. I must be off" — Ruth glanced at her watch — "and so must you. Don't forget we're having Aruna to dinner tonight. Last night was hardly a reunion, what with the Führer hanging around drooling over her . . . That *was* strange, wasn't it? Ah, well. No telling what our beloved Herr Hitler will do next." She kissed his forehead. "Good-bye, my love. See you tonight." She was gone.

John stood up and put on his robe. Abruptly he sat down again. There must have been quite a bit of champagne indeed, last night . . . Where was Ruth off to, anyway? Probably she had once again agreed to meet with some Jewish family that was trying to get to America. Living in Nazi Germany had brought Ruth much closer to her "irrational superstition." Her Jewishness, he thought, was now the principal outlet for the deeply compassionate soul that Ruth really was, the woman under the acerbic mask who cared for humanity as she cared for her own sons.

That was fine. If he could get to the bathroom and take some aspirin, his headache would improve. He wanted a cigarette. Where were they? He vaguely remembered borrowing someone's cigarettes last night and pocketing the pack. His evening wear was still crumpled on the chair where he had piled it, so John staggered over to it and began hunting through the pockets. He found the cigarettes, a pack of the good German kind, and tried to dig one out. But for some reason his fingers couldn't get into the pack, although it was torn open. Was he so clumsy this morning? No . . . a small piece of paper, a folded piece, had been inserted in the open pack, covering the cigarettes. John pulled it out and unfolded it. Something was written on it in neat, precise German. John found his reading glasses by the bed and put them on, and the message popped into focus:

Pergamon Museum
Tomorrow
5 P.M.

John's headache was suddenly worse. What kind of nonsense was this? Someone had gotten drunk last night and played a silly joke on another drunk, himself. Germans had such odd notions of humor . . . He was about to throw the note away when he remembered something more about the cigarette pack. Someone in Aruna's party had given it to him, he wasn't sure who. But why would some brilliant physicist play silly practical jokes on a foreigner he had just met? German physicists were lucky if they had any humor at all, especially nowadays . . . He stood staring dumbly at the note, his temples throbbing, wondering what to do. Then the telephone rang, breaking his reverie. It was probably his secretary, wondering where he was.

"Hello?"

"Good morning, John Dev-leen." The honeyed voice sang in his ear.

"Aruna?"

"Yes. How are you?"

"Oh, uh, I'm fine. Ruth and I are looking forward to seeing you tonight."

"Yes, I am looking forward to it also. Can you come to my house this afternoon?"

"This afternoon? Yes, I think so, but, uh . . . won't we all be seeing each other tonight?"

"Yes, we will. Can you come?"

John looked down at the paper in his hand. *Five* P.M.

"I'll come at three," he said.

*

Precisely at three John rang the doorbell at the address Aruna had given him. It was a very large villa of prewar, imperial vintage, surrounded by pretty flowerbeds, in a good neighborhood. A maid dressed in street clothes met him at the door and hung up his hat. As Aruna came downstairs to meet him the maid let herself out.

"One afternoon a week she has free for the cinema," explained Aruna. "So I am told by my hostess." John was startled to find her again wearing native Indian dress, a beautiful yellow sari. His heart beat faster; his brain cursed the maid for leaving them alone.

"Ah. Where is your hostess?" No one else had appeared.

"In Delhi, at my father's house," said Aruna, "with her husband, my host. He is a very famous scholar, a Sanskrit scholar, who has known my family for years. When I received Doctor Werner's invitation they were already staying with my parents, and they insisted that I stay here while I was in Berlin."

"Very kind of them." John could think of little else to say until the crucial question had been answered: why had Aruna asked him here?

"Come see the house." Had she invited him for a tour? No. She led him perfunctorily through parlor, dining room, and sitting rooms filled with the strange statuary of India. She did not speak of the furnishings. "I always wanted to tell you, John, that I was so very glad when Ruth wrote me from Harvard that you were getting married. From the very first moment I knew you two were right for each other."

John laughed. "How could you? As I recall, at the very first moment Ruth and I were at each other's throats."

"Were you? I suppose. But really, I think it is right. A dreamy man like you, dear John, whose mind is always soaring high, needs an anchor, a hardheaded Ruth, to keep his feet on the earth."

That was certainly true, but why were they talking about his marriage? John began to feel uneasy. What was she really getting at?

He parried her thrust. "I trust that your marriage is also a good one."

"Oh yes, it is," said Aruna. "Chandor is very kind, very attentive.

Our children are a joy. And Chandor's family is an excellent one. The alliance is of benefit and pleasure to both sides. Which is, of course, why Chandor and I were engaged, sight unseen, by our fathers' agreement. That is what marriage is in India — the fulfillment of social position, a contract between good families. I think it is a good arrangement, but then I am Indian. It must seem very strange to you Westerners, who always marry for love."

On her last words she turned and looked straight at him with her deep black eyes. John stiffened. Why did she look at him like that? What was she implying with all this talk of marriage and love? Aruna was not only still beautiful after ten years, she was still baffling; he had no idea what she thought. But he had the feeling that her statements were really probes, efforts to dig around in his brain, to try to elicit something. What? That he didn't love Ruth? Of course he did. What sort of game was this? Was she trying to get him to admit what he knew was true, what she must know was true — that he had married Ruth on the rebound from his rejection by her?

"Look, Aruna," he said coldly, "what are you — "

"Shall we have a look upstairs? It is most interesting." Before he could reply she had taken his arm and led him up a staircase. "Look."

John looked, and saw a long, dark, high-ceilinged hallway. On the left side, the street side, was evidently a series of large windows; heavy closed curtains hung over them and permitted only weak haloes of daylight to penetrate around their edges. On the right side, barely visible in the curtained twilight, some odd black shapes like people stood in various attitudes along the wall.

"Come see," whispered Aruna.

"How can I see if there's no light?" John laughed. He started to draw the nearest curtain, but Aruna reached out and caught his hand.

"In an elegant old house one must respect the shadows."

She was standing very close to him. In the dark he could feel her presence more than see it, and in spite of all his resistance the feeling intoxicated him. Instantly he became the ardent schoolboy again, burning for the voluptuous, unattainable Aruna . . .

She did not let go of his hand, and although a voice inside him was shouting to him to pull it away, he did not.

"Come," she said, and propelled him along the silent curtained hall. The black people-shapes loomed up next to them. John gasped; they were strange gods, many-armed, exotically garbed, carved from stone. Their inhuman smiles emerged ghostlike from the gloom.

"The great gods of India," Aruna whispered. "Are they not beautiful?"

John nodded. He was looking at her. In the dark she was no longer a woman; the other, greater, unknown thing she was, the "more" he had always sensed in her, emerged now in the darkness and possessed them both. An Indian goddess had come down from the wall, transformed from stone into perfect flesh. Her great eyes stared into his. *She is the eastern queen, who has no army but wields power with her glance . . .*

At the end of the hall was a large lacquer cabinet. Aruna moved to it and opened its doors. Hidden inside was a statue that made John stare, a statue of a god who held a wildly voluptuous goddess in his arms. Their embrace was hardly the serene dance of the divinities along the wall. The god's member, hugely erect, was inside the goddess, and his left hand squeezed the nipple of her breast; there was a smile of sheer wanton pleasure on her lips . . . Aruna's lips . . .

"John." She breathed his name, her liquid lips touching his, and she pressed against him. In the dark, in the silence, he felt her high firm breasts against his chest and shuddered with desire. For ten years, the years of marriage, of children, of career, he had wanted only this . . . He crushed her to him and kissed her deep and hard. His hands moved over her breasts. Aruna trembled and moaned. In one swift movement she had his jacket off, in another his tie; with almost frenzied fingers she undid the buttons of his shirt. Then her hands, her lips, her tongue ran over his chest.

"Wait." John reached for his sleeves, to unbutton them. But they had no buttons; his fingers touched the cool gold of his new cufflinks. The memory of his thirty-first birthday, of Steven and David and Ruth, hit him like icewater.

"Wait." This time he spoke loudly, angrily. He pushed her away. The look the great eyes gave him was more of confusion than of hurt; he saw that she was nearly lost in deep arousal.

For a long moment they stood panting and staring at each other in the near darkness. Then John began buttoning his shirt.

"I'm sorry," he said. "I can't." She said nothing. At dinner tonight she would say nothing, and neither would he.

"I must go." He picked up his coat and tie and went downstairs, dressing as he walked. His mind was calm, and steady in its conviction, but beneath his mind every cell of him still shuddered and longed for her.

On the street outside Aruna's house John glanced at his watch. It was a quarter past four. He hailed a cab and told the driver to take him to the Pergamon Museum. In another hour, he said to himself, he would perhaps feel very foolish.

By five o'clock John had already paced the galleries of the Pergamon Museum for fifteen minutes, largely ignoring the exhibits. He was wondering about who he was to meet here, and why; and he was thinking about so much else besides. The business with Aruna had shaken him badly. What was he going to do, now that she had once again disrupted the pleasant harmony of his life? The consequences were so much greater this time. He was no longer an obscure Harvard undergraduate; he was married (to one of her closest friends!), he had sons, he was a public servant of the United States, with a reputation to protect. And he *did* love Ruth . . . He knew perfectly well that all this was absolutely true. Then why did it also seem so completely irrelevant? A tide of unthinking desire again and again swept over his convictions, carrying him to Aruna . . . He sighed deeply in disgust. He was a lust-ridden pig. *Men claim to have brains,* he thought, *but they think with their balls.*

Having condemned himself, he immediately reconsidered. This whole damned business was *Aruna's* fault. *She* had tried to seduce *him.* Why? Surely she could not have come all the way to Berlin for that? What about her marriage? And why *now,* ten years too late, when she could have had him any time at Harvard? Certainly it had been different then; there had been strict campus regulations governing the relations of the sexes, and they had been so inexperienced, so young. At least, he had; about Aruna one never knew. All that spring at Harvard he had not known. And now . . . first the bizarre incident with Hitler last night, and today this.

With Aruna anything might be possible. There was a power about her that had obsessed him years ago — and yes, damn it, it *still* did, and he resolved to resist it. But he wondered how they could both possibly sit through dinner with Ruth as if nothing had happened.

From behind a hand grasped his arm. He turned and saw a man standing next to him, a man he instantly recognized.

"Doctor Werner!"

"Thank you for coming," said Karl Werner. His gaunt face cracked into a thin smile, without warmth.

"How did you find me in such a big museum?" asked John.

"I've been following you ever since you arrived. I wanted to make sure that no one else was following you."

"I see." Out of respect for Werner John did his best not to laugh. Such cloak-and-dagger nonsense from a man of Werner's stature! "Care for a cigarette, Doctor Werner?" John reached into his jacket for the pack. "Apparently they're yours anyway — I stole them from you last night."

Again Werner smiled grimly. "I made sure that you did. In any case, there's no smoking here. And I don't smoke. When I received an invitation to the embassy I had to devise a method of communicating anonymously with you while I had the chance. Anything more explicit would have been too dangerous."

John nodded. He forgot his urge to laugh. Dr. Werner had been very clever, and, clearly, very desperate. Why?

"Why meet here?" John asked.

"Look around you," said Werner.

John looked. They were standing in an obscure rear gallery of the museum; glancing at the exhibits, John guessed it was a wing of the Assyrian collection. And it was after five; the museum would close within the hour. Except for the long-dead Assyrian emperors whose cruel faces glared down at them, John and Dr. Werner were quite alone.

"You see," said Werner, "here we may talk." He led John to a small bench and they sat down. Werner smiled again. "The Reich has not yet thought to plant its spies among the ancient dead."

"What does your message mean?"

Despite his previous assurances, Dr. Werner cast a glance around the room before he spoke. John remembered his Harvard lecture and pitied him. The man was a genius, a thinker of inspired boldness, a guiding light in Western civilization — and because he was also a German, he lived in fear.

"Mr. Devlin," said Werner, "have you ever read a novel entitled *The World Set Free*? It was written by the English science-fiction writer H. G. Wells."

"No." John was puzzled. He had not expected a discussion of literature.

"Wells wrote this novel in 1913. It is the story of a worldwide war that is fought with a new and very terrible weapon, a bomb made from the tremendous power that is locked inside the atom."

"A bomb out of atoms? I don't understand," said John. "I thought atoms were just sort of, uh, invisible little building blocks . . ."

"Please listen," said Werner impatiently. "It is true that atoms are the foundation of matter. But as you said last night that you attended my Harvard lecture, you might remember that I said there that what seems solid matter to our eyes is really only a frozen energy. Therefore, it is theoretically possible to convert a material atom into energy. And theoretically, the energy contained in a single atom is also of an unbelievable magnitude of power."

John rubbed his chin thoughtfully. "So Wells's novel is more than fiction?"

"Precisely," said Werner. "It is a tribute to Mr. Wells's genius that he was capable of foreseeing the practical application of what in 1913 was apparent only in the remotest theoretical outlines. The rest of us are just now catching up to him."

John's hand came to a halt on his chin. "You mean these bombs really exist?"

"No, they don't," said Werner. "Not yet." He looked straight at John with his deep, holy eyes. "But it is only a matter of time — and not much time."

For a moment John sat silent, trying to grasp the full meaning of what he had been told.

"Just how powerful would these bombs be?"

Werner held him in his gaze. "As I have calculated it," he said quietly, "a single atomic bomb could destroy the modern city of Berlin and everyone in it, down to the last building and the last innocent child."

"*One* bomb?"

"Yes, Mr. Devlin. One bomb."

John was stunned. But the practice of diplomacy had taught him to recover quickly from the unexpected. "Your news is terrible indeed, Doctor Werner. But I'm baffled by the melodrama. Why go to all this trouble to tell *me,* of all people?"

Dr. Werner smiled. "Oh, Mr. Devlin, I think you know why."

"No. How could I know?" John asked, startled.

The smile spread wider. It was rather unpleasant on Werner's fleshless face, like the grin of a skull. "Because, Mr. Devlin, what you once called esoterica is about to change forever the governing of nations and men."

John was astounded at Werner's memory.

"Quoted verbatim from that stupid question I asked you at your lecture," he said ruefully. "Ten years ago. You can't hold me to that, Doctor Werner. I was only a kid, and — " The memory of what had happened immediately after he had asked his question came back to him. He looked into Werner's remarkable eyes, and they held him.

"Yes, it was an especially stupid question. And something happened right after you asked it. Isn't that right?"

"No. Ah — what do you mean?"

Werner focused his gaze on John, as if to pierce his lie. "Excuse me, Mr. Devlin, you *did* see something. Something unseen. I knew it immediately. I could see it in your eyes. Since then I have been waiting for the inevitable moment when we would meet again. And I assure you, it *was* inevitable."

"I don't know what you're talking about," John said angrily, standing up, fighting a rising fear. *How in God's name . . .*

Werner stood up too. "Come with me, Mr. Devlin," he said pleasantly. He took John's elbow and pulled him gently forward. "I want to show you what I brought you here to see."

John obeyed. As Werner steered him between displays and through adjoining galleries he said nothing, while his mind shouted silent questions. He had gained the diplomat's instinct not to open his mouth until he had a grip on his fear and his shock and had reestablished control. If he talked before that, he would soon blab his innermost secrets to a man he scarcely knew. And how could he know what the real point of this bizarre meeting was? Perhaps Werner was actually some sort of Nazi agent trying to trip him up, to blackmail him, to get a source of information within the American embassy. It seemed absurd, but at this moment, he told himself, anything was possible.

How in God's name did Werner know? He had written nothing down, or almost nothing; certainly nothing about the Werner lecture. He had told no one.

"So. We are here." Werner brought him to a halt and released his arm. They were standing in a long, spare gallery dominated by a single exhibit. "It's beautiful, is it not?" asked Werner, gazing upward.

Preoccupied as he was, John heard himself answer "very," and mean it. Directly before them, towering up some fifty feet, was the magnificent façade of an ancient city gate, built entirely of glazed bricks, all of deep ocean blue. A border of yellow bricks ran around the edges and framed the perfect half-circle of the central arch. Through the sea of blue brick floated strange processions of mythical beasts: huge horned bulls, claw-footed dragons.

"The Ishtar Gate," said Werner, still gazing upward. "The crowning glory of the walls of ancient Babylon. Brilliantly reconstructed in Berlin. Do you know why it is here?"

John thought for a moment and gave the only answer he could, the historian's answer. "At the turn of the century German banks built a railway for the Turks to Baghdad. Did they also purchase this?"

Werner chuckled and shook his head. "Let me tell you a story, Mr. Devlin, the story that in the biblical days of King Nebuchadnezzar was enacted annually before this gate. Imagine, Mr. Devlin, that we stand before the Ishtar Gate in Nebuchadnezzar's time, in the month of Akitu, the Babylonian festival of the New Year. What would we see? A long procession winding past us out of the city. At the head of the procession, escorted by the king, is the image of the great god of Babylon — Marduk the Warrior. Behind Marduk all of Babylon marches, a gigantic column of people in ecstatic adoration of their god. As Marduk enters the temple the air is charged with anxiety and hope. On the day of the New Year time collapses in Babylon, and for a terrible moment her people hover between life and death, survival and extinction. For a moment they exist before time existed, in the realm of myth; they become spectators at the great battle their lord Marduk fought before heaven and earth existed, to establish his supreme authority over the universe."

Werner turned his gaze upward again, toward the blue gate. As he spoke his eyes grew so large and luminous that John, watching him, began to believe that he actually was seeing what he was describing.

"The terrible battle between Marduk the Warrior and his mother, Tiamat, decides the fate of the cosmos. The young god comes shining, striding over the clouds. The lightning flashes in his hands, and the howling storm winds play about him like eager hounds. Before him like a mountain lies the grotesque bulk of his mother, the Leviathan, womb of the universe. Tiamat advances on her offspring to devour him, but the young god sends his winds into her gaping maw and inflates her like a balloon. In an instant he has nocked a shining arrow into his great bow. He aims into the hideous mouth and shoots; Tiamat is dead. Marduk straddles his mother's carcass and splits it into perfect halves. From one half he creates heaven, from the other earth. He measures the trajectories of the stars and fixes them in their orbits, and he invents the laws of the operation of the planets. From Tiamat's vanquished blood and flesh he creates mankind. He rules alone and supreme in a cosmos constructed by his own will and genius. He is Marduk the Warrior. His word is truth, his might is law."

For a moment Werner remained staring up at the blue ocean of ceramic brick — *swimming in its depths,* John thought, mystified. If Werner wanted something from him, he seemed to have forgotten it in the course of this bizarre recitation. Or was the tale a trick to throw John off guard, to lure him into confessing his own unstable past? He stood still in the middle of the deserted gallery, wondering what to think, what to do.

Abruptly Werner turned and saw John's puzzled stare. He chuckled again.

"Poor Mr. Devlin! He hears a hardheaded scientist spinning silly fables and he cannot believe his ears! But you see, Mr. Devlin, a hardheaded scientist *does* believe in silly fables, because he knows that they are neither silly nor fables. And so, Mr. Devlin, do you!"

"I've already told you, I don't know what you're talking about."

"Don't you?" For a long moment Werner stared at him. "Very

well then, you don't. Allow me to explain. The silly fable, the myth, is the mask, the necessary filter for our poor earth-clouded senses. Behind the mask, inaccessible to the senses, is the archetype — the fact, the thing that is, that exists. Our puny senses cannot perceive what exists without dressing it up in odd rags and bits of costume, and so we do. We call it the Warrior and the Virgin and the Mother and the Father and the Holy Ghost, and we make up silly fables about it. Then we mistake the silly fables for the facts they reveal, and we forget what they really are. But from time to time a few of us are reminded. And there is a reason for it, as you know. As I *know* you know."

John had had enough.

"Doctor Werner." He stepped forward and gripped the German's arm. In his big football player's hand Werner's slender bones felt lean and light as a bird's. "I don't want to hear any more of this," John said in an even, menacing tone. "I want to know exactly why you lured me to this place, and what you want. A few minutes ago you told me something about a terrible bomb that could destroy an entire city. Is that what you wanted me to know? If it is, tell me more about it, please, because I want to know if such a horrible thing can really be. If it isn't, then let me go home to my dinner. But for heaven's sake stop this cryptic nonsense about — "

He stopped. Werner was eyeing him very curiously.

"Is it possible," said the German after a moment, "that you really *don't* know?"

"That's right, I *don't*. And please stop telling me that I do," John said angrily, releasing Werner's arm, hoping the German would believe him.

Werner folded his arms across his chest and began to pace the gallery. He frowned, thinking.

"Mr. Devlin," he said finally, "do you remember that in my Harvard lecture I spoke of evolution?"

"You mean Darwinism?" John did not remember that.

Werner smiled. "No, not quite. I spoke of an evolution that is now in the hands of the human culture which biological evolution once brought into being. You may recall that I postulated that our culture would soon transform itself — indeed, would *have* to transform itself — as its science probed deeper into the atom, into the fundamental nature of matter. That is what I meant when I spoke of evolution. I 'lured' you, as you say, to this place today because ten years ago, when you and I stood face to face at Harvard and you asked me your stupid question, I looked at you and I saw — " Werner's face seemed suddenly to cloud over at the memory. John remembered his horror-stricken look at Harvard. "I saw that the time of transformation was very near at hand. And then the voice — you *do* know the voice, don't you?"

"I told you, I don't know about *anything*," John said quickly, too quickly, feeling the flush of panic spread over his face. *Now Werner must know I am lying,* he thought, and he decided that his best tactic from now on was to say nothing. *How in God's name did Werner know about it? Did he also have . . . ?*

"The voice told me that you would be the one," Werner said quietly, looking very hard at John.

"The one what?"

"The one who will bring about transformation."

"What?"

"*Are* you the one, Mr. Devlin?" From their deep sockets the hard eyes bore into his.

John turned to go.

"I'm sorry, Doctor Werner," he snapped over his shoulder. "I've had enough. This is sheer madness — "

"Mr. Devlin!"

Something in the voice compelled him to stop.

"I want to tell you more about the bomb."

John stood still and thought. If Werner was really going to change the subject, he would stay. And if the new subject was the mysterious bomb that could threaten a city, he *should* stay. He turned around and walked back to Werner.

"All right. *That* I will hear."

Werner nodded. "Good. As I mentioned to you earlier, it is only a matter of a little time before it is built. And unless I am very wrong, which I doubt, it really will be powerful enough to destroy an entire city. Now, to the point: the chances are excellent that it will first be constructed here."

"In Berlin?"

"In Germany. In the Third Reich."

"Which means it will be Adolf Hitler's bomb."

"Exactly."

For a moment neither man said anything. Werner looked at John. John thought. Werner had just ended all the dinner-party debates about the future of nazism.

"That mustn't be allowed to happen," John said finally.

"Right again, Mr. Devlin," Werner said. "But it is also most important that you understand *why* it must not happen. Do you understand why?"

"Well, of course I do," John replied, annoyed that the cryptic questions were returning to Werner's conversation. "Because Hitler is a man of bellicose temperament and possibly unstable faculties" — even John instinctively looked around the room for listeners — "and he's a blatant expansionist to boot. A lot of innocent people would die if such a weapon fell into his hands."

Werner shook his head. "There is an even more important reason than that one, Mr. Devlin."

"What do you mean, more important? If you're saying that the lives of so many people — "

"It is the same reason we are standing here at this moment. It is the reason the Ishtar Gate is now in Berlin."

"Forgive me, Dr. Werner, but I'm afraid I don't see the connection between something as ancient as this gate and a bomb that doesn't even exist yet. I haven't got time for games."

Werner caught his arm. "Oh, but there is a very *deep* connection."

John felt the grip on his arm tighten. Angrily he yanked his arm away.

"Stay another moment, Mr. Devlin," Werner said quietly, but in a tone that was more command than request.

"Why should I?"

"Because if you don't listen to me right now," Werner whispered, glancing around the room, "the atomic bomb I have just described will most surely be possessed by Adolf Hitler."

"I'm sorry to hear that," John whispered back. "I don't see what I could possibly do to prevent it."

"I will tell you what you can do. All you have to do is make one railroad trip to Copenhagen."

"Copenhagen? Why on earth — "

"Because in Copenhagen," said Werner, "there lives a close

friend of mine, a man named Carl Pedersen. Do you know the name?"

"Yes, of course." The whole world knew the name. Carl Pedersen was a Nobel laureate physicist and an outspoken humanitarian, bitterly anti-Nazi.

"I thought you might," Werner said. "I brought you here today to ask you to pay a visit to Carl Pedersen."

"Why?"

"I want you to tell him what I've just told you."

"About atomic bombs?"

"Exactly."

Again John was baffled. "But Doctor Werner, why on earth would you entrust the revelation of something so . . . *scientific* to a layman like me? Why would a man like Carl Pedersen believe anything I said?"

Werner shook his head. "Don't worry, Mr. Devlin. You need only go to Pedersen in my name and tell him what I have told you — that the possibility of an atomic bomb will soon exist in the Third Reich. He'll understand the implications perfectly well."

"I still don't understand. Why do you need me? Why don't you go yourself?"

"That, too, is very simple, Mr. Devlin. You're an American. You have freedom of movement. I'm a German, and moreover a German scientist in a prominent position. My movements are watched, especially by those in the government who would like to remove me from my Kaiser Wilhelm position and replace me with one of their lackeys. I refuse to endorse the Reich's belief that the proper job of a German physicist is to serve the Reich as a technician and cease from further "Jewish" speculation about the nature of the universe. Because of this I have made many enemies. But for you it's a simple matter. A weekend holiday with your wife, a few days away in charming Copenhagen . . ."

"I understand that," said John. "What I don't understand is how in hell my merely telling Carl Pedersen that a Nazi atomic bomb might someday exist will prevent its existence."

Karl Werner held up a finger. "That, too, is extremely simple. One week from today Carl Pedersen leaves Copenhagen for a lecture tour of your country."

"And?"

"And in the course of this lecture tour he will visit several prominent American universities, at each of which there is at least one person just as capable as anyone in Germany of inventing an atomic bomb."

"There is?"

"Of course there is, Mr. Devlin. Don't be stupid. The refugees — most of them Jewish, all of them brilliant scientists. Thanks to Hitler, America has them now. When Carl Pedersen alerts them to the possibility of an atomic bomb in Hitler's hands they will panic."

"And get down to work building their own bomb, right?"

"Exactly right."

"And you and I pray that the refugees in America are just a little faster than their German colleagues and invent their bomb first, so at least Hitler will have to think twice about the consequences for Germany before using his bomb."

"Correct again. Except that Hitler will never have his bomb as long as I am alive."

"What do you mean?"

"When the time comes, the bomb development project must be directed by me, because by that time I will probably be the only scientist of any talent left in Germany. And I will make sure that development proceeds very slowly. For just this reason I have made up my mind that whatever happens I will not join my colleagues in America. I will stay here and delay Hitler's bomb until he has destroyed Germany and himself, as he inevitably will."

John found himself really listening to Werner. In his years of diplomatic work he had developed a generally accurate ability to distinguish true conviction from mere boasting, and he felt sure that Werner had conviction. It was perhaps the reason that in ten years Werner had aged so much, to his present skeletal gauntness. He had decided to sacrifice himself when everyone else was running for his life.

"All right, Doctor Werner," John said finally. "I believe that you mean what you say. I'll go to Copenhagen."

Werner's face lit up, as though he had been expecting a no, and he clasped John's hand in both of his.

"Thank you, Mr. Devlin — "

"But," John went on sternly, withdrawing his hand, "I'm not

going *anywhere*, not one step from this spot, until you clear the air of all the nonsense you've just been insinuating about me. If I'm to speak to one of the world's great physicists, I'll damn well not look like a fool doing it. If you want my help in this, you'll have to give me a better explanation of what this is all about. And please don't take me through any more of this mythological nonsense."

Karl Werner's forehead split into furrows, and on his face appeared the despairing look of a man who suddenly realizes that on a matter of ultimate significance he has failed to make himself understood.

"But Mr. Devlin, it's *not* nonsense. Not at all. Don't you see? It's everything *else* that's nonsense."

John sighed and looked at his watch, thinking of Ruth fuming over the hors d'oeuvres at home. "Look, Doctor Werner, I really don't have time . . ."

Again Werner reached out and gripped his arm. Again John moved to brush him off, but this time he found to his surprise that despite his considerable advantage in size, the German's grip was unshakeable. Werner's eyes stared straight and unwavering at John, like twin arrows striking a target.

"Stay only a moment longer, Mr. Devlin," he asked, or rather commanded, "and you shall understand. Remember I spoke of evolution. Evolution is the inevitable process that connects all things on our planet, and all times. Past, present, and future are merely the links in its chain. Evolution changes the forms that existence takes through time. First clouds of gases, then water, then amoebas, then humans, then . . . But however many forms it assumes, existence itself never changes. The fundamental forces that constitute reality remain inaccessible to evolution, to time. 'Forces' is what a contemporary physicist calls them; other people, earlier people, would call them gods. The epic squabbles of science and religion over which of these two nicknames is correct mean absolutely nothing. They are merely disputes over perception, not essence. Do you understand this, Mr. Devlin?"

John made another attempt to free his arm, and failed. "I understand what you're saying," he answered. "I have no idea at all what, if anything, it means."

A disturbing smile once more fractured Werner's fleshless face into a thousand tiny wrinkles. John thought of ice cracking, or glass shattering.

"Very well," Werner said, with mock solicitude. "I won't tell you that in fact you *do*, because it seems to upset you so. It means that the historical events that we call epoch-making, that have moved the evolution of the species forward, have actually been the periodic eruptions of the fundamental, universal, eternal forces of this galaxy — the gods — into time. Whenever the gods have intervened, the species has entered the next phase of its destiny. Culture is transformed, and a new mythology makes sacred the memory of that transformation. The myth I have just told you, the Marduk myth, is an example. It is the national myth of an imperial civilization, the urban civilization of the ancient Near East, which came to flower in Babylon but first burst upon the world much earlier, about twenty-three hundred years before Christ. It occurred in the lifetime of one extraordinary man — Sargon of Akkad, who created it singlehandedly, out of his own genius and will. Sargon overthrew the older Sumerian civilization of independent city-states and forged the first true empire in the West. His power was irresistible because his mind had touched the raw nerve of reality. Sargon saw past the mask to the fact. The archetype lived in him, acted through him, and the species evolved. Sargon was the first. He was the Warrior. Since him there have been others. Now there is one here in Germany."

John was astonished. "You mean *Hitler?*"

"Yes. He too has seen past the mask."

"But I thought you despised him."

"I despise the man. Not at all do I despise what lives in him, what possesses him — that makes the little man Adolf merely insane."

"Wait a minute, wait a minute," John objected. "You're making him sound like —"

"Like a prophet?" Werner's smile spread further. "Indeed I am, Mr. Devlin. Very perceptive. Indeed he *is*. A god lives in his flesh."

"What?"

"As a god lived in Sargon's flesh. It is not coincidental that the Ishtar Gate has passed from Babylon to Hitler's capital. The mantle of the Warrior now rests on the Führer."

"You are crazy, Dr. Werner!" John cried. He pulled his arm with every ounce of his strength away from Werner's hand, pulling so hard that he yanked Werner off balance and brought him stumbling against him. But somehow, impossibly, the emaciated German held on.

"Mr. Devlin!" he hissed, clutching John's shoulder with his other hand. "You *must* listen to me! Understand that your presence here is also no coincidence. You were brought to Berlin because you are one of us, one of the people the gods have chosen. I saw that. I *know* it. If *you* do not accept it, now, all is lost. Hitler is a mistake, the Galaxy's mistake. The Warrior can bring the species no further. From now on he can lead us only into cycles of greater misery and destruction. A new god is needed. Hitler is filled with the old god. He is a mistake. He must be eliminated. He must not have the new bomb. The time for the test is not yet. We are not ready yet. Only when *you* are ready will the time come for the test. When you have opened yourself and the new god fills you . . ."

John pulled his shoulder free and drove his fist into Werner's stomach. The German doubled over and at last let go of John's arm.

"You are *mad,*" John whispered, almost in awe. Then he left the room.

Behind his back he heard Werner gasp, the wind knocked out of him, and croak: "Go to Copenhagen."

5

The Buddha's Heart

JOHN DEVLIN MADE IT HOME for dinner with Aruna without being disgracefully late, and it was extraordinary, but true, that despite everything that had happened to him that day, he managed to behave in a perfectly normal manner in front of Aruna and Ruth. In fact he seemed to enjoy himself; he laughed heartily at even the mildest of his wife's witticisms, and reminisced about Harvard with Aruna in a tone of innocent warmth. But the laughter and the reminiscences, the savoring of past trifles, really were lifelines (and threadbare ones at that) to which he clung desperately. Inside, as he chatted, he fought down his panic and one echoing thought: *What the hell is happening to me?*

Only one day ago everything had been fine. He had been a devoted husband and father and a stable, responsible man. And now, within the hours of one working day, he had galloped to the very brink of adultery with a woman he hadn't seen or even corresponded with in ten years, and immediately afterward been subjected to the patently lunatic ravings of a man whom all the world regarded as a brilliant physicist. In the moments during dinner when Ruth and Aruna fell into their own reminiscences and he could turn his attention inward without being noticed, he tried desperately to sort it all out.

About Aruna he could fathom nothing beyond what he had already puzzled over that afternoon in the museum. He looked at her loveliness across his table, heard the music of her laughter evoked by Ruth's barbed recollections of their Radcliffe classmates, and resolved on the spot that he would never, *never* be alone with her again. At least for that problem there was a simple solution. But what about Werner?

Hours later, after they had driven Aruna home (John of course had to pretend that he didn't know the way) and Ruth had gone to sleep, John slipped out of bed and sat in the big armchair in his study, thinking about Werner again. Without question the man was mad. John reached for this simple conclusion time after time and each time tried to cling to it; and each time, though he desperately wanted to believe it, he slipped away from it. What made him let go was the undeniable fact that Werner *knew*. Not everything, apparently. Not John's secret. But he knew *something*. He knew that something very strange had happened to John after his Harvard lecture. Maybe anyone could have guessed that; John thought that disturbances in his face and eyes could have hinted at something odd going on in his mind. But Werner also — how was it possible? — knew the *voice*. The same voice? It had to be. Werner had also heard it after the lecture, when John had, which carried an implication that cheered John. If Werner had heard it too, the voice might not have been John's hallucination, which would mean at least that he, John, might not be as periodically nutty as he thought. But it might also mean that there was another man in the world as nutty as himself. And if the voice wasn't someone's hallucination, then what, for God's sake, could it be? John thought hard, trying to keep his reasoning afloat above his fears. There were other explanations. He had to be brave, to face them, if he was to understand.

One possibility — all too possible on the face of it — was that Werner hadn't actually said the things John had heard him say. Perhaps John had imagined them. It couldn't be ruled out; it had happened before. How much had he imagined? Maybe all of it — maybe Werner hadn't really been in the Pergamon Museum at all. Perhaps John had taken a cab there and wandered among the exhibits, talking and shouting to no one. Perhaps there had not ever been a real note . . . Was he *that* mad?

For a moment John lost his battle with his panic and bolted from his chair into the bedroom. Tiptoeing past the sleeping Ruth, he went into the closet, where his trousers hung on a peg, and hunted fearfully through the pockets, half-expecting to find nothing. But the note was still there, and its message was the same. John breathed a sigh of relief and immediately grew anxious again. If everything at the museum had actually happened, what was he going to do about it?

His pragmatic self, the self that had rescued him from New Bedford, conquered Harvard, and brought him success in diplomacy, was at last presented with the crisis framed in terms it could grasp, and it immediately took command. It issued an order that the frightening question of how Werner knew the voice, and the positively terrifying question of what the voice *was,* if it wasn't a mere hallucination, remain unanswered until the concrete situation at hand had been dealt with. John had made a promise; he had agreed to go to Copenhagen and talk with Carl Pedersen about atomic bombs. Copenhagen was a real place. Carl Pedersen was a real person. They were the only real things in his whole encounter with Werner. If he was going to come to grips with this thing, perhaps he should start with what was real and work from there. Should he therefore keep his promise and make the trip? Would it tell him something? Immediately he realized that the answer depended on the reality of all this business about a bomb. If what Werner claimed was true — if bombs powerful enough to destroy entire cities were about to be produced for Hitler — then he'd damn well better make the Copenhagen trip and find out more about it, and pass the information on to Washington right away. But what if the whole thing was some delusion of Karl Werner's? What if Werner was simply the lunatic he appeared to be, and lived in a private world threatened by . . .

For an awful moment John imagined himself in Copenhagen, babbling nonsense at a baffled and annoyed Pedersen. There couldn't be any trip until he had verified Werner's story about a bomb. *Get the Wells book,* he thought suddenly, sitting up and snapping his fingers. Then he slumped back, crestfallen at the realization that the Wells book proved nothing. Whatever was in it could have served merely as a catalyst for Werner's delusions. What had to be verified was the impending reality of Wells's prophecy, and how in hell was he going to do *that?* He couldn't just call up other physicists, in his public capacity as a diplomat, and ask about science-fiction bombs, and make a public fool of himself if he was wrong. And worse, if there *was* something to it — and even if there wasn't — once the Nazis got wind of his investigation they would be only too delighted to embarrass America by ejecting him from Germany on a charge of espionage. And that would be the end of his career.

He had to verify the bomb discreetly, privately, through someone he could trust. But who? He didn't know any scientists. Well, that wasn't true; he knew — no! It was out of the question. He had promised himself . . . But in another hour, when he finally slipped back into bed, John had retracted his promise. He had no choice. In the morning, as soon as he was alone, he telephoned Aruna.

When she opened her door he was relieved to see her dressed in sensible, unalluring Western clothes. "Where's the maid?" he asked. "Are we alone?"

"When you said you wanted to see me privately I gave her the day off," Aruna said. He had expected her to be serene and unruffled, as always, but today she was keeping her mesmerizing eyes mostly fixed on the floor. She actually seemed contrite. John felt that she wanted to clear the air.

"Listen, Aruna," he said, "before I explain why I've come, I want to say something —"

"About yesterday? Please, let's just forget about it." Her eyes stayed on the floor; she rubbed her hands together nervously. Her voice was brisk and sad, full of remorse. John was astonished. The dazzling Aruna had never seemed so . . . vulnerable. Immediately his male gallantry sprang forth, as if on command.

"Of course we'll forget it."

"And be friends?" She raised her eyes to his, and in them he saw only pleading sincerity.

"Of course we'll be friends."

"I am so glad." She seemed relieved to the point of tears.

John felt his original purpose in coming endangered by the prospect of a long emotional scene. He told himself to be gentle but firm, masculine, to take charge of things.

"Let's sit down somewhere where we can talk." He patted Aruna's shoulder affectionately.

She led him into the parlor. When they were seated he told her about his meeting with Werner, leaving out, of course, all of Werner's probing references to his own past.

Aruna heard him through without once interrupting — without in fact reacting much at all, even when he hesitated over the stranger parts of his story. She sat attentively beside him, absorbing everything he said with equal composure. *Damn,* John thought, *you can just never tell what she's thinking. She's wasting her time in mathematics. She'd do well at diplomacy. No, better, at poker . . .*

"What are you going to do?" Aruna asked when he had finished.

John launched into the plan he had thought through in his study the night before. "Well, if all this atom-bomb business has any truth to it, I have no doubt about what I'm going to do. Before I go anywhere, and that includes Copenhagen, I'm going to the ambassador and tell him everything I know. Werner assured me that he'll single-handedly keep the bomb from Hitler's hands, but that's not good enough. Even if there's only a *possibility* that the German government could possess such a weapon, Washington has got to know about it. I'm going to recommend to the ambassador that we blow the lid on this thing right away — lodge an official protest, bring in the League of Nations, and so forth. Make Germany's neighbors aware of the danger and get them involved. Apply economic sanctions and demand disclosure of secret research. Hitler will kick up a fuss, to be sure, but ultimately he'll have to give in. He just isn't strong enough right now to take on everyone at once. Then, when the whole world knows about the danger, I'll recommend to Washington that America go Karl Werner one better. Werner wants an American bomb to checkmate Hitler's bomb. Again, I don't think that's good enough. Once a bomb like that exists it'll be used, no matter who controls it. We need an international agreement banning the development of anything resembling such a horrible weapon. We need laws, domestic and international, to curtail dangerous research. We need a watchdog team of top scientists drawn from all countries to catch violations. I know that making Hitler's bomb public will probably put Karl Werner in danger, but I'm sure that once he sees the international wheels turning to stop the Nazi bomb he'll find no more reason to stay in Germany. I can arrange for his asylum in America, and from America he could tell the world . . ."

He stopped. Aruna was no longer looking at him. She was staring down at the floor, sadly shaking her head.

"What's the matter?" he asked.

Aruna looked up at him, and John could see the expression of pity on her face. He realized immediately who the pity was for.

"There's no bomb?"

Again Aruna shook her head, and her eyes filled with tears. "No," she said in a husky voice. "I'm afraid Doctor Werner is deeply . . . distressed."

John sat back in his chair.

"This really is crazy," he said softly, looking at Aruna.

Aruna looked back down at the floor. "It's so very, very tragic," she said. "I am afraid that the change in the German government was responsible. Karl has been under such terrible strain since the Nazis came to power. You know, like all geniuses he is not a very practical man. He doesn't understand politics or politicians. When he witnessed the ruin of his colleagues' careers, and the universities stormed by hoodlums, and German intellectual life destroyed . . ." She got up and began to pace across the parlor, her hands pressing on her temples, her eyes still on the floor. "And their lackeys hound him ceaselessly, you know, trying to find a Jew in his bloodline or some other nonsense, some way of disgracing him before the Reich. He lives in dread of that, because he believes so strongly that without his position he will be powerless to stop . . ."

Aruna halted her pacing at the French doors. Staring through their windows she took a deep breath, composing herself, then turned back to John.

"When he invited me to Berlin," she said, "I came not really for professional reasons but because I was worried about him. You see, he had begun to write me about the Wells novel and about this bomb. I can tell you, John, that there is not a jot of scientific evidence to support Mr. Wells's speculation. In fact, atomic scientists have all but reached the opposite conclusion. In order to release the tremendous amount of energy required for the bombs Mr. Wells describes, we must break apart the core, the nucleus, of an atom. And no one has succeeded in doing that. Two years ago, in Rome, Fermi transformed a uranium atom into new elements when he bombarded it with some weak particles called neutrons. But that is not at all the same thing."

"What you're saying," John broke in, "is that atomic bombs aren't really possible."

"Exactly," Aruna said. "They shall remain forever where they are now, and should be, in Mr. Wells's gallery of imagined horrors. But Karl has . . . he has forgotten this. You remember his Harvard lecture. You remember what hopes he had for physics and for the world."

"Yes, of course."

"When he saw the Nazis extinguishing those hopes, sending Germany back into ignorance, into darkness . . . I'm afraid that something happened to his mind. In his letters to me, which had always been about strictly scientific matters before, he began to speak of the necessity of keeping an atomic bomb out of Hitler's hands. Had I not also read the Wells novel, at his suggestion, I might have remained completely baffled by his references. But as I had, it is all too clear to me that . . ." Her voice quivered as she brushed a tear from her cheek. "That in Karl Werner's poor strained mind the plot of the novel and scientific reality have become permanently confused."

John looked glumly down at his hands. "I'm sorry," he said. "After yesterday I had suspected something like this. I had hoped it wouldn't be true."

"Oh, it is very, very bad." Aruna sighed deeply. "Until I came here I had no idea how bad it really was. He has started to imagine all sorts of things. Yesterday he invited me to lunch at his home, and I was scarcely through the door before he began saying the most unbelievable things about you."

John looked up. "About *me?*"

"Yes." Aruna sat down again. "One embassy party and he's already worked you into it! While I tried desperately to act as if we were having a perfectly normal lunch, he carried on about how you had been chosen by the gods to save the world."

"Oh, my God . . ."

"Yes, it's awful, isn't it? I'm not sure he means you personally. In his mind you may be confused with the country you represent. He has such great admiration for the freedoms of America. And as you now know, he is obsessed with the belief that this atomic bomb must belong to America, because he believes that America, with its high principles and respect for human life, would never drop it on anybody but only keep it as a threat to the enemies of freedom."

"So it's really America he's talking about?"

"I think so. But I might be wrong. He was so insistent about certain things, very queer things."

"What things?" John tried not to sound alarmed.

"He said something about a voice, a voice only you and he could hear, that comes from the gods and directs the fate of men . . . And that you were someone who had visions and saw the future. Didn't he say these things to you in the museum?"

"Uh, no. He — no, he didn't."

John saw Aruna's puzzled look and hoped mightily that she would interpret his sudden change as concern for Werner. *Dear God. How many people has Werner told?*

"How strange," Aruna said. "He raved on about such things with me yesterday, just before he saw you. He seemed quite obsessed. I don't understand why he wouldn't —"

"Why didn't *you* tell me?" John broke in, remembering that an offense is the best defense. "When I came here yesterday you had already seen Werner. I wish you had said something to me about this. A man in my position can't have someone going around saying that —"

"Oh, I don't think that he does," Aruna said quickly. "I'm sorry not to have told you. I had some hope of protecting the reputation of a man who has been my friend and mentor. Until perhaps something could be done for him. Of course, it is different now that he has publicly accosted you . . ."

"I understand." *Then why the hell did you insist that I come here alone yesterday? Was it some mad passion for me? No, impossible. Then what?* For once he saw her revealing agitation, in her face and movements. Clearly her story about protecting Werner was not the whole truth. He decided to press the question hard with her now, to bully the real answer from her while she was briefly vulnerable. But an instant later he felt like a cad and stopped himself. Besides, he had found out the essential thing he had come to learn. Why complicate matters by causing a tearful scene or perhaps even a quarrel? For Ruth's sake he had to maintain good relations with Aruna (and Ruth would instantly divine the reason behind a sudden, mysterious falling-out). Better to honor his promise to Aruna and forget about yesterday. He had just handled one crisis; no sense in giving himself another one . . .

"Well," he said briskly, rising from his chair, "I guess I have the answers I need. Obviously there's no point in going to Copenhagen, or to the ambassador."

Aruna rose also. "No, none whatever."

"Needless to say, I'm relieved." John smiled at her. "I think the world can do without an H. G. Wells future. Of course," he added quickly, seeing that Aruna did not return his smile, "I'm very sorry about Werner. If there's anything I can do for him, please let me know. I'm sure he'd be welcome in America, if he ever changes his mind about staying here. It sounds like getting out of Germany would be the best thing for his mental health."

"Yes, you're probably right." Aruna was staring at the floor again. It was clear to John how deeply disturbed she was by Werner's madness.

"I'm sure things will be all right. Remember, if he needs any help — with emigration, or with any kind of treatment — please let me know."

"I will."

For a chaste instant he grasped her hand. "Thank you."

They stood awkwardly in silence for a moment until John, feeling once more that he had to take charge of things, said, "I hope you can come for dinner again soon."

Aruna nodded sadly. "Of course."

"Good." There was another awkward silent moment between them. Then John spoke. "Well, thank you again. We'll see each other soon, then. Please don't bother — I'll see myself out."

He turned and walked through the open parlor doors.

"John, wait."

Keep going, he said to himself. He pretended not to have heard her.

"John!"

She had called him loudly, urgently; he could not pretend he had not heard. He turned and walked back to the parlor doors. Her eyes seemed to plead with him.

"John — please stay a moment more. I have found something in this house that will interest you."

No. "I really must go. Perhaps if Ruth and I came for dinner . . ."

"Of course." She cut him off, her voice trembling. The great black eyes filled with tears. She gave him a long, miserable look and began to cry. Immediately he felt like a heel.

"Oh, John," Aruna said through her sobs. "I am so sorry. I don't know why I behaved like that yesterday. All of last night I lay awake in my bed and thought of Ruth, and of my children, and of poor Chandor, who was so kind and allowed me to come to Berlin . . . When I saw you again, so much feeling came rushing into me . . . I didn't know I had it, it just . . . overwhelmed me, and I . . ."

Aruna was wringing her hands, and her sobs were becoming more violent. In another moment, thought John, she might become hysterical. Filled with pity for her and with guilt over his own intransigence, he crossed the room and gingerly held her shoulders in his hands.

"Aruna, don't do this," he said gently. "We're both guilty. But it's done with. Let's just forget it, as you said, and be friends."

She said nothing, but her sobs grew quieter. He released her shoulders. "I have to go now." He turned to go, then turned back, trying to do more. "How about if this weekend the three of us —"

"But you don't *believe* me!" Suddenly the eyes flashed through their tears. Aruna's anger came like sudden lightning. "You do not believe it is possible for me to be your friend. If you did, you would stay now, and not be afraid."

For a moment John simply looked at her. Her anger had caught him completely off guard. She was right, he decided; he had to demonstrate his faith in her, and in himself. And he had to help her do the same. It was clear to him: she was asking him, without saying so, for his help. She was weak, and she was asking him to take charge.

"You're right," he said. "It's silly of me to run away like this." He smiled at her. "Okay. What did you want to show me?"

Aruna delicately wiped the tears from her cheeks. She smiled too, for the first time since he had arrived, and gestured toward the doors with her arm.

"Come into the study."

It was the same unbelievable smile, the same exquisite movement of the arm, like a dancing god's. It was the same passion, unchangeable, undeniable, they awakened in him. As he followed her through the parlor doors he was thinking, and denying it, and thinking it again: *I should have gone . . .*

Unfortunately the study turned out to be upstairs, past the curtained hallway of provocative statues, but now John did not dare refuse to follow her. He had to show his faith.

Inside the study it was also dark, but Aruna immediately drew the curtains. Daylight fell on what looked like a room full of ghosts. All of the furniture was covered with white sheets.

"Here is what I wanted to show you." Aruna led him to an alcove formed by an arching space between bookshelves, behind the desk. Hanging in the alcove was a framed page from an ancient manuscript, with rows of strange characters surrounding a central illustration.

"The letters are Sanskrit," said Aruna. "The manuscript is perhaps from the ninth or tenth century, and the man in the picture is the Buddha. Look closely at him."

John bent his head under the bookcase and looked. The Buddha sat in the familiar lotus position, preaching to monks, his graceful hands gently expounding the Eightfold Path. Behind him were bright concentric rings, haloes of holiness, and on his breast . . .

"A swastika?" John said, surprised. On the breast of the Buddha whirled the ancient symbol, identical to the one on the Devlin watch.

"That is what I wanted you to see." He heard Aruna speaking quietly behind him. "For Buddhists also the swastika is important. They call it the Heart of the Buddha. The Heart of the Buddha is the innermost Truth, the mystical essence of his message to the world. It is existence, the eternal round of being, endless, infinite, containing everything that is."

Aruna was silent. John prayed that she would keep talking. He continued leaning into the alcove, pretending to stare at the swastika. He dared not turn around to look at her; just feeling her near him, merely standing in her atmosphere, had set the irresistible tides rolling in him again. And he *had* to resist them.

Without turning around, he said, "I've always wondered why the Nazi swastika goes in the opposite direction from the one on my watch." The swastika on the Buddha's breast, like the one on John's watch, whirled counterclockwise.

"My father's friend," replied Aruna, "whose house we are in, told us a story about it. He said that when Hitler formed his Nazi party the swastika was already familiar all over Germany as a symbol of the ancient pagan Germans and their simple warriors' virtues. Apparently the Germans were one of the last European peoples to be converted to Christianity, and then only by force, by the Franks under Charlemagne. Before that they worshiped some sort of terrible warrior god who was quite bloodthirsty and demanded human sacrifices from them all the time."

"Sounds as if Charlemagne did them a favor," John commented.

"Well, perhaps." Aruna smiled. "But according to our friend, a few years ago quite a number of Germans didn't think so. The passage of time had romanticized their pagan past for them and they felt a powerful longing to rid themselves of their urban, industrial, Christian present and return to it. Hitler wanted the German people to identify their longing to return to their ancient virtues with his party's message, so he made the swastika the Nazi symbol. But he changed its direction."

"Why?" Still John did not look at her.

"It's very curious," Aruna said. "My father's friend said that at that time, in the early twenties, many people associating with Hitler had studied India because they believed it was the original homeland of the so-called Aryans. They told Hitler that what he had done would bring bad luck to the party, because in India a clockwise swastika points away from God, toward extinction and death, whereas a counterclockwise swastika points toward God and God's creation. But for some strange reason Hitler would not listen to them. He insisted on the clockwise swastika, the symbol of death. An odd story, don't you think? Evidently Herr Hitler has defied the gods. But, well, perhaps he *can* defy them? Contrary to expectations, his reversed swastika seems to have brought him only good fortune."

John found the swastika story intriguing, but it was not at the center of his thoughts. As she had told it Aruna had moved, unconsciously no doubt, nearer to him; he could feel her standing just behind him, almost touching him. And for him Aruna's closeness had the potency of an embrace. The inner tide was a roaring wave now, sweeping him toward her in spite of everything. With every ounce of self-control he had he was trying not to be swept, but the conflict was consuming him. He began to shake from the sheer tension of it.

"John?" He felt Aruna's hand touch his arm. "What is wrong with you?"

"Nothing." But her touch was the end. His resistance broke, and the roaring tide swept through. He turned from the strange painting on the wall and looked at her. Ten years ago he had turned from a strange painting on a wall and looked at her for the first time. He was still in that moment: nothing had changed.

"Aruna —" He started to say something, but there was nothing to say. He pulled her to him. For a panicky instant he came to his senses and feared she would be angry and push him away. But Aruna melted into him wordlessly, completely. He felt her desire, as strong as his, and was lost. They said nothing. In moments they had stripped one another. Then John fell upon her and entered her on the carpeted floor.

Aruna's passion was at least the equal of his. She brought him inside her with an eager thrust and held him hard in place, her hands locked together in the small of his back, pulling him deeper into her, deeper than he could possibly go, devouring him . . . Her body began to move up and down mechanically, pumping like a piston in rhythm with her deep, soft moans, her gasping breaths. Her hands and legs kept him locked inside her, serving her, but she no longer knew him, or herself; her conscious mind had dissolved into a dark, ancient ocean of feeling, wide and deep, that swept over her. She rose toward climax; her body thrust harder, faster, almost out of control. John rode atop her helplessly, like a man on a runaway horse. In the final moments he heard a word, a strange word in an alien tongue, whispered and moaned, and at the end shouted in a voice that was not her own honeyed voice, a voice from very far away: *Arjuna. Arjuna. ARJUNA!*

The last time she screamed the word; her body arched and shuddered and she came, her long sharp fingernails slicing John's back. And he came too in that instant, his mind exploding. A drop, a tiny drop he was, in her bottomless well.

In stillness they lay locked to one another on the carpet, surrounded by ghostly sheeted furniture. He could feel her heart racing. He held her tight. Her mouth hung open and she gasped for breath. Her black hair lay plastered in sweat around her closed eyes and over her forehead, where his cheek had smeared away her elegant dot of rouge.

After a few moments, when her heart beat more slowly, he rolled gently off her onto the floor. Her eyes did not open. She had forgotten him. For a long time she lay still, breathing in long, shuddering gasps, and for all that time he sat quietly and watched her and wondered, as he had always wondered, who on earth she was.

April 22, 1936
Berlin

This morning the ambassador summoned me to his office, to personally deliver the telegram from Washington announcing my promotion and my transfer to the embassy in Tokyo. Steven and David took the news well enough, with their children's wide-open curiosity, but I think Ruth is unhappy to be leaving Berlin, although she is pretending enthusiasm for my sake. Unlike me, Ruth pretends nothing very well. And (although I didn't say it to her) that virtuous quality of hers may be one reason that my career has advanced again, out of the blue, and advanced both of us away from Germany and halfway around the world to Japan, where Jews are not persecuted because there are so few Jews. I assume that word of her outspoken public efforts on behalf of people seeking exit from Germany, which make her an admirable American and an unstable commodity in the eyes of the Foreign Service, has filtered back to Washington from our embassy, and possibly from German protests. If that's true, the ambassador has been kind enough to say nothing about it. What Washington doesn't understand is that Ruth's compassion isn't limited to her own people. It just happens that in Germany the Jews are most in need of it. In Japan, I'm sure, others will be, and they'll be damned lucky to meet my wife, and Washington be damned!

Personally I am delighted to be going. The Tokyo assignment really is a plum. Things are heating up over there, and Washington wouldn't be sending anyone they didn't consider a first-rate man. And Tokyo will take me away from Aruna, thank God. We sail from Hamburg in a week. If I am busy enough and my excuses clever enough, I may be able to avoid seeing her at all before we go. I hope so. I don't know what, or who, "Arjuna" is. I don't want to know. If I stay in Berlin, my marriage and probably my career are finished. It's as simple as that. If I am near her, she possesses me; I am helpless. After yesterday I can only explain her in archaic terms, as a medieval demon, a succubus who fastens herself sexually to a man and steals away his soul. It's almost no exaggeration to say that I would fear just that if I remained in Berlin, for Aruna has a power over me that overwhelms all defenses and reaches into the very core of me to take possession. And it isn't love at all; it's power.

So my promotion could not be better timed. Once again Fate takes a hand. I am almost beginning to believe in Fate, since so much of my puzzling existence seems to be interlinked. Germany sinks the Lusitania *after I have hallucinated the tragedy. In college I attend a lecture by a German physicist, and after ten years of perfect mental health I suffer hallucinations again, on the spot. On the same day I meet two girls. Ten years later, when I have been rejected by one and have married the other, the first travels to Berlin, where I am posted — and once again all hell breaks loose. And it's also in Berlin that the same German physicist has become quite mad and raves to me about the gods and about impossible weapons only the gods could wield. I hope Aruna is right in her opinion that it's all only poor Dr. Werner's madness. Much as I want to believe that, I can't quite get rid of the uneasy feeling that in the Pergamon Museum I was once again involved in a bit of hallucination. I hope not. At any rate, there might be yet another good reason to leave Aruna and Germany: my sanity. The combination doesn't seem to be good for it. But somehow, given the course of my life so far, I find it hard to believe (much as I would like to) that I'll never see Berlin again. If I ever do, I'd damn well better keep a grip on myself, and hope to God that my lovely succubus is nowhere in sight.*

On the afternoon of April twenty-second, the day after John and Aruna had lain together on the study floor, the Berlin–Copenhagen express pulled out of the Zoo Station precisely on time, as the government of Adolf Hitler had promised. If he had not been dissuaded from his trip to Copenhagen by Aruna's revelations, John Devlin might well have been on board. As it was he was not; he was across town in his apartment, guiltily keeping the day's events from his family and trying hard to make some sense of them in the private pages of his diary. But someone he knew was on the train.

She was no longer sad and teary-eyed. As the train picked up speed and jolted west through the Berlin suburbs she serenely studied the swastika flags that fluttered everywhere over Hitler's capital, the swastika drapings on lampposts, the swastika posters on walls. *How odd,* Aruna thought. *The most ancient of symbols obsesses the most modern of nations. The Nazi Hitler points his swastika toward death and gives a dying Germany new life. How odd. After all, their "Aryan" posturing is such nonsense. But what of it, if it serves them well? And it has, for in one respect Adolf Hitler is right: his people are pagan warriors, converted only by force to the cross. Their true god is not Jesus but Wotan, god of mystic terror and of death, and neither Rome nor its soft-hearted Christianity has vanquished him from their souls. In death they shall always seek their god and find their life. I shall rely on them.*

The express was out of the city now, moving at full speed, clicking smoothly along among orchards and farms. The dying sun slanted over the rich green of the spring fields and the new leaves of the trees. Aruna stared into the setting sun. She would go to Copenhagen. She would visit Carl Pedersen, and tell him that Karl Werner and his Berlin research group had begun intensive work on the possible development of an atomic-energy bomb, on the orders of Adolf Hitler. Pedersen, noble man that he was, would believe every word and rush off to America in a fine panic to plead with the refugees to invent an atomic bomb before Germany did. The refugees, terrified men, would commence work at once, and throw their misgivings to the winds. And John Devlin, who could have upset everything by telling the world, would be none the wiser.

The sun sank lower in the sky, to the rim of the flat North German plain. The express was traveling almost straight toward it. The sunlight was weak now, and for a long time Aruna's enormous dark eyes gazed tranquilly upon the fiery ball, upon its uncounted atoms transforming themselves into energies beyond human grasp. At length she smiled. She thought of the men who would soon sit down in America and try to bring those energies within human grasp, to put them into a bomb. They would succeed, too, she was sure. If the Americans didn't, then the Germans eventually would. It didn't really matter. The bomb would be invented. Humanity would have the power of gods, to use as it would. It would have the sun.

How odd it was, she thought. Humanity was no different from every other little strand of evolution: it moved forward, inexorably, whether it liked it or not. It did not move backward or stand still. And yet these strange idealists, these John Devlins, the most intelligent of the species, tried to hold their own evolution back, because of what individuals might suffer. Because of suffering they ran to their governments and their leagues of nations and whatever other little powers they believed in, to try to stop that which must be.

It was the great Western delusion, this obsession with the individual. Indians had seen things with such greater clarity, for a much longer time. Aruna thought of the *Bhagavad-Gita,* the Song of God, the greatest poem of India. Its hero, Prince Arjuna, the mighty warrior, refuses to shed the blood of his brethren. The divine savior, Krishna, shows him that true impiety is to refuse to play his part in God's holy destiny, and once Arjuna understands, he rides to the slaughter with a song in his heart. How different from their Western Bible, with its hero's whining about the one lost sheep!

The individual is a fly on the face of the planet, swarming by the millions, thought Aruna. *Swat him down and a hundred will take his place. He is nothing; he can be reproduced. Evolution is everything. Destiny is everything. Destiny is bringing the power of the sun to the earth, into human hands. And Karl Werner and John Devlin and Carl Pedersen will all play their roles in this.*

Poor John, she thought, her lovely lips breaking into a smile. *How he squirmed when I held his darkest secrets up to him! He is still in flight, my stubborn Jonah. Werner was easier to break — but I knew a scientist would be. My hardheaded diplomat still won't accept his fate. But he's cracking, you can see that. How eagerly he gobbled up my lies about Werner and the bomb! John Devlin still needs his fairy tales, like the rest of them. They are like so many children who refuse to grow up. They don't want to see the Truth. But he will, in time. I will see to that. And when I have broken open his puny little mind and the horror of the Truth has flooded in, I shall stand beside him in his hour of need, as Krishna stood beside Arjuna; and like Krishna I shall sweep away the illusions once and for always. For the individual's puny illusions do not move Destiny. Destiny is the Will, the transcendent Will, that every so often finds pure expression in a human life. And that life — John Devlin's, or Karl Werner's, or whoever's — will make the difference.*

The sun had set; Aruna's compartment was dark. Her great black eyes stayed open, savoring the night. There was no one else in the compartment, but if there had been, and if his mind had been of the right sort, he might have looked at Aruna now in the dark and seen the curious luminous glow that emanated inexplicably from her beautiful eyes, as if they had somehow kept within them the last rays of the setting sun, or the first flash of light at the beginning of Time.

6

The Hero

UNDER THE MOON the Mediterranean waves rolled black and dense, their great swells sweeping rank after rank toward the beaches on the western edge of Sicily. The waxing moon, shining ripe and brilliant over the sea, coated the black waves with its shimmering silver glow. Through the ocean of silver a tiny black spot slowly moved: a fishing boat, a chip of wood swept along by the waves, its sputtering engine lending some puny assistance to the ocean's power.

Twelve men were crowded onto the little boat; most sat slumped against piles of nets or lying stretched out on the deck. The luminous beauty of the moon did not entrance these men; they cursed it, and stared nervously out over the bright silvery waves.

"Paratrooper's moon," said the eldest, the one in command. He was about fifty years old, short and built like a beer barrel, with black-stubbled jaws and tiny, piggy eyes. He leaned out of the wheelhouse window and spat into the wind. Then he drew back and went on: "Sonsabitches won't jump at night unless they can get one all lit up for 'em. So the rest of our poor dogfaces hafta walk up the beaches right into the fuckin' Krauts by the light of the silvery moon, and get their asses creamed — for the goddamned paratroopers!"

"The moon will set at midnight," said a younger man who stood next to the one who had first spoken. This man was a good head taller than the beer-barrel major and was lean and clean-shaven, with his dark red hair shorn into a military crew cut.

Two other men were in the wheelhouse: the owner of the boat, who steered, and his son, who stood by his father's side. These two said nothing, because they did not understand what was being said; they were Italians, and the men next to them were speaking English.

"The Allied planners in Algiers picked this night for the invasion because tonight the moon will set at midnight," the younger man repeated. "So the first wave, the paratroopers, can jump under the conditions that suit them best, and the ground forces, which will land after midnight, will have the advantage of darkness."

He stared calmly forward as he spoke; he did not look at the major. But when the major heard the tone of condescending patience in the polished voice he shot his companion an angry look.

"Listen, Lieutenant," he growled, "I'm a soldier. I was leading doughboys against Kraut trenches in France before you could jack off. Nobody has to tell me why your Limey buddies in Algiers picked tonight for D-Day — 'cause the faggots love paratroopers, that's why." The major laughed from deep in his belly, a grinding, unpleasant noise. "When I see that moon go down," he went on, "I'll believe it, and not before. And if it ain't dark when we get to Sicily, I'll make sure *you* have the honor of point position all the way to the dump. Capish?"

"The moon *will* set, Major," the younger man reiterated quite calmly. Still he did not turn his head.

"Who is this one that speaks so coldly to you?" The owner of the boat asked in Italian.

The major laughed again. "He is a first-class bastard," he answered, in Italian. "A college man, an aristocrat, who comes to read books to us about how to kill Germans."

The two Italians burst into hard laughter.

The lieutenant grimaced. He knew not a single word of Italian, but he got the idea.

"Permission to be excused, sir," he said stiffly. "I thought I'd check in with everyone before we sighted land."

"Sure, sure, go check in." The major snorted. "Do whatever the hell you want."

The lieutenant shouldered past him, out of the wheelhouse door. "Hey, Devlin!" the major called after him. "Just don't fall overboard, okay?"

With the major's crude laughter rumbling behind him, Lieutenant John Devlin, United States Navy, climbed forward over nets and several large black boxes toward the bow of the boat. He stepped very carefully over the boxes. They were all marked DANGER: EXPLOSIVES.

The fishy smell of the little boat, the creaking of its timbers and pitch of the deck under his feet, made John Devlin feel warmly nostalgic. He shrugged off the minor unpleasantness of the major and ambled happily along the deck, inspecting the fittings. So many summers he had spent on a boat so much like this one — Father's boat, before Harvard and then the Foreign Service had taken him from New Bedford and made him a landsman for good. It was why the Navy had seemed right for him when he had at last returned from Tokyo and volunteered.

Unfortunately, not every naval officer was right for the Navy. Kneeling in the very bow of the boat and clutching the bowsprit like an abject figurehead, Lieutenant Matthew Engels, M.D., was puking his guts out.

John placed a sympathetic hand on Engels's shoulder. At John's touch the seasick man heaved himself around and slumped against the pitching gunwale, gasping for breath.

"I won't ask you how you feel," said John. "I can tell."

"Jee-sus Christ," Engels replied with a moan. Even in the silver moonlight he looked sickly green. He rolled his brown eyes toward John. "How in hell did I get on this frigging boat?"

"You volunteered, remember?" John chuckled.

"Yeah, I remember. And I remember who talked me into it."

"I didn't say it wouldn't be dangerous."

"You only mentioned death. You didn't mention *this,* you swine." Engels struggled up onto one elbow. " 'Say, Matt,' " he suavely intoned, impersonating John, " 'I hear that some of you medical boys are interested in going into combat to observe stress reactions. Why don't you come by my office for a chat sometime?' The next thing I know I'm committing my internal organs to the deep. If God had meant for Jews to sail, he wouldn't have raised them in Brooklyn. I mean, all my life I've never liked more water than my bathtub could hold. And even that makes me feel not too terrific. Ohhhh . . ." The boat leaped in a swell, and Engels found it necessary to cease his tirade and seek the gunwale again.

"Poor Matt." John shook his head, chuckling. His friend Engels was terrific: sick as a dog and still making jokes. He had liked him the moment they had met, in Algiers. John felt much in common with Engels; both of them were men from humble origins whose own efforts had brought them far in the world. When Engels had taken John's suggestion and volunteered for the mission, his dossier had revealed his accomplishments: Columbia, Harvard Medical School, two years of study in Switzerland with Jung. But Engels was not only smart, he was practical and direct — unusual qualities in a psychoanalyst, especially one who had spent time poring over alchemical arcana and discussing life after death with the controversial mystic of Zurich. They were Ruth's qualities, and John also found them attractive in a man. Now, however, the great Dr. Engels was wretchedly ill, and very much in need of help.

"I have a suggestion," said John. "Go back amidships, just behind the wheelhouse, and lie down. It's a smoother ride. You're getting the worst of the pitching up here. Come on, get up — I'll help you."

"Oh, another one of your brilliant ideas? Of course, sure. I'll be happy to do you a favor sometime, John, old buddy . . ." But Engels gripped John's offered hand and pulled himself to his feet. John held on to him to help him keep his balance on the deck, and they started aft. As they passed the wheelhouse the major stuck his stubbly face out and gleefully chuckled.

"Hey, whatsa matta, Lieutenant Engels? Pork chops a little greasy tonight? Hahaha!" The beer barrel rolled back into the wheelhouse, laughing maliciously.

"Eat shit, D'Angelo," Engels muttered into the wind. "Your father was an organ-grinder's monkey."

John heard this and burst into laughter.

"How can you think anything about D'Angelo is funny?" asked Engels morosely. "You catch more hell from him than anyone else, and it never seems to bother you."

"You're funny. He's not." John let go of Engels and cleared a space for him on the roof of the low cabin, just behind the exhaust funnel. "Up we go." He boosted Engels onto the roof. "Now just lie there and keep still until it's time to land."

"You expect me to fox-trot?" Engels flopped back and threw an arm over his eyes. "Anyway, I don't see how you can take

D'Angelo so calmly. If you were my patient, I'd say you had a reality problem."

"An occupational hazard." John rolled easily with the boat, steadying himself with a hand on the cabin roof. "Diplomacy, at least in its public aspect, deals more in fantasy than reality."

Engels chuckled. "Well, my diplomatic friend, if you can handle D'Angelo, you can handle anybody. We had a lot of his kind in my old neighborhood. They all grew up to be good soldiers, but none of 'em joined the U.S. Army, if you know what I mean."

John smiled wryly and nodded. He knew very well what Engels meant, although he couldn't officially admit it, to Engels or anyone else. In May, only two months before D-Day, the Navy had discovered a serious flaw in the carefully prepared plan for the invasion of Sicily. The plan called for the rapid development of captured harbors into fully operational naval bases, but it had suddenly dawned on the planners that such development could not possibly succeed without the cooperation of local civilian authorities. And everyone knew what ancient criminal organization constituted all "local civilian authority" on Sicily. The Navy had then further discovered, to its dismay, that not a single one of its intelligence officers assigned to the Sicilian invasion even spoke Italian.

So there had been a frantic search through the personnel files of all Allied services, and the service records of men like Major Louis D'Angelo had begun to accumulate on the desks of certain intelligence officers in Algiers, among them John Devlin. John had read through Major D'Angelo's official file and found him to be a career soldier, with a record distinguished for bravery under fire (which should have made him a colonel by now) and marred by several ugly incidents of brutality to men under his command (which had kept him a major). Then John had read a great deal more, all of it quite unofficial, and found exactly what the invasion planners were looking for: a man closely related by blood (and, the Adjutant General's Office suspected, by some questionable Army supply contracts) to several of the biggest Mafia names in New York, men implicated in prostitution, drug rings, labor racketeering, and scores of murders. John had forwarded all his information to the senior planning staff, who had liked what they read and immediately pulled the major from his command to lead a D-Day diversionary strike on the beaches west of the actual landing sites. Thereafter he was to remain on Sicily as a liaison between the first Allied assault waves and local civilians. The admirals and generals had given him a team of commandos to carry out his diversionary mission and left the rest to him.

And D'Angelo had proved to be the perfect choice. On the waterfront at Tunis, with Sicily only ninety miles away, he moved easily among the scores of Italian smugglers who ran their fishing boats with impunity between Axis-held Sicily and Allied-held Africa. He met distant relations, made new friends, learned things. The commandos owed the boat they sailed on tonight to him, as well as the detailed information about the German ammo dump they were going to blow up and the local partisan contact who was waiting on the beach to guide them to the dump. No one but D'Angelo could have arranged all this. So John did his diplomatic best to tolerate the major's sense of humor. Even on paper the man had been repugnant to him — but he was indispensable for Sicily. And now, in the summer of 1943, Sicily was everything.

A series of low moans came from Lieutenant Engels, whose arm still covered his eyes. He seemed as comfortable as he could be and quite indisposed to further conversation. John glanced aft where the commando team lay nonchalantly stretched out atop more boxes of explosives. No point in going back there, he thought, although he vaguely felt that as official second-in-command of the mission he ought to say something to the men before they landed. But these men didn't need any words of wisdom from someone on his very first combat mission; they knew perfectly well what they were supposed to do and how to do it. They were taciturn country boys from the South and West, veterans of North Africa, experienced killers. The opinions of ninety-day-wonder lieutenants whose every utterance broadcast Harvard did not interest them.

John glanced at his watch. Eleven forty-five. The moonlight was noticeably weaker. Sicily should be visible soon. He went forward again and sat on the bow hatch, searching the moonlit horizon for a glimpse of land. He could see nothing yet, so he watched the waves rolling before the bow and soon fell to thinking. It was July 1943, and everything that he, John Devlin, had once sworn so gravely to prevent had happened. The world was once again plunged into war. The brazen Harvard boy who had boasted to coeds of his intention to save the world single-handedly from another August 1914 had been caught completely off guard, like everyone else, on the morning of December 7, 1941. To make matters worse, he had actually been at the American embassy in Tokyo, participating in the diplomatic conversations which the Japanese had kept up even as their fleet steamed toward Hawaii. Within hours of the attack on Pearl Harbor, John had been locked into the embassy compound with Ruth and his sons and everyone else, and there he had languished for six helpless months of internment while negotiations for an exchange of diplomats dragged on. And now, not quite one year after the Swedish liner *Gripsholm* had finally brought him and his family into New York, he was a soldier — an occupation he had once intended to render obsolete. At the age of thirty-eight he was on his way to Sicily on a dangerous mission behind enemy lines, with six trained killers and one seasick psychiatrist . . .

"May I join you?" The polite request was jarringly out of place on this boatload of toughs. John looked up at the man who had uttered it. He had forgotten: six trained killers, one seasick psychiatrist, and Major Franklin Forsyth. It was easy to forget Major Forsyth, who scarcely said a word to anyone; the only remarkable thing about him was his presence on the mission, which was a complete mystery to all involved.

"Of course, sir." John made room for the major on the hatch. Major Forsyth sat down rather heavily as the boat plunged into a trough. He was not noticeably seasick, but he kept his balance with difficulty on the pitching deck. *So would I,* thought John, *at his age;* the white-haired major must have been sixty years old. What was he doing here?

"Excuse me for disturbing you, Lieutenant," said Forsyth, "but I wonder if you'd mind going over the particulars of our mission one more time with me. You see, my orders came on such short notice that I didn't really have time to familiarize myself with what is intended, and Major D'Angelo — ah . . ."

"Isn't the easiest man in the world to talk to." John finished the timid major's sentence for him. "I'd be happy to review the mission with you, sir. We're headed for a small promontory about thirty miles northwest of the main landing beaches at Licata and Gela. The boat will bring us to within a mile of shore; Major

D'Angelo has arranged for a local Allied sympathizer to meet us on the beach and guide us to a German ammunition dump located on the promontory heights, just over a small fishing village. Major D'Angelo's men will plant their explosives and blow up the dump. The idea is to create a diversion, some confusion that might draw enemy attention away from Licata and Gela just before the invasion. When we're done we'll paddle back to the fishing boat, sail down the coast, and link up with the invasion fleet."

"I see." Forsyth was quiet for a moment. "I suppose," he said at last, "that there will be some fighting involved."

"I doubt if the Germans will invite us in to blow up their ammunition," John replied with a laugh.

"No, I guess not." Forsyth smiled nervously. He said nothing more, and looked out toward Sicily with his blinking eyes, twisting his liver-spotted hands. *Poor old guy,* thought John, *he's scared.*

John wasn't scared. At least he didn't think he was. He thought he had no right to be; he was going on this mission because he had pestered his superiors in Algiers for months for a front-line assignment, anything to get away from a desk that was piled high every day with captured German documents to be translated and analyzed. He had volunteered to fight, he told them, not to sit. But until now his education and his career had condemned him to serving his country in a stifling office, while others did the real work of crushing Hitler. At least, that was the way he saw it. Someone else might have seen it differently. Yuzawa saw it differently.

Yuzawa was his Japanese friend. They had met on an extraordinary day in 1937, a year and a half after John's posting to Tokyo. The Japanese military, then rampaging through China, had deliberately bombed and sunk the U.S.S. *Panay,* a gunboat ferrying American civilians out of the besieged city of Nanking, and machine-gunned the survivors. Within hours of the announcement of the *Panay* massacre, while the American ambassador and his staff worked frantically to avert a break in relations, ordinary Japanese had appeared at the embassy in droves to express their personal shame and disgust at their leaders' actions. Yuzawa, a young Buddhist monk, had been among those John had received.

From the first moment John had found him fascinating. His head was shaven clean in obedience to his vows; he was small in stature but muscular and handsome. They had chatted for an hour, Yuzawa speaking flawless English with a pleasant manner and a charming laugh. John had been amazed; the monk knew as much as he did, if not more, about the history and culture of the West. When he marveled aloud at this Yuzawa laughed and explained that all his life he had lived in Nagasaki, an industrial city on the island of Kyushu, in the far south of Japan. Nagasaki had a large Roman Catholic population — the result of years of missionary work among the Japanese there — and the largest Catholic cathedral in Asia as well. Yuzawa had attended mission schools and had been groomed for the priesthood. Then, at eighteen, he had shocked his teachers by suddenly entering a Buddhist monastery.

Yuzawa saw it differently. Their conversation had been brief that first day; John had been busy. He had invited the charming monk to call on him again. Yuzawa had smiled and bowed and taken his leave, and John had not seen him again for four years. And then, six months after Pearl Harbor and two weeks before the *Gripsholm* was to sail, despite the locked gates and the state of war between John's country and his own, Yuzawa had somehow materialized one day in the embassy garden to say good-bye . . .

"May I ask, Lieutenant, the name of the promontory we're headed for?"

It was the timid voice on his left. John realized that once again he had forgotten Major Forsyth.

"It's called Capo Granitola. It's just about the closest point to Africa on the Sicilian coast."

"Ah. Well, that makes *some* sense, then," said Forsyth, more to himself than to John.

"Do you know Capo Granitola?"

"Yes, quite well. As you may have guessed, Lieutenant, I'm not a career Army man." The major and John exchanged ironic smiles. "For the last thirty-five years I've taught classics at the University of Pennsylvania. The only reason I was called up was that before the war I did extensive archaeological research on Sicily. I was put in charge of a cartographic section in Algiers, drawing maps for the invasion. Then, two days ago, out of a blue sky, I was ordered to join your mission. Let me tell you, it was the shock of my life. I'm just too old for this sort of thing. When

I asked for an explanation, I was told that the mission was in an area of Sicily I knew well. I was to function as guide in case the commandos became lost in the dark. And now I see that the orders make sense. Before the war I did excavate for several seasons around the temples of Silenus, which aren't far from Capo Granitola. Good Lord, I hope the Germans haven't stored their ammunition in *them*, as the Turks did in the Parthenon! At any rate, I do know the area quite well. But now you tell me that Major D'Angelo has arranged for a local guide. I must confess I'm quite confused."

A shout came from the wheelhouse. John and the major looked back and saw the old man, the steersman, leaning out and pointing a bony finger toward the land.

"Capo Granitola!" he shouted to the men on the bow hatch.

John and the major stared into the night and caught just a glimpse of a single light, rhythmically flashing. It was the prearranged signal from their guide.

Forsyth stood up, grabbing at the forestay to keep his balance. He looked at the tiny light flashing in the darkness, and in his timid voice recited: "Rough years I've had: now may I see once more my hall, my lands, my people before I die."

"Where's that from?" John asked.

"Homer's *Odyssey*, Book Seven. The prayer of a weary old man on a tiny ship, driven among these islands by a hostile fate. Facing his death when all he wanted was to go home. Odysseus." Forsyth reached down and loosened the pistol belt buckled tight around his sagging middle. "Well, Odysseus, wiliest of men, tonight I invoke your courage and your craft. I've read your story so many times that I know it by heart, but only now do I understand what you are saying to me."

"Forsyth! Devlin! Move your butts!" D'Angelo was shouting from the wheelhouse.

"Well, Major," said John, "time to go." Instinctively he checked his watch. He could no longer read the dial. The moon had set; it was midnight. The paratroopers had jumped. In three hours the invasion would begin.

Major D'Angelo's Sicilian guide proved to be excellent. In scarcely an hour's time, exactly on schedule, the commando team was crouching in the darkness just outside the perimeter of the ammo dump. Whatever was going on elsewhere in Sicily at that moment, word of it apparently had not reached the Germans at the dump; only token sentries were on duty, and the compound, darkened against air raids, was quiet.

D'Angelo hissed out orders. "Dixon. Mackey. Reconnoiter, and take care of those sentries. Be *quiet*. Use the wire."

Without a word two of the silent commandos put down their rifles and wrapped thin silver strands with leather handles around their fists, then faded noiselessly into the night. As they brushed past him John glanced at their expressionless faces. Added together, their ages would probably just equal his.

D'Angelo turned to John and Matthew Engels. He grinned unpleasantly. "Ever seen what the wire can do? Once around the neck, and pull!" He crossed his hairy fists and violently jerked them apart. "Goes right through the windpipe. On a little guy, like a Jap, it'll take his head off. Wanna try it sometime, college man?"

Everyone waited in silence while Dixon and Mackey accomplished their work: three minutes, four minutes, five minutes. John tried very hard not to think about what the wire could do. Then the two young commandos silently materialized.

"We're in luck, Major," said Mackey, in soft southern tones. "Damn Krauts 'r all snorin' like babies in the barracks, right where you said they'd be. Must've had quite a night on the town."

D'Angelo nodded. "Sentries?"

Mackey looked at Dixon. "Ah got mine." He grinned.

Dixon grinned back and gave the high sign. "Me too."

John saw that there was blood on Dixon's hand — the fresh blood of a murdered man. He felt something he had not expected to feel: cold curiosity. What was it like to die in an instant, alone in the night, without even a chance to fight? A peculiar feeling began to rise in him.

"Demolition team, go!" D'Angelo whispered. The other four commandos, their packs laden with explosives, disappeared.

"Okay, this is it." D'Angelo faced John, Engels, and Major Forsyth. "We're going up to the barracks. In five minutes the charges will blow. You three just stay behind me and my boys and run when we run. Forsyth, did they give you something to shoot with?"

Forsyth nodded and held up a pistol. Its barrel shook noticeably in his hand.

"Okay, okay," said D'Angelo in disgust. "You just stay next to me. And try not to shoot anyone who isn't a German." He looked at his watch. "Four minutes. Mackey, take the point, then Dixon, then me with the major. Devlin, you and Doctor Engels bring up the rear. Anybody makes a noise and Dixon will use the wire on them, pronto. Got it, Dixon?"

The boy nodded, still expressionless, not appreciating D'Angelo's humor. John felt the sensation rising in him rise a little further. This kid was an automaton, he thought; he was no longer fighting a war for his country, he was simply killing whoever D'Angelo told him to. Was that what combat did to you?

"Move out." Everyone got up as quietly as possible, crouched low, and formed their column.

"Get out your notebook, headshrinker," D'Angelo said to Engels. "In exactly four minutes you're gonna see what you came to see."

Mackey led them to the neat hole he had cut in the barbed-wire fence just outside the barracks. With its few scattered buildings and vehicles, the dump compound was indeed so quiet that it seemed uninhabited, but a few faint snores coming from the barracks building confirmed the German garrison's presence. At D'Angelo's command everyone lay flat on the ground just outside the fence. John stared across the compound at the long camouflaged ammunition sheds. In less than a minute they would explode. He was pleased to discover how calm he was. The pistol in his hand, an Army-issue Colt .45, was not shaking. In the face of danger he was in control, as he had always known he would be. One last time he mentally reviewed his assignment. *Aid combat troops in securing barracks. When barracks are secured locate administrative offices. Quick-check German documents in office for information on enemy coastal batteries. Capture all relevant documents for detailed examination by naval —*

KABOOM! In an instant the black of the night had turned to red. The ground trembled. Where the sheds had been there was fire, nothing but fire billowing into the sky. A wave of force and heat struck John's face and he stared openmouthed, forgetting everything else.

"*NOW!*" D'Angelo screamed in his ear.

John leaped to his feet. Everyone else was already through the fence. Clutching his pistol, he ran for the hole. He was through. A door crashed open just ahead of him. He heard shots and shouts, English mingling with German. He was through the door, inside a large room weirdly lit in red and black by the exploding ammo. He saw Dixon, Mackey, and D'Angelo kneeling — for some stupid reason he thought of Mass — and spraying gunfire all around the room. Forsyth and Engels were crouched behind them. And in front, in the path of the bullets, the enemy, the hated Nazi, was dying.

He was meeting his death not in his famous steel-gray uniform but in his underwear. The Americans' surprise had been complete. Their gunfire had already killed many of the Germans in their beds. The others were scampering madly about, grabbing for weapons. John saw one man, wearing nothing but boxer shorts, running almost straight at him, heading for some light machine guns racked against the wall. He pointed his pistol at the German. The man's eyes snapped from the machine guns to John. "*Nicht schiessen! Nicht schiessen!*" he yelled, throwing his hands over his head. He was scarcely ten feet away.

John pulled the trigger. The kick of the Colt nearly knocked him off his feet. An enormous ragged hole opened up in the German's chest and he flew backward, his feet leaving the floor as if a powerful wind had picked him up. John gripped his pistol with both hands and fired again. The dead man's arm came off at the shoulder. John fired again. Suddenly his whole body was shaking violently, almost uncontrollably. He fired again. The mangled body slammed against a bed.

Another German was crouching down, behind the bed, hands up, shouting. John fired. He was shaking and the shot went wide; one of the German's upraised hands disappeared. The man screamed in agony and fell to the floor. John locked his shaking arms and took aim at him. He pulled the trigger, and the pistol snapped harmlessly. *Empty*. He threw the Colt away and raced to the wall, to the machine guns. He grabbed one and turned back to the Germans. A naked man was racing for a window. John fired the machine gun. The recoiling gun jumped wildly in his untrained hands, but he hit the fleeing German, who pranced grotesquely in front of the window as if held up by the force of the bullets which tore holes in his naked flesh.

There were three others, huddled in a corner, hands empty and raised high. They were shouting at him, *"Wir kapitulieren, kapitulieren!"* His mind heard the phrase and understood it perfectly: *We surrender.* He swung the gun over to the corner and fired. The three Germans fell and he kept on firing into them, feeling the power of the gun kicking in his hands, exulting in it, hearing a voice, his own voice, shouting loudly in the air, or perhaps only in his mind — no, not shouting, singing almost, a paean . . .

"Devlin! Your left!"

John spun left at the warning; the blazing gun cut down one more man, a man almost close enough to strike John. At that range he was nearly cut in two. John pumped bullets into him, panting hard through clenched teeth. He felt relief. This man might have killed him; he was fully clothed and armed. Armed with a pistol. A Colt. The uniform was not steel gray. It was olive drab. *Forsyth.*

"Devlin!"

It was D'Angelo shouting at him. John felt the hot gun, still firing, being snatched from his hand. In the sudden silence he stared wildly at D'Angelo. He felt very cold. His body trembled and his teeth chattered uncontrollably. His fatigues were drenched in sweat. D'Angelo held the gun. He smiled at John, a smile of pure contempt.

"Nice going, Lieutenant. You just killed Major Forsyth."

John stared. It *was* the major on the floor. Blood pumped out of half a dozen holes in his chest. His eyes and his mouth were wide open. He looked very surprised. And he was dead.

"You bastard!" It wasn't D'Angelo talking now; it was Matthew Engels. John turned to his friend. Engels was livid with rage, but he wasn't looking at John. He was looking at D'Angelo.

"You bastard!" Engels yelled again. "I saw you! You pushed him!"

Major D'Angelo's smile disappeared. He turned slowly to Engels.

"Lieutenant," he said with quiet menace, "that's a very serious accusation. Are you accusing your commanding officer of murder?"

"You pushed him!" Engels ignored the threat in D'Angelo's voice. "I saw you, you sonofabitch! You reached out your arm and pushed Forsyth in front of *him.*" Engels pointed at John. "And then you shouted to make him fire to the left!"

D'Angelo's face flushed red with anger. "Listen, you smart-ass kike," he snarled, "don't tell me what happened. I'll tell *you* what happened. Your egghead friend here lost control. You wanna talk about murder, you talk to him. Ain't that right, boys?"

John saw the faintest flicker of doubt pass across Mackey and Dixon's faces before they stiffened up and said, "Yessir." John's body was still shaking; his mind was absolutely numb.

"Now get the hell outta here, Engels," D'Angelo said coldly, turning away.

"You bastard!" Engels shouted. He did not move.

D'Angelo spun around. He leveled the machine gun at Engels. "Lieutenant — I said *go.*"

For a long moment Engels stared contemptuously at the muzzle of the gun pointing at his gut. Then he turned and stalked out of the barracks.

Slowly, by degrees, John's mind was becoming less numb. He remembered seeing something in the corner of his eye just as he turned left . . .

"You *did* push him," he said suddenly to D'Angelo, looking at him in quiet surprise.

D'Angelo turned to him. His smile came back and he swaggered over until his smirking face was only inches away from John's. "Listen, Lieutenant," he said, his voice mocking, "I got one thing to say to you. We get back, it's your word against mine. And considering what just happened here" — he waved an arm at the slaughtered Germans — "I think I know who an Army court would believe, don't you?"

John said nothing. He stared past D'Angelo, at Forsyth. D'Angelo grinned.

"Hey, cheer up, Devlin," he said jovially, turning to look at Forsyth. "Our valiant major has not died in vain." Hunting for something in the pockets of his combat jacket, he walked over to the dead man. He found what he was looking for and held it up to show John.

"Phony documents," he said, grinning again. "Didn't your buddies in Algiers tell you? Plans for a second American landing at Capo Granitola, three days from now. When the Krauts find 'em they'll tie up half their troops on the island over here, waiting for us to show. Only we ain't gonna show." D'Angelo knelt beside Forsyth and carefully inserted the false documents inside his jacket. "Trouble is," he went on, "the Krauts'd hafta find these documents on the body of a high-rankin' officer, somebody in charge. And since I was the only high-rankin' officer on this mission, and since I didn't particularly feel like volunteerin' for this particular job, your buddies in Algiers looked around to see who they could, ah, 'spare' — and sent me Major Forsyth." D'Angelo smoothed down Forsyth's pockets and stood up. He looked at John with his mocking smirk. "You mean they didn't tell you?"

John stared at Forsyth. He said nothing.

"Listen, Devlin." D'Angelo walked toward the barracks door. "I don't like to see you so upset. Tell you what I'm gonna do. When we get back I'm gonna tell everybody how the major cleared this barracks of Krauts single-handed, before he bought it. I'm gonna put him in for a decoration. Feel better now?"

John said nothing.

"Hey, c'mon, Devlin," the smiling D'Angelo cajoled. "Look at it this way — you did the guy a favor. He was nothing, a loser. Now he's a hero. His family'll be sorry he's dead, but they'll be proud of him too, a hell of a lot prouder than they were before." D'Angelo paused at the doorway. "So don't be glum, chum. Tonight you made a man outta Major Forsyth."

The look in John's eyes, which showed that D'Angelo's obscene humor had struck home, evoked another of the major's vicious laughs. D'Angelo started to leave the barracks, then stopped. "Oh yeah," he said, "I almost forgot. The crowning touch." The German machine gun was still in his hands. He leveled it at Forsyth and squeezed off another burst. Forsyth flopped over onto his side as the bullets struck exactly where the documents were planted. They would now be bloody and full of holes.

"Can't let the Krauts think we planted those landing plans on a *dead* man!" D'Angelo laughed again. He turned to John and added with mock politeness, "When you're ready to join us, Mr. Devlin, we'll be in the office, rifling the files." Then he tossed the machine gun back to John, who instinctively caught it, and left.

As soon as he had caught the machine gun John threw it away.

His eyes traveled around the silent room. In the blood-red light, dimmer now that the ammo explosions were subsiding into fires, the eyes of the unarmed, naked men he had slaughtered, open and glassy, met his.

Dear God, he thought stupidly, numbly. *What have I done?*

He heard footsteps behind him and turned. It was Matthew Engels. For a full minute the two men stood side by side, staring at the carnage, not speaking. Then Engels turned to John.

"You sonofabitch," he said, and he struck John in the face.

7

The Dead

April 12, 1944
Naples

One year from today I shall reach the middle of my life. I shall be forty years old. But I will never see forty. I will be dead.

The dream came again last night. It comes every night, seven days in a row now. I had thought the horror was over. It will never be over.

At first, on Sicily, it was worse. Three weeks after it happened I was in Palermo, sitting in a café with the rest of our troops. They were all drinking and eating and grabbing girls. They were glad to be still alive. I was hungry too, and thirsty. I raised a glass of clear red wine to my lips. Suddenly the wine was cloudy and sticky and warm; it was blood. I threw it away from me. Then a waiter brought me food. He removed the cover from the plate, and there was a man's head on the plate, Forsyth's head. He looked up at me with his old sad eyes, and in the middle of the café crowded with soldiers I screamed. I ran away. After that I kept to my quarters. Everywhere I went I saw them. When I sat in cafés they sat near me. In the streets I saw their faces in the crowds. I woke at night and saw them crouching in the corners of my room. After a while I began to talk to them. "What do you want?" I asked them one night, as they all sat quietly around my bed, staring at me. They said nothing. "Do you want to know why?" I shouted. "I don't know why!" But the dead said nothing; they only stared at me with their dull accusing eyes. If they had come to me many more nights I am sure I would long ago have gone mad.

But in October Naples fell, and I was transferred. The dead did not follow me. I didn't see them anymore. I thought I had left them behind on Sicily, ghosts of the place who would trouble me no more. But now, suddenly, the dream. In the dream it is Sicily again and I am in the barracks. They are in front of me again, naked, and again I am killing them; but in the dream I have no gun. I am eating them alive, like an animal, a predator, tearing off their living flesh and gulping it down, while they plead with me to stop . . . For seven nights I have had this dream. Last night I was afraid to close my eyes. I dare not sleep.

Just before I left Tokyo, I asked Yuzawa if he thought me a sinner because I intended to fight. Yuzawa said that after frightful sinning a man sometimes finds the Buddha in himself. All of us are Buddhas, he said, only we are blind; perhaps when we have sinned enough we shall cleanse our vision and the Buddha will be there. And then, he told me, we will know this world to be a blazing sea of fire, an endless ocean of suffering, and this dreadful knowledge will make us serene and compassionate. Well, I am burning now; the ocean of hell is closing over me. And I don't know a goddamned thing. I don't know why I killed those men. I don't know why they come to me at night. I don't know why I once saw an ocean liner sink a week before it actually did. I don't know why an undertaker turned into a monk and whispered rhymes to me. I don't know why I broke a man's ribcage in some stupid football game. It's as if there is something inside my mind, something black and horrible like a disease, that takes control of me whenever it wants to . . .

I will make one last effort. Beginning today, as I turn thirty-nine, I will write everything down in these pages, everything I can remember of my strangeness from my childhood, when I dreamed of the storm and of Grandfather in the tree. In a year's time I shall either have understood this black thing that seizes me, and beaten it, or I shall kill it with a bullet through my brain. Forty years is long enough. I can endure no more.

The flies were having a party. Around the rim of the glass they danced, licking up sugary, sticky whisky. Suddenly a giant hand swooped down, and the party was over. John Devlin had located his glass.

Four glasses later, each of them full of straight Scotch, John heard a knock on the door of his quarters. " 'S open," he muttered.

Not hearing this, the man at the door waited a discreet moment before walking in anyway. John looked up from his chair. Matthew Engels was looking solemnly down at him.

"Hello, John," he said.

"H'lo, Matt," said John. He tried to concentrate. "Sit down. " 'S been a long time."

"Yeah, a long time," said Engels sadly, pulling up a chair. "Over a year. A year and eight months, to be exact. Since D-Day Sicily."

"Yeah." John nodded. He remembered clearly; the whisky, as it always did, removed the pain.

"I just got transferred to a hospital in Rome," Engels went on. "I'm on my way there and I got held up for a few days, waiting for transportation. Someone said you were here and knew where you lived. I thought I'd look you up."

"Sure." John sat cocooned in his alcoholic haze. He had nothing to say to Engels. He had nothing to say to anyone.

"I wanted to see you," Engels continued, "to apologize for the way I reacted back on Sicily, at the ammo dump. I've thought about it ever since and I feel really bad about hitting you, and I'm sorry." Engels held out his hand.

" 'S Okay." John did not take it.

"I guess," said Engels, withdrawing his hand, "that everybody was more or less out of control that night. When I thought about it later I realized that when I hit you I really wanted to hit D'Angelo, whom I couldn't punish because he outranked me and was holding a machine gun. You were just the substitute. After we took Sicily I did my damnedest to get that bastard D'Angelo arrested. I yelled my head off to everyone from the MPs to the military courts, but nobody would even open an inquiry. 'Bring us corroboration,' they said, and I knew those kids Mackey and Dixon wouldn't talk, and I didn't want to involve you . . . Anyway, I finally wrote to Ike himself. After a while I got a nice letter back from somebody on his staff, thanking me for bringing such a serious matter to Ike's attention. They had checked the records and discovered that the whole thing was a dead issue — literally, because D'Angelo had been killed. Bought it on Sicily a week after D-Day, just outside Agrigento. There's one GI casualty I won't mourn. I only wish I could have killed him myself, instead of leaving him to the Germans."

"D'Angelo's dead?" John stirred in his cocoon. "I wonder if I'll see him too now."

"Huh?" Engels gave John a long, critical look. "Listen, John, you don't look too good." He noted the empty bottles lying around the room and piled into the trash can. "Pardon me for asking, but do you drink like this every night?"

"Oh, no." John dropped his head back and chuckled. "Certainly not. Not *every* night. Only on *special* nights. Tonight is a special night." He heaved himself out of the chair and lurched across the room to his bedside table. "A special night . . . here." He waved a piece of paper in the air. "Got this letter today from home. From my boy Steven. Oldest boy. Fifteen now." John brought the letter very close to his blurry eyes and began to read. " 'Dear Dad, we read in the papers that you have just about beaten Hitler and will come home to us soon. I am so proud of you. When we took Sicily you were part of it. And now we've really got the Axis on the run, and you're part of it too. David and Mom send their love and feel as proud as I do, and we all hope we'll hear something from you soon.' " John stopped. He crumpled up the letter and threw it into the trash.

"My wife and sons, you see," he said, lurching back toward his chair, "think that I am a hero. They remember good old Dad, good old decent, upright Dad, who joined up with a square jaw and a smile on his face and went off to do his duty. And soon good old Dad will be coming home to them. And everyone will be proud. And one night good old Dad will just lose control again and kill them all in their beds."

"John! Stop it!"

John had picked up his glass to pour another drink. Suddenly he threw it savagely across the room. It smashed to pieces on the floor. He turned on Engels.

"How in hell can I go home to them?" he cried. "I'm not their dad anymore, I'm not their hero. I'm a . . . a monster. I shot those men even after they were dead. And I couldn't stop myself . . . I killed Forsyth . . ."

"*D'Angelo* killed Forsyth."

"I don't care what D'Angelo did. I'm the guilty one." John collapsed in his chair. He buried his face in his hands. "I can't go home, Matt. I can't hide what I've done, not even from myself. Nearly two years have passed, and still I have . . ." He hesitated; never in his life had he told anyone, not even Ruth, about his secret. "I have . . . dreams."

"So do half the guys in this war who've seen any action," Engels said firmly. "I treat a dozen of them every day. In their sleep they relive all the horror they've seen. And the other half don't give a shit — they kill Krauts and then go guzzle wine and gobble pasta and sleep soundly at night. That's the way it is. That's the human condition." Engels was quiet for a moment. "Try to forgive yourself, John," he said more gently. "It's a war. You're not alone. A lot of guys do things they don't expect —"

"You know," John interrupted, suddenly laughing again, "you're too late, Doctor Engels. Somebody else already gave me this lecture. You see, my dreams just won't go away. So about a month ago I had an idea. I was raised a Catholic. I was taught to confess my sins and ask absolution from God. So in desperation I did something I hadn't done in years — I went to confession. To a Navy chaplain. I told him all about the ammo dump, about what I did. I even told him about Forsyth, and what D'Angelo did. And you know what he said?" John reached for his whisky and, his glass broken, took a pull from the bottle. " 'God forgives you all,' he said, 'for an excess of zeal in performance of righteous duty in his name.' Then he gave me some prayers to say, to make my dreams go away. And now you're telling me the same damn thing, without the God and the ritual. Or are you going to prescribe pills instead of prayers?"

"Maybe the chaplain was right," said Engels with a wry smile. "After all, historically, God has forgiven a lot."

"That's not the point!" John sat up. His anger brought him out of his stupor. "The goddamned priests don't know anything about God. Do you really think that God forgives me for massacring those men because I'm an *American?*" John jumped up from his chair and paced across the room, dangling the whisky bottle from one hand. At the wall he wheeled around, and in one long burst shouted at Engels: "Dammit, Matt, I was a decent man! An educated man! An intelligent man! A man with a successful career! A family! *Children,* for Christ's sake! I was everything a man is supposed to be! Things like this are not supposed to happen! I'm not supposed to lose — to lose . . . control! And, and everything else — why should it have happened to *me?* It wasn't patriotism, it was that . . . that *thing!*"

"John." Engels was giving him a hard, questioning look. "If my hunches hadn't been right a hundred times before, I'd say I was wrong, but I have the feeling that there's something more to all this, something much more than Sicily. What is it you aren't telling me?"

At the question John froze. He had said too much. No one

must know. They'd lock him up and throw away the key. In his rising panic he lashed out at his friend. "Oh no, you don't!" he shouted. "Don't you get professional with me, Engels. Thanks for the apology. Now leave me alone. I don't need any damn psychiatrist, any more than I need a priest. All my life I've handled everything myself, and I'll damn well handle this thing myself, or I'll —"

"What? Blow your brains out?" Engels stood up and confronted John. The Brooklyn street kid punched through the professional calm of the Park Avenue practitioner. "That's exactly what you're planning to do, isn't it, Mr. High-and-mighty-brought-so-low John Devlin?"

John looked away, angrily clenching his jaw. Engels saw he had been right and kept after him.

"You think that'll solve it? You think you'll make it up to Forsyth and a bunch of dead Krauts by killing yourself? Are you gonna play Jesus Christ like a good Catholic boy and go to the cross for D'Angelo's sins?"

John's head snapped back to face Engels. "They're *my* sins, goddammit!" he bellowed.

Engels clenched his fists and shook them in John's face. "Good God, man! The Krauts you shot would've killed you in your bed and been proud to do it! And D'Angelo — shit, people like him aren't worth a damn! Sicily was *evil,* John — yes, it was *evil.* There is evil in this world and in every one of us, and God permits it, and yes, you're right, the priests never have an answer for that one! But there is also good in this world, and if you're thinking of destroying all of the considerable good that's in you just because you found some evil in there too, you damn well should feel guilty about it! Should your sons not have a father? Should your wife not have a husband? Should a world pulling itself out of the rubble of war not have the talents and compassion of one of its finer diplomats, one of the few who believes in something more than screwing his neighbors? If you want absolution, sure, you won't get it from a priest. But you won't get it from death, either. Love your children, love your wife, love the world. Let your good triumph over your evil. That, my friend, is absolution!"

Engels had finished, but for a long moment he continued to stare angrily at John. For a long moment John stared back, silent also; then he brushed past Engels and walked to the small writing desk that stood opposite his bed. In the drawer of the desk were his diaries, where everything was written. Grandfather in the tree. The *Lusitania*. The monk in Mr. Watkins's carriage. Karl Werner's Harvard lecture. The Pergamon Museum. Aruna. His secret. He had never told anyone. In the tree he had promised Grandfather. But Matthew Engels was right: he had to live. And he could not live any longer unless he understood, until the power of the thing inside him was broken.

He opened the drawer. The black volumes were stacked neatly inside. He felt Engels's eyes on him, watching. *Promise me, Johnny . . . whenever ye get a look into the infinity of things, that you'll not tell a livin' soul. Promise.* It was March 1945. Late March. He had written everything down. For a year he had thought, remembered, analyzed. He had not understood. In three weeks he would be forty; in three weeks he would have to keep his vow. He would have no choice.

"John? Are you all right?" Engels was standing by his side. "My God, you've gone white as a sheet."

John grabbed the stack of diaries and shoved it into Engels's hands. "Yes, Doctor Engels, you were right," he said, his voice on the edge of breaking. "For the hundred and first time you were right. There *is* more. A lot more. It's all in there. Please read it. And if you can make one damn bit of sense out of it, for the love of God, please tell me what it is."

The day after his visit from Engels John received new orders. They were not from the Navy but from the Department of State, a sure sign that the war was ending. In one week's time a conference would be held at Syracuse, in Sicily, where representatives of all the Allied nations would discuss the possible political and economic directions of the postwar world, especially of the defeated Axis nations. John was ordered to attend.

His orders included transportation to Syracuse on a PT boat scheduled to make the trip from Naples later in the week. Reading them, John had a panicky moment. Engels had gone to Rome, with the diaries. How would he get in touch with his friend if he left for Syracuse? How long would he be tied up at the conference? What if he were ordered elsewhere afterward? He *had* to know what Engels thought. But in another moment he got a grip on himself and simply cabled his address at Syracuse to Engels in Rome.

Once John had calmed his fears the trip promised to do him good. The Neapolitan sky was a beautiful burning blue when the PT boat left the harbor for Syracuse. Again John felt the roll of a small craft in a giant sea and experienced warm memories of his youth. The good weather held for most of the voyage, all the way to the Strait of Messina. But as the PT boat entered the strait, just at evening, the weather changed.

"Damn," said the skipper, a very young lieutenant j.g., as he eyed the blackening sky. "You never can tell when one of these squalls will blow up. Happens all the time around the strait. Bad place to sail . . ."

The skipper and his crew hurried to batten down their craft as best they could, leaving John behind the wheelhouse spray shield. He stood thinking of his telegram to Engels, hoping it had gotten through. A squall was a squall. He had been in worse with Father . . .

But he had not. An hour later the PT boat was fighting for its life in the worst storm John had ever seen. Gigantic waves smashed into the wheelhouse and stood the boat on its side. The wind shrieked and drove the rain and the pounding waves. The sailors, giving every thought to the survival of their craft, had no time to panic, but John, who had no duties to distract him, was terrified. He was seaman enough to understand the risk to the boat in weather like this. Hanging on to the wheelhouse, trying to keep himself from being swept overboard, he squinted into the night for a glimpse of the cliffs of Sicily, or of Italy; they were only two miles apart in the Messina Strait. He thought he saw rocks looming dangerously close. Would the boat be driven ashore and pounded to bits? He could not be sure. It was so very dark, absolutely black, and the rain and the spray made it hard to see . . .

Forsyth's invocation filled his mind: *A weary old man on a tiny ship, driven by a hostile fate . . . only now do I understand what you are saying to me.* Odysseus had nearly drowned in this strait. Scylla and Charybdis, monster and maelstrom — death inescapable on either side . . . There was something dead ahead, right at the bow of the boat. A rock. Scylla's rock. Call the captain. No, wait — not something, some*one*. Standing on the bow. Who? John wiped the spray from his eyes.

John. Come to me.

He could no longer feel the rain. He could no longer hear the wind. He was enveloped in darkness, sinking slowly, tranquilly, into quiet, liquid depths. It was very cold and very wet. He managed a thought: *I am overboard. I have drowned.* He must already be dead. It was so very peaceful. He felt no pain at all, only calm. He drifted downward, waiting for the nothingness of death.

But instead he felt his feet touch bottom. It was still very cold, but suddenly quite dry. And, he suddenly realized, not so dark. There was a kind of gray twilight. He could see.

What he saw was an absolutely flat and featureless surface, extending apparently forever. It was unnaturally flat, more like an ideal shape, a geometric plane, than actual earth. All around was only the gray twilight, which might have been air, or cloud, or nothing at all.

John.

His mother stood before him. She looked as he had last seen her, just before he left for Africa, just after Father's funeral: her raven hair shining silver, her milk-pale skin wizened and old. He tried to speak; he could only think. But she heard his thoughts and answered them.

Where are we?

In the Land of the Dead. The very border of Matter and Spirit. The living flesh can go no further than this.

Are we dead?

I am dead. I died an instant ago, in New Bedford. I wanted to see you one more time.

Mother . . .

The dead are freed from their bodies; they know everything. Now I know what Grandfather Michael knew, what he told you in the Tree. I know now what you have to do. You must live a little longer. Good-bye.

Mother! How do you know —

She was gone; she had faded into nothingness before him. There were others taking shape. John knew them in an instant, to his horror.

Forgive me.

It was Forsyth his thought went to, Forsyth who stood before him in his bloody uniform, his torn body. Behind him were the Germans, some in their underwear, some naked, arms and hands missing where John had shot them off.

We have come back into Matter to speak with you. We must enter it as we left it, as we were at the last moment we were in Time.

Forsyth had read the horror in John's mind. Again John's plea went out: *Forgive me.*

Forgiveness is a matter for the living. We do not forgive, we do not accuse. Only do not forget us.

They had vanished. There was someone else. An old man with a tangle of white hair, seven feet tall.

Grandfather.

He was standing motionless, wearing the clothes he had worn thirty years ago, on the day he died, when John had watched Father O'Reilly close his eyes.

Grandfather. It's me, John.

John felt himself running toward the tall old man, but after a few steps he stopped. It was not Grandfather. It was Grandfather's body, but it had no face. Under the tangled hair there was nothing, nothing at all, only a black void.

Who are you?

Inside the void two white-hot eyes blazed up, burning into John's. *I am frightened,* he thought, and felt no fear. They were the eyes he had seen all his life, whenever the thing had seized him.

Who are you?

From the void there now came a voice: a horrible voice, a terrifying voice, the voice out of nowhere that had spoken riddles to him time after time.

The time of your service is very near. The next time I call, you must answer me.

How?

The white heat of the eyes grew even whiter and hotter, until the eyes were all that John could see, and more than he could bear. *Stop . . . please stop.*

Very soon I shall call to you once more. If you are worthy, you shall answer. Remember Jonah . . .

All was white, infinite white, white without end — maddening, mind-eating nothingness.

Who are you? Who are you? WHO ARE YOU?

"Well, I'll tell you who I'm not, Lieutenant. I'm not your mother, that's for damn sure."

John sat up. He was in a bunk, below decks in the PT boat. The boat floated still and calm. Above him, through an open hatch, he saw blue sky, and heard a city.

"Whoa! Easy, Lieutenant." The sailor at his bedside grinned. He wore a medical corpsman's insignia. "Don't get up just yet. Skipper's sent for a doctor to check you out. Might be some weird strain of fever or something."

"What do you mean?" John could remember nothing.

The corpsman whistled softly through his teeth. "Hoo boy, Lieutenant, you must've really been out. You mean you don't remember what you did last night?"

"No." John lay back obediently in the bunk.

The corpsman laughed. "Well, hell, in the middle of the worst Mediterranean storm in ten years you started crying, 'Mama! Mama! I'm coming, Mama!' just like a little baby boy. And I'll be damned if you didn't try to make a run for the bow! Good thing the skipper got to you first. Damned if you weren't about ready to leap overboard."

The Navy doctor checked John and pronounced him free of fever or any other sickness. Avoiding the skipper's eyes, John thanked him for his quick action, dressed, and disembarked. A car was waiting for him. The crew stood in a little knot on the foredeck of the PT, whispering and watching him. As his driver opened the door for him he heard a burst of laughter behind his back.

The car took him through medieval streets clogged with soldiers and rubble, to the huge old villa where the conference would be held. On the way the driver told him that the storm had thrown the conference schedule into disarray. Most of the other participants had been delayed by the bad weather, so the opening meeting had been postponed for a day. John leaned back against the big leather seat and stared at the ruins of Syracuse passing by. He was grateful for the unexpected gift of a day; he needed whatever time he could find to pull himself together.

But no sooner had he taken possession of his room at the villa than there was a knock at the door. Frowning, John opened it. Immediately his frown became an astonished smile.

"Matt!"

Engels walked past him into the room. "Yes, you *should* look surprised, Lieutenant Devlin. It's a miracle I got down here. I had to give my boss in Rome the most cockamamy story . . ." The psychiatrist dumped his briefcase on the bed and began rummaging through it, looking for something. "Anyway, they told me downstairs that your conference has been put off a day. That's good. We might need all of today, and even tonight."

"For what?"

Engels had found what he was looking for. "For these," he said, turning around. John's diaries were in his hand.

Without further explanation he made John sit down and respond to a solid hour of questioning about all of his hallucinations. When he finally paused, John ventured to ask a question of his own — the central one.

"Look, Matt, it's very kind of you to take all this trouble, and I'm very grateful, but please just tell me one thing: am I crazy?"

"Let me ask you a question," Engels replied, as though he had not been doing exactly that for the past hour. "Do you know what a shaman is?"

"A shaman . . . Isn't that a sort of magician, or some kind of high priest, in a primitive tribe?"

"Magician, maybe. Priest, never." Engels leaned forward in his chair and stared intently at John. "Primitive peoples, the most primitive ones, don't have priests. Priests come with civilization. But what primitive peoples do have, in every generation, are individuals to whom God, or the gods, speak directly and openly, as I speak to you. One day in their youth these people unexpectedly receive an initiatory vision — an annunciation, as it were — in which the god appears to them as an animal or as the spirit of a great shaman of former times. After that their lives are never the same."

"What do you mean?" John asked nervously.

"The god gives them superhuman power, wisdom, and sometimes knowledge of the future. He teaches them the hidden secrets of the universe. He allows them to visit him. It's as though these people can see and hear with absolute clarity things that most of us cannot see or hear, or at best catch only snatches of in dreams. It's as though the gods have chosen them."

"What are you getting at?" But even as he asked, John had an uneasy feeling that he knew. Crazy Karl Werner had said that . . .

"What I'm getting at, John, is that what's in these diaries of yours reads a hell of a lot like what these primitive shamans would write, if they could write."

"But Matt, that's ridiculous! Obviously I'm not some primitive, I'm a man of the twentieth century."

"Which means nothing, as far as the psyche is concerned."

"What?"

"In Zurich years ago," said Engels, "in the seminars with Jung, I became convinced of one thing: that the psyche, the human mind, is ultimately timeless. Every phase of what our conscious intellect sees as the long march of history, and of endless prehistory before that, and of the unknown future to come, coexists simultaneously, right now, in you and in me and in General Eisenhower and in anyone else you'd care to name. Outside of what our consciousness can perceive, in the darker regions of the unconscious, all of this exists — "

"Hold it, please," John said, putting up his hands in protest. "All of this is very interesting. But frankly, it still doesn't answer my original question, the only one that matters a damn to me at this point. *Am I crazy?*"

Engels looked at him. "Yes, you are," he said evenly. "But only in the sense that Jesus of Nazareth was crazy. Or Elijah." He smiled. "Or Jonah."

Jonah. John had not told Engels about the Land of the Dead. He wondered if he should, and decided to wait. "Do you really believe that?" he asked.

At the question Engels seemed suddenly less certain. He got up from his chair and began to pace the room. "God, John, I don't know," he said quietly. "I admit it all sounds goofy as hell, from the rationalist point of view." He shook his head. "You know, it's really incredible. You can bullshit all you want with the great Jung, and you can dazzle the Park Avenue ladies with your profound explanations of their mundane little dreams. And then one day in the middle of a war you chance to meet John

Devlin and suddenly it's real. You meet a perfectly normal civilized man who for all the world appears to be an honest-to-God shaman. And suddenly you just don't know." Engels stopped pacing and looked at John across the room. "Do *you* believe it?"

"No, I don't," said John wearily. "Yes, I do. No, I don't. Yes, I do. For Christ's sake, Matt, I haven't known what to believe for forty years. At this point I'm afraid even to think about it. You brought up this shaman business — you tell me if it's true."

Engels leaned back against the wall, put his hands over his eyes, and furrowed his forehead. For a full minute he was silent. Then abruptly he dropped his hands and opened his eyes and came away from the wall. He walked over to John and looked straight at him.

"Yes," he said, "it is true. It has to be true. If it isn't, everything I know about the mind is just a lie. And it *isn't* a lie. I have to stake everything on that, and by God, I will. You *are* a shaman. You *are* a prophet. The voice that spoke in Elijah and Jonah, Jesus of Nazareth and William Blake, speaks in you." Engels continued to stare at John, a bit defiantly, as if he knew what was coming. And it did come. John exploded.

"*Damn it,* Matt!" he shouted, striking his chair with his fist. "Talk sense to me! This is serious! You're not in some Jungian bull session here, you're not brown-nosing your big man in Zurich! You're talking to a flesh-and-blood man who's at the end of his goddamned rope!"

"I stand by what I said," Engels replied firmly.

"Oh, Jesus, Matt. Sure, of course you do, you've got your professional pride. But do me a favor and drop your pride for a moment and help me out. Now let's analyze this rationally. First of all, I'm not a prophet, or a poet. I'm a diplomat — "

Engels broke in. "And that is the most extraordinary thing about what's happened to you. Unlike every other shaman who has ever lived, you are an insider, not an outsider. A Jonah with connections. Yes, a diplomat, one with a shaman's vision, one who could work *in* the world in quiet, unobtrusive ways and get practical results, instead of railing at civilization from the outside and winning converts through martyrdom."

A puzzled, frightened look appeared on John's face. "Oh, come on now, Matt — "

"For God's *sake,* man," Engels said, his voice nearly a whisper, "look at your diaries!" He flipped through one of the black books. "There is a window open in your otherwise normal diplomatic mind, a window such as only the great shamans have had, and through it all your life you have received a series of cryptic but cohesive messages." He shut the book and stared decisively at John. "One of the things that rubbed off on me at Jung's place was the belief that such things appear for a reason. They have a purpose. And they intensify right around forty, at midlife, if that purpose has not been fulfilled. Your dreams and visions, and your strange experiences in love and war, were designed to give you the self-knowledge, and therefore the power, to fulfill your purpose."

"And what is that purpose?" John asked warily.

"On the way down here I gave that one a lot of thought. Finally I decided that the clue lay in the reference to the sun in your Harvard vision. The sun is an optimistic symbol — enlightenment, a new day. I think in your case it's a symbol of some laudable goals you've expressed to me before and that show up over and over in your diaries. Like using diplomacy to end war and build a world government and so forth." Engels hunted through the diary in his hand until he found the correct page. "Yeah," he muttered, studying it. "So the unconscious is pointing you toward success. *If* you can learn from Sicily."

John hung his head morosely. "But what can I learn from Sicily, except that I'm not worthy to achieve my own ideals? That I'm . . . evil?"

"That's exactly what you learn," Engels cried, "that you're evil! That evil really exists. Evil not conceived in the abstract but *experienced,* as horror. When the darkness in you overwhelms the light and upsets everything you thought was true, you begin to grow wise. A man who has truly experienced evil, in the world and in himself, and holds evil with good in one sorrowful embrace, is the only truly compassionate man, the only man who is truly whole. If you can be that man, John Devlin, and bring that compassion to your diplomacy, then you *will* be worthy of your ideals; you *will* catch the sun and bring its light to earth. You will bring the world out of the darkness of war into a new, enlightened order of things — the dawn of the day. The realization of your noble goals."

Do not forget us. The words of the dead echoed inside John.

"Are you saying," he asked, "that if I began to work publicly and single-mindedly toward my ultimate goal, to the exclusion of other, lesser ones, that my visions and dreams would go away?"

Engels looked at him in pleased surprise. "I think you're getting the idea."

John leaned back in his chair and closed his eyes. For the first time in two years he felt hope. He would not tell Engels about the Land of the Dead. Perhaps it would not be necessary. Perhaps the eyes and the voice would not come again. Not if he answered their call. He opened his eyes and looked at Matthew Engels.

"Now you're talking sense to me," he said, and smiled. "I'll begin tomorrow."

And John Devlin did begin the next day, and kept on throughout the week. When the conference on the future of postwar Europe commenced he argued for compassion toward the defeated Axis powers. Some applauded him, but others told him angrily to his face that he was soft-headed and bound to bring on another war by advocating policies of weakness. It was his first taste of the fate of the prophet, the one he had avoided for so long. But at the end of the week a letter arrived from Ruth, telling him that his mother had died a week before in New Bedford. *It's all real,* he reminded himself, and he stuck to his position to the end of the conference and thereafter, in the months to come, as Germany surrendered and projected policies became realities. He discovered to his inexpressible relief that his hunch, and his friend Engels's diagnosis, had been right. The dead came to visit him no more. His dreams disappeared. He slept peacefully without alcohol. A happy tranquillity filled him by day, even when angry generals denounced his policy positions. He had answered the call. Odysseus, long journeyer through dark oceans of mind, was home.

After V-E Day John Devlin was eager to go home, but the Navy and the State Department kept him on active status while they debated sending him to the Pacific, where the war was not yet over. Finally he was told simply to go home and await further orders. Late in the summer he came back to New Bedford, to the old white house Grandfather had built. Ruth and the boys were there to welcome him, and his first day home was a continuous, delirious celebration. Steven and David took him sailing, tried on his uniform, and pestered him with a thousand questions. Ruth had the makings of a feast roasting and baking in the kitchen. When he got a moment free from the boys he crept up behind her at the stove and took her in his arms. She looked wonderful. He felt wonderful. His fears of facing his family had vanished with his nightmares. He was the happiest man alive.

"Don't you think, my darling," Ruth said, turning inside his arms and kissing his chin, "that your homecoming banquet is missing something?"

He thought for a moment. "Champagne?"

"Exactly." Ruth pulled him closer to her. "Why don't you send the boys into town for it? I'll call in the order. Steven got to be a pretty good illegal driver while you were away. But he's under strict orders to drive very slowly, which means they'll be gone for a while. Which means that we . . ." She pulled him closer.

John kissed her cheeks, her neck, her ears. "Let me go," he said tenderly. "I'll be fast. I'll get two bottles of champagne, and we'll save one for after dinner."

Ruth smiled. "Brilliant as ever. Off you go."

Twenty minutes later John returned from town and parked the station wagon in the little garage built by Grandfather as a stable some distance from the house. Carefully cradling the champagne in his arms, he started for the kitchen, but stopped for a moment to admire the gold of the summer sunlight on the leaves in the garden and the old oak tree. The universe of his youth. It was the evening of his first day home, August 5, 1945. But on the other side of the world in Japan, where the United States was still at war, it was the morning of August 6. And at the precise moment that John Devlin stood in his New Bedford garden contemplating the evening sun, the clocks of Hiroshima read 8:15.

At the moment the first atomic bomb exploded over Hiroshima a strange thing happened. All over the world, sometimes thousands of miles from ground zero, certain people changed. Some of them dropped dead. Others went mad. Most of them simply felt odd for a moment, before their innate defenses shut them off from what was happening in their minds. In New Bedford, staring at his garden, John Devlin felt the beginnings of something like an internal earthquake.

His first thought when it began was that something seemed to be trying to push itself out from inside of him. For a puzzled moment he thought of a woman giving birth. The next instant he went mad. Everything that had ever been, everything that was then, and everything that would be appeared simultaneously in his mind. *Everything.* He saw other dimensions — four, five, six, dozens of them, all at once. An infinite number of places and moments, every possible combination of space and time that could exist, raced through his neurons in a single flash. The champagne fell to the ground as he clutched his head and screamed. The strain was too much. In another moment he would die.

Feeling itself approaching disintegration, his physical organism frantically went into action to save itself. His heart raced, his lungs pounded, his bowels let go. His brain crackled with electrical energy. Chemicals sped through his system, calming him, exciting him, all to no avail. He felt his very cells coming apart. He was dying . . .

In front of the trembling, twitching, jerking body in the garden a figure in a black hooded robe suddenly materialized. Two hands clamped onto the dying man's skull and held it, pushing hard. John felt the hands crushing the bone of his skull and screamed again, but the hands kept his body and his mind from total disintegration. They drew off into themselves the immense power that was consuming him. In another moment the hands suddenly released his head. John collapsed onto the ground, into puddles of his own feces. His heart and lungs and pulse had stopped. He was dead.

The tall robed figure stood quietly for a moment over the limp body on the ground, then gently knelt by its side in the excrement and cradled it in its arms. Rocking slowly back and forth, it began to sing in its terrible voice: a simple children's tune, a lullaby for infants.

After a few moments John Devlin opened his eyes. He began to cry. He made colicky sobbing noises. His mind was no longer dead, but it was an infant's mind, reborn.

The hooded figure held him, rocked him; it soothed his cries and whispered nursery rhymes into his ear. Step by step, at an accelerated pace of years in minutes, John Devlin's mind was being rebuilt. In the hooded figure's arms he learned again to speak, to reason, to retain memories, to control emotions. In a few minutes his cries had ceased. The hooded figure rose from the filth on the ground and set John on his feet. John said nothing; he only stared with solemn eyes at his faceless savior. His mind and body were restored, he was whole and adult again; but he was not the same.

The sun has fallen. It is time. Will you serve me?

John said nothing. He did not know what to say. He had thought he was free.

The god in you is free.

I'm no god. I'm a man. A madman . . .

Serve me, embrace the god, and the man shall live.

I don't want to live . . . Madness, madness . . .

He shall live as his hero Jesus lived, bowed with the burden of a god set free inside weak flesh.

Madness . . .

Refuse me, and the god shall consume you. For one instant the man shall know everything — everything that is — and then he shall die.

Madness, madness . . . I want to die . . .

The god shall be free, the man shall be gone. There is no more time. Choose now.

God, god, god, why me? Why ME?

Before I chose others. Now I have chosen you.

No, no, NO . . .

Answer: will you serve me? Or will you die?

John fell back to his knees. He put his shaking head into his sweaty, filthy hands, and sobbed.

"I shall serve," he whispered.

8

Jonah

November 30, 1956
Hay-Adams Hotel
Washington, D.C.

Dear Steven,

Have you heard from your brother lately? Your father and I are very concerned. We haven't had a word from David for more than six months, and then all we had was a postcard, telling us that he'd left M.I.T. and giving some godforsaken Air Force base in Nevada as his new address. That's all. Since then, not a word. Do you know anything about what he's up to? Your father tried to find out through some of his connections, and for the first time in his life he got nowhere at all. We've tried telephoning the base a dozen times, and somehow we always seem to catch him "out." We leave messages but he never returns our calls. I wonder if he even gets our messages. I've never trusted the military and I never will, not even to deliver a telephone message. If you've heard anything at all from him since he disappeared, please let us know. I know he's an adult now, but sometimes I think he just barely qualifies as one, and I'm worried about what he may have gotten himself into.

I hope that you're well and not finding your final months of study too onerous. I don't know why you should now — you never have before. We are down here for various as-yet confidential reasons following Ike's re-election. I do my best to keep my mouth shut, since for some reason the Republicans are busily courting your father, but sometimes it isn't easy. I can't say that I've ever liked Republicans any better than generals. Diana seems to have adjusted nicely to being away at school and went back quite willingly after Thanksgiving break. Which means that things are fairly quiet around the house (currently the hotel); not, however, as quiet as I would like. David isn't the only member of the family I'm worried about — your father is acting up again.

Yesterday morning I found him sitting on the floor in the living room of our suite, in the center of a circle of bright yellow daisies. Where he got daisies in Washington at this time of year is mysterious enough. But he was stark naked. When I approached him he picked up one of the daisies, held it up to me, and slowly traced the circle of petals with one finger, looking at me with the most idiotic smile on his face. He said, "You see? Like the sun!" And then he said something about how I was a sun and he was a sun and we were all of us suns, and then he started muttering that damned stupid Hindu phrase, tat tvam˙asi, *the way he always does when he gets like this. At that point I went back into the bedroom, got dressed, and went out. After eleven years I have finally learned not to try to stop him when he acts like this. But that doesn't mean I have to accept it, either. So I went out for breakfast and a walk, and when I came back he was showered and dressed and heading out the door for a round of meetings, as normal as anyone could be. Having also learned in eleven years to expect these sudden returns to reality, I simply kissed his cheek and reminded him that we had a dinner party in the evening. He nodded and smiled and was off, looking brisk and distinguished, the very picture of the man he is supposed to be.*

I breathed a sigh of relief and assumed that once again it had passed — but of late your father's personality has become so truly mercurial that even I cannot predict what he will do. Of course last night he made a thoroughly dignified entrance to the party, and everything was fine until it was time to leave, when I looked around and realized he had disappeared. After much discreet searching I finally located him in our host's study, standing under a lamp. One look at him and I knew that he'd been standing motionless, just that way, for some time. You know how he does that. He seemed to be looking at something, but his back was toward me, so I walked over to him to see what it was. And do you know what it was? A rock. Not even a beautiful or unusual one, but just a rock, a plain, dull, gray, stupid rock. He must have picked it up in the driveway. He was holding it up to the light between two fingers and staring at it with total concentration. He didn't even know I was there. I looked at his face and almost choked. Tears were running down his cheeks in two great streams. Over a rock! At that moment he finally became aware of my presence, but he just stared at me for one long moment, and then looked back at the rock. Then he said another of those things he says — this time I think it was "the heart of the Buddha" — and new tears began to trickle. I guess he meant the rock, although I'll be damned if I know what he means by anything anymore. Anyway, after a minute or so he suddenly looked at me again and whispered, "Take me home."

You can be assured that I complied with his request and got him out of there as quickly as I could.

So it's the same old story. Last night I went to bed thinking, as I have so many times in the past eleven years, that the man lying next to me was an absolute raving lunatic. As always I lay awake until I had resolved, for the hundredth time, to get him to see a doctor. And as always, this morning it was as if nothing had happened. He is an absolutely normal man — the same man I married nearly thirty years ago, the same father you and David and Diana have always known. The same man the State Department has entrusted with one embassy after another. What doctor in the world would believe me?

Well, enough. Don't say your mother never gave you valuable practice as a confessor. You've heard all this so many times before. I guess now that he's settled down again he'll stay that way for a good long while, as he always has, and things will be fine until the next time. I just wish I understood him. At first we all ascribed it to the war — you remember that as soon as he came home it was obvious that something had happened to him in Italy — but good Lord, the war was over eleven years ago! Since then his career has gone so well, and he couldn't have been a better husband to me or a kinder father to Diana, except at these unpredictable moments when this "other" man appears, and God knows what he will do . . .

But then again, unpredictability seems to be an inherited trait among the males of our family. And I don't mean David. I know, I know, I can almost hear you saying it, you've said it so many times: your vocation is none of my business. I forgive you for saying it because you always put it so charmingly when you do. But even now, nine years after you went off to that seminary, whenever I think of you I still picture you where I always did, in some gorgeous Manhattan law office with a view and a secretary — not as a Jesuit, wearing your clerical collar. Somehow it just doesn't add up.

Enough said. Take care of yourself and let us know what, if anything, you've heard from David.

Love,
Mother

December 10, 1956
Pontifical Ecclesiastical
Academy
Vatican City

Dear Mother,

I've just received your letter of November 30. Your concern for my well-being under a scholastic burden is much appreciated and quite unnec-

essary. Even speaking modestly I can say that as I near graduation my star is shining here brighter than ever. I'm at the top of my class and have been singled out for special praise in languages and debate. More important, I have learned well the invisible, unacknowledged curriculum of a Vatican diplomat's education: the art and science of patronage. The key men in the Secretariat of State, the men who every year hand out the choicest diplomatic assignments to the stars of each academy class, know my name and my work — I've made sure of that. Come graduation I'm assured of an appointment to Paris, or at worst Vienna.

They say of the academy that it's produced five popes, ninety-eight cardinals, hundreds of bishops, and not one saint. Despite what you say, it has certainly been the right place for me.

Now, as to David: the last time I heard from him must have been when you did, about six months ago. Only he didn't say anything to me about an Air Force base. He wrote that the government had invited him out to some island in the Pacific Ocean — I can't remember the name — to participate in some sort of test. He didn't say what they were testing, but he didn't have to. Anyone who reads a paper knows what they test on those islands. But you know David. People all over the world are always inviting him to do things, and half the time he gets absorbed in his cello or in some problem and misses his plane. Have you tried calling his apartment in Cambridge? He probably never left it.

I'm sorry to hear that Father's been putting you through all that again. I heartily agree with you: the war was over eleven years ago, and it's high time we stopped excusing him on that basis. For God's sake get him to a competent doctor, even if it means legal proceedings. For your sake, if not his. It's not fair for you to suffer just to protect his hallowed career.

My best to Diana, and to David, if you ever hear from him again.

Your loving son,
Steven

The pocked white ball rolled smoothly over the plush office carpet. The office was a famous one, of oval shape. For the past four years its occupant had elevated the lowly golf ball, as previous occupants had elevated beards and stovepipe hats, teddy bears, and long cigarette holders, into a symbol of the American presidency. The recent election had just confirmed the symbol for another four years.

With gyroscopic precision the unswerving ball joined two of

its twins inside a drinking glass laid lengthwise on the carpet. Across the oval room the famous golfer resumed his conversation. He was talking to John Devlin.

"Well, John," he said, "I can't tell you how happy I am that we've finally found some time to chat. I wanted you to know how pleased I've been with the really wonderful work you did for America during my first term in office."

"Thank you, Mr. President." John sat on a couch, his feet perpendicular to the neat line of golf balls on the carpet. There was nothing strange about him today, in looks or behavior; he sat as he had sat through other conversations in this office: calm, professional, wearing the dark, dignified clothing of a statesman, his temples graying handsomely. In his fifty-second year, he was a man who seemed quietly secure in the knowledge that he had succeeded in rising to the top of his profession, and that that success had brought him power.

The President lowered his putter behind another ball. "*I* should thank *you,* John. It's rare that a man who rose under Democrats should work so diligently for a Republican President. I'm sincerely grateful to you for that." The President settled his feet a little farther apart. The wavering head of the putter suddenly became rock-still. Then, swiftly, it was drawn back and sent forward again, and with a soft *thunk* another golf ball traveled straight and true from its place in line right into the glass.

"You know," said the President, looking up at John again, "when you've been a military man all your life, as I have, and then suddenly you find yourself a politician, you have to get used to so many differences, whether you like it or not. What I *cannot* get used to are these darned party politics. A soldier like me is trained to serve his country and get the job done. Politicians, as far as I can tell, serve only their own party, and do only what will further their own party's interests. When they get power they use it to block the minority party's programs, and the minority party blocks theirs, and meanwhile no one's doing much of anything for his country. By God, if we'd fought Hitler that way . . ." The President shook his head.

"Anyway," he went on, smiling, "at least we are blessed with a few men like yourself, who put service to country over advantage to party. Let me come to the point." Once again the putter was lowered behind a ball, the last one. "It's been a year since you've had an ambassadorial post." The President carefully squinted an invisible line between ball and glass, and aligned his feet with it. "They tell me that now you've had your fill of lecturing and writing and that you're ready for another job. Well, that's why I wanted to see you." Again the President locked the putter head into position. "I want to give you a new job — the big one. I want to give you Moscow."

On the last word the putter head swung back. John said nothing. The President assumed that Ambassador Devlin would politely wait for him to finish his putt, but at the moment the putter came forward, the *thunk* was drowned out by John's sudden reply.

"Thank you, sir. I'm afraid I can't accept."

The final ball went wide of the drinking glass by a good two inches. The President stared at John.

"You can't — you don't *want* Moscow?"

"That's right, sir," said John firmly.

The President leaned on his putter and thought. "I don't understand," he said after a moment. "Forgive me, but I thought — well, you've worked so hard and so successfully all these years. I assumed that what you were aiming at was — "

"Of course. What every ambitious diplomat aims at: the top." John stood up. "Mr. President, please understand that I'm deeply honored by your faith in my abilities. And you aren't wrong — I *have* been aiming at something big all these years. But it hasn't been Moscow."

"Well then, what *is* it, for heaven's sake?" The President's face wore a baffled expression. It simply did not make sense that a man in John Devlin's position would refuse the crowning honor of his diplomatic career.

"It's bigger than Moscow. Bigger than anything else. I want to work directly with you, sir. As your policy assistant on nuclear disarmament."

"On disarmament?" The President exchanged his baffled expression for a worried one. "Well, John, I don't know . . . Disarmament is a little out of your bailiwick, isn't it?"

"With all due respect, Mr. President, I think what you're saying is that my views on nuclear disarmament are known to clash with those of Secretary Dulles. That's quite correct. Secretary Dulles wants to preserve peace by standing on the brink of a nuclear war with Russia. I've always maintained that his 'brinkmanship' policy is the surest way of getting us into a nuclear war."

The President shouldered his putter and stared at the carpet. "I don't know, John," he repeated. "You'll have a heck of a fight on your hands from Foster."

"I'm not suggesting that you choose between us. I'm suggesting that a policy as extreme as Secretary Dulles's needs a corrective counterpolicy within your administration, because despite what the secretary says, the disarmament issue isn't a simple matter of keeping a god-fearing America stronger than godless Russia. Nuclear war and nuclear weapons have made strident nationalism out of date — *dangerously* out of date. And I suspect, sir, that you'd agree with me on that."

At John's last words the President looked over at him. Then slowly, thoughtfully, he crossed the carpet and leaned down to pick up the errant golf ball.

"All right," he said, and tossed the ball to John. "Foster will hit the roof, but you're on. You have the job."

"Pardon me, Ambassador. Would you like to order now?" The maitre d' inclined himself solicitously toward John.

"No, I'm afraid not, André," John replied. "Our party hasn't arrived yet." He checked his watch. "He's already twenty minutes late."

"Very well, sir. I shall return in a few minutes. May I say also that you possess an extraordinary watch?"

"Oh, thank you. Yes, it is unusual, isn't it?" John held the enormous, ancient pocket watch up for André's perusal. "Would you like to have a look at it?"

"John, *please,*" whispered Ruth.

"Go ahead, take it!"

The maitre d' gingerly held the watch John had thrust into his hands. When he closed the cover and saw the design on it, he suddenly cleared his throat.

"Ah. I assume, Ambassador, that this watch is a memento of your service in the war?"

"Oh, no," said John, laughing. "Many people think so. But actually the swastika has been an emblem of my family for generations."

"*John,*" Ruth hissed.

·André's eyes widened. "Of — of your *family,* sir?"

"Yes," replied John. "My grandfather had this watch when I was a boy. The swastika was a very special symbol to him. It represented a link with things that to him were . . . eternal, and, I think, quite beautiful as well."

As he listened André's smiled never waned, but his eyes acquired a discomfited glaze. "I see. Very interesting, sir," he said with elaborate politeness, and he quickly returned the watch to John's hand. "Excuse me, please." He executed a little bow and a gesture that said, *Unfortunately, I am so busy . . .* "Madame." He bowed again to Ruth, and hurried away.

"For God's sake, John," said Ruth, "if you insist on carrying that thing in public, don't make a display of it. People will think you're some kind of Nazi."

"Will they?" John chuckled as he thoughtfully chewed an olive. "Well, my dear, perhaps I *am* sometimes."

"John! Please, for once, don't go cryptic on me, just when — " Ruth stopped. The smiling André had returned to their table.

"Ambassador, Madame, your party has arrived." André indicated with a small flourish the tall, red-haired young man with thick spectacles whom he had escorted across the room.

"Hello, David," said John, getting up.

"Hello, dear," said Ruth.

"Hello, Dad. Mom." David Devlin shook his father's hand and went around the table to give his mother a kiss. Both of his parents were already studying him. To their eyes he seemed absolutely normal — to Ruth, a little too thin, as always, and to John, rather abominably dressed in violently clashing plaids and cheap trousers, as always. At least he had worn a tie, albeit one that in combination with his sport coat produced something like motion sickness in an observer. If David had forgotten the correct time for meeting his parents, at least he had remembered that at his father's favorite Georgetown restaurant something resembling correct attire was expected.

So he was, superficially, unchanged; as he took his seat, and as André took everyone's order, John and Ruth relaxed a little. Despite his mysterious disappearance and sudden reappearance, David was reassuringly himself, studying the French menu in baffled consternation and finally asking for onion soup, a croque monsieur, and chocolate ice cream, as though he were ten instead of twenty-four. John smiled. He had come to indulge his younger son's stubborn peculiarities, and in this he was not alone. Lately his badly dressed, habitually late offspring was being courted by the world.

Over the years John's wish had come true: Grandfather Michael's communion with natural things had blossomed in great-grandson David into a formidable scientific ability. At twenty-four, David Devlin held a Ph.D. in theoretical physics and a faculty position at M.I.T. He was well on his way to international recognition in his field. What had astonished John as he had watched his son's reputation grow was the fact that as David became more and more famous, he became less and less worldly. And he had not been very worldly to begin with — indeed, since childhood the greater part of his being seemed to have been occupied by his peculiar genius, leaving little room for ordinary human abilities. As a result David's absent-mindedness went beyond lack of taste in clothes and an inability to catch planes; while absorbed in a mathematical problem or in playing his beloved cello, he seemed to be capable of severing the connection between his mind and the physical world. In an earlier age, John thought, watching David bend over his hot soup, his younger son would have been a Pythagorean or a Platonist of the most extreme variety, absorbed in the mystical properties of pure number, despising gross earth. David ran the same risk that a true Pythagorean ran in every age — the risk of perishing in the "real" world of human affairs, if perchance he strayed into it.

John began to worry again. Yes, it was true that David appeared to be quite unchanged, but there were still unanswered questions: his sudden departure from the M.I.T. cloister; his apparent evasion of all contact with his family for six months; and then, out of the blue, a telegram announcing his arrival in Washington within the week. What was he up to? Through the first course, as the three of them chatted cheerfully about safe and pleasant subjects, John and Ruth stifled their curiosity. They both knew how stubborn David was, as only a truly unworldly person could be; if they pounced on him with questions, he would withdraw and say nothing. They had agreed before dinner to let him enlighten them on his activities. But when the main course had been served and the family pleasantries exhausted, Ruth began to lose patience.

"Well, David," she declared as she cut into her steak, "you've been a hard man to find these days."

For a few silent moments David applied himself to his croque monsieur. John and Ruth exchanged a glance.

"I sent you my address," said David at last, with surly finality.

"Yes, dear, I *know* you did," said Ruth, trying to keep anger out of her voice. "What I mean is that we've known where you are, but we haven't been able to reach you. We called so many times, and you never called back. Didn't you get our messages?"

David's face went blank. "Messages?"

"I *knew* it," cried Ruth, losing what little restraint she had left. "The damned military has been lying to us." She banged her fist down on the white tablecloth.

David did not start. He had seen his mother pound a table at least once a week for the last twenty-four years.

"What are you doing mixed up with the Air Force, anyway?" Ruth cried. "You've never had anything to do with those people."

"Are you telling me I shouldn't?" David snapped.

"Oh, I know better than to do *that,*" his mother snapped back. "You never listen to me or to anyone else about anything, even when you should. *Especially* when you should. But now it seems you've been listening to somebody. One day you're at M.I.T., thinking all your woolly thoughts in your academic sanctuary, and the next day — literally — you've vanished, and we, your parents, can't find you, and you tell your brother that you're somewhere in the South Pacific, and us that you're in Nevada! And then after six months you suddenly reappear like this, and aren't even so courteous as to offer your parents an explanation!" Ruth's ire, fueled by half a year of maternal worry, was now fully aroused. "Let's have an end to all these mysteries, here and now. What in heaven's name have you been up to?"

David gave his mother a flat, annoyed look. "I'm sorry, Mother," he said. "I'm not permitted to discuss my work with anyone. For security reasons."

Oh, come now. All this time John had said nothing, watching his son withdraw behind a shield of stubborn silence. *Come now, David. We know what your work is. I know. Mother knows, but she won't admit she knows because it repels her. A top American physicist doesn't go to a Pacific island for a suntan. He doesn't go to Nevada to gamble. He goes to test bombs.* MIKE *and* BRAVO *and* TEACUP. PLUMBOB *and* REDWING *and* KNOTHOLE. *Funny little names for a very big death. The biggest death. H-bombs.* He looked at his son, the genius in mismatched plaids. *Your reputation outgrew the cloister, didn't it? Big men in Washington, men you had never heard of, heard of you. They tempted you. They took you to a blasted atoll and showed you what the big toys really could do. Then, while you still were wide-eyed with amazement, they asked you to build them new toys, giant missiles with guidance systems of their own, pilotless missiles that could set an H-bomb down on top of a Russian city halfway across the world. I know what they've asked of you. And you said yes, didn't you, my woolly-headed, cloistered, cello-playing, Pythagorean son?*

"Have I ever told you," John said suddenly, "about my trip to Nagasaki?"

In an instant Ruth and David had stopped glaring at each other and were staring openmouthed at him. John gave them both a pleasant, questioning smile. They both returned looks of stunned surprise.

"Why, no, dear, you haven't," said Ruth, smiling uneasily. *Are you kidding?* she thought. *Since the war the mere mention of Nagasaki in this family has been absolutely taboo.*

"It was really quite a fascinating experience," John went on, oblivious of David and Ruth's stares, as though he were simply steering the conversation away from further unpleasantness by changing the subject. "Although as I recall, when I received the orders to climb back into my Navy uniform and go to Japan I was not very happy about it. After all, I'd only been home with you for about three or four weeks, I think. Didn't I get home from Italy right around the bombing of Hiroshima?"

"That's right," Ruth and David both said quickly. And both of them had virtually the same thought: *You mean you don't remember? I will never forget. You came home on August 5, 1945, the most frightening day of my life.*

"Yes, I thought so," John went on. He smiled, looking off into space. "You know, I still remember how great it felt to be home, that first evening."

Ruth and David exchanged a wide-eyed glance. *You felt great?*

David thought. *There you were, my father, home safe and sound from the war. And then all of a sudden my father became a — to this day I still don't know what you became.*

Good God, thought Ruth. *After all these years you suddenly break silence to tell us you felt great? That's not what I remember, and believe me, my dear, I remember that evening as if it were yesterday. My perfectly normal husband goes out for twenty minutes to buy champagne and returns in a state I still find indescribable. Covered with — at first I thought you had been beaten up in the street. Then I had a good look at your face, your eyes, and almost shrieked. I still don't know what I saw there, but since then I have seen it again, so many, many times . . . We hadn't made love in nearly three years, and that night you raped me. You threw me on the bed and rammed inside me, over and over . . . and I conceived Diana.*

"When our military-civilian commission got to Nagasaki," John was saying, "it was mid-September, about six weeks after the bomb fell. Our job, you see, was to survey the impact of the new weapon on the entire community. We had military engineers to assess damage to buildings and materials, we had doctors to study the injuries and physical health of the survivors, and we had psychologists, and a few diplomats who, like myself, had served in Japan, to study the bomb's impact on people's mental health and social attitudes. It was quite a distinguished group — some very big names. Our study was to be completely scientific. You might say that Nagasaki was our laboratory, America's, that is. This wondrous new American invention, the atom bomb, had been the experiment, and a grandly successful one, and now we, the experimenters, were going to find out just exactly what we had done to the rats."

"The rats?" asked literal-minded Ruth.

"Oh you know, the Japanese. The guinea pigs. Because that's what they really were, you know. After the bomb was first tested, in New Mexico, there was a plan to demonstrate it to the world, specifically to the Japanese military — to pick an uninhabited spot somewhere and set it off, you see, so that the Japanese would understand what would happen to them if they kept on fighting. Somehow the plan got voted down by the scientists and the government. Everyone said that the Japanese were too fanatical to surrender after a mere warning. So we made demonstrations out of Hiroshima and Nagasaki, without warning. Afterward some of the scientists admitted that they had wanted to see just what their new creation could do. And you couldn't find that out just by blowing up the New Mexico desert, could you? You needed the real thing. You needed guinea pigs. As a scientist, I'm sure you'd agree with that, wouldn't you, David?"

David gave his father a puzzled look. "Well . . . sure."

"Right. So six weeks later, after Japan had surrendered and was safely occupied, everyone hurried over there in great excitement to see the results of their handiwork. It *was* impressive, let me tell you — but of course I don't need to, do I, because you're a physicist and you already understand, in *theory,* what such tremendous force can do." John shot a sly smile at his son. "To witness the application of the theory, of course, is even more impressive. But you've never seen an actual atomic explosion, have you?"

David looked very quickly down at his plate before he shook his head.

Oh yes you have, you guilty liar. And it thrilled you to death, the thing you always dreamed of, alone in your room with your books and your cello. Nature's ultimate secret. The mystic core of Matter. The very borderline between the perceivable and the unimaginable. Plato and Pythagoras could only spin tales of it, but you saw it. And straightaway you made your pact with the ones who had tempted you.

"The first thing we saw," John said aloud, "was the 'big picture.' We stood on a mountain and looked down at the city of Nagasaki. Or rather the *absence* of Nagasaki, because that's exactly what it was. A very large space from which a major section of the entire city had simply been removed." John put his open hand on the table top and moved it slowly across. "Almost as if a giant hand had just swept it into the sea." John's hand bumped into a full wineglass. He did not stop it, and it pushed the wineglass over. The spilled wine fanned out blood-red over the white tablecloth.

"John!" said Ruth. "Be careful, please!"

"Below us there was nothing," said John, ignoring her, "nothing at all, anywhere, except the outlines of foundations, block after block of them, an endless grid as far as you could see." His narrowed eyes focused on the wine stain, watching it spread. "Here and there the frames of very large buildings still tottered, crazily bent and buckled. They looked like mansions built by some very demented prospectors who had gone mad living in a flat and featureless desert. Other than these, there was nothing. Only the grid where the city had been, and the white ash that filled the grid, like pretty new snow — the ash that once had been buildings, and people too."

John looked at David. David looked at his plate and stabbed defiantly at his croque monsieur.

"There were some names you'd know, David, on the team with me, some of the Los Alamos people who helped build the atom bomb. When they looked down at what the bomb had done they got very quiet. Of course *all* of us were, but for them, the ones whose genius had actually produced what we were looking at, it was something special. They just couldn't believe what they had done. I think up there they felt a sort of quiet elation, something almost mystical, when they saw how their puny human minds and hands had found the power to command the omnipotence of nature, the force of the universe itself."

A solicitous waiter appeared with a towel and mopped the wine stain.

"Thank you," said John, watching David.

And that elation, my son, was the last they felt. From above, from the hills, the destruction was an abstraction, a neat grid of objects destroyed. Force against mass: quantifiable, analyzable, repeatable. The ultimate experiment on the ultimate subject. Then we went down.

"Excuse me," said Ruth indignantly, "but *I* wouldn't feel elated at all. A city destroyed in an instant. All of those innocent people dead. It's ghastly."

"But Ruth, you must understand that scientists don't look at it that way. Their methods train them to think dispassionately. They have a horror of human emotions, which elude their measurements and remind them of the long, dark age when science was shackled by superstition. Now, of course, the shackles are removed, and the scientists achieve such incredible things! And all because they are *dispassionate*. Of course it *was* difficult for our team to be dispassionate, once we descended from the hills into Nagasaki. The Japanese were still digging people out of the rubble, you see. All of them dead, of course. The really astonishing ones were the blast victims — not a mark on any of them, but all their internal organs smashed, from the huge compression of the blast wave. You could tell them, too, by the way their eyes popped right out of their sockets. They always looked very surprised, the blast victims, and I can't say that I blame them, do you, David?"

"John!" Ruth put down her fork. "You're becoming disgusting." She turned to her son. "Now look, David," she said, "I want the truth, and I want it now. I'm your mother. Security regulations do not apply to me. If you've gotten yourself involved with — "

"Ruth, dear." John interrupted her with the same maddening pleasantness. "Did I ever tell you who the Occupation authorities assigned to guide us at Nagasaki? Extraordinary coincidence! Remember my old friend Yuzawa, the monk?"

"Yuzawa?" The coincidence *was* extraordinary, and Ruth was genuinely startled.

"Yes, Yuzawa!" said John emphatically. "You probably don't remember Yuzawa," he said to David. "You were so young. I met him when we were in Tokyo before the war. At any rate, Yuzawa, you know, had lived all his life in Nagasaki. He was born and raised a Catholic, too, near the Nagasaki cathedral, but he later became a Zen Buddhist. I assumed that he had been swallowed up by the war, so you can imagine my complete astonishment when up he rode in a U.S. Army jeep to greet us! It turned out that he had been out of Nagasaki on the day the bomb fell, visiting some of his old Jesuit cronies in the suburbs. And lucky for him that he was, because the bomb burst right over his old neighborhood, the old Catholic neighborhood of Nagasaki. Right over the cathedral. His parents and brothers and sisters and cousins and friends were all simply vaporized. He told me later that he couldn't even find their bones."

"My God," said Ruth. "And after that he was your *guide?* I'm surprised he didn't murder all of you in your beds. He must have hated you."

"Now that, my dear, was the interesting thing. Yuzawa didn't hate us. He was just as I remembered him — as charming, witty, polite as ever, although disinclined to excessive conversation. But that of course is normal in a devotee of Zen."

"Well, whatever Zen is," snapped Ruth, "it obviously doesn't preach courage." She attacked the final portion of her steak.

"But Yuzawa wasn't the only Japanese who felt that way," said John. "The remarkable thing was that so many people in Nagasaki bore us Americans no ill will whatever. Especially the injured, if you can believe it. The Japanese, you see, believe strongly in an old oriental tradition called the law of karma. Karma is a kind of eternal spiritual give-and-take, which keeps the cosmic account books of good and evil balanced for all souls. If a soul does good, then more good comes to him. If he does evil, more evil. So many people in Nagasaki believed that the atomic bomb wasn't America's work but God's — that God had merely used America to punish them for their evil attacks on China and Pearl Harbor. There really wasn't any question of revenge, because in their eyes we were only the agents of God." John stared off into space, thinking. "You know," he said after a moment, "it really was remarkable to see how people clung to that conviction through such terrible suffering. We interviewed survivors in the burn wards. Their flesh was charred black and held together only by bandages; it was more like slime than skin. If you accidentally touched someone or tried to shake his hand, black slime came away on your fingers . . ."

"John!" This time Ruth slammed down her fork. "Enough!" John looked blankly at his wife.

"I won't hear any more of this!" she cried. "Please, David, I'm asking you once more. Before your father revolts us both, just please tell me, what have you been doing for the Air Force these past six months?"

"I'm sorry, Mother," David said. "I can't discuss it."

The Devlins ate their dessert in silence. John thought about Yuzawa. *A man in a hurricane grips a tree to stop the winds from blowing him away. Yuzawa was the tree. We sat in the rubble, in the wrecked cathedral, and I told him everything: the dreams and the visions and what had happened in the garden. I told him I was mad. I begged him to help me. And he told me what I had to do . . .*

You were strange when you went away, thought Ruth, *but you were stranger still when you returned. The next morning I noticed that the old sailing dinghy was missing. Then I saw smoke rising from the island. I thought I understood. You had seen something horrible at Nagasaki, and you wanted to be alone for a day or two. But John — dear God, you were gone more than a week on that little ocean rock! A dozen times I nearly called the Coast Guard. But every day at evening I saw the smoke from your fire and didn't call, and then one day you came back and showered and shaved and put on a suit and went straight down to Washington with a smile on your face, and wangled an embassy out of Jim Byrnes. And not a word to anyone about Nagasaki or the island, though I asked again and again.*

On the island, thought John, *I did what Yuzawa taught me. At first it hurt so much I could only sit a few minutes at a time. But I sat. I sat and I breathed, in and out, in and out, as Yuzawa had taught me, until I had reduced the world, the universe, the sun and the moon and the trillion trillion stars, to an inhalation and an exhalation of air. In and out. God's breath. Birth and death, creation and extinction. In and out. And I held my mind to a single question, the one Yuzawa had asked me in the rubble of Nagasaki: what is the purpose of a shadow? An absurdity, I protested . . . Answer it, Yuzawa had said, and the god will be free in you . . . The diplomat tried to answer it. The historian tried to answer it. The humble fisherman tried to answer it. The frightened schoolboy tried to answer it. I screamed and wept and begged God for an answer, and still it eluded me. I went without food, without sleep. Do not stop, Yuzawa had said, whatever happens to you! I don't know how many days . . . I saw the sea full of the* Lusitania's *drowned, and the dead of Sicily gaped in my face. Long after Time had gone and the place around me had disappeared, an autumn leaf fell, and I knew . . . I had no words left, no words at all, but I knew, when the leaf fell I knew. I did not know. The answer was, wordlessly. I was no more. The god was free in me. I am his vessel. I am his dancing ground. He is free in me, and I serve him.*

John stirred his coffee and contemplated David, eating his chocolate ice cream in sullen silence. *I know what you're thinking. You're not going to listen to me. Not to your strange father who can't comprehend things only the Olympians of science can know. But listen you will.*

"Well, David," John said affably as dessert was cleared, "you remain a mystery to us. As you wish. Will you be returning west soon, or will we have the pleasure of your company for a while?"

"I'm leaving the day after tomorrow," David said. "I'm very busy."

"Ah! Too bad." John reached into his jacket for pen and notebook. "I wonder if you'd do me a small favor on your way back?"

"Of course, if I can."

"Good! Thank you." John scribbled briefly on a piece of paper. "An old friend of mine, a scientist, is teaching at a college not far from where you are — not far by western standards, anyway. In northern Arizona." He handed the paper to David. "Here's his name and the name of the college. I wonder if you'd look him up and give him my regards? It's been a long time since we've —"

"Mannheim?" David was staring incredulously at the paper, reading the name on it in an unbelieving tone. "*You* know Howard Mannheim?"

"Why, yes." John smiled his pleasant smile at his gaping son.

"How?"

"From Nagasaki, of course," said John. "Don't you remember? He was on the commission with me."

"Oh, sure," mumbled David. "It's just that you never spoke of him . . ."

"Will you look him up for me?"

Suddenly David's sullen flatness returned. "I'll . . . I'll try. I'm very busy." He pocketed the note. John nodded and smiled. *Oh, you're busy, David, but you'll go. Then come and tell me how busy you are!*

Dinner was over; the check was paid. Smiling André ushered the ambassador and his family to the door. David and Ruth kissed each other, to make up a little, and David rode off in his own cab, to his own hotel, still nursing his mystery. John watched him go. *No, my silent son, your secret is not safe. In your simplicity you made a pact with them, and I will not let you keep it.*

9

Einstein's Hint

DAVID DEVLIN LEFT WASHINGTON for Nevada on schedule, after three days, but it was another six months before he kept his promise to his father. He told himself that he was busy, and he was. But the name, and the promise, nagged at him.

Howard Mannheim. What had happened? Everyone in science wondered that. Mannheim had been a lifelong star of American physics, teenaged *wunderkind* at Princeton, dominator of Göttingen doctoral seminars, dazzling teacher at Chicago. An arrogant man, a hard man, but a true genius. It had justly been said that the only thing bigger than Howard Mannheim's ego was his brain. Then, with the war, had come Los Alamos and the ultimate challenge. Mannheim had been assigned to the team of geniuses building the atomic bomb, and among that team, and the scientific community at large, it was now universally if sometimes grudgingly acknowledged that without Howard Mannheim's incredible intellect and driving will the bomb might never have been built. Mannheim had met the ultimate challenge and had conquered it, as he always had conquered. As the war ended and he prepared to return to academic research, there had been a betting pool among top physicists trying to guess the year he would win the Nobel Prize.

But then the inexplicable had happened. Two weeks after Japan's surrender a grateful American government had extended to certain Los Alamos scientists the opportunity to tour Hiroshima and Nagasaki and study the effects of their bomb. Howard Mannheim's name had been at the top of the list of those asked to go, so

Mannheim had gone to Japan with the joint military-civilian commission and had then returned to America and duly taken up his research. But it had not been research in physical science. The arrogant giant of American physics suddenly changed fields. At the age of thirty-two he resigned his teaching position at Chicago, left his stunned wife, and without a word of explanation to his colleagues, buried himself in the biology department of an obscure state college in the volcanic ponderosa-pine country near Flagstaff. After that, the man had lived in complete seclusion for ten years. Phone calls from reporters and friends were not returned; letters were sent back unanswered. The legends of Howard Mannheim's rise faded away and were replaced by whispers, rumors that filled the black void where his star had shone with all the dark reasons for his fall.

David Devlin, a student during Mannheim's days of greatness, had heard all the rumors time and time again, and he reviewed them mentally in June of 1957 as he bounced in a rented car along the dirt road leading to Mannheim's Arizona home. They were all the usual ones: alcohol, drugs, crossing the thin line that divided genius from insanity. All clichés, David concluded, whose paltriness merely confirmed the true mystery of Howard Mannheim's behavior. A man at the pinnacle of success, and a man who makes no bones about loving his success, throws it all away. The solution to that problem was worth knowing.

The car cleared the top of a ridge, and through the red dust on the windshield David saw a small house in a clearing among the pines below him. It had not been easy to find. For ten years the college had not disclosed Howard Mannheim's address to anyone, so David had had to deduce a likely location by interrogating local urchins. Now he had found the house. But would Mannheim speak to him?

As he drew near the question vanished from his mind. Surprise took its place. He had expected Howard Mannheim's house to be neglected and trashy, a mere roof sheltering its owner's boozy dereliction. What he saw instead appeared to be an immaculate cottage worthy of an English country parsonage. The cottage was actually a sturdy cabin of local design, constructed of the dark volcanic rock of northern Arizona, which had been cemented together in irregular patterns; but bolted to the rock surrounding its windows were varnished pine shutters and a front door to match, all in perfect repair under a tidy timber roof topped with neat rows of shingles. The house formed the hub of an immense encircling garden of vegetables and bright flowers, through which rough crooked paths ran from several directions toward the house, each one marked out by lines of exquisite roses, a different subtle color for each path. It was like some sort of labyrinth, David thought, getting out of his car. For a moment he just stared at house and garden, dumfounded. The European, domesticated symmetry was so utterly out of place in the wild mountains of Arizona. Whatever else Howard Mannheim did, or didn't do, he obviously worked very hard to maintain himself here. To be self-sufficient. Where in country like this did he get enough water for a garden this size?

"There's an artesian spring behind the house," came the answer. David jumped. The voice had come from behind him, and he turned around to see a man standing there.

"Of course, there's also the snow melt," the man went on. "I have cisterns up the mountain." He pointed behind the house, through the trees. "And underground pipelines downhill, right to the garden. I'm never short of water."

He lowered his finger until it pointed straight down at his feet. His stare followed it, toward the ground. A few moments passed. The man kept pointing at the ground and saying nothing. After a while David, not knowing what else to do, stared at the ground too.

Suddenly the man looked up. "It took me a whole summer to lay in those pipes," he said with pleasant matter-of-factness. "The ground here's very hard. Old lava, most of it."

David nodded. The man smiled at him.

"David."

"Ah, yes," David said, a little taken aback. He did not recall introducing himself. "You're Howard Mannheim?"

"I'm Howard Mannheim." The man extended his hand and David shook it.

"My father must have called you to say I might be coming," David said.

Mannheim smiled again. "I don't have a telephone." He gestured toward the house. "Come in."

David walked behind Mannheim on the narrow paths through the garden. The man whose name he had read dozens of times in dozens of books and articles but whom he had never seen was tall and hawk-faced, with a sharp nose and dramatic eyebrows that gave him a stern stare like an eagle's. Above the brushes of his brows his cephalic landscape was devoid of any further growth until its far side, behind the ears, where a fringe of crew-cut hair began. The clean dome of skull gleaming between brows and fringe was so prominent that it drew one's attention away from the rest of Howard Mannheim. But David noted that while Mannheim was dressed in old clothes, there was nothing slovenly about him — nothing of the drunk or the addict or the madman of the rumors. His tanned, stout, middle-aged body seemed firm and fit, and his step seemed sure. Then why in God's name was he hiding out here?

David felt a sudden sharp pain in his thigh. He looked down to see the thorns of a rosebush snagged in his trousers.

"Hold on," he said, tugging at the bush.

Mannheim turned around to look. "Careful!" he shouted angrily when he saw David pulling at the rose. Quickly kneeling and roughly pushing David's hand aside, he disengaged the thorns from the trousers himself, while he snapped at David: "Careless moments are *always* destructive. I don't want to see any more carelessness!"

"I — I'm sorry," David stammered.

But Howard Mannheim was no longer angry. His instant wrath had instantly vanished. He had succeeded in freeing David's trouser leg from the rosebush, but he remained kneeling by David's leg for several more seconds, pinching the trouser leg between his fingers and holding it a few inches from his eyes, inspecting it with myopic concentration. David stood stiff and nonplussed until Mannheim suddenly jumped to his feet and said, with his former pleasant sincerity, "You know, those pants of yours really are abominable. A Woolworth's year-end sale, I'll bet. Doesn't the Air Force pay you guided-missile boys what you're worth?"

David got stiffer. "What do you mean by that?"

"Guided missiles. You're in Nevada developing guided missiles. Don't they pay you for it?"

For a panicky moment David tried to think of how to deny the truth; then he decided simply to say nothing. He stared at Mannheim and tried to look noncommittal and not defensive.

"Come on." Mannheim chuckled and waved him forward. David

followed him into the house, wondering what to expect and how in hell Howard Mannheim knew so much about him.

The house inside was as neat and tidy as the house outside — neater and tidier, in fact. *Too* neat, *too* tidy, David thought, gingerly taking the seat Mannheim offered him. The chair was large and sturdy enough, but he lowered himself into it very carefully, as if it were made of glass; such was the immediate effect Howard Mannheim's living room had on him.

It was not an unusual room in size or furnishings. There were chairs around a table, an Indian patterned rug on the polished wood floor, a long row of bookcases along the back wall, a stone fireplace, a blackboard covered with mathematical work. All of it was utterly predictable for the home of a talented physicist. What made David instantly anxious, what in fact engendered in him something like an urge to scream, was the atmosphere of nearly maniacal order. The flowerpots in the window bays, the precise rows of books on the shelves, and even the bowl placed at the exact center of the large central table had an air of being "just so" — that was the phrase that occurred to David. They seemed like strands of some invisible system of things that was uniquely Mannheim's, some tensile energy web that had him as its ever-shifting center, and that charged the room. A careless movement might tear this fragile web, which seemed to contain something immense. David had been warned already about careless movements, so he sat carefully. He had the feeling that if in sitting he accidentally shifted his chair a single millimeter to the left or right, the entire room would suddenly fly apart and all its objects whirl madly in a vortex of chaos, and that Howard Mannheim, now staring serenely at him from a chair across the table, would suddenly scream and explode into a raw white heat.

David leaned back in his chair, and to avoid Mannheim's penetrating stare, he glanced at the equations on the blackboard. Although they were obviously unfinished work in progress, they were written in rows squared and blocked into perfect symmetry. The individual numbers and signs looked more typed than handwritten. David winced inwardly. It was all very, very tight, very, very weird.

"Do you see what I've been working on?" asked Mannheim, following David's gaze to the blackboard.

David concentrated on the numbers for a few moments. "The Einstein-Podolsky-Rosen Effect?" he finally guessed.

Mannheim smiled. "Yes, exactly. EPR. You seem to be as good as your reputation."

"Thank you," said David, and returned the compliment: "I'm honored to meet you, Doctor Mannheim."

He expected Mannheim to go on talking about the Einstein-Podolsky-Rosen Effect, but Mannheim merely shifted his gaze back to David and resumed staring at him. Mannheim sat completely still, not shifting his body or moving his hands or even his mouth in the normal small, unconscious ways people did when they were sitting quietly. He didn't even blink. His self-containment was complete and inhuman. He smiled a subtle smile at David, never looking away from him, his unblinking eyes calm and steady. The smile was so unlike the fierceness of his eyebrows and eyes that it gave his upper and lower face an unrelated, composite look, as though he were two different beings. David thought of a picture he had once seen, a picture of some Hindu god whose left side was anatomically male and whose right side was female . . .

"My father asked me to find you and give you his regards," David said, not knowing what else to say. "But I suppose he's told you that," he added quickly, feeling foolish, since Mannheim had known his name. Obviously he at least had had a letter from Father.

"Who's your father?" Mannheim asked pleasantly.

David was stunned. "Don't you know?" he blurted out.

"No. Who?"

"Well — John Devlin. He said you knew one another. In Japan."

"John Devlin?" Mannheim sat perfectly, completely still. Anyone else would have scratched his head or shifted in his chair or moved in some other way, fidgeting, trying to remember. "Yes, of course I know John." He said nothing more; he lapsed into his self-contained silence again, watching David, faintly smiling. A full minute passed.

Maybe the rumors are true, David thought. *Maybe this guy is just plain nuts.*

"Then my father wrote you I might be coming?" David finally prompted.

At last Mannheim's body moved. He shook his head.

"No," he said, smiling still. "I haven't heard from John Devlin since 'forty-five."

He's definitely nuts, thought David. *Or I'm definitely nuts.* He fought down a sudden rise of fear and asked quite calmly, "But Doctor Mannheim, if you haven't heard from my father, how did you know my name?" He deliberately made no reference to the even more astonishing fact that Mannheim had known what was a closely guarded government secret, a secret even from his father: the exact nature of his work in Nevada.

"Where did you see it?" Mannheim asked.

"I beg your pardon?"

"The burst. The nuclear fireball. Where did you see it? Out in the islands, I assume. Which one?"

The words "I'm not permitted to discuss it" formed routinely on David's lips before he realized the futility of dissembling on one point with a man who already knew everything else about him.

"Eniwetok," he said. "The Redwing series. May of 'fifty-six."

"Right. And what did you think, when you saw it?"

"What did I think? Well, I . . ."

"I mean," said Mannheim with some urgency, "what was the *very first thing* that you thought? Your gut reaction?"

"Well, since you ask . . ." David thought for a few minutes. "It wasn't very profound," he said finally, "or even particularly rational. It was just an old platitude: 'Behold the face of God.' "

He expected the great genius Mannheim to sneer at his cliché, but instead Mannheim's smile became slightly broader. "Good," he said in a pleased tone. "It's what I'd thought."

"What is?"

Mannheim stood up. "Why am I working on the Einstein-Podolsky-Rosen Effect?"

David's patience with these unexpected conversational twists was thinning. "I don't know why you're working on it," he said testily. "How could I?"

Mannheim reacted not at all to David's displeasure. "It's what I came out here to do," he said matter-of-factly, as though that information were sufficient for David to understand everything.

"But Doctor Mannheim," David said, "you could have worked on the EPR in Chicago! You could have built your whole career around work like that, and published it, and won a Nobel Prize for it. Excuse me, but I fail to see any connection at all between your work and this bizarre exile of yours. If you're serious about your work, you publish it. You share it with your colleagues. You make useful contributions to science. You add to humanity's knowledge. You haven't done that since 1945. Whatever you're doing out here can't be anything but . . . sterility. If what they say is true, and you came out here just to drink yourself to death, that's one thing. But please don't ask me to believe you're doing anything of value in a place like this!"

His outburst over, David had only the briefest instant to recall the stories of Howard Mannheim's legendary temper before Mannheim was upon him. With a panther's smooth motion he had somehow leaped the table between them and now sat on its edge, gripping David's head in his big hands and pulling it close to his face.

"I am here," he said quietly, "because *I* am awake. *You* are asleep."

The first rush of shock and panic subsided inside David. He stared into Mannheim's face, felt Mannheim's warm fingers on his temples. *He isn't angry,* he thought, astonished. There was great force in the hands but absolutely no painful pressure. No urge to hurt. There was great power in the face's expression, but that expression could have conveyed a powerful joy just as easily as a powerful rage.

"You are asleep," Mannheim repeated, drawing David's face even closer to his own. "Do you understand?"

"No," David gasped. He was bent far forward in the chair, and Mannheim's hands on his jaws made talking difficult. But he hesitated to push Mannheim away. The sheer force of the man, even if it wasn't anger, frightened him.

Abruptly Mannheim let go of him. He sat back in the chair and repeated, as calmly as he could, "No. I don't understand."

Mannheim got up. He stood still for a few minutes, looking down at David, his hawklike face still radiating its peculiar, indefinable intensity.

"You will," he said finally, in the same calm voice, and then he went to his blackboard. He stared for a little while at the mechanically neat series of numbers descending its surface before he turned back to David and asked, in the voice of a teacher interrogating a student, "What is the controversy surrounding the Einstein-Podolsky-Rosen Effect?"

David rattled off everything he knew. "The Einstein-Podolsky-Rosen Effect was described in 1935 by Albert Einstein, Boris Podolsky, and Nathan Rosen, in a paper entitled 'Can Quantum Mechanical Description of Physical Reality be Considered Complete?' This paper was one of Einstein's many attempts to counter the Copenhagen interpretation of quantum mechanics, which stated that physical reality cannot be described objectively, that is, independent of the subjective observations of the person who describes it. Einstein, Podolsky, and Rosen attempted to prove that certain physical phenomena do have a real existence even when not under observation. The best evidence for their position is the unexplainable behavior of two streams of subatomic particles traveling in opposite directions when they pass through a Stern-Gerlach magnetic field. If the magnetic field is oriented along an up-down axis, a particle passing toward it will be deflected and spin upward, and its twin traveling away from the field will spin downward. If the field is oriented on a left-right axis, one particle passing through it will spin right, and its twin will spin left. The Einstein-Podolsky-Rosen Effect occurs when the axis of the magnetic field is changed from up-down to left-right *after* the two streams of particles have been released. This causes particles passing through the field to change their spin from up to right. Immediately the particles traveling away from the field switch their orientation from down to left."

"Correct," Mannheim said impatiently. "Now the controversy."

"The controversy," David went on, "stems from the theory that the shift in the spin of one stream of particles would instantaneously result in the spin shift of the opposite stream, even if the two streams were so far apart that not even a beam of light could travel from one to the other 'instantaneously.' This implies that there is something in the universe that travels faster than the speed of light. Einstein of course denied this conclusion, since his whole physics — our physics — rests on the principle that nothing in the universe travels faster than light. He and his collaborators insisted that what happens to the two streams of particles is *simultaneous* but in no way *connected,* and is therefore independent of any changes the experimenter makes in the magnetic-field orientation. In other words, the quantum theory, which describes everything as a mere set of observations dependent on the actions of an observer, is inadequate, because it cannot describe a phenomenon that exists independently of what the observer does."

"Right!" As David finished, Mannheim began nodding his head vigorously, almost rhythmically, as if keeping time with the climactic end of a symphony. He jumped in as soon as David stopped. "But Einstein left us a little hint, didn't he?"

"Hint? What do you mean?"

Mannheim had left the blackboard and was running his finger along the books in the shelves. He pulled a worn volume from its place and held it up to David.

"In his autobiography," Mannheim said, "Einstein tells us that the only alternative to *his* conclusions concerning the Einstein-Podolsky-Rosen Effect is to deny that two separate events have any reality independent of each other — to believe instead that everything seemingly separate is in fact fundamentally connected."

David frowned. "If I recall that passage correctly, Einstein declared that alternative to be unacceptable. He also wrote, ironically of course, of a possible telepathic communication between the particles, to show the depth of his scorn for such conclusions, I think . . ."

"Exactly." Mannheim whipped the book back into its place on the shelf and strode back to the blackboard. "Now come look at this."

The blackboard was a standard university one, free-standing, double-sided, on wheels. Mannheim flipped it to show David the other side. David saw that the second side too was covered with equations, the long lines of numbers as maniacally neat as their counterparts on the front.

Mannheim beckoned him forward. He got up from his seat and approached the blackboard.

"Take your time," Mannheim said, pointing to the numbers.

David began mentally working his way through the equations. He was not far along before he appreciated the reality of Howard Mannheim's legendary genius. Though David's own mathematical powers had been described more than once as little less than supernatural, he found himself laboring through Mannheim's figures like an English major forced to take elementary physics. But he struggled on, compelled by his own pride and by Mannheim's piercing presence beside him, and as he reached the bottom of the blackboard he broke through struggle into pure astonishment.

Mannheim saw the changed look on his face and chuckled. "Well, David," he said. "What do you think now of Einstein's scorn?"

David had already started over again, reading the equations from the top, checking for mistakes. But he did so reflexively, as a trained mathematician. He knew there were no mistakes.

"You've done it," he said finally, turning to Mannheim. "You've actually proven it."

"Yes," said Mannheim, coming forward. "I actually have."

For a few moments neither Mannheim nor David said anything. David stared at the neat numbers on the blackboard as though they were the first excavated hints of an incredible and hitherto wholly unsuspected civilization. He felt Mannheim next to him fairly crackling with excited energy. The intensity emanating from him was so powerful that David expected him momentarily to spin away from the blackboard and fly about the room. But when David turned to look at him, he saw in his features only the same impossible calmness, the same superhuman control. Mannheim's powers seemed to flow from him as hotly and effortlessly as energy from a sun.

Mannheim met his gaze with a smile. "You see," he said quietly, "poor Albert couldn't help himself. Underneath all his scorn, underneath everything Einstein the scientist despised, perhaps feared, he knew that something was up. He knew it. He couldn't help knowing. And in spite of himself he left us a hint of it." Mannheim moved closer to the board, until his face was only inches from his equations. His voice dropped to a near-whisper. "And I have taken the hint. And look what I've found out. *Look* what I've found out."

"Superluminal connections really *are* there," David murmured, studying the numbers, his face parallel to Mannheim's.

"Faster than light," Mannheim whispered. "Faster than light. *Beyond* light. Beyond light, all is connected. The particles are not separate. They move as parts of One. Where we cannot see, where we cannot measure time or space, they dance. All is One. Light is not the end. It's only the boundary. On one side, our side, the known. On the other side, the . . ." Mannheim gestured toward the blackboard. "He knew it. He didn't *want* to know it, because it frightened him, but he knew it, and he left us a hint. . . ."

"You've got to publish this right away," David cried.

Mannheim turned to him. This time the look on his face was unambiguously angry.

"*Idiot!*" he hissed, and in the twinkling of an eye his heavy arm moved so swiftly that it scarcely seemed to move at all and struck David hard across the face, so hard that David staggered against the blackboard and nearly knocked it over.

"What the hell — " Instinctively David struck back.

Mannheim caught his arm in midair and gripped it hard.

"Are you *crazy?*" David shouted, struggling to free his arm.

"Are *you?*" Mannheim asked calmly, tightening his grip.

"What's that supposed to mean?" David's nose and cheeks throbbed with pain. Involuntary tears filled his eyes. His arm hurt in Mannheim's grasp.

"What it means, idiot, is that you're no damn different from the rest of them! Asleep, asleep!"

"Look, Dr. Mannheim." David rubbed his arm. "All I said was that you should publish. I would think that would be obvious, to say the least. My God, when people read what's on this blackboard they'll have to throw everything — everything! — out the window and start all over again! I mean, it's as if . . ." David forgot his anger for a moment and stared again at the numbers on the board. "It's as if . . . everything that we believe is real . . . might only be just . . ."

"A dream." Mannheim finished the sentence. "You're afraid to say it, aren't you?"

"Call it whatever you want!" David snapped at him. "But publish! You can't keep something like this to yourself! You're a scientist, dammit. You have a duty to your science, to humanity!"

Mannheim threw back his head and began to laugh so hard that his eyes filled with tears.

"*Duty!*" he roared. "Duty!" His laughter came even louder, belly-shaking, with his usual force. David stared at him, his anger evaporating into perplexity. Howard Mannheim was without a doubt the most mercurial character . . .

With some difficulty Mannheim got hold of himself, wiped his teary eyes, and gave David (who winced instinctively) a friendly slap on the back.

"You know, David," he said with a chuckle, still catching his breath, "you're right. I have a solemn duty to my science and to humanity, and it's high time I performed it." He paused theatrically, barely able to suppress another laugh, and then added with great dignity, "And I'm going to do my duty right now."

He knocked the blackboard flat on the floor, unzipped his fly, and urinated on his equations.

David was too stunned to do anything but watch the orderly rows of numbers wash away. When Mannheim had finished a fan-pattern of wet chalk was splashed across the board. A good third of his proof of superluminal connections had dissolved into urine and dust.

Mannheim zipped up his fly. "There. Thank you, David, for bringing me to my senses. Humanity can be grateful to me now."

He turned and stalked out through the front door, into the garden.

David stood very still, looking down at the blackboard. For a moment he felt nothing, his emotions frozen by his internal emergency alarms. A moment later he had an overwhelming urge to flee, to get back into his car and escape from this madman and his mad little kingdom in the woods. With great difficulty he fought it down. He was a physicist; he *had* to stay until he had convinced Mannheim to publish his theorem or understood it well enough to bring it to the public himself. But would that be possible? David knelt down beside the blackboard and, his nose wrinkling at the odor of urine, inspected the damage. It had been sufficient, he concluded; the theorem was unintelligible. One struggling pass through its mind-crushing mathematics was hardly enough to imprint it in his own brain. Mannheim still held all the cards.

David stood up. Through the open door of the cabin he could see Mannheim standing among his flowers, hands in pockets, staring down his hillside at the pine forest before him and the mountains and sky beyond. The summer sunlight shone on his gleaming bald skull, inside which, David thought, the entire future of physics now lay. He had to stay. Steeling himself for whatever might happen, he walked from the cabin into the garden and stood by Mannheim's side.

For a while neither of them spoke. David took in the view. It was midafternoon by now, and the sun struck at an angle through the crystalline Arizona air, warming the mountains' colors, deepening their shadows. Atop the ridge that shielded Howard Mannheim from the world, stands of aspen shimmered above tumbled piles of porous rock.

"A few hundred million years ago," Mannheim said suddenly, "that ridge of rock was a wave of lava rolling down from those mountains. Liquid, solid — which is its 'real' state?" He spoke evenly, calmly, not looking at David. "In a place like this you are so much closer to the Truth. You see that humans live by clinging to illusions. Illusions of permanence. Of certainty. All we've really known, in all these millennia of our civilization, has been a dream. A movie — yes, more like a movie, a movie that is being projected so slowly that for all our time on earth we've only watched a single frame of it. And during all those millennia we've mistaken that single image, that snapshot, for reality, when in fact it is only one insignificant frame of the movie, the changing flow of a million images, all connected, all One." He looked at David and smiled. "Any first-year geology student could have told you that. The really profound thing is what I just pissed off that blackboard. The really profound thing is that even the *movie* isn't reality. It's only a movie, a visual dream, and the camera, endlessly filming it, creating it, is our mind."

David took courage from Mannheim's gentle mood. "Don't you think, Doctor Mannheim, that humanity should be told of this incredible thing?"

Mannheim's face darkened, and David braced himself to ward off another blow. But Mannheim did not strike; he stared very hard at David, as if debating whether it was worth pummeling such a fool once more. Then he seemed to give up the idea and simply turned his face away to stare at the aspens on the ridge.

"I've already told them."

"You *have?*"

Mannheim's face snapped around again, and it was angry. "What the hell do you think Trinity was all about? Hiroshima? Nagasaki? Eniwetok? The rest of it? You said it yourself! 'Behold the face of God!'"

"But I don't see how that — "

"We should have been on our *knees!*" Mannheim shouted to

the aspens and the mountains. "On our goddamned *knees!*" He bent down and began yanking stray weeds from among his gorgeous roses. "Until the last second no one, not even I, knew whether Trinity would work. No one dared to believe it. Then the night sky was suddenly brighter than the day . . ." He looked up from his weeding, down the pretty line of roses, out to the Arizona wilderness. "And the light was . . . it was every color imaginable, red, gray, lavender, blue . . . the blazing gold of the sun. It was light . . . we had cracked open Matter, all of *that.*" He swung his arm across pine forest, volcanic ridge, and mountain peaks. "We had cracked it open like a goddamned *nut* and looked inside. And we saw light . . . We were at the boundary. At Trinity and Hiroshima and Bikini, and all the hundreds of times since, we've stood at the goddamned boundary. Everything that you assure me the precious so-called scientific community, and this wonderful species of ours as a whole, has been so desperately eager to learn has been in front of their damned eyes since 1945."

He stood up and tossed the weeds into a little wheelbarrow. "And what have they done with it? What have they *done?* At Trinity I showed them a crack in the wall. A tear in the veil. Reality. The end of the movie. Time to wake up. But did they wake up? Did they stop their centuries of dreaming when I shined the light of Truth right into their eyes? No. They just turned away from my light and kept on dreaming, dreaming a new variation on the endless nightmare they love so well to dream. In their sleep, each of their stupid little nations dreams itself the final winner, the conqueror of all the others, of the planet itself, with its almighty *bomb* . . . That's what they've done with Truth, you know. Made a bomb of it. Made a *thing* of it, an object. Frozen it into Matter, trapped it in Time. Dragged it down into their prison, the goddamned dungeon of space-time. And all their wonderful scientists, all their bright little boys like *you,* are the goddamned jailers."

"Just a minute," David interrupted. "Don't let yourself off so easily, Doctor Mannheim. If that's what's eating you, you're responsible. *You* gave us the bomb."

"I gave you the Truth!" Mannheim shouted. "They gave me money and men and told me to solve their little war-problem. Well, I took their money and their men and I solved their damned problem, and I showed them the Truth. The moment I saw it — Trinity — I was awakened. And I have been wide awake ever since." Again Mannheim turned his stare on David. "Don't tell me you don't know what I'm talking about. You woke up too, when you saw it. You saw the face of God — "

"Jesus Christ!" David turned away. "Forget I ever said that! I told you, it's just an old platitude! Inadequate language. All it means is that for an instant I got excited. I couldn't think of a rational description of what I felt when I saw the fireball, so I fell back on some archaic religious image. I don't really believe that I saw the face of God. So please stop throwing it back in my face."

Mannheim was upon him again. David felt his chin seized and swiveled to the left. Mannheim held it in his hand, firmly but with his peculiarly unmalicious force. He was forcing David to stare right into his face, only inches away, so close that his breath warmed David's cheek as he spoke.

"You're lying to me, David Devlin. You're lying, because you're scared. You're a little bit smarter than your fellow sleepers, aren't you? There was a rent in the veil and for an instant light poured in and you stirred in your slumber. You and a few others. You know there's something behind it all, something beyond all we can see and measure and know. The old mythic image for it is as precise as any mathematics: it *is* the face of God. And like God it will not be trapped in Time. Stuff it into bombs and it will destroy us. But if we reverence it, open our minds to it, awaken at last from our sleep to reality, we will someday become what it tells us we must be." His voice rose and his hand tightened on David's chin. "You understand that I am awake now. I see these things that you hide from in your slumber. I have known who you are for years, what you have done before you did it, what you have left to do. And I know more: I know that if we survive our bombs and let our minds mature, there will be a future physics very different from ours, and you and I will no longer be jailers, destroyers, servants of a nightmare. We shall rule an awakened world . . . we shall be priests."

David knocked Mannheim's arm away.

"I'm leaving you now, Doctor Mannheim," he said icily. "There's no point in my listening to more of this. I came here to give you my father's regards, and I have. I also came, frankly, out of curiosity, to see what had really happened to you. Now I see that the rumors were right. Your mind has slipped from its pinnacle of greatness into some very dark depths indeed. I'm sorry. It's a profound loss for science."

To David's surprise, Mannheim said nothing. He looked sadly down at his roses. David turned to go, but Mannheim's apparent dejection made him feel bad. "Look, Doctor Mannheim," he said more gently, turning back. "I understand what you've been through. I'm sure that seeing what you did at Nagasaki, and knowing you were responsible, was a real shock — "

"Nagasaki," Mannheim broke in, "was inevitable." His voice was a voice of steel. "Nagasaki was necessary. It was part of the plan."

"Plan? What plan?"

"It was the prelude to the test. If we fail the test, we do not awaken. We turn aside from our evolutionary destiny . . ."

"Wait a minute. What test? The Trinity test? How could Nagasaki be — "

"If we fail the test we shall sleepwalk into our own extinction. I know this. Unless we wake up, when the test comes we shall die in our sleep."

For several very long moments Mannheim simply stared at David, as if to let what he obviously regarded as a life-changing revelation sink in.

David stared back, with a frown that conveyed his own total bewilderment, before he blurted out, "What in hell are you talking about?"

Mannheim smiled. "If it took one more, or five more, or one hundred more Nagasakis to awaken the world, then I would give the world a hundred more Nagasakis. I am awake. I am free of delusions. I can do what is necessary. The power of God is free in me."

"You're a lunatic." David turned away in disgust and walked toward his car.

"You know everything I'm talking about, Devlin," Mannheim called after him. "You knew it long before the generals made you one of their jailers. But you're worse than the generals you serve. *They* sleep so soundly that the dream is all they know, but you woke up, and then you went right back to sleep. Because you're afraid, Devlin. You're afraid that the Truth will overwhelm your puny little human mind. So you keep a tight lid on what you know. You live in a tight little world with your cello and your mathematics, because somewhere you know goddamned well that there's something in you that could blow any time. Just as it blew in me. When it blew I woke up, and I'm not afraid."

David had reached his car. Mannheim raised his voice nearly to a shout. "And if you think you can sneak a safe little peek at the face of God by building the generals' playthings, and never have to look at him full in the face and see the Truth, you're as doomed as the rest of them!"

The final accusation was in fact exactly right. David, who had been trying to ignore Mannheim's tirade, spun around at his car door as if struck by a bullet and shouted back, "And what do you suggest I do, Doctor Mannheim? Wake up to madness, like you?"

Glaring up the hillside, squinting into the declining sun, he saw the silhouetted figure of Mannheim start toward him. *Jesus Christ,* he thought, *I've had it with this guy.* He grabbed the handle of his car door to open it.

"Devlin!"

Mannheim was nearly running down the hill, closing fast. David saw that he would have no chance to leave before Mannheim arrived unless he was prepared to beat a hasty and undignified retreat, which he was not. He kept his hand on the door handle and waited for Mannheim. *If he so much as touches me again —*

"Devlin." Mannheim arrived, panting slightly. "Listen to me."

"All right." David let go of the door handle, turned around, and looked once more into Mannheim's peculiar aquiline face. He saw there nothing but the same strange intensity, and immediately regretted that he hadn't just gotten in the car and driven away.

"Do you really want to know what you should do?" Mannheim asked, peering closely at David, his great brows plunging to a V over his nose.

"I don't think so." David sighed.

"Stay here with me," Mannheim went on, ignoring the answer. "Stay here three days, or two days, or one day. Or one hour.

Only an hour, as long as you *listen*. As long as you're not afraid of what I'm saying."

"I'm sorry, Doctor Mannheim. I think I've already heard everything you have to say." David turned and put his hand on the door handle again.

"Devlin!" Mannheim bellowed at him. "If you're going to go, then go. But only go if you don't believe in what I've said. Don't go just because you're afraid."

"Dammit, I'm *not* afraid," David snapped over his shoulder.

"That's exactly what you're doing," Mannheim bellowed on, ignoring him. "You're leaving because you're afraid. You're afraid of what you know is true."

"No! I'm leaving because you're crazy."

"You can only leave if deep down, under all the fears that are frantically sounding their alarms, ordering you to cling desperately to the safety of human slumber — if underneath all that, at the core of you, where your tiny little human being blends into being itself, you don't believe me. If that's true, then go!"

For a moment there was silence between them.

"I don't believe you!" David said furiously. But he took his hand off the door.

January 21, 1961
New Bedford

Dear Steven,

A new decade, a new era. Yesterday the Democrats returned to power with a handsome young lion at their head. Whatever else young Kennedy may or may not be, he is charismatic, and now that we're in the television age charisma, or the lack thereof, may be what makes or breaks all presidential candidates. I don't mean to sound cynical. I like Kennedy, and your father worked hard to help get him elected. As you know, he even took a leave of absence from his job with the White House to have more time during the campaign. At the time I wondered why he had suddenly become so interested in domestic policies, and I thought the real reason for his leave might be sheer exhaustion, after all those years of battling Dulles over disarmament policy. Frankly, I was very relieved when Dulles died — if he hadn't, I'm sure that by now we would have found him and your father dead together, their hands locked around each other's throats. Whatever the press has said, as of yesterday I suspect that your father had the final word. If the Rome papers carried our outgoing President's farewell address, you'll know what I mean. I'm sure that to many, Ike's warning to resist the growing power of what he called the "military-industrial complex" seemed to come right out of left field, but if I didn't hear your father talking there (and all through that speech), then I've spent my life married to a man I don't know.

Anyway, whatever your father's reasons for taking a leave, I'm glad that he did. Last year his bouts of strangeness came less and less frequently, and in the past few months they seem to have vanished entirely (knock on wood). I can't tell you how relieved I am to be finally at ease with him, after so many years of wondering when the next episode would strike and whether he would recover from it. In the past three months there's been only one incident strange enough to mention.

Right after the election Kennedy was at Hyannis, relaxing after the campaign, and he decided to drive over here and thank John personally for all he had done for him. We had just finished dinner when the President-elect arrived unannounced, surrounded by his entourage! Your father took the whole thing in stride, or so I thought, until he suggested to Kennedy that the two of them take a walk on the beach. You realize that it was mid-November and after dark, and that we had already had the first snow flurries. Someone in Kennedy's party laughed and said that maybe it was a little chilly for that, but your father was already out the door, in nothing warmer than a sport coat. That did it. If you've read anything at all about our new President, you'll know what I mean — if he sees that a man who is thirteen years his senior isn't bothered by cold, then by God he isn't bothered by cold either. So Kennedy followed John out the door and the two of them walked up and down the beach for what must have been an hour, while I gave hot coffee and dessert to the punier constitutions who had stayed indoors. When they finally came back Kennedy's sport coat was buttoned all the way up and the collar was turned up around his neck, and he looked a little blue around the lips, but he flashed his dazzling smile and told everyone how bracing and beautiful the beach had been, how lovely the full moon was, etc., as if it had been the best idea in the world. (I handed him coffee so he wouldn't have to ask for it.)

After Kennedy left I asked your father why on earth he had kept the President-elect out so long in the cold and wind. What could they have possibly discussed for an hour? "The moon," said your father, with that odd look of his that spells trouble, a look I hadn't seen in months. "The moon?" I said. "For an hour?" *"You'd be surprised what people don't know about the moon," he said, and that was that. I wasn't aware that your father knew enough about the moon to discuss it for an hour with* anyone, much less with a man who was probably distracted by thoughts of pneumonia or freezing to death. But anyway, since Kennedy didn't get pneumonia or freeze and has now been duly installed as President, and since your father after that night has been happy and cheerful and absolutely his old self, I can't really complain.

So your family charges on into the new decade in relatively good shape. Diana is happier than ever at school and displays an incongruous dual aptitude for dramatics and science. Even though I've missed her, I'm glad we sent her away — she's been spared your father's pathological interludes and thinks of him in a positive, if somewhat idealized, way. I suppose all daughters worship their daddies at some time or another, especially daddies they only see on vacations and at Christmas.

But our other scientist seems even more lost than ever, and worries me deeply. You remember that right after he finally kept his promise and went to see Howard Mannheim, he disappeared again. We had just succeeded in establishing that he really was at that Air Force base in Nevada when suddenly he wasn't. Finally we got a long letter from him, postmarked from some town in California that I had to look up in the atlas. It turned out to be the only town for miles in a huge blank spot in the Mojave Desert. The letter admitted that what we had suspected all along was true: that David had left M.I.T. to do nuclear weapons research and that he had eventually resigned from his project and decided to have nothing more to do with the military. Of course we were happy to hear that, but when we wrote to ask him what he was doing in the middle of the Mojave Desert and when he was going back to M.I.T., he replied that he was never going back to M.I.T., nor would he work for the government or the military ever again — that he had seen something horrible and false in them all and wanted nothing more to do with any of them. He said he had found a house in the desert and a job teaching math in a high school, and that he had work to do. Four years later I still cannot discover what that "work" is, and neither, apparently, can anybody else.

Poor David. His career as a scientist is surely finished. Even a reputation like his can't sustain him forever. Who would take him seriously now, no matter how brilliant he is? I fear his woolly head has at last done him real harm. He blunders from the cloister into the real world, discovers that it is less than perfect, and ruins his life by fleeing to the desert in an anchorite's protest. Such a waste of brains. But you know how he is; no one can say anything to him. Apparently he simply stays home when he isn't teaching and "works." Probably he's playing his cello, playing his life away. I don't know anymore. We haven't heard from him in months.

Well, enough about us. I want to hear more about you, my worldly confessor. Your last few letters have been awfully thin. You used to write such funny ones, and now all I get from you is vague references to "important assignments" and the like. What happened? Do your Jewish mama a favor and spice it up again. You know the old yenta loves nothing better than a peep at the Pope's dirty linen . . .

Love,
Mother

At the end of May 1961, as cold New Bedford clothed itself in the warm green garments of a new spring, John Devlin received an unusual telephone call. The caller was his son David. It was unusual for David to call, and it was unusual for him to be very communicative if he did, but for once David had plenty to say. He told his surprised father that he was calling from Washington; he had left California, left teaching, left the desert. Something very exciting had happened. Early one morning a week before he had stopped at a roadside café, as he did every morning, to eat his breakfast before reporting to school. That morning the café's television set had been on, and everyone else had been watching it. President Kennedy was making a speech. At first David had not watched; since 1957 he had resolutely ignored every utterance made by a public figure. But a little of what Kennedy was saying had finally compelled his attention. The speech had been not about politics, but about space. Kennedy had called for a long-range program to wrest from the Soviets the leadership of the new adventure in space, requesting the necessary funds from Congress and asking his country to organize its talents and its resources toward one monumental goal: to land a man on the moon, and bring him safely home, by the end of the decade.

The speech, David told his father, had electrified him. He had not even bothered to go to school that morning, but had rushed home to telephone NASA and offer his services to the moon program. Those services had been gratefully accepted, and David was still living in the afterglow of his elation.

After David had hung up John told Ruth he was going for a walk on the beach. In fact he went no farther than the garden and the Tree. He stood at the spot of his terrible revelation, sixteen years past, and felt the satisfaction glowing within him. He had only had to wait and to watch until young Kennedy's rising star had appeared on the horizon. And then, on a wintry walk under the full moon, Kennedy's mind had proven fertile ground for the planted seed, just as John had guessed it would. Now the seed had flowered into an epoch-making speech, a clarion call for America to turn itself from cold war to the peaceful conquest of the moon and the new mystery of space. The call had now been answered by precisely the person for whom it had actually been sounded: David Devlin. John had prepared Kennedy; Howard Mannheim had prepared David. In both of them — young, impressionable, imaginative — the opportunity for a step forward had come.

The new warmth of the sun shed its blessing on the grateful earth. Deep in thought, John scarcely noticed. He had promised to serve, and he was serving well. He was thinking ahead, as far as a man's mind could. *Kennedy will turn their minds away from nuclear war for a little while. For a little while, that is where their minds must be. For a little while.*

IO

The Grail

EARLY IN THE MORNING of the last day of May 1968, David Devlin found himself sitting in a very uncomfortable plastic chair, trying to get some sleep. His body had just been flown through the night and deposited in a waiting lounge at Orly Airport, outside Paris, where the clocks read 9:00 A.M.; but his own internal clock was still set for Houston, his home. In Houston it was 2:00 A.M. . . .

David yawned and stretched very carefully, trying not to tip over the briefcase propping up his feet. He had not slept on the flight. He had worked all the way across the Atlantic, trying to finish in advance the calculations he would need in a week, when he returned. Now he wished he had slept instead. In his youthful prime the *wunderkind* of M.I.T. had put in days and nights of sleepless work without noticing it. Now, at thirty-six, he noticed. His body, the Platonist's eternal enemy, was beginning to let him down. But he had had no choice except to work. It was a bad time to take a week off from NASA. When was there a good time? He didn't know; it had been over a year since he had even asked himself the question.

David kept his eyes closed and tried to ignore the airport bustle. In the blackness columns of numbers and Greek letters paraded before him. For anything else, he thought wearily, he would not have left the space program, even for a week. But it *was* his parents' fortieth wedding anniversary . . .

"Do you think he'll come?" The loud question on his left arrested David's descent into slumber.

"Mmmm . . ."

"David! I said, do you think he'll come?"

David gave up and opened his eyes. "Don't ask me," he said, yawning again. "You heard from him last. Did he say he was coming?" He turned to look at the person on his left, who had asked the question — his sister, Diana.

"Oh, I don't know," said Diana, puffing fretfully on her third cigarette in twenty minutes. "He *said* he was, but you know, Steven is always so mysterious about these things. That's what bothers me. Until he actually shows up you can't be sure." Diana took another drag on her cigarette. When she blew out the smoke she threw her head back dramatically, a habit she had acquired while rehearsing a Noel Coward play in her undergraduate days.

Not knowing this gesture's origins, David found it affected, and he shut his eyes again as much from disapproval as fatigue. But as he drifted down toward sleep once more the parade of equations before his closed eyes was disrupted by an unbrotherly thought: his sister, whom he hadn't seen in years, looked terrific. She was twenty-two now, out of college and a year into graduate school, and she was tall, like the Devlin men, and graced with the smashing combination of her mother's alabaster skin, her father's blue eyes, and her great-grandfather Michael's flaming red hair. She was a scientist too, apparently a good one; she had just finished her master's degree in cell biology at Johns Hopkins, where they trained some of the best. And she was wearing one of those summer dresses that was no longer than an untucked shirt . . .

"*Pardon,* you are the children of Ambassador et Madame Devlin?"

David sat up. A Frenchman in a chauffeur's uniform was standing over them, hat in hand.

"Yes, we are," Diana replied. "Who are you?"

The Frenchman gave a little bow. "I am sent to drive you to your parents' 'otel."

"A limo." David yawned. "Great." He lifted his feet from his briefcase and stood up.

"Wait a minute," said Diana. "Don't you think we ought to hang around a little longer? In case he comes?"

"The last time I waited for Steven," David said through a hand covering his yawns, "all I had to show for it was an apologetic telegram two days later."

"Please." The Frenchman gestured toward the glass exit doors of the lounge. Through them David and Diana could see a black car that had opaque one-way windows and was at least twice the length of an ordinary automobile. Twin French tricolors fluttered from little flagstaffs over the headlights.

"Let's go," David said. He picked up his bags and started forward. The driver took them from him and hurried ahead to open the door.

Diana stared at the car. "Oh, wow. Oh, no," she said. "Do we really have to ride in that thing?"

David gave her a puzzled look. "What's wrong with it?"

"Well, Jesus, David, we'll look like *pigs* . . ."

David sighed. At this moment what he wanted to do more than anything else in the world was to stretch out in an enormous, silent limousine and fall asleep.

"Look, Diana," he said, "if the limo bothers you, take a cab and tell the driver to follow us. Maybe everyone will think you're a famous urban guerrilla, stalking her next target."

Diana gave him a nasty look and lugged her bags outside, past the car, toward a taxi stand. David followed the driver and stretched himself out gratefully inside the waiting behemoth. A moment later there was a tap on the window by his head. David pressed a switch and the smoky glass descended, softly purring. Diana peered in at him, still scowling.

"I can't take a taxi," she said.

"Why not?" asked David.

"I don't have any French money."

"Get in the car," David said, sleepily chuckling.

Diana picked up her luggage and started for the open trunk, but the indefatigable driver raced around to meet her and take her bags.

"*Merci, non,*" said Diana, yanking them away. "I can carry them myself."

The gigantic limo whisked them noiselessly along the Orly exit routes. At the same moment, in Paris, John Devlin was also riding in a limousine, crossing town on his way to the morning session of the "official conversations" between the United States government and the Democratic Republic of Vietnam. Negotiating with Hanoi had been his daily business since the beginning of the month.

And a very bad business it was, he thought as he saw the old Majestic Hotel, site of the talks, looming up ahead. The negotiators had spent weeks bogged down in mutual intransigence and procedural trivia, while in Vietnam, day after day, people died.

He checked his wristwatch. The children had landed by now; the driver so kindly provided by the French was bringing them to the hotel, where he would see them that night. He knew what to expect. David, woolly-headed as ever and plunged into space work, would scarcely be aware of what his father was doing. Diana, who had leaped passionately from college theatricals onto the stage of the worldwide youth revolt, would take him to task for having anything to do with Johnson's war of genocide. And Steven — was Steven coming? John tried to remember. Steven was very busy these days. Had he said yes or no? Had he said either?

John had had so much to think about — how to salvage the talks, how to salvage the world. In the spring of 1968 the whole world was Vietnam, a battlefield where societies and their peoples stumbled about chaotically and violently clashed. Kennedy's death in 1963 had started it. There was something about that death that John did not want to know but knew nonetheless. When Kennedy had died he had felt at first only the sorrow millions had felt, though deeper perhaps, because he had known Kennedy and had had great hopes for him. But then a dark, dispassionate thought had taken form in him and grown cancerously, until at last he had had to acknowledge it. He knew who had killed Kennedy. Not Oswald, who had fired the gun; not Castro, not the Mafia, not the FBI or the CIA or any of the hundred other groups accused every week since November of 1963 by whomever wished them ill. John knew who — or what. The god had killed him. The old monk. The voice, the eyes, whatever it was. The thing that had driven his own poor flesh until at last it had gotten free in him. He had seen no burning eyes nor heard a voice (he had not done so in years, thank God), but he knew what was true. The god had killed Kennedy, and therefore Kennedy's death had not been chance, any more than John's strange life had been. But it had taken John five years to understand *why* it had not been chance.

Nearly a month ago, when he had arrived in Paris and had caught a glimpse of the savage street fighting of the May Revolt, it had dawned on him that perhaps this was what Kennedy's death had been intended to accomplish. Perhaps the deaths of Pope John XXIII and, that spring, of Martin Luther King had been intended to accomplish this as well; in all three cases the effect had been the same. *At the end of a decade of deadlocked cold war,* he thought, *the god gives humanity inspiring leaders who call upon the human spirit to fashion a new and better world. Millions respond, as if they had been waiting all along for the call, and the young American President, the articulate black minister, and the aged pontiff become symbols of a quest and objects of a nearly fanatical devotion. But after a few years the first rush of excitement has passed. The symbols of a new world are in danger of being recognized as merely human, and so, with exquisite timing, they are purged of their humanity, lifted into heaven, where they remain perfected symbols forever. The young, the minorities, the poor are spared disillusionment and left with the hope of a new order of things and a smoldering rage that their heroes have been taken away. In their minds the deaths become the final proof of their world's essential evil, the final granting of license to meet its violence with violence of their own.*

Now, in 1968, the gathered momentum of that assault was finally snowballing in every aspect of life, from mass politics to an individual's single act, from the street barricades of Paris to the shrinking length of women's skirts. It was phoenix time. Everywhere, in Paris and Berlin and Milan, in Newark and Watts and New York, in Saigon and Biafra and Prague, the old world was burning, tottering, about to collapse; and inside of the blazing hulk, in the chrysalis of its ashes, the young, embryo of the future, were setting new fires, scaring away the corrupted flesh of the womb, killing their own parents to burn a way out to something new.

He could see it in his children. They were all driven by it. Diana went about these days holding aloft a blazing torch on behalf of everyone denied the utopia of her radical vision, and stood ready to hurl it without hesitation into any edifice of the established order that blocked the utopian path. David followed a completely opposite path with equal fanaticism, avoiding any political engagement whatsoever, singlemindedly pursuing his commitment to the dream of space. And Steven — well, who ever knew what Steven really thought? John's eldest child had learned from the Jesuits to move from one position of certainty to another, and so he did, perpetually, with a dazzling intellectual fluency. But what was he *really* up to, behind all the jesuitical brilliance? Hard to say. Steven had always been difficult to read, even for John. How could anyone fathom a young man who, worldly and clever and assuredly destined for Harvard Law and Wall Street or the State Department, had at nineteen suddenly declared his vocation and become a priest? Perhaps, John thought, he was sometimes too skeptical about Steven's vocation; it was hard for him not to be, given his early lessons in the value of priests. He was glad that Grandfather Michael didn't know what had become of his first great-grandchild . . .

Or *did* he know? In the inexplicable fate of his eldest child John saw more clearly than anywhere the hand (and perhaps the humor) of the power he had known all his life, the power that now was quickening the pace of whatever it intended for the world. It was phoenix time, time to evolve. A cycle of evolution was coming to an end. Karl Werner's watershed had crested and broken and flooded the world in fire. The young of the species, the crown of creation, were literally blazing a desperate path through the ending world, looking for a place to go. Time to evolve.

He had arrived. The car door opened and he stepped out. During the past five years he had come to understand how an old world had been made to die; now, in Paris, he must discover what the new world would be. He knew only that he would not find it among the old ideologies of capitalism, communism, fascism, or religion, reappearing in new disguises. All of these were parts of what was dying. He must sift through their ashes for a sign of what was coming. When he had found it he would follow it, and join forces with evolution to serve the god.

In front of the Hotel Majestic there were always TV crews, and behind them and the barricades of police a small crowd of more or less quiet antiwar demonstrators. But today, as John walked the daily gauntlet from car to hotel, he heard a sudden scuffle to his left. John looked just in time to see one of the demonstrators break through the police barricade and rush toward him. At his heels were several beefy gendarmes, one of whom caught him in a choke hold with a nightstick just as he reached John. Another gendarme pulled his arm behind his back, and a third yanked his head back by his long tangled hair.

"*Attendez,*" said John to the gendarmes. "Thank you, but let him go, please."

The policemen looked for instructions to their sergeant, who hesitated for a moment before shrugging his shoulders and nodding. They let go of the struggling youth, who immediately assumed an air of smirking insouciance and sauntered over to John, producing from his pockets a pack of Gaulois.

"Cigarette, *cochon?*" said the boy, smiling pleasantly.

"*Merci,*" said John, smiling back. He took a cigarette and sized up the owner of the pack. He looked about twenty-one and no different from every other scruffy university kid John had seen on the streets of Paris.

"Light?" the boy said casually. Around them the cameras had closed in and were whirring and clicking. The gendarmes had backed off a few feet and were cooling their heels, waiting to clobber the kid when the important American grew bored with him.

"Sure," said John. The boy produced a lighter and flicked it into flame. John suddenly had to remember that he was being filmed for television, and tried not to laugh. The cigarette lighter was a bright pink penis. When the boy stroked it a thin flame shot out the hole in its tip.

"You like it? Keep it." The young man saw John suppressing a smile and tossed the phallic lighter to him. "Take it home to LBJ and tell him he can fuck himself with it."

At the four-letter word the gendarmes grabbed the kid again. John held up his hand.

"*Attendez, attendez,* please," he said. Again the puzzled cops withdrew.

"Anything else?" John asked.

"Yeah. Tell Uncle Ho he can fuck himself too."

John was startled. "I thought Uncle Ho was your hero."

"Ideology is death," said the kid without hesitation. He turned to the television cameras and struck a theatrical pose. "And now, ladies and gentlemen, a terror-poem brought to you by the Commandos of Dada Death. Dada Death commands LBJ to purge space-time of all karmic diseases. When LBJ fucks himself with my megaton lighter, space-time implodes and spontaneity makes a daring escape. Space-time humps imagination and Taoist pleasure giggles at infinity. History meets itself on the curve of space and duality dies of fright. Surprised into unity, all things become One, and there is Dada every day, Dada every hour, Dada every minute — "

"Fucking space case," a reporter said to his cameraman. "Shut it off. We can't use this."

"Monsieur Devlin!" The French protocol people were waiting for him.

"Thanks for the light," said John, and walked on.

"Screw you, *cochon*," the boy shouted cheerfully, just before the gendarmes grabbed him.

All that day, as John sat through yet another futile session of American–Vietnamese bickering, he thought about his encounter with the lunatic kid. By the end of the day he was convinced he had found the sign. Whatever the species was evolving into, this young man was the first step. Not as an individual, of course, but the sign was hidden somewhere in his pseudosurrealist nonsense, like Ariadne's thread. Since John had been in Paris, ninety-nine percent of what he had heard from the barricades was the usual tired leftist cant about workers' councils and the dictatorship of the proletariat and the like, all of which had failed in Russia in 1917 and would fail again, and again and again . . . Today for the first time he had heard something different, gibberish though it was. He laughed to himself. *Dada every day . . .*

As he rode home that night John decided to find out who among the Parisian revolutionaries was talking this way. Whoever they were, chances were they were holding forth at the Sorbonne, occupied since mid-May by an army of student radicals. John decided to go fishing among the Sorbonne factions until he found the one he wanted. *Not an easy thing for an old* cochon *like me,* he thought, *but fortunately I have some very tempting bait.*

"Oh, God, Dad, do I *have* to?" Diana moaned during dinner. It was Monday, three days after John's encounter with the strange young man. John and Ruth's anniversary was Wednesday. On Friday David would return to Houston; Diana, the student, could stay another week or so if she liked. That night John had come home from the talks and announced to his daughter that an old French friend of his had had a splendid idea.

"Just have lunch with him, dear," he said. "For my sake, please. I really couldn't refuse his father. Since your mother and I have been here, Frédéric's been very kind to us."

"I know, but — "

"Besides, you might like Charles. The La Portes are a very interesting family — one of the oldest in France, I believe, and very distinguished. Frédéric was born a *comte,* although he doesn't use the title. A very unassuming, cultured man, which is probably why he's been so successful as a diplomat. He's not a bad historian, either. So his son — "

"Is probably some unbearable snotty French prig."

"Diana!" said Ruth.

"I'm sorry, Mother, but I really don't want to do this. I really don't. I've got only so much time to spend in Paris. There's a *revolution* going on here, in case you haven't noticed, and I want to see it happen, not spend my week smiling at some conceited jerk while he babbles about wines or some crap like that."

"I'm not sure you would," John said blandly. "From what Frédéric tells me, Charles is just your type. Very committed to social change. Did I tell you he's part of that business at the Sorbonne?"

"He is?"

"Yes. He's on the philosophy faculty there. I think Frédéric told me that his specialty is something modern, existentialism or something like that. Anyway, he's one of the younger people on the Sorbonne faculty — or he was, until the students took the place over. But when they did Charles decided to join them. His father tells me that he's very much in sympathy with their goals. Not that Frédéric is particularly happy about it."

"Are you sure about this?" Diana looked skeptical. "Those don't sound like the politics of anyone whose father has a title . . ."

"And where did you acquire *your* politics, my dear?" John asked pleasantly. "At Miss Porter's?"

"Look, Diana," Ruth broke in. "Whatever his politics are, Charles is the son of a friend. Frédéric is a very dear man who has thoughtfully arranged for you to spend a little of your vacation with someone your own age. It won't kill you to have lunch with him."

"Okay, okay," Diana muttered. "I'll have lunch with him once. *Once.*"

The next evening Charles La Porte telephoned the hotel, and Diana, trying to sound polite, accepted his invitation to lunch the following day. After she had gone to meet him Ruth dragged the protesting David out to buy him some decent clothes for the anniversary dinner. By the time they returned that evening and John arrived home from the talks, Diana had still not come back, and a letter from Steven was waiting.

"Well?" asked John. He had walked in to find Ruth reading and David peering over her shoulder.

"He's not coming," Ruth said. She scowled and handed the letter to John. "He's very sorry, of course, just the way he always is . . ."

John read. The letter was on the stationery of a hotel in Prague. Steven wrote that he had abruptly been sent to assist in negotiations between the Catholic Church in Czechoslovakia and the liberal Dubček government, whose "Prague Spring" had permitted Czech Catholicism to emerge from twenty years of underground existence. As was more and more the case with Steven's letters, the details were sketchy.

"Well, at least he wishes us all happiness," John said ruefully, handing the letter back to Ruth.

"Terrific," Ruth snapped. "What would make me happy is seeing my son, the Great Enigma, materialize in his empty chair tonight. Just *once* I wish he'd show up for something."

"Speaking of showing up," said John, consulting his wristwatch, "where do you think Diana is? We're due at the restaurant in an hour."

Behind John the front door burst open.

"Hi, everybody!" Diana breezed into the room. "Hope I'm not late. You will *never* guess what I've been doing!"

"Discussing wines?" asked Ruth.

"Are you kidding?" Diana laughed, missing the irony. "I was at the Sorbonne!"

"Is that right?" said John, looking pleased. "I gather, then, that the young La Porte's convictions resonate with your own?"

"*I'll* say." Diana beamed. "Charles is really together."

"Is he cute?" asked Ruth, smiling.

"I couldn't tell you, Mother," Diana said coldly. "I didn't really notice. We were discussing issues." She turned back to her father. "I really like him, Dad. He took me to the funkiest little place in the Latin Quarter, right in the middle of the barricades, and it was full of workers and, you know, *real* people, and we talked for hours . . . and then he showed me around the Sorbonne. You know, he's *really* together."

"You mentioned that already," said Ruth.

"Well, it's true," Diana shot back. "Charles may be a philosopher, but he's into action. He *worships* Sartre. He believes that even in an absurd world the individual can find meaning through action, as long as it's committed social action."

"Like what?" asked Ruth.

"Well, like . . . like what he's trying to do at the Sorbonne. While we were over there today he said it was time for him to teach his afternoon class, so I said, 'Okay, where's the classroom?' And he said, 'Wherever we are in this moment.' And then he just sat down, right there in the courtyard, and said to a couple of people who were standing nearby, 'I feel like talking about philosophy now. Can you join me?' And people really got into it! When Charles started talking, more and more people came over — some students, some workers who were on strike — and we sat and talked for about an hour, and some people asked questions. The workers asked some of the best questions, too. At least that's what Charles told me later. I couldn't follow a lot of the French . . . Anyway, as long as people felt like it they stayed, and when they didn't they left, and no big deal. It was really far out!"

"Hmph." Ruth frowned. "Sounds pretty flaky to me."

"Oh, Mother! You just don't understand — "

"Why does meaningful action have to be *social* action?"

It was David who asked. Diana broke off glaring at her mother and gave him a puzzled look.

"What other meaningful action is there?"

"Well," said David, "my work isn't 'social,' by your definition, but I consider it very meaningful."

"Oh, *your* work!" Diana tossed her flaming hair. "You're half-right, David. Your work does *not* benefit society, that's true."

"Sure it does, in the long run."

"I suppose you think that siphoning off millions of tax dollars for some useless trip into space is of some mysterious benefit to the poor, and everyone else whose dreams are a bit more mundane than yours?"

"I'm sick of hearing that kind of crap!" David exploded. If anything ever got the unworldly Devlin child angry, it was an attack on his raison d'être; and angry he now was. "There seems to be an epidemic of irrationality these days. My God, Diana, we're going to put a man on the moon! Can't you understand what that will mean for humanity?"

"Not much, except to a few fat-cat technocrats like you!"

"For Christ's sake, Diana, don't be ridiculous."

"Ridiculous?" Diana replied angrily. The actress in her owed much to a talent for tirade inherited from her mother. "Who's being ridiculous, David, me or you? Take your eyes off the stars and look at what's really going on around you! Go ask some black kid who can't get an education or a job because the system that supports you doesn't care how thrilled *he* is about your precious space program! Go tell his parents that their kid will just have to go on the streets and steal because you need all the money to put a white man on the moon! Go on, tell them! And then tell me *I'm* ridiculous!"

"Diana — "

"Oh, I know, they don't have to worry, right? Because all we have to do is land a man on the moon and poverty and racism will just disappear! Right?"

"Hold it!" Ruth placed herself between Diana and David. "I have two things to say. The first is that I married your father forty years ago today and I would like to remember something more pleasant about this occasion than a lot of internecine bickering. The second is that if you two don't stop this and get dressed now we'll never make our reservation."

In the next room the phone was ringing. John, who had been standing quietly listening to his children argue, got up to answer it.

"Probably the driver," Ruth said, "wondering where we are."

"Maybe it's Steven," Diana said as she headed off to her bedroom. An instant later the full impact of her elder brother's absence fully dawned on her. "You mean he never showed up?" she cried, turning at her door, "Why, that — "

Diana broke off as her father returned and she saw the look on his face.

"Dad, what is it? Was that Steven?"

John sat down, rather heavily. "No, dear, it wasn't. It was Frédéric La Porte."

"Oh yeah? Wanted to know how the big date went, huh?"

"No, it wasn't that," John said quietly, looking at her. "He wanted to know if we'd heard the news."

"What news?"

"Robert Kennedy has been shot."

The Devlins did arrive for their dinner on time, but the aniversary celebration was a subdued one. A triple pall hung over the celebration: Steven's empty seat, David and Diana's smoldering argument, and, above all, the terrible news from home. When they returned to the hotel John ordered newspapers and turned on the television, and everyone sat up in front of it well into the night, watching for bulletins from Los Angeles. When it was confirmed that Kennedy had died, John and Ruth and David said goodnight and went to bed. They left Diana slouched on the sofa, staring vacantly at the bright TV screen.

The next morning she was gone. John and Ruth found a note on her pillow:

Dear Mother and Dad:
I'm sorry to sneak away in the night like this but I think it's best that I do. Otherwise we might have a fight and there's really no point in that. I've gone back to the Sorbonne. Please don't worry. I'll be with Charles La Porte, and he's not as big a flake as you think.

After last night, nothing makes sense except revolt. Look what happens to people who try to play by the system's rules.

Diana

"What should we do?" said John.

"What do you mean, what should we do?" Ruth cried. "I'll tell you what we're going to do — we're going right over there and bring her back!"

"Why, Mother?" David asked in surprise. "She's an adult, she can do as she likes."

"David," said Ruth, "if you'd been here for a month, as I have, you'd know what a dangerous place the Sorbonne is. Every night those kids go out and get their heads cracked open by the police."

"But if she believes — "

"Pfft! She *believes!* She's just miffed because I didn't like her new boyfriend." Ruth's voice was scornful, but her eyes were welling up with tears. "And that's nothing to get hurt for." She turned fiercely away from David, eyes blinking, hunting for a tissue. "Poor Bobby's is enough death for one week."

John had been facing away from Ruth and David, staring out the window of Diana's bedroom, listening. Ruth was absolutely right. If Diana went out on those barricades, she stood an excellent chance of being hurt, or worse. Besides, the Sorbonne rebels' days were numbered. In the past two weeks De Gaulle had worked a miracle and snatched victory from almost certain defeat, getting the French people back on his side. The revolution was finished. Probably it had only days to live. If he was right about that, he could take the chance . . .

"You know what I think?" he said, suddenly turning to Ruth. "I think David's right. Diana's an adult. She's too old to be rescued; like the rest of us, she now has the privilege and peril of making her own decisions. I don't think we should interfere."

Ruth stared at him in disbelief as he walked past her and out of Diana's room, carrying the note. After forty years John certainly knew his wife well enough to know that the matter was very far from settled, but he thought he could prevail, or at least stall until the revolution failed and Diana brought herself home. What was important was that she be there as long as she could . . .

In the other room, where his family could not see him, he permitted himself a smile. He had lowered the bait. Or rather, the bait had been lowered. He had only made a small arrangement; the rest of the credit belonged to . . . John dropped Diana's note on top of the newspapers whose headlines announced Robert Kennedy's death. It was a simple case of cause and effect. Another hero lifted to heaven at exactly the right time. Still smiling, John contemplated the note and the newspapers and sent a silent thought into the deepest depth of himself and to the outermost galactic star: *Thank you.*

Diana was gone for ten days. John just managed to forestall Ruth from going to her rescue, but only just. At night the sirens of the gendarmes' paddy wagons wailed in the streets and Ruth couldn't sleep. John convinced her to wait until they had talked everything over with Frédéric La Porte, who told Ruth that his son was an intellectual, not a street fighter, and that as long as Diana was with him her presence at the barricades was doubtful. This reassurance bought John time, but the day after David departed for Houston Ruth heard a report that a high-school student had been killed in a demonstration outside Paris. It took a reassurance from Diana herself, who fortuitously telephoned to say she was all right just as her mother was leaving the hotel for the Sorbonne, to keep John's plan intact.

A week later Diana called again, this time from a police station. Charles La Porte was with her. The gendarmes had swept in and cleared the Sorbonne. Could John and Frédéric please come bail them out?

It took the combined diplomatic skills of the two fathers plus a great deal of string-pulling on Frédéric's part to secure the release of their children from the clutches of the gendarmes, who were not in the least inclined to be merciful to rock-throwing radicals. At the station John got his first look at Charles La Porte, who was a very handsome young man with longish dark hair and a turtleneck. No one said much. Diana and Charles were both nursing some nasty welts acquired from police batons during the final moments of the occupation, and they wanted to go home. When Diana got into her father's limousine she fell asleep almost immediately. At the hotel John helped her upstairs, where she slept for another ten hours.

"When you walked into the occupied Sorbonne," she said later, as she sat over some breakfast, "the first thing you thought was wow, what a fantastic place!! It was like some kind of far-out festival. The courtyards were covered with slogans and *amazing* posters, and there were flags flying and music playing everywhere, and people making speeches and having meetings . . . There was so much energy, and it all seemed so terrific."

"But it wasn't?" John asked sympathetically.

Diana stared down at her breakfast, thoughtfully rubbing her left arm, which sported a very large and particularly nasty welt.

"No, it wasn't," she replied. "After you'd been there a day or two you began to see beyond the posters and the music. You went to the open meetings to see some direct democracy in action, and instead you spent hours listening to rival factions denouncing each other. You started noticing other things too, like all the garbage just lying around everywhere, and the filthy bathrooms, and eventually you came to see that all the energy there was an energy of chaos. There was no form to it, no direction; it was just . . . energy. Very violent energy. A lot of the people I met weren't students or workers, they were just thugs using the Sorbonne as a refuge from the police. They terrorized everyone . . . Finally there was a big fight in the courtyards and the students threw the thugs out. By that time I had just about had it. It wasn't a revolution, it was a free-for-all."

"Poor dear," said Ruth. "Why didn't you come home sooner?"

Diana looked sheepish. "I guess I was too proud for that." She put her hand over her mother's hand and patted it. "I'm sorry if you were worried."

"Worried? You think I was *worried?*" Diana's safe return had brought out the old Ruth. "Why would I worry? In the middle of the night my daughter sneaks out to take part in an insurrection. Why should I worry?"

"And Charles La Porte was a disappointment too, I gather?" asked John.

At the question Diana brightened up. "Oh no, Dad, not at all. Charles was the only one I knew at the Sorbonne who was *doing* anything. While everyone else was screaming abuse at each other he was writing proposals to the government on how to reform the university system. Some of his ideas are really good."

"Let me guess," said Ruth. "First of all, nobody has to show up for class unless he really, really wants to . . ."

"Oh, Mother, no." Diana laughed. "Charles's proposals are more realistic than *that.* And the government seems to be taking them pretty seriously. That's why Charles still thinks the occupation was a success. He says that in one month he learned a lifetime's worth of lessons in what works and what doesn't. He sees now that after the old academic rigidity it was necessary to have an explosion of pure spontaneity before real change could occur."

"Well, dear," John said, "I'm glad you'll at least have a pleasant memory of him to take back to America with you. You're a bit overdue, you know. This came a few days ago from Baltimore." John picked a yellow envelope off a nearby table and handed it across the breakfast table to Diana. "I hope you don't mind — since you weren't here I took the liberty of opening it. Your adviser is wondering where you are. Of course your mother and I hate to see you go, but you shouldn't get yourself in trouble . . ."

Diana was studying the telegram rather longer than was necessary to absorb its contents. "Well, you know, Dad," she said finally, "I was thinking . . . They don't really need me back at the lab for another couple of weeks. If you and Mom don't mind me hanging around, I thought I'd see a little more of, ah, Paris . . ."

"We'd *love* to have you stay!" cried Ruth.

"Whatever you wish, my dear," said John, beaming.

A year later, after an impassioned transatlantic affair, Charles and Diana were married in Paris. The groom's father gave the reception at his country château, where John, ferrying champagne in both hands, wandered through labyrinths of shrubbery and past tables of guests who raised their glasses to his happiness. He felt very pleased with himself — not because his daughter was getting married, though of course her happiness did please him, but because of something else, something that made him hum a little as he threaded his way across the guest-covered lawn. What pleased him most today was the man with the goldfish.

John had noticed him first at the church, dressed respectably and sitting quietly in one of the rear pews, solemnly cradling in his lap a round vessel containing a single enormous, goggle-eyed goldfish. Thereafter John had found it hard to pay attention to his daughter's wedding and not look back at the mysterious ichthyophile in the rear of the church. He had wondered how many of the guests were also thinking about him, a question made irrelevant early on at the reception, when the bearer of the goldfish had suddenly drawn everyone's attention to himself.

Climbing atop a chair and balancing his companion in its bowl expertly atop his head, he had harangued the startled guests for a full minute. The exact content of his speech had eluded everyone present — at least the whole of it had, although people had caught certain parts of it, depending on how many languages they knew. In a one-minute speech the goldfish man had switched with lightning speed and theatrical fervor, almost word-to-word at times, from French to English to German to Italian and back again, like a Berlitz instructor gone mad at Pentecost. Then, amid the astonished mutterings of the older guests and the scattered applause of the younger ones, he had jumped down from his chair, caught the plummeting goldfish bowl neatly in his arms, presented it in solemn silence to the giggling bride, and vanished.

That had been five minutes ago; around the tables people were still speculating on who he was. As John brought champagne across the lawn to the bride and groom, he was thinking that he knew. He had pieced together enough of the harangue to guess that whoever he was, the goldfish man must be a friend of the boy with the phallic lighter and the message for LBJ.

"Here we are." John extended the champagne to Diana and Charles.

"Thank you, sir," said Charles. "Please, I'm sorry about the —"

"The goldfish man?" said John.

Diana giggled again. At her insistence the fish had been given a place of honor at her table, where it now swam around and around in its bowl, its goggling eyes ogling the bouquets.

John held up a reassuring hand to Charles. "Not at all. Very interesting fellow. A friend of yours?"

"Well, yes." Charles grinned at Diana. "He belongs to something called the Dada Commandos. We got to know them at the Sorbonne."

"It was hard not to get to know them." Diana chuckled. "Even at the Sorbonne they stood out."

"I'm sure they did," John said. He had never told his family about his own encounter with a Dada Commando. "May I ask you two experts for an interpretation of Dada Commando behavior?"

"The Dada Commandos," said Charles, "are perhaps the oddest subspecies of our generation."

"I'll say," Diana chimed in. "They're so far out it's unbelievable."

"And they have respectable revolutionary ideals?" asked John with a grin.

The newlyweds looked at each other and smiled.

"The Dada Commandos," Charles said, "are devoted to the destruction of all ideals. I believe their devotion encompasses revolutionary ideals as well as conservative ones."

"True," said Diana. "They want to destroy *everything*. One of them once explained to me that since Hiroshima, reality is just a joke. You know, the world is such a tragedy that it's finally flipped over into comedy."

"But a comedy without meaning," Charles said, "resembling most of all a bad slapstick, a silly farce. So they prefer to — to — what is the phrase?" He turned to Diana.

"Call a . . ." Diana prompted.

"Ah, right! I know, call a shovel a shovel. They want to behave in a way consistent with present reality; that is, they want to behave insanely. This is why they act and speak outside the common social and linguistic structure."

"That's putting it mildly," John said with a chuckle.

"What? Oh, yes, to put it mild." Since meeting Diana, Charles had been working hard on his English idioms. "What they are saying is that all of those things, those fundamental structures, are no longer true, and we should stop dreaming that they are and acknowledge the reality of our present chaos by living chaotically. Supposedly, they have an earnest hope that someday everyone will join them. But it's hard to tell how serious they are, since they are never serious. As of now it all comes down simply to this, with them: the world is a joke, so always be joking."

"Indeed!" said John. "That doesn't sound like anything you two would have much sympathy with."

"Well, I don't know." Charles looked suddenly glum. He took a gulp of champagne. "At least they *do* something, even something silly." John saw Diana give Charles a pained look. His own political inaction since the Sorbonne uprising was apparently troubling him.

"But Charles, I mean, some of them are just a little too weird," Diana said. "You know, like . . . what was that old guy's name?"

"Oh! You mean the one everybody called Doctor Einstoned?" Charles laughed.

"Einstoned?" John asked incredulously.

"Yes," Charles said, still chuckling. "One in a million he was, that one."

"Oh, Dad, you would *die* if you met this guy." Diana giggled. "How he got to the Sorbonne I could never figure out. He certainly wasn't a student — I mean, he was your age, Dad. And he wasn't a professor. He wasn't even French."

"No? What was he?"

"An American. Somewhere along the line he had really tripped
out. He was a great big guy with absolutely not one hair anywhere
on his head except behind the ears, where he had these two . . .
like *tufts,* that were all white, and he had let them grow long
and they stuck out like . . . like two shots of steam, you know?"
Diana had to stop to give in to a wave of helpless laughing. She
put her hands up to her ears and pointed them outward to illustrate
her point. Charles and John burst out laughing too.

"You used to see him whipping around the Sorbonne courtyards
with his Dada Commando disciples at his heels, talking a mile a
minute, and it looked like his head was about to explode." Diana
tried to go on, but the memory had reduced her to quivering
mirth.

"You know," Charles continued as best he could, "his head
did actually explode one day, in a way. The things that came
out of it were beyond anything any of us — all of us who considered
ourselves intellectuals — had ever heard."

"Such as?" John asked.

"Well, such as — what we all heard a few minutes ago. The
goldfish man. The most incredible mélange of science East and
West, philosophy East and West, religion East and West, and
history East, West, North, South . . . The man knew *everything.*
Everything and more, I sometimes thought. Because he didn't
lecture to people about what was known — he took everything
known and whirled it into some fantastic system of his own, one
that ignored logic and yet seemed completely convincing, as though
logic were some obstacle it had righteously overwhelmed. And
always it came to the same conclusion: if you are alive, if you
know the Truth, you are completely outside the world. You inhabit
a separate reality that is absolute, and therefore you have absolute
freedom in what the unenlightened masses call the world, because
for you that world is not real. You have the same freedom that
someone has in a dream, when he dreams. No laws apply to you,
legal, moral, or physical."

"I can see why your Dada Commando friends found him inspirational," John remarked.

"The Germans especially adored him," Charles said. "Because,
I suppose, being Germans, they couldn't help but admire anyone
who had made a metaphysical system out of sheer anarchy."

"But there were other reasons too," Diana broke in, having finally regained her power of speech. "Einstoned was practically a German himself. He spoke the language flawlessly, and someone told me that he had been a student at some German university."

"Perhaps he *was* a German," John suggested.

"No, I'm sure he was an American. You could tell from the way he spoke English. But beyond that it was hard to know what he was, there were so many rumors about him. Ten different people would tell you ten different things, and each would swear only he knew the truth."

"Right," said Charles. "One day I was told he was an ex-priest. The next day I heard he was ex-CIA. I also heard a long story about his days in China in the forties as one of Mao's inner circle, and another one that he had once been a very famous American physicist, a real genius, who had finally become — you know . . ." Charles spun his index finger around his ear.

"Crazy," Diana said.

"Yes, crazy. I guess that's how he got his name."

"What was his real name?" John broke in.

"I never knew," Diana said. "Did you?" she asked Charles.

Charles shook his head. "I don't think that anybody knew."

"Where is he now?" asked John.

Charles shrugged. "I don't know that either. Just before the police came, he disappeared."

"Anyway," said Diana, "whoever he was, it's certain that he was a hero to the Dada Commandos. Most of their antics and their philosophy, if you can call it that, were inspired by him — "

"Excuse me, daughter." Frédéric La Porte came up to Diana and kissed her cheek. "I am stealing your father for a moment."

"Of course, Papa." Diana rose on tiptoes to kiss him back. Until she had met her future father-in-law, the campus radical had pictured him in the only way she could imagine a French aristocrat, as a character from *A Tale of Two Cities:* a nasty man with a powdered wig and a beauty mark, laughing as his speeding coach ran down peasants' children. But at their first introduction Frédéric, who was tall and silver-haired and possessed neither wig nor beauty mark, had dissolved the caricature with his charm and won an instantaneous victory over Diana's political convictions.

"Remember, you promised me a walk," he said to John.

"Ah! I certainly did. I see you've brought me champagne." John accepted a glass from Frédéric's hand. "How can I refuse?"

Frédéric and John strolled back across the crowded lawn, accepting kisses, handshakes, and toasts as they headed for the quiet of the shrubbery beyond.

"I'm sorry that David couldn't come," Frédéric said as they entered the labyrinth.

"Oh, so am I," John replied, "and so is he. He's not really the cold-hearted scientist he appears. Unfortunately, Diana and Charles chose to get married at the very moment that ten years of his work were coming to fruition."

"Of course I understand."

They walked in silence for a moment. Carefully, leaning forward, they sipped champagne. A painful topic hung in the air between them.

"And Steven — ?" Frédéric said finally.

"Still no word." John looked at the path, not at his friend.

"I'm sorry." Frédéric stopped. "Nothing at all?"

"A few weeks ago some friends of mine in Moscow finally found out what happened," John said. "He was picked up on the street in Prague last August, five days after the Soviets invaded. The KGB hustled him into a car and drove him away. That's all. He has simply disappeared, and no one will tell me or my Russian contacts where he is. But they don't have to."

"You think he's in the camps?"

"Where else would he be?" John said bitterly. "Unless he's . . ." He turned away and started walking again.

"Ah . . . such a pity." Frédéric shook his head and followed John. "It's not right for them to treat a diplomat that way. Especially a papal one. What would a Vatican monsignor have been doing in Prague to invite their horrors?"

John turned to his friend with a wan smile. "Well, quite a bit, apparently. I also have some contacts in the CIA. As you can imagine, they were monitoring the Prague situation pretty carefully in the spring of sixty-eight. They think that the KGB had been tracking Steven for some time, at least since he first arrived in Prague."

"But why?"

"My CIA friends tell me he was going rather far beyond his

official Vatican duties there. They have some pretty compelling evidence that he was organizing underground resistance cells among the Czech clergy."

"Resistance against Dubček?"

"To the people Steven was working with, a Communist is a Communist, no matter how liberal he is. The Czech clergy have had it pretty rough under communism." John shook his head. "My CIA friends claim that there are people in the Vatican curia who could have ordered his actions, but that seems very farfetched to me. Frankly, I've begun to wonder if my son doesn't have some CIA connections of his own. At least that would finally give me a rational explanation for this vocation of his. Of course, it could also have been entirely Steven's idea. Knowing him, I suspect that his drive for a cardinal's hat might have affected his reason. But now . . ."

There was nothing more to say, except to draw the conclusion John dreaded.

"I'm sorry," Frédéric said again.

The two friends walked in silence for a while, listening to the chatter of the lawn fade into the music of fountains in the labyrinth. Frédéric sighed.

"It's odd," he said. "You know, just now I was thinking of these children of ours, and of their generation. Do you know the legend of the Holy Grail?"

"Of course," said John, and quoted: " 'That which heart of mortal man cannot conceive, nor tongue relate.' "

"Precisely. The Grail, the mystical vessel, undefinable symbol of the Ultimate Mystery, the grace of God. Out from Arthur's court rode his knights of the Round Table, Lancelot and Percival and Galahad — the flower of chivalry — to find the Grail and bestow God's grace upon a fallen world."

"Right." John smiled. "Rushing forth in full armor and full ardor, flinging themselves into the splendid quest to end all quests —"

" — and failing, because they confused human prowess with spiritual strength."

John saw the point. "Steven and Diana and Charles. Now another generation of ardent youth seeks the breath of grace for an exhausted world."

"Just what I was thinking. This generation of our children, does it not remind you of the generation of the Grail? Charging out to vanquish evil and pave the way for a splendid new world . . . and stumbling over the sad old truths of human existence. Curious that it should happen again, just now."

John studied the bubbles in his champagne. "Perhaps the world is getting ready to evolve."

Frédéric chuckled. "Evolve? Good Lord! You of all people are not a Marxist determinist, are you, Devlin?"

John grinned. "No, not a Marxist, just someone who believes in evolution . . ."

Frédéric looked at him. "Well, *that* I had not thought of." He reflected a moment. "It's possible. When the Grail legend arose we were just breaking up our medieval world and moving into the Renaissance. That was evolution, but it wasn't obvious for another three centuries." Frédéric thought for a moment more. "Of course, there is one difference. In the medieval world a Galahad, a man of perfect spiritual purity, was possible. Only Galahad was pure enough not to confuse a quest for things of the Spirit with earthly conquest and adventure."

"And therefore only Galahad was granted a full vision of the Grail." John sipped his champagne. "You don't think our new generation can find a Galahad?"

Frédéric frowned. "I don't think so," he said. "Everyone these days looks for the Grail in politics, where, according to all the legends, it most certainly is not. So perhaps this time we shall have no Galahad who can bring us to grace." Frédéric's frown became an ironic smile. "What do you think, eh?"

John shrugged and smiled and drank his champagne. *My dear, wise old friend,* he thought, *I suspect that you are wrong.*

A month later John knew that Frédéric was wrong. After their American honeymoon Diana and Charles joined Ruth and John, but not in New Bedford. They met in Houston, at David's invitation, to see the United States land a man on the moon.

The family stood behind David at Mission Control and watched as the monitors showed the dust of the moon coming closer and closer and closer, until it suddenly stopped. *The eagle has landed.* Cheers erupted around them. A dozen grown men threw off their headsets and rushed to pound David on the back. John saw that even Diana was staring at the monitors in unabashed awe. *Here's your new Galahad,* he thought, looking at David. *The rest of you rushed madly about setting fire to the world, and he kept to his own vision, the vision of an unearthly mystery. Now he has given you the Grail. He has changed our destiny forever. Who among you can say as much?*

John saw tears forming in Ruth's eyes and knew that she cried not for the mystery but for the child who was not there, her favorite child, her charming, clever Steven, who had tripped himself up and fallen into hell and would never come back again. John moved to her side and put his arm around her and cried with her for the son they had lost. A voice came to them from the moon. *One small step indeed,* thought John. *Humanity leaves the earth. We shall gaze back in wonder at ourselves, at our tiny planet floating through infinity, and Spirit will awake in us again.*

He looked fondly at his younger son, who disappeared and soon reappeared with a case of champagne. *You have given us a mystery. You have wrought a revelation in our fallen souls, and we are ready to evolve. And you gave us your mystery because years ago I sent you to a madman in the desert, and walked on the freezing beach to put a thought of my own into poor murdered Kennedy's mind. I did that because . . .* John thought of what he knew, of the secret certitude that, unknown to anyone, guided his life. Eight years ago he had planted a seed, and now it had blossomed; in the meantime he had watched and waited amid a dying world to see how next to serve. Now there were others serving too, although they didn't know it. David was one, and Diana, and perhaps someday Charles might play a part. And poor Steven too, if only he hadn't . . . John fought down his emotions and kept thinking. There were others as well. Thanks to Diana's adventure at the Sorbonne, he was sure of it. *Doctor Einstoned indeed.* As the champagne corks popped all around him in Mission Control, he turned his thoughts again to the man with the goldfish.

II

Lazarus

IT WAS A VERY QUIET STREET in a rather poor part of Paris, quieter still because dawn had not yet come. The people who lived along the street were asleep in their mammoth new apartment buildings, whose sheer concrete faces were interchangeable with others in any city of the world. This was not the face of old Paris, the Paris of the romantic past; it was the face of a different Paris, the Paris of 1985.

The people in the buildings slept, dreaming of their drab jobs and of escaping them, dreaming of husbands and wives and of others whom wives and husbands did not know, dreaming of things too dark, or too bright, to comprehend. The mutter of engines on the street below was so faint that it woke no one. No one saw the three cars creep to the curb beneath them. No one heard the oiled doors noiselessly open. No one heard the men get out. No one heard them take their places around the front doors of a huge apartment building. No one heard them speak, for none of them spoke. No one heard them check their weapons.

One of the men, indistinguishable from the rest in his down jacket and running shoes, jabbed his finger in a circle through the sharp October air, counting heads. When he was satisfied that everyone was in place he looked upward for a moment at the cliff face melting into darkness above him. One hundred and fifty apartments made up that face, but only one interested him. For a year and a half he had been looking for it. Three days ago he had found it.

His eyes fell to the front door. "Let's go," he whispered.

Six men followed him; the rest stayed where they were. The door was locked, but the man who had whispered, the leader, had a key. They came silently into the building and moved without noise along the featureless corridors of the ground floor, reading by the dim night-lights the numbers assigned like codes in an experiment to the anonymous black doors: A-115, A-116, A-117 . . . The leader wanted A-121. He found it. The six men following him formed an arc on his right. They leveled six automatic weapons at the door.

On the other side of the door, inside A-121, six other people were sleeping, their dreams perhaps like their neighbors' dreams, perhaps not. One of these people was a young woman in her twenties, who slept by herself in a small bedroom off a hall. The rest were men, none of them older than thirty-five, three of whom slept in the larger bedroom at the hallway's end and three in sleeping bags on the living-room floor. All of them were young, but they were hardly innocent. They were terrorists. Several of them had been terrorists for five years or more. For five years or more the men in the corridor outside had hunted them in a dozen cities. Until this moment they had always escaped.

Slowly, almost reverently, the leader in the hallway nodded his head. Six automatic weapons opened fire on the door of A-121 and splintered it. The leader crashed shoulder first through the wreckage and raced into the living room, then dropped low and pivoted left, hunting for the wall switch. Two days ago he had come to the building on the pretense of apartment-hunting and had learned every detail of the standard layout. From the doorway six machine guns poured fire into the living room. The leader found the wall switch and flicked it on. In the burst of light he saw three long forms, black and sectional like caterpillars, pink faces poking out of them. Two of them were dead men's faces, eyes and mouths frozen open in a last look of shock. The third caterpillar was still alive, despite a row of bleeding holes in him. His hand groped toward a pistol on a coffee table. The leader stood up and shot him in the face.

The police commandos were inside the apartment now, racing down the hallway, shooting the locks off the bedroom doors. There were shouts at the end of the hallway, and the leader ran toward them. Three of his men had stormed the large bedroom, but the shooting in the living room and the locked door had given the three men inside time to open a window and escape. The girl in the smaller bedroom had not been as fast. The leader found his men in a standoff with the girl, their weapons trained on her from the doorway. She had just had time to grab her pistol before the commandos burst in. Now she sat up in her bed, pistol in hand, and stared sullenly at the men in the doorway.

"Don't shoot," said the leader. He had a list of questions and he needed someone to give him the answers. "Let me through."

The men stood aside and the leader walked into the room. He stood over the girl on the bed. She was very young, he thought, probably not yet twenty-five. She did not look at him.

"It's finished," he said. She stared past him. He held out his hand for her gun.

She raised the pistol, and now too she raised her eyes to his, but her stare did not change. It was emotionless, blank, as if her eyes were already dead. The commando leader kept his hand out, patiently waiting for the pistol. But she did not give it to him. She brought the barrel to her temple. The shocked commando grabbed for her arm, but not fast enough. Even now the girl's dead eyes showed nothing. She pulled the trigger.

"Jesus!" The leader grimaced. Blood sprayed over his outstretched hand. "Shit, shit, *shit*. Damn, damn, *damn*. Somebody get me a towel or something."

One of the men disappeared into the bathroom. The commandos who had stormed the larger bedroom were consoling themselves for their lost quarry by ransacking the apartment for information. One of them ran to the doorway just as the man returned from the bathroom with a towel.

"Look at this," he said. He held a piece of paper up to his chief, who wiped his bloody hand and took the paper. The man who had brought it saw the girl lying on the bed with the gun in her hand and half of her head blown off. "Jesus Christ," he muttered.

"Here it is again," said the leader. He studied the paper, which had three telephone numbers written on it. Above one was written *Rome,* above another *Tokyo,* and above the third *Istanbul.* At the top of the page was something none of these veteran terrorist-hunters could explain: a drawing of a winged man under a blazing sun. And underneath it a single word: *Icarus.*

The leader shook his head. "We'll run the phone numbers," he said, and handed the paper back to the man who had found it.

"Why bother?" the man said. "They'll be dead ends, as always."

"Just do it," said the chief wearily. He sighed deeply as the man shrugged and pocketed the paper, then looked at the dead girl on the bed. *She* could have told him. She had killed herself without an instant's hesitation, rather than tell him. For ten years he had been ambushing terrorists all over Europe, and suddenly, in the past year, he had begun to find on so many of the younger ones this winged man, this blazing sun . . . It was not the first time one of them had killed himself rather than explain it to him. There was a new strain of terrorist in the world these days, one as indifferent to its own life as to the life of others. Was it Icarus, the winged man, who inspired this? Was he their leader? Who was he? The leader slumped against the doorway and folded his arms over his chest. In ten years he had never failed to crack the cover of his prey; sooner or later, someone had always talked. Now, for the first time, he was failing. No one was talking. They were all choosing death instead.

The dead girl's blood soaked the white sheets of her bed and now dripped from the mattress onto the floor. The commando leader leaned his head against the doorframe and shut his eyes. *Icarus.*

"Shit, shit, *shit,*" he whispered. "Damn, damn, *damn.*"

A few hours later, at dawn on the other side of the Atlantic, John Devlin awoke in his New Bedford home. The early light had awakened him; from his bed he looked out the window and saw that the day would be pale-bright but cold and blustery. This year winter was early. John looked to his right, at Ruth's bed, and saw that she was still sound asleep. As quietly as he could he climbed out of bed and dressed, pulling on a thick sweater over his heavy shirt. Last April had been his eightieth birthday, and if it was cold he felt it.

When he had dressed he slipped out of the house and struck out into the chilly wind, heading for the beach. Whatever the weather, a walk had been his morning's ritual for the past week, as it was whenever he had something very important to decide.

Half an hour later the beach in front of the Devlin house was lined with parallel sets of footprints. One set broke abruptly away from the rest and headed back toward the house. Behind the house, at the ancient oak in the garden, the Tree of his childhood, John Devlin had ended his walk. He leaned against the gnarled tree-flesh, old before he had been born, and felt his eighty years to be an infancy in comparison. That was why he had come to the Tree morning after morning for a week, breaking off walks that had begun on the beach. The Tree was hundreds of years old. When he had been a boy, so very long ago, he had lain in its oaken arms and its rustling leaves had whispered to him . . . and then he had run to Grandfather, and Grandfather had told him everything it said. Inside him nothing had changed in eighty years; he was back in the garden, a solitary, reverent listener, waiting for the ancient Tree to speak. He needed so much to hear . . .

At his feet oak leaves swirled in the wind. Fallen leaves, autumn leaves, russet and brown. John studied the random movements of their dance. *The leaves are mocking me.* He was a man; he saw with his eyes. His eyes could not detect the pattern hidden in the dance of leaves; the senses saw crudely, saw only the random surface of things. To his brain they told the lie of chance, which the Mind in him, the god, knew to be merely the veil, the illusory barrier that divided his sense-imprisoned brain from infinity. For a week he had been standing at the Tree, watching the dance of leaves, listening, waiting, trying to rend the veil. There was something he needed to know. He needed so very badly to see once more what the Tree had hinted at, what had nearly killed him in 1945, after the bomb.

With a sudden movement he trapped a dancing leaf. There was something he had to know. He held the leaf against the sun, and like a ghostly X-ray the intricacies of its ribs and veins became visible. The pattern in the leaf. Seventy years ago, on this very spot, Grandfather had rent the veil and had come back from death to show him the pattern in the leaf, microcosm of macrocosm, miniature of infinity. The revelation. It had come again after the bomb, and nearly killed him. All things interconnected, beyond what the senses could perceive; a shaman's vision of what is and was and shall be. Could he have the vision again? He stared at the leaf. Not today. Today a leaf was only a leaf, an autumn color to be perceived, a crackly parchment to be crumpled in the hand. John crumpled it and threw it away. He *had* to see again, one more time, beyond the veil.

There was something that he had to do, and there was not much time in which to do it. He was eighty now; soon his time would run out. If he didn't do what needed to be done, who would? *I chose others before. Now I have chosen you. Will you serve?* "I shall serve," he had said, and serve he had, for forty years. He had done his best to prepare the species, to lay the groundwork for what must happen. For the test. Because he was an old man and his body would soon die, it was time to do what he had to do. *I have chosen you.* It was time to put humanity to the test, and he could not. For forty years he had known the moment would come; now that it was finally here, he was afraid.

The pale sun shed its weak warmth; the whirling leaves danced. Whatever god was in him, whatever else he had heard and seen and been at this spot, today he was nothing but a doubting man. *How dare you?* The whole idea was preposterous. Put the species to a test — preposterous and, worse, insane. For one awful moment he saw the past forty years as a delirium. He was no shaman, whatever Jungian mind-games Matthew Engels had played with him — just a garden-variety lunatic. *I have chosen you.* What nonsense, what sheer hubris! The fervid imaginings of an unstable mind. He had been unstable since boyhood, he knew it. By sheer will he had hidden it from the world. Looking back, he could see how wrong he had been. All of his strange life he had been plagued by megalomaniacal fantasies and the tawdry spooks of a Catholic upbringing, old monks and the like, and in his silliness he had dignified these as revelations and believed in them. Even what had happened in 1945 had been . . . a *breakdown*. A severe one, but only a breakdown, a wholly internal affair . . . Well, the important thing was that now he would stop. At the last moment he would yank himself back from the precipice he had been rushing toward in delirium for forty years. He would not make another mistake, the worst mistake he could make, and inflict his mad hubris on the world.

John left the Tree and started toward the house. He walked six steps and stopped. *No.* It was not as simple as that. It couldn't be. He wasn't mad, he was afraid. He couldn't bear the responsibility of what was to come. *You are an insider, not an outsider. A Jonah with connections. The voice that spoke in Jesus speaks in you.* Engels had said all that. *Well then,* John thought bitterly, *if I speak with Jesus' voice, I shall speak as Jesus spoke: Let this cup pass from me.* He was *not* Jesus of Nazareth; that was the worst hubris of all. Jesus of Nazareth had been God; he was a man. Responsibility for testing humanity was God's, not any man's.

But as soon as he tried to cling to this thought, the fundamental tenet of his pious Catholic youth, the words of his revelation rose up and haunted him. *He shall live as his hero, Jesus, lived, bowed with the burden of a god set free . . .* That, he knew, was the truth of it, the lifelong curse of it. The man John Devlin feared what the god in him would do. The man John Devlin felt the horror of it; the god felt nothing. The man Devlin alone could not act beyond his human limits; the god alone would have no limits. It was an agony to be both. In an inspired instant John thought of ending it all — not suicide, exactly, only a choice between alternatives. He could give the god full play again, have another revelation — for one instant see everything, and then die. Or he could make the other choice, be consumed and be done with the whole damned business. Let the god go his way and do his work. John had served enough.

"John!" Ruth was standing at the back door in her robe and slippers. "It's cold. Come in, I've made breakfast."

He could see the worry on her face. Seven mornings in a row she had found him outside. He had to decide, and to quit acting like this. He had put her through too much already, in the past forty years.

But are they ready? he found himself thinking as he came in to eat. In spite of everything he had decided, the conviction persisted: it was time for the test. He had made his preparations; he hoped they were ready. *But how dare you?* Again his debate began. Again the man quailed before the god . . .

His indecision prolonged itself into the afternoon, while he made a show of working on what every retired statesman was expected to inflict upon the world — his memoirs. Just after lunch the telephone rang. It was the President, calling from Washington. Would John temporarily come out of retirement to serve as a special presidential envoy? Someone was needed to talk to the Japanese. As he knew, the previous administration had encouraged Japanese rearmament, so Japan had rearmed itself, continued its dazzling economic growth, and grown more powerful each year. Now the South Koreans were becoming nervous. The Indonesians were becoming nervous. Even the Australians were becoming nervous. The President wanted to send someone to Tokyo, someone with John's knowledge of Japan and his sixth sense about foreign affairs in general, to assess the situation. Did other Asian countries have reason to worry or not? Should America change its Japanese policy? And so on.

As John listened, he tried to think of a tactful way to say no; the squabbles of nations no longer interested him. But as the refusal formed on his tongue, a sudden thought struck him so forcefully that he cut right into the President's sales pitch to say that yes, he would go to Japan. The President sounded a bit startled but thanked him and asked him to come down to Washington as soon as he could to discuss the trip.

After the President had hung up, John told Ruth that he was going to Japan. He then went back to his memoirs. When he had closed the door of his study behind him he gave a long sigh of relief. He would take no more cold morning walks; now he knew how to resolve his problem. He would go to Japan. He would speak one last time with Yuzawa.

A month later he was in Tokyo. In 1946 Nagasaki had been an empty horror; in 1985 Tokyo was a frantic one. John toured incredibly efficient factories and sipped whisky at government-industry receptions. He had "frank discussions," which were anything but that, facing smiling human masks across tables. He heard speeches, made speeches, clapped, laughed, stood up, sat down, shook hands, bowed. Robots hummed, cars flew off assembly lines. The miracle of Japan: an American dream bought at gunpoint by the Occupation and sent back cheaper and better. He longed to be through with it and go to Yuzawa.

In a week his talks were concluded and he was free. As fast as he could he fled to Kyoto, away from robots and speeches and into a jumble of six hundred temples and the exquisite emptiness of sand gardens. It had not been hard to trace Yuzawa. John had been mildly astonished to discover how many foreign ministry officials and Tokyo executives had heard of him. Since the day Yuzawa had sat with John in the rubble of Nagasaki, the monk had risen to become senior abbot at the foremost of Japan's Buddhist temples.

Following the advice of his friends in Tokyo, John avoided the main gate, where the tourist buses stopped, and slipped into the temple compound through a quiet side gate. He walked up an ancient stone pathway between vibrant pines and the fiery leaves of November maples. His inquiries of passing monks led him along other stone pathways, under the graceful curves of Chinese gates, past serene expanses of white raked sand and gnarled rock. He expected to come momentarily upon some magnificent dwelling hidden at the center of these splendors, where Abbot Yuzawa dwelt in aloof sublimity, the oriental sage wrapped in clouds, closer to heaven than to earth. When he found no such building and realized that he was beginning to retrace his steps, he began to wonder if he hadn't misunderstood his directions. He spotted an elderly monk on his knees, pulling weeds in a small vegetable garden near a toolshed, and approached him, hoping that the old man understood at least a little English. Whatever Japanese John had picked up in his Tokyo days was nearly fifty years old.

"Excuse me," he said hesitantly. "I am looking for the abbot. For Abbot Yuzawa."

"Yes?" The old man looked around and up at John.

"For Abbot Yu —"

The elderly monk had risen from his knees to his feet. When he stood up John saw that the old man humbly pulling weeds *was* Abbot Yuzawa.

"Yuzawa! It's —"

"John Devlin." There was pleasure in Yuzawa's voice, but not a hint of surprise. This calmness at the sudden reappearance of an old friend after forty years threw John into confusion. For a moment the master diplomat was at a loss for words, but then he realized that there was really nothing to say. Obviously he had come to see Yuzawa. So John simply bowed, in silence. Yuzawa bowed too, and got back on his knees.

"Excuse me, please, for one moment," he said, resuming his weed-pulling. "I must just finish."

John stood about awkwardly for a few minutes while Yuzawa cleared his garden. It was so odd to be kept waiting in these circumstances that John began to wonder if he hadn't made a mistake in coming. Perhaps in his old age Yuzawa had become truly monkish and reclusive, and wanted no visitors.

But the instant his weeding was finished Yuzawa rose again to his feet and said, "Come and have tea." He bowed again, and gestured with his arm. John looked at him. Yuzawa was at least seventy-five now, but his movements and his manner still had the compelling charm of his youth.

A few minutes later John was sitting cross-legged within the white-paneled simplicity of the senior abbot's quarters, watching Yuzawa prepare tea. Yuzawa's smallest movement was precise, unified, contained; merely watching him calmed John's anxious mind and prepared him to say what he had come to say. When the tea had been made and served, he began to build up to it.

"Teacher, I hope you have been well."

Yuzawa inclined his head. "I am well, thank you. I trust you are well also. You have come to ask me something." He looked straight at John, a pleasant look inviting him to come to the point.

John wondered how to begin. With the simple truth? "I'm an errant and inconstant pupil who is deeply troubled and in his trouble seeks his master."

Yuzawa smiled and nodded again. "How are you troubled?"

John hesitated; from here on the truth would not be simple. He sighed deeply and went on. "Teacher, it has been nearly forty years since we last spoke. And in forty long years I have seen what you told me I would see."

"What have you seen?" Yuzawa gently asked.

John gave his friend the speech he had rehearsed a hundred times on his way across the Pacific. "I have seen that this world is a blazing sea of fire, an ocean of suffering, and that its suffering never ends. I have seen that the souls of men and women lie trapped in such a world, prevented from evolving to a higher consciousness because of history, which is the payment of karmic debts incurred by the actions of their nations. And now, since Hiroshima, the nations have the greatest debt to pay, and I believe that I see humanity giving up its struggle to evolve under the burden of this great debt. Because of this I see today the signs of an age of darkness beginning in the world. I think that in its despair humanity is turning its back on its own evolution and descending into lower realms of existence, deeper and deeper into hells of ignorance. I have been deeply troubled by all this, and I have thought about it a great deal, until at last I have conceived a way to prevent the age of darkness and help bring about instead the evolution of humanity to a higher realm . . ."

Again John hesitated. He was dodging, and he knew it.

Yuzawa, thinking he was finished, smiled. "Why are you still troubled if you have discovered how to achieve such a great good?"

John's speech did not include an answer. He groped for the right words. "Because . . . because to achieve this great good I fear that I must do something . . ."

Yuzawa's pleasant face showed no reaction. "What is it that you must do?"

John forgot the rest of the speech, took a deep breath, and told him.

When he had finished Yuzawa was silent for a few moments, and then said simply, "This is indeed a difficult thing you propose to do. Are you absolutely sure that there are no alternatives?"

It was the question that John most dreaded, not because he didn't know the answer, but because he feared so much actually to say it. He was quiet for a very long time before he did. "No. There are none."

Yuzawa was silent. After a moment John went on. "The worst of it is that I'm not sure it will work. And then it will have been for nothing, such a terrible waste . . . Beyond all else I fear to take responsibility for that."

Yuzawa suddenly stood up. "Come back tomorrow morning," he said firmly. Then he strode forward with a younger man's energy and lightly helped the startled John to his feet. Before John could say a word his old friend seized both his hands and shook them warmly, then said, "It is so very good to see you again!" He bowed and disappeared. A few moments later a novice appeared and escorted John back to the gate.

John spent a very long and sleepless night in his hotel, wondering what on earth had possessed him to come to Kyoto and blurt

out his innermost secret, and why Yuzawa had disappeared so
abruptly, and what was awaiting him the next morning. Before
dawn he again walked through the temple's side gate. He found
Yuzawa in the eating room of his quarters, finishing a breakfast
of pickles and rice with the novices. The abbot smiled to see his
friend so early.

"Good morning, John Devlin. You are keeping our temple
schedule today. That's good."

John bowed and tried to smile in return.

"Come with me," said Yuzawa.

He led John through the sliding panels of his rooms. Presently
they came to a room that clearly was reserved for meditation.
In fact somebody was meditating in this room, somebody robed
in the flowing black of the temple monks. He was facing away
from the entrance, but as John entered he could see immediately
that despite his robes the sitter was neither a monk nor an Asian;
he had the larger Caucasian build and an unshaven head of graying
hair.

An instant later, hearing someone enter behind him, he ended
his meditation, stood up, and turned around to greet them. John
stopped. The man was Caucasian: a little shorter than John, very
pale, and lean nearly to the point of emaciation. John had never
seen him before, but . . . but the eyes in the sunken face somehow
prodded his memory. Then the stranger smiled, and with a shock
John knew who he was.

"Steven!"

His elder son hurried forward, black sleeves flowing, to embrace
him.

"Father!" Steven hugged him close. "So it's true! I couldn't
believe it when Yuzawa said you had shown up here yesterday,
out of the blue."

"But . . . but . . . *You* can't believe . . . ?" John could scarcely
gasp out the words. Since 1968 no one had heard anything of
Steven. It had been seventeen years. The Vatican had offered its
condolences, there had been a funeral Mass . . . John grabbed
the folds of his son's robes and felt them in dumb amazement.
Then he looked, stupefied, at Yuzawa.

"How —?" he gasped again.

Yuzawa beamed happily, bowed, and withdrew.

John turned back to Steven. "You're — you're supposed to be . . ."

Steven laughed. "Dead? Yes, I know. But instead I'm resurrected. Not a bad *imitatio Christi,* eh?" He laughed again, but saw the disoriented expression on his father's face and quickly became serious. "I'm sorry, Father. I've been out for a long time. I couldn't tell you, or Mother. I couldn't tell *anyone.*"

John was still groping through his shock. "Out of . . . ?"

"Out of the Gulag," Steven said. "I was in the camps for five years before my superiors in the Curia could get me out. Not an easy thing to do, even for them." He released John from his embrace and stepped back to examine him. "You look *great,*" he said heartily. "I can't tell you what a wonderful thing this is. I was sure I'd never see you again before you . . ."

"Wait a minute." John's first coherent thought was almost an angry one. "For God's sake, Steven, why didn't you tell us?"

Steven put his arm around his father's shoulders. "Come on, let's walk," he said gently, "and I'll tell you why."

They walked. Steven steered John through a doorway into a long open-air gallery of polished wood that faced one of the oceanic sand gardens. John allowed himself to be steered. Everything he looked at seemed different, unbelievable. He thought, *This is what a miracle feels like . . .*

But the shock was wearing off. He could feel that the arm around his shoulders was a real one. He looked at his son. Without doubt the Gulag had left its mark: Steven, his mother's favorite, had his mother's looks, her sleek black hair and her handsome pale features, but five years in the camps had eroded deep lines in his handsome face and stripped off the plumpness that the old Steven's love of good food and drink had maintained. The black hair was full of gray, mostly gray . . . No doubt the years in Siberia were also responsible for that. But John remembered that his boy must be . . . what? Fifty-six? That was old, but Steven looked even older. More coherent thoughts took shape. Five years in the Gulag; seventeen years of silence. What about the missing twelve?

"Your mother will be overjoyed to see you," he said. "Overjoyed? There's no word that can do justice to what she'll feel. And David and Diana . . ."

"Father." The arm around him squeezed his shoulder gently. "I'm afraid I have to ask you to do a very difficult thing. I don't want you to tell *anyone,* not even Mother, that you've seen me."

"*What?* Steven, how can you?"

"Please, listen." A benchlike step led down from the gallery into the garden. Steven drew John down to sit on it, and sat beside him. "The first reason is that my release from the Gulag wasn't entirely, ah, official."

"What does that mean?"

"It means that the Curia secured my freedom only with the help of a few discreet gifts given selectively at the middle levels of Soviet bureaucracy. Along with the gifts went a promise that my release would never be made public. The official KGB records still show me rotting away in their hellholes, and as long as nobody knows otherwise, everything is fine. But if they discover I'm out, a lot of people will be in danger."

"You mean the Russians who released you —"

"And I mean me, and you, and our whole family. So for the time being, at least, I must ask you to say nothing."

John thought for a moment. "You said that was the first reason. Is there a second one?" The old suspicion surfaced in his mind. "Have you been working for the CIA all this time?"

Steven laughed and shook his head. "No, no, it's nothing so nasty as that." From under his robes he produced a gold cross that hung on a chain around his neck. "I serve only one master," he intoned piously, "and he is not of this world."

"Then what the hell have you been so damned secretive about ever since you joined the church?"

Steven smiled. "I'm going to have to begin at the beginning. Otherwise you might not believe me." To his father's surprise he produced a pack of cigarettes from his monk's robes. "Not that I'd blame you if you didn't," he said, lighting up. "Anyway, I'm going to take you back to 1957, the year I graduated from the Pontifical Ecclesiastical Academy and became a Vatican diplomat."

"Well, I *do* remember that," John said.

"What you will not remember is something I don't believe I ever told you. I graduated at the very top of my academy class, with all kinds of honors and so forth, and I was really quite full of myself. I took it for granted that my first assignment in the

Secretariat of State would be the kind they always hand out to the best of each academy class: junior secretary to the nuncio in some wonderful and important European capital. In my own mind I was so sure of where I would be going that before any appointments were announced I actually went to the railroad station and bought a ticket for Paris."

"That sounds rash."

"Indeed it was. Well, the next day the appointments were announced, and I got the surprise of my life. They had given Paris to some pleasant, earnest fellow whose work had been obviously inferior to mine. And me they had assigned — to this day I can still feel the shock when I remember — me they had assigned to the secretariat *archives.*"

"The archives?" John grimaced. No wonder Steven had always been loath to talk about his early Vatican days.

"The archives. You can imagine how I felt. They might as well have entombed me alive in some basement crypt. Of course I went to everyone I could and demanded an explanation. No one would give me one. My razor-sharp professors all put on their masks of simple piety when I showed up and told me that any service to Christ and his church was sufficient glory for a man."

John chuckled. "I'll bet they did."

Steven shook his head and puffed on his cigarette. "For about a month after that I was completely numb," he went on. "Every morning I descended into my tomb of dusty tomes and languished there. The incredible dullness of the work made the job a genuinely purgatorial experience . . . except for Monsignor Ravelli." Steven exhaled reflectively and smiled.

"Who was he?"

"The senior archivist. Ravelli must have been already in his seventies when I went to work for him — one of those venerable gnomes who scurry through the subterranean regions of the Vatican. Or so I thought, in my despair. But it turned out that Monsignor Ravelli wasn't at all your average gnome. From his ancient little body there sometimes shot beams of truly penetrating intelligence. Not so much in the performance of his duties — any idiot could have done those — but in the stories he told: endless, funny, fascinating stories, sometimes quite scandalous, about the not terribly spiritual history of the holy church. I think he had committed the entire Vatican archives to memory. I used to live for his stories. Ravelli was very kind to me, almost a grandfather. In my misery I fancied that in fact Ravelli *was* me, from an earlier time — that the church punished very bright clerics who had shown insufficient humility by hurling them into the lowest circle of archival hell, and that fifty years before Ravelli had graduated at the top of his academy class and bought a ticket to Paris . . . How beautiful."

Steven broke off for a moment to stare at the rocks floating in the ocean of sand. The sun had risen now and the dew was glittering along their dark ridges.

"So entombment was not completely unbearable," prompted John.

"No," said Steven, "if only because of Ravelli. Then, after a while, I began to notice some rather odd goings-on in the archives. I think I had been there about two months when one day I had some trivial question for Ravelli and found him in his office meeting with some foreign visitors. That in itself was certainly not odd, given the incredible scope of the Vatican archives; Ravelli was always receiving scholars from all over the world. But these people were different. First, they were talking with Ravelli in a language that I, the great linguist, didn't understand. I caught only a few words of it before they clammed up and Ravelli asked me, in his usual kindly way, if I wouldn't mind coming back later. That was the second unusual thing: I had always been allowed to interrupt Ravelli's meetings for any reason. Why not this one? But of course I left, and as I was closing the door they started talking again and I caught a few more words, and suddenly I realized what their language was. *Russian.* Can you imagine my surprise?"

"Indeed," said John. "Not a popular language at the Vatican."

"Especially not in 1957. The church and Moscow hadn't had diplomatic relations in more than twenty-five years, and Pius XII was carrying on his own thundering version of the cold war. Anyway, after my first shock I concluded that the Russian visitors must have been emigrés. But then why hadn't they been speaking French or German? Why was Monsignor Ravelli fluent in Russian? Later that day they left Ravelli's office, and they never returned; they hadn't even come to use the archives. I was baffled. I had no idea what their visit meant."

"The beginning of your road to Prague," said John.

"Exactly," said Steven. "But more, much more." He had finished his cigarette; he crushed it out very carefully on the flagstones at his feet. Then he bent down and brushed the ashes off the stone and put the butt into a little plastic bag he withdrew from his robes.

"Here the monks are permitted to smoke," he said. "They are not permitted to litter." He put the bag away. "Not long after I discovered Russians in the archives, something happened that was stranger by far. It began with yet another of what I then was sure were deliberate humiliations. The secretariat granted me my dream and sent me to Paris — for one week, as an errand boy, to pick up some documents stolen from the archives by Napoleon and recently rediscovered. So I spent a delirious week there, feeling like a man on leave from prison and vowing that someday I would have the Paris nunciature and my revenge on whoever had tried to deny it to me. At any rate, on my last night there I left my hotel and went out for dinner at a very charming little restaurant I had discovered nearby. At the door I stood aside to let several elderly monks pass through on their way out. But these monks were Buddhists, Southeast Asian monks in bright saffron robes, all chattering loudly together in some incomprehensible tongue. There was an Occidental with them, also elderly, dressed very well in a gray suit and hat, speaking their language. At first I couldn't get a look at this curious Frenchman who kept such exotic company; the man's hat was wide-brimmed, and he was quite short. But as he jostled past me in the doorway he looked up and said, *'Pardon, merci,'* and I nearly dropped from shock. It was Ravelli."

"You're joking."

"Absolutely not. While I stood there with my mouth open he nodded his head and walked on. By the time I recovered myself he and the monks had gone. The next day I went back to Rome in a complete daze. It occurred to me that months of anguish and boredom in the archives might be affecting my sanity, so as soon as I got back I hurried to Ravelli's office to reassure myself that I had been seeing things in Paris. But Ravelli wasn't there. I was told that he had left for a vacation. So for several days I was left in an agony of doubt. But then one night I awoke and saw Ravelli standing over me, holding a lighted candle. 'Come with me,' he said in his usual kindly way, and you can be sure I did, once I had blinked a few times to make sure I wasn't dreaming."

"Where did he take you?" asked John, who was thoroughly caught up in the story.

"Through the galleries," said Steven, "and the museums, the repositories of the Vatican's ancient treasures. In the dead of night, by candlelight. It was incredibly eerie to walk those corridors in darkness and silence and see the hard faces of Roman emperors, and Greek gods, and animal deities of Egypt, leaping out through the candle flame. It reminded me of a passage through some primordial tribal cavern, some primitive shrine where they keep the ancestors' skulls and the images of the gods and initiate the young. Then Ravelli started talking, and I was initiated. I found out the deepest secrets of my Vatican tribe. My real career began that night."

"You mean your diplomatic work?"

"Well, yes, that, but so much more. That night I learned what the church really was, and would become. Among the skulls of his ancestors, the emperors of Rome, Ravelli made me understand clearly for the first time that the church had come into being as a way of saving the tottering Roman Empire, by infusing its institutions with the new spirituality that had replaced Greek skepticism in the world. The human species does not long tolerate an absence of spirituality. That, Ravelli told me, was what the old men of the Curia had learned over two millennia. Whenever spirituality had been in danger of dying out, progressive elements in the Curia had saved the church by re-creating it in a new form in tune with the times, a new vessel that could once again contain and give form to the inevitable spiritual impulse. Amid the barbarism of the Dark Ages the progressives created the deep and simple piety of Benedictine monasticism. Amid the horrors of the church's own Inquisition they created the loving gentleness of the Franciscans. Amid the humanist and scientific revolts of the Protestant Renaissance they created the Jesuits, an order of Renaissance men: rugged individuals, exacting intellectuals, trained with a military discipline. And now, said Ravelli, in the twentieth century, spirituality was once again in danger, this time from a godless materialism and the sterile skepticism of science. The church was about to undergo another transformation to save spirituality and thereby save itself. While Pius XII dreamed uselessly of past glories, of papal armies and kings kneeling at his feet, the Curia progressives were reaching out secretly to the forces that were bringing spirituality back to a dying world.

"What forces?" asked John breathlessly, as if Steven had been telling him a terrific ghost story. Before them the sand garden looked more beautiful than ever in the slightly higher sun. But John had forgotten all about the garden; he had almost forgotten his shock at seeing Steven. What he was hearing now might be just what he needed to know . . .

"Marxism, the new religion of the West, and Buddhism, the old religion of the East, which in the 1950s was just starting to take the West by storm. The old men of the Curia saw it coming. They knew that in whichever direction humanity was evolving, the tide of those two forces would carry it there, so they prepared a two-pronged move of their own. One prong was to separate 'good' Marxism, the pure Marxist humanism that was in fact very Christian in its ideals, from the monstrous perversion of Marxism that was present in the Soviet Union, the atheist, materialist Russian empire. It was in the rash pursuit of that goal, when I confused my own ambitions with my real work, that I blundered my way right into the Gulag."

"As I always suspected," John said. "But the church hasn't given up on that goal?"

"Oh, no. In fact, the church is harder at work than ever to undermine the Soviets. You can trace the whole history of it very easily, if you know how."

"How?"

"Well, think about it. Weren't you surprised when Pius XII died — less than a year after the night I'm describing to you now — and the cardinals elected that aged nobody Angelo Roncalli to succeed him?"

"Well, yes, of course. Everybody was."

"Right. And then everyone was even more surprised when Angelo Roncalli became John XXIII, a truly spiritual pope who melted the cold heart of the church and revolutionized its dogma. The first revolutionary thing Pope John did was to declare that the church has no enemies and to extend an open hand to communism."

"Aha." The old diplomat John was beginning to understand. "The surest way to defeat your enemy is first to make him your friend."

Steven smiled. "Exactly. John XXIII achieved the double victory of getting the Soviets to drop their guard and making the church suddenly attractive to Marxist humanists who had supported Russia for lack of any alternative. Then, after John had drawn the Soviets into good relations and stolen away their supporters, the Curia hit them with a new pope, Paul VI, a veteran diplomat who could follow up John's loving overtures with some hard-nosed negotiating. With Paul the war of concession and attrition began. And then the Curia progressives bided their time, looking for the right man for the next stage of their plan — and in 1978 they found him."

"John Paul II?"

"A Communist Pope. The masterstroke. The progressives elected a pontiff from inside the Soviet empire. Suddenly every Catholic in the world owes allegiance to a pope who has struggled for freedom under Russian rule. His struggle is now their struggle. And this pope is every inch a crusader, cast from the mold of the warrior-popes of old. John opens the door; Paul holds it open, then John Paul marches through it, cross aloft, step by step to victory. In 1968 Moscow crushed Czechoslovakia; it dare not crush Poland as long as John Paul is Pope. Step by step we are winning. And it is only the beginning of what needs to be done."

"You mean the other prong, the Buddhists."

"I mean the Buddhists. That was the other thing Monsignor Ravelli told me in the dark of night, when I found out at last that my assignment to the archives was not a humiliation but a recruitment by the Curia progressives. Ravelli confirmed that it was he I had seen in Paris. In 1957 the Vatican progressives were already engaged in negotiations with Buddhist leaders, negotiations so secret that only three or four people in the world knew about them. This is why: they were negotiations toward the goal of founding a new religion."

Steven was silent for a moment, contemplating the beauty of the garden. John was silent too, contemplating the incredible thing he had just heard. It really was a day for miracles. In his terrible doubt his long-dead son had risen from the dead to show him the way.

"What sort of new religion?" he asked presently.

"The best of East and West," said Steven. "A very holy alliance of the deep, direct spirituality of Zen and the organization of the Catholic Church."

"You mean an *official* alliance?"

"I mean exactly that. Buddhism has got to be the spiritual vehicle of the future, there's no doubt of that — it's the only path that can reconcile all the divisions that are tearing us apart, the divisions between science and faith, between God and human existence, between civilization and the earth. In a way you could say that it's the way forward to our origins, because in Zen you find the subtlest, most refined expression of our original primitive relationship with God, a relationship of immanence, in which God and humanity and all existing things are holy and One."

"Eden before the Fall," said John.

Steven looked over at his father. "Yes, right, exactly. Ever since the Fall, when we sundered ourselves from God, we've been trying to regain that original innocence. That's the *point,* you see." Steven's voice grew emotional, and he struck his fist on his knee. "They've *got* to understand that they need to regain their innocence if they're going to survive. The peoples of the earth must *somehow* be made to understand . . ."

Steven stood up and began to pace back and forth in front of his father. "In the camps, you know, in the Gulag, it happened to me. I hit bottom, just as the world has done now. I became indifferent to God and myself and everything, because everything, I felt in my misery, had become indifferent to me. For days on end I existed in a kind of mental blankness, a time void. Now I can see that it was the void left when the Gulag destroyed my arrogant ego. My whole life, my whole reality, had been only my puny ego, which was so easily crushed. But at the time I knew nothing except the profoundest alienation imaginable — an emptiness that lasted for weeks, until I seemed to exist only as an eating, sleeping, and working body, nothing else. If one of the guards had pointed his gun at me, or if someone had told me I was free, I don't think I would have reacted much, either way.

"But then, after weeks of this despair beyond all despair, I was loading rocks into a truck one morning when the spring thaw had begun, and everything changed. I saw the morning sunlight shining on a bank of wet pebbles. Only that — a miracle! — and suddenly it was as if something just fell away inside of me, like a rotting old house that finally collapses after years of neglect. And then a feeling of the most unbelievable joy flooded through me. Would you believe it? There I was, condemned to hard labor in Siberia for the rest of my life, no one knowing where I was or even whether I was alive or dead, and I started to laugh! Not madly, but quietly, and tears began to pour down my cheeks, tears of purest joy . . . It was like what I imagine a balloon feels like when it's filled with helium and soars into the sky. I was filled with Spirit. The barriers between me and the universe had crumbled. I looked at the wet pebbles again, shining in the sun, and I was looking at *myself*. But not my old self, Steven Devlin the brilliant Jesuit — my *real* self, it seemed to me, the self the Jesuit had never known. And this real self was a pebble on the ground and a bird in the air and a fish in the sea and a star shining ten billion light-years away — and a human being stuck for life in a Siberian labor camp."

Steven stopped pacing and faced his father. "After that, whatever happened to me, I felt the continuous presence of God. But I was also enough of an intellectual still to know what kind of experience I'd had, so after my release, when I'd recovered my strength, I asked my superiors to assign me to Japan — to Yuzawa, who's been working with them on the new religion for years. I came here over a decade ago, and I've been sitting here ever since, absorbing Zen. Ten years isn't very long to do that, but Yuzawa is kind enough to say I'm making progress."

Steven smiled at John and was silent. He turned away, squatted on his haunches, and looked into the unanalyzable whiteness of the garden sand. The simple movement, so oriental, so unlike the old Steven, impressed itself on John more than words. The old Steven had had his clerical suits custom tailored and had carried his cigarettes in a gold case to match the expensive crucifix around his neck. The old Steven, John thought, had always reminded him less of a priest than of an exceedingly ambitious young executive with an odd taste in collars. The new Steven, humbly rocking on his calves, had at last become a man of God, after a lifetime in the priesthood. If a man could be pleased that his child had suffered, John was quietly, compassionately pleased.

"I hope you understand why I couldn't contact you," Steven said. "My presence here is a secret kept even from the Vatican. As far as the church knows, I'm still in Siberia and presumed dead. Only a few people I report to in the Curia know the truth. That's the way it has to be while Yuzawa and I try to lay the groundwork for the new religion. You can imagine the uproar in Rome if our work were discovered. But when the time is right, when we encounter the one person, the one event — the thing we now are waiting for — with the galvanizing power to carry our new faith, then Rome, and the world, will know of us. Until then — " He turned abruptly to look at John. "I hope you're not angry with me," he said. "I hope you understand. I know you're a man who has lived in what is called the real world. When that world was my world, I would have sneered at anyone who talked the way I'm talking now, and called him crazy, or at best an idealistic fool." He chuckled and shook his pale, gaunt head, running his fingers through his close-cropped graying hair as if remembering the exquisite barbering he had once demanded. "Funny how . . . Well, anyway, I hope you understand." He turned back to stare at the garden again, then reached into his robes for another cigarette.

"I do," said John, staring with him at the ocean of sand.

John and Steven spent the rest of the day together. Steven outlined the plan for the new religion. "Zen Buddhism," he repeated, "has to be the core of it. But Zen is fundamentally an esoteric practice for the mystical few. To reach humanity at large we need the occidental genius of Catholicism, the power of a worldwide spiritual institution, to create what no previous religion, especially Christianity, has succeeded in becoming: a cult of the masses that retains its spiritual purity and doesn't succumb to secular politics."

"Question," said John. "How are you going to pull in all the millions of rational skeptics out there?"

Steven grinned slyly. "Well, Father, I won't. David will."

"David?" John felt himself reentering shock. "You mean he's part of this thing too?"

Steven nodded. "Of course he doesn't know about me yet. You're the first. David thinks he's in it only with Yuzawa. When the time is right Yuzawa will bring us together, just as he brought you and me together today."

"*Yuzawa?*"

"Yes," Steven said blandly. "The connection surprised me too when I first learned of it. It seems that for years my brother's been doing some amazing work on his own, aside from his NASA job. He's developed a mathematics that seems to show beyond any doubt that some fundamental reality exists beyond what we can see. Beyond light. At least, that's what he tells Yuzawa he's proven."

"Beyond light?"

"Beyond light. According to Yuzawa, David conceives of it in religious terms, as a fundamental unity, and says that all things we see and experience are merely distortions of it. Which is why Yuzawa knows about his work. Apparently David got very curious when he discovered that all his mathematical work was simply restating a Buddhist view of the universe, so he found his way to Yuzawa. To others, too — apparently the Jungians are very high on him. They think he's found an objective confirmation of their hero's synchronicity principle, which posits connections between minds and events outside everyday cause and effect —"

"Wait, wait a second," John interrupted. "Why didn't he ever tell *me* about this work?"

"Good question. Actually, he's been very odd about it. He doesn't even claim credit for it. He says that someone else actually did the work and passed it on to him. He refuses to say who that someone was. He'll only say that he, David, is waiting for the right moment to make it public."

"Why?"

"I don't know. I don't think he's afraid for his reputation among his hard-nosed NASA engineer friends — David's never been like that. All he will tell Yuzawa is that he has more work to do before he's ready. I guess he does — I'm hardly the one to judge a mathematician's progress. But I'm glad he hasn't published; his secrecy plays right into our plans. When he's ready, we'll be ready, and we'll hold up his work to the skeptics who won't hear my arguments of faith."

"And all these years he's never told me," John repeated, dumbfounded.

"Well, as you know, Father," Steven said with a wink, "David's always been the best among us at keeping a secret."

Second best, John thought with an inward chuckle, but he said nothing, and listened much more, and grew happier as the day went on. They were all in it, they were all serving. He had not been wrong.

That evening, when father and son had taken dinner together with Yuzawa and his monks, Steven withdrew to meditate, and Yuzawa took John into another room.

"Thank you," said John when they sat down.

Yuzawa smiled. "Are you less troubled now?"

Confronted with the direct question, John was suddenly not so euphoric. The final doubt, the ultimate one, remained.

"I see now," he said cautiously, "that there is a chance they will be ready. A *good* chance. But . . ."

For a while the two old men sat silent, facing one another in the emptiness of the Japanese room, a room without distractions, where the essence of a thing could not be avoided. Finally Yuzawa said, "You cannot decide this thing if you think about good and evil. Good and evil are not absolutes. You must weigh them in the balance of Truth. The good of a thing may outweigh the evil of it, or the evil outweigh the good, but if you really want to act from Truth, you must embrace both the good and the evil of what you must do."

John nodded sadly. "Yes, teacher, I know, but it is very hard for a man —"

"Yes, exactly," said Yuzawa. "Hard for a man. A man's mind is small and ignorant and cannot know the Truth. Only when he experiences the Buddha in himself, which *is* Truth, can a man know what Truth is. Therefore you must remain here tonight, in this room. You must do as you did once before."

John sighed deeply. Yuzawa meant his vigil on the island. Another revelation. "I know, teacher. I came here knowing that, but suddenly I am old and tired and afraid."

"Do not be afraid," Yuzawa said gently, but very firmly. "Tonight, and tomorrow, and as long as you must, you will do *zazen,* as you did before. You will sit until you have quieted your doubts and your fears and all the frantic questions of your man's mind, the ego-mind. When you have done that you will realize the Buddha in you. When you know the Buddha in you, you will know the Truth, because the Buddha is Truth — ultimate, universal, timeless, and indivisible Truth — and when a man knows the Truth it is impossible for him to doubt."

So John did as he was told. Yuzawa brought him a comfortable robe and a cushion, and he folded his old legs painfully under him and sat erect and vowed, before he put away all thoughts, to sit until he had become the Buddha and conquered doubt. Before he began he did one more thing. From the pockets of his suit he drew what looked like an old rag wadded into a lump, and unwrapped it. Then he took what was inside the rag, Grandfather's ancient pocket watch, and made its chain into a loop by fastening the free end to the top. When he had made a necklace of the watch he hung it around his neck with a certain ritual care, so that the old design, the swastika, rested over his heart.

12

The Buddha

A WEEK LATER John left Kyoto and Japan. Before he left he called Ruth in New Bedford and suggested that they meet in Paris, to visit Diana and Charles and their son, Timothy, who would be turning ten that month. A visit to Paris and her grandson was not hard to sell to Ruth. With the greatest difficulty John kept himself from telling her about Steven. He felt awful about it, but he had promised. For his part, Steven had promised to reveal himself to his mother as soon as he could. And in fact John was grateful to have no distractions. He had succeeded; he had conquered his doubt. He had decided to go ahead.

In Paris John enjoyed the food and bought Timothy birthday presents. When the first excitement of her parents' visit had subsided Diana stopped cooking for them and taking them out and got back to work at the Louis Pasteur Institute. With typical spirit she had managed marriage, a child, and her doctorate, and now was engaged in cancer research. John had time to enjoy his grandson.

Timothy La Porte had the quiet Devlins in him. He was a very bright boy, very bookish, gifted in mathematics like his uncle David and blessed with his father's dark good looks. With his grandfather, whom he seldom saw, he was reticent but not timid; he showed John some drawings of buildings he had done, strange, ingenious, Escher-like structures, always set in the brilliant landscapes of unknown planets. John was pleased. The boy was bright, but he also had imagination; and imagination, not the soulless genius of technocrats, was what the future would need.

At the end of a week, when Diana was busy again and Timothy had had his birthday party, John found himself alone one evening with Charles, not entirely by accident. They sat by the fire drinking coffee, chatting, and reading the papers.

"What do you make of this?" John asked. He pointed to a headline on the front page of the *Herald Tribune:* ICARUS TERRORISTS STILL A MYSTERY.

"Oh, well," said Charles, smiling vaguely and shaking his head, "I don't know what to make of all that. I mean, I have my guesses, but that's all they are." He went back to reading his magazine.

"But I'd like to hear your guesses," said John. "At this point that's all anybody is doing — guessing. I'm sure your guesses are as good as anyone's."

Charles put down his magazine. "All right. I think I know something about what Icarus is because some of the terrorists, the ones they've killed and identified, were people I knew. Diana knew some of them too."

"Is that right?" John said, leaning toward Charles. "How would the two of you ever meet people like that?"

"A long time ago," said Charles, "in 1968."

"Aha. The Sorbonne?"

"Exactly. Do you remember the man at our wedding with the goldfish bowl?"

John chuckled. "Ah, yes. Not an entirely normal young man. What was his name?"

"You weren't introduced," said Charles, "but we told you where he came from: the Dada Commandos. Remember?"

John leaned back in his chair and stared up at the ceiling. "Yes, of course! The Dada Commandos! What a bizarre group. Whatever happened to them?"

"Well," said Charles, "that's my guess — that some of the Icarus people are former Dada Commandos."

John dropped his eyes from the ceiling to Charles. "Well, *that's* an interesting conclusion. Are you sure of it?"

"As I said, it's a guess. But obviously, I read in the papers the identity of dead people associated with Icarus, and more than once they've been people who in 1968 were more or less involved in the Dada Commando happenings. A lot of them were foreign students, Germans mostly. And there are other reasons that a Dada Commando-to-Icarus evolution makes sense."

"What sorts of reasons?"

"Well, philosophical ones. Doctrinal ones, if you can speak of a doctrine in their case. Do you remember the Dada Commandos' view of life? Life is a meaningless void, an absurdity; Hiroshima, the bomb, the impending destruction of the planet canceled out meaning. So the Dada Commandos filled the void with every form of silliness imaginable, because they wanted to shock people into seeing that there *was* a void, that everything that was supposed to matter really didn't anymore, that all of society's beliefs and morals and institutions were just dead weight, a sort of putrefaction that had to be cleansed from our minds before — well, before the world could become a better place. I hesitate to say that, because no Dada Commando would ever have admitted to such a bourgeois ambition as wanting a better world. But knowing them as I did, I am convinced that such a hope was there. They were people of the sixties, and for all of its violence the sixties was fundamentally a time of optimism, of belief in the impending dawn of a new and better world. I don't think even the Dada Commandos were immune to that optimism."

"I agree," said John. "Certainly you and Diana weren't."

At the remark something showed for an instant in Charles's amiable eyes — something, thought John, like sunlight glinting on steel. He noted it. "But it's a rather big step, isn't it, from goldfish bowls to international terror?"

"Not as big as you might think," answered Charles. "That's the really fascinating thing. After all, what is a murder or a kidnapping but a more spectacular prank? Especially in a world that lives every day in fear of instant annihilation? From the Icarus point of view, it must now be the generals who are the real master Dadaists."

"Aha . . . I see," said John. "A Dada Commando becomes an Icarus terrorist when he loses hope."

"In a sense, yes. The sixties failed, the world didn't get better, humanity persisted in clinging to its dead illusions. Now we are all standing naked before the apocalypse, waiting passively, as far as anyone can see, to be wiped out, like Jews lining up for the gas chambers. So why not act, if only to *act,* and join the apocalypse? Anything is better than just chewing your cud and, you know, buying cars and houses and going to the beach, and just waiting for the end."

John tried hard to be cautious, not to jump to conclusions. "Hmmm. Interesting. Whatever happened to the old boy who was their guru?"

"Doctor Einstoned?" Charles chuckled at the memory. "After the May Revolt he went underground for some reason. I don't think he had committed any crimes, but he vanished. In 1970 Diana and I met some old Sorbonne comrades who told us that Einstoned's German disciples had spirited him away to their country. But that was fifteen years ago, and we've heard nothing about him since. Maybe he went back to China to visit his old friend Mao."

"I thought he was a physicist," John said.

"A physicist?" Charles smiled. "Oh, perhaps. One never knew, exactly. In any case, that was a long time ago. Whoever he was, wherever he went, I doubt that he's still alive."

"Probably not." John sipped his coffee. "But he did leave a sort of legacy behind, didn't he?"

"Legacy?"

John got up from his chair and stood by the fire, bringing his coffee with him. "Allow me to tell you my own guess as to what Icarus is."

Charles looked surprised. "By all means."

John took a sip of coffee. "If I am a typical Icarus terrorist I am, let us say, forty at the oldest, and perhaps much younger. The point is that I have never known a world that didn't live with the daily terror of nuclear war. I am a child of Hiroshima, of Nagasaki, of Eniwetok, of Bikini Atoll. I have therefore never known a world that has not been slightly mad, because living in continuous terror eventually causes madness. In my salad days, in the glorious sixties, I believed in a revolutionary new world that would eliminate that terror and madness — it was the only sane thing to do, in the midst of madness. Now, however, I see, just as the Doctor Einstoneds of my youth told me I would see, that the world has in fact rejected sanity. It has rejected the call to wake up, acknowledge its madness, and be cured by revolution. Instead the human species seems to have chosen terror; it remains trapped in a destiny pregnant with apocalypse, and while it is fully conscious of that destiny, it is still unable (perhaps even unwilling) to change it. And if *that* isn't the ultimate absurdity, I don't know what is."

John finished his coffee and set the cup carefully on the fireplace mantel. "So then, if I am of the post-Hiroshima generation, and if I see that an insane humanity can't or won't get itself off the track of its own annihilation, I may become a terrorist, for any of several reasons. First, because I am enraged at humanity for its suicidal failure, and I want to punish it. Second, because by definition I am, after all, one of those who failed, since I am human; so perhaps my rage is also against myself, and I am just trying to commit suicide. Or third, at a more subtle level, I am attempting to bring about the only remaining solution to the burden of my terror, by acting out my own doom and the world's catharsis. Is there any more of that delicious coffee?"

Charles got up and fetched the coffeepot. "Bravo, John," he said as he filled John's cup. "Your analysis is quite convincing. But you still haven't explained what Icarus means."

"Thank you," said John, sipping carefully from the hot cup. "Yes, that is what's really got the police baffled, isn't it? This bit of Greek mythology, Daedalus' winged son, suddenly popping up all over the world in the hideouts of international terrorists, and all of them preferring suicide to being asked to explain their fondness for it." John took another sip and set the cup on the mantel again. "Well, I can tell you exactly what Icarus means."

"Oh, you can? Well, good Lord — please do," Charles replied in a tone of friendly disbelief.

"Icarus," John said, "is simply the single unifying image of everything I've just described. Remember the myth?"

"Not well enough to guess what you're getting at."

"Daedalus, a technological genius, frees himself and his son, Icarus, from imprisonment in a mad king's labyrinth by inventing artificial wings so they can fly away. Father and son leave the maze of their suffering and soar, free and uninhibited, above the earth. But Daedalus, old and wise, flies close to the ground. Icarus scorns his father's caution and revels in his freedom from the ties of earth. He soars higher and higher, ecstatic, defiant, until he flies up to the sun, that is, to God. You might say that by doing so he elevates himself to God's level, that he even challenges God. Of course the divine heat of the sun melts his wings, and from the heights of heaven he plummets to his death. Our terrorists have not failed to see the symbolic parallel."

"Which is?"

They have accepted Icarus' fate. They intend to fly into the sun and die."

Charles furrowed his brow. "Pardon me, I don't see —"

"*Nobody* sees!" cried John, suddenly agitated. He left the fireplace and began to pace about the room. "What is the sun?"

"The sun? Well, it's — it's heat . . ."

"Heat, yes! And what makes that heat?"

Charles thought for a moment. "Hydrogen, I believe."

"Hydrogen! Exactly! The fusion of hydrogen atoms produces the sun's tremendous heat! And what has clever man made within your lifetime and mine from the same fusion of hydrogen?"

It took Charles a moment to understand, but when he did his face suddenly darkened. "Good God," he said softly. "You don't mean . . ."

"Don't you see?" cried John. "They're laughing in our faces while they prepare our doom! These Icarus terrorists have decided, as you put it, Charles, not to wait around for apocalypse. They're going to play God in a godless void and give this failed world the day of judgment it so richly deserves. The final happening, the consummate prank. The ultimate act of the ultimately alienated mind."

"But where . . . ?"

"I don't know," said John. "Have any guesses? After all, they were your friends."

"No, no, I don't — I mean, it's been years. I don't know them anymore."

Charles looked distraught by the possibility John had raised, but John saw again that hard glint in his eyes. Now he permitted himself to proceed to conclusions.

"Well, wherever they set it off, it'll be a horrible disaster. I don't think I can go public with anything I've said, because I really don't have proof. But I do think it's high time for a counter-push, an escalation of efforts to *control* our bombs. Let me tell you about a splendid idea that occurred to me in Japan."

The next morning John telephoned the President and repeated to him everything he had told Charles about his idea. The President agreed that it was splendid, and advised him to go to work on it. John and Ruth flew back to Washington, where John was given an office at State, and he began to write letters and make phone calls. Six months later, in May, the idea had become a reality. John had organized a summit meeting of unprecedented proportions: a NATO–Warsaw Pact conference on nuclear disarmament. His sixty years in diplomacy had garnered him enough international influence to bring together the leaders of the United States and Western Europe and their Communist counterparts for a three-day debate on the disarmament deadlock. Of course, John thought to himself with an inward smile, there had been factors besides his own international repute. The real stroke of genius had been arranging for worldwide television coverage; *that* had brought the President and his European counterparts flocking, since no elected Western leader could afford to pass up a chance to show himself to his worried constituents on television, advocating peace and friendship. And the Soviets, who played to the Western press as diligently as the President did on matters of nuclear weaponry, had jumped at the chance to debate on camera.

As John kissed Ruth and headed for the airport he had every reason to feel good. At eighty-one he had not lost his touch. In three days, with the whole world watching, he would personally convene the greatest public effort yet toward nuclear disarmament, and he would convene it in the city he had chosen six months ago, when the whole thing had been only the last dream of an old man who wanted to do good: the divided city, Berlin, where the East–West rift was most dramatically visible. Here was a neat symmetry, John thought — a career begun in Berlin, a career ended there.

On his way to Germany John stopped off in Paris to see Diana and Timothy and to pick up Charles. From the start Charles had been quite enthusiastic about the conference. He had even made several trips to Berlin for his father-in-law to lay the groundwork. Now he had arranged to attend as an observer, representing a group of activist European university professors concerned about nuclear war. John, of course, was delighted that his son-in-law was as interested in the conference as he had hoped he would be.

In Berlin John busied himself greeting elder statesmen, most of them old friends, and making sure all was in readiness for the President. Charles disappeared. He had several meetings to arrange for his professors' group, he said, which intended to caucus and prepare a resolution for submission to the conference. John smiled and nodded and said he thought that was a good idea. Then he went back to his greeting duties, thinking all the while of what he would say when the conference convened.

The moment came that he stood at the podium. Around him sat the assembled leadership of the nuclear powers of the world. Behind them he saw the staring eyes of the television cameras; through those eyes the entire world was present. Again John permitted himself an inward smile. He had brought them all to Berlin; he had succeeded. He cleared his throat and began to address the world.

"I should like to convene this conference by dedicating it to a very brilliant man: my late friend, the atomic physicist Howard Mannheim, who created out of his driving genius the desperate imperative that brings us together today. Today, in death as in life, Howard Mannheim's soul is burdened with the responsibility for what he did — a burden that some say broke him and finally drove him mad. But it would be unworthy of this conference to do as so many have done and make Howard Mannheim the scapegoat for our tribal crime, to load him with our collective guilt and drive him, as his own tortured mind drove him, out into the desert. It is true that Howard Mannheim's genius gave us the atomic bomb; but a genius, like the rest of us, is only a wrinkle in a greater Mind."

John paused and looked out over his audience. They were all listening — the leaders of the world in front of him, Ruth in New Bedford, David in Houston, Steven and Yuzawa in Japan, Diana and Timothy in Paris, Charles and his group at the back of the room, and a billion more around the world. Now he would say what he had wanted to say to them for forty years. Now it was time. There would be no more secrets.

"It is that Mind, you see, the one great Mind of our human species, and of all life, which has worked through Howard Mannheim, and through others, as the gods worked in the fairy tales of our species' infancy, to bring us to this moment of ultimate crisis. I, who have lived a very long time upon this earth, say to you now that our species has been brought to this crisis for a reason. Forty years ago, standing amid the rubble of Nagasaki, Howard Mannheim told me about the night the first atomic bomb was tested, on the desert at Alamagordo. In the final seconds scientists were praying — praying, of course, that all their efforts would be successful, but more than that, Howard said: just praying, praying to God. Then the bomb exploded and the very foundation of the universe revealed itself to us. And we prayed to it. It seems that our long evolutionary journey 'up' from our animal origins had ended where it began, in union with God. As animals, before we became humans, we lived completely at one with our planet and the universe, innocent, without an inkling of an 'other.' But then we embarked on the unprecedented evolutionary path of mastering our environment, and at the moment we took that path we began to divide ourselves from the planet and the universe. We made the rest of existence into an object that was not us, and then we attacked it, dominated it — and now, on the brink of the twenty-first century, we stand poised to conquer it. From our path of division we have reaped a nearly omnipotent technology. We have also reaped a spiritual devastation that is nearly complete. If we allow that devastation to come to completion, our technology will destroy us."

Scattered applause from the back interrupted John. He looked up to acknowledge it, and his eyes wandered to Charles, who, with his colleagues, was vigorously clapping.

"But now, as we cast frantically about for a way to halt this final deterioration of Spirit in us, we find to our astonishment that the key to our reunion with the spiritual may lie in our most terrifying technology. That is the lesson of Alamagordo, if we can learn it. It is no accident that there were those at Trinity who prayed to their bomb as to a god. The power of the bomb *is* the power of a god. It is the power contained in the nucleus, the invisible essence of all existence. So let us learn the lesson. Let us learn to see our terrible nuclear weapons not as the end of the world but as a beginning, as a first crude approach to the boundary between the material universe, which we can sense and measure, and that awesome secret beyond Matter, the mystery of Spirit, which our alienated souls have dreamed of and yearned for for so very, very long. We can come full circle now, if we choose, back to the unity we lost. If we choose, the science of the atom may someday reunite Matter and Spirit, and thus humanity and God, and reverse at last what our myths have called the Fall of Man — our alienation from the universe, the source of our suffering, our conflicts, and our false tribalistic loyalties, from which have sprung our terrible wars. But this can only happen if we discard the bombs, if we no longer put the science of the atom in the service of war, the age-old symptom of our alienation."

More applause. John glanced over at the President, who was clapping hard and smiling, but somewhat vacantly, as though he hadn't understood a word John had said. Probably his press people had just ordered a close-up and told him to react. John noted similar behavior at the Soviet table. They must have ordered close-ups too. He cleared his throat and went on.

"A nuclear war will, despite all military advertisements to the contrary, inevitably destroy all combatants. It will also be our human species' final act of collective suicide, the ultimate expression of our alienation, the dead end of our evolutionary path of unchecked domination. We know that it is not inevitable that we trudge that path to the bitter end. As we approach the year 2000, our science, that beautiful invention which we have so misused, is concluding what our religions have always known: that we are at home in the universe, not strangers to it. This discovery is perhaps the most significant of all the discoveries science has made. It closes the circle; it brings us, old and well evolved, back to the point where we began. It announces that a new phase of evolution, perhaps beyond anything we can now comprehend, may be about to begin.

"The choice is ours. If we throw away our nuclear arsenals and choose life, if we choose to evolve, we shall send a message to that immense, mysterious, spiritual Mind that has nurtured us to this moment — and believe me, that Spirit is waiting now, to see what we will do. We shall send a message that we are worthy to continue our evolutionary destiny. But we must choose this now, before it is too late and the sheer sadness, the insanity, of our alienation leads us to choose death. If we choose death, Spirit is finished with us. We are a failed experiment. Spirit will go on, evolution will go on, the universe will go on; and we must be content with our own annihilation. This is the test we now must pass. Let us pass it. Let us choose life. Let us show that we are worthy. Let it be done now. Let it be done here."

He had finished. There was the expected storm of applause.

People were standing and cheering, honoring an elder statesman's final plea. Not that they had understood it. John looked at the President and saw him smiling less forcefully now, more uneasily, as though he were wondering whether Devlin hadn't at last gone a bit senile on him. Speeches about God and peace were fine, but the great Spirit . . . Well, thought John, they will understand soon enough. He looked around for Charles. Charles was not in his seat. John spotted him at one of the microphones set up at intervals in the huge conference hall so that members of the audience could address the floor.

"Mr. Chairman," Charles said into the microphone, "the Professors' Committee against Nuclear Arms would like to read a statement to the conference."

"The representative of the Professors' Committee against Nuclear Arms may come to the podium and address the conference."

John watched Charles thread his way toward him, holding a sheet of paper in his hand. Unless he had been very wrong, it was going to happen now. He didn't think he had been wrong. But he had said what he had wanted to say. He was ready.

Charles climbed to the podium and shook John's hand. John saw his other hand drop the paper and move to the side pocket of his sport coat. *It's now.* John dropped Charles's hand and swung around to face the audience, standing erect. He had assumed the stance of a cooperative hostage before Charles had got the pistol from his pocket and put it to John's temple.

There was a sudden, bewildered hush before the podium; it spread backward as more and more people realized what had happened, and then it gave way to a pandemonium of shouts. Charles walked John forward to the podium microphone.

"What's up, Charles?" John asked calmly.

"I'm sorry, John," said Charles. He leaned toward the microphone. "All right, everybody, be quiet. Be quiet. Be *quiet,* or I shoot."

The uproar in the audience subsided. In a few moments it was perfectly still; everyone sat frozen, and the cameras rolled.

"All right," said Charles. "Now everyone listen. The group known as Icarus has taken command of this conference. All of you are our hostages. At this moment in the city of Berlin a nuclear device is armed and ready to explode. The power of this device is over one megaton. If it is exploded, it will annihilate this conference and most of Berlin. The bomb is in the control of Icarus. The people who control it are watching me now on television. If the television cameras in the room are shut off, or if anyone shoots me or tries to arrest me, they will instantly detonate the bomb. If you think that we don't have the will to die along with you, think again. Time and time again we have shown that we do."

Charles gripped John's arm tightly near the elbow. John could feel him trembling. John himself was completely calm. He studied the frightened faces in front of him. They reminded him of the faces of the drowned, the *Lusitania*'s drowned. He thought of the horrible shock that Ruth and Diana and Timothy must be suffering, in front of their televisions. *I'm sorry.* Under his shirt he could feel the cool metal of the pocket watch against his chest. He closed his eyes and quieted his mind and began, as he had practiced so hard in Yuzawa's quiet room, a meditation on the image of the swastika.

Charles kept talking. "We of Icarus are not afraid to die, because all of you will kill us anyway with your bombs. At least if we die today, we can ourselves choose to die and not wait for you to decide for us." The microphone echoed Charles's voice around the hushed room. "Are you frightened now? I sincerely hope so. Your fear is a gift from the people you have terrorized for years. You have failed them. You have brought your people to the brink of death, and any day now you will be a little clumsy and push them over, and then all of you will just dive into your cozy little bunkers and come out safe and sound in three months and say, 'Ooops! So sorry.' Well, *I* am sorry, but I must tell you on behalf of a billion terrified people that you do not make a very inspiring leadership."

John was very far away, at the core of the turning swastika, the heart of the Buddha, image of all that is.

"But don't feel bad," Charles was saying. "Today Icarus offers you a chance to redeem yourselves, to show that you have real qualities of leadership. Icarus offers you a chance to atone for your failures." Charles let go of John's arm but kept the gun pressed tight against his temple. With his free hand he pulled a paper from his pocket. He held it up for all to see. "Icarus declares to the Conference on Bilateral Disarmament that everyone in this room is now to be held responsible. The generals and the politicians and the scientists are responsible. Responsible for Hiroshima. Responsible for Nagasaki. Responsible for the horror of the world. You in this room, you are the real terrorists. Today we of Icarus modestly hope to be worthy of you."

Charles began to read from the paper. "To the Conference on Bilateral Disarmament, now held hostage: Icarus agrees not to explode its bomb if the following conditions are met. First, before the world, on television, this conference must pass a resolution that it shall destroy every nuclear warhead now in existence anywhere in the world. Second, the Conference shall order this destruction to take place immediately, in front of television cameras, for verification by the world. The conference participants shall continue to remain the hostages of Icarus until the destruction of the last warhead has been verified. Third, no nation on earth shall ever again construct a nuclear weapon on pain of suffering the detonation of an Icarus bomb inside its capital city. We repeat: if anyone attempts to interfere with our representative, or if the television cameras are turned off, the bomb in Berlin will instantly be exploded. We ask the chairman of the conference, Ambassador John Devlin, for an answer to our conditions."

All eyes were on John. John opened his eyes and looked back at them. In them he read his instructions: *Buy time, while we find the damn bomb and disarm it.*

"For the conference," said John, "I accept the conditions laid down by Icarus." He heard an entire roomful of people exhale in relief. "The goals of Icarus and of this conference are fundamentally the same," he added.

"I know," said Charles sadly, taking the gun from John's temple. "*Your* efforts have always been for the best, John. Even we of Icarus know that. We know you'll do your best to make sure our conditions are met. I'm sorry it had to be done this way. Your conference is a splendid idea, but it's a gentleman's idea, an obsolete idea, out of step with reality. The only way you'll get disarmament is by scaring the hell out of *them.*" He waved an arm toward the hostage leaders of the world.

"Perhaps you're right," said John. "I confess I don't know anymore, in this world, what's right and what's wrong. But let that pass. The conference has agreed to your conditions; let's begin drafting the resolution without delay. But before we do, I have one stipulation of my own."

"What is it?" asked Charles in surprise.

"Whether Icarus' methods are right or wrong, Charles, I am still a civilized man — a gentleman, as you say. I refuse to conduct a conference of statesmen at gunpoint. I insist that you surrender your gun to me for safekeeping while we carry out your conditions."

Charles hesitated. "I can't do that, John."

"Oh, come on, Charles," John said. "What have you got to worry about? No one can harm you, because the instant they do your friends will explode the bomb and we'll all be dead. It's a symbolic gesture, for an old man who clings to outworn notions of how people should conduct themselves. For my sake, please. Give me your gun."

Charles hesitated another moment. "Well, all right." He held out the gun to John.

John stared at it. He read the thoughts of the people around him. Thank God for Devlin. Devlin's got the situation under control. The old fox has already got something up his sleeve. *Well, I do,* thought John. The image of the swastika, symbol of all that was, filled his mind, giving him vision, giving him strength. *Yes, I do.*

He was outside of Time now, free mind unchained from an old man's body, locking thoughts with another mind, the mind of another old man who had lost his chains forever. That old man's disciples were very near, their eyes on a television screen, their hands on the detonator of the bomb that, as his final lesson, he had shown them how to build.

Forty years, Icarus. Forty years, Dr. Einstoned. Forty years, Howard. Forty years since we walked together in the ruins of Nagasaki. Forty years since we looked at one another and knew that what one had seen, the other had seen. Forty years since we first knew that this moment would come. We are brothers, you and I, and all those who know what must be. We are the shamans. We are the goldfish men. I have served; you have served. Now together we shall test them.

Mind rejoined body. John looked at Charles, still holding the gun out to him. One millionth of one second had passed.

Yes indeed, Charles, we shall scare the hell out of them, and we shall see if they are worthy.

It was time. After forty years, it was time.

I feel you all in me now, not as the dying memories of an old man but as parts of one Being, one Being that forever is. Forgive me, dearest Ruth; to Wotan's city I bring your people's holy sacrifice of fire, to win a Promised Land. Stand by me, Matt, we are going to the cross now, all of us, for one man's sin is all men's evil, and all men must be cleansed. Aruna, Krishna, truth I could not see, we meet again in our Berlin, and now I understand. It is your hand I have always held, your hand that has led me, led us all, to this place, that has led me since I stood in the dusty street and held out Mr. Watkins's hat to you. You are the guide to Truth — benevolent, terrible, my charioteer. All the while I fought against you like a spoiled child, but now I understand. Joyfully I surrender to you . . .

His left hand grasped the barrel of the gun. "Thank you, Charles. And now, together let us make . . . a world set free." He took the gun in his right hand, by the stock.

Well, Johnny lad, in truth 'tis a fearful, fearful thing to be chosen by God.

He pointed the gun at Charles and shot him between the eyes.

There was time for one loud, shocked gasp from the leaders at the conference, from the watching world. Then, their conditions betrayed, the Icarus terrorists exploded their bomb. In that instant John Devlin saw, and knew, and wondered at all his life had been, and marveled at all that was to come; and was released.

Timothy Devlin sat on the couch between his mother and his grandmother. Every day for two weeks he had sat this way, between them. Sitting on the couch had become his world. On his left, sound; on his right, silence. Mother hadn't stopped crying in two weeks. For two weeks Grandmother, whom he had never known to let five minutes pass without having something to say, had said nothing. She had scarcely greeted them when they had arrived from Paris. Since then she had just sat and stared at the television. She looked very sick.

Two weeks ago, in Paris, he had seen his grandfather shoot his father on television, and then the bomb in Berlin had gone off. The television screen had gone black and Mother had screamed and screamed . . . In a little while the television picture had come back, and a man had said that Berlin had been destroyed by the bomb and that everyone at Grandfather's conference was dead. About an hour after that a man from the American embassy had come to their apartment with a car and told them to get in right away, not even to pack. The man said he was going to put them on a plane that would take them to America. Timothy hadn't wanted to go to America, a place he scarcely knew, and said so. The man had grabbed his arm and shoved him into the car after Mother. Once the car was going he had been nicer, and had tried to make friends. Timothy had looked away from him, out the window of the car. All along the sidewalks were people who had poured out of buildings at the news from Berlin. They stood in crowds but didn't speak to one another; they didn't run or walk or even move. They just stood. They looked like people in a snapshot, a still photograph. There had been no traffic in the streets. Everything had been quiet; everything, even people, had stopped.

Then they had flown to Washington, where some very angry people had asked Mother a lot of questions. When she couldn't answer any of the questions they had flown them in another plane up to Grandmother's house. Washington and New Bedford had looked just the way Paris had, like snapshots, people standing still in the streets, saying nothing, doing nothing, not even looking at one another . . .

Since then he had sat every day on the couch at Grandmother's house. Mother had cried, and Grandmother had not spoken. In front of them, every day, the television showed Berlin. It was just a big mound of rubble. Men in silver suits and helmets were clearing away the rubble. They looked like the old pictures of the first astronauts Timothy had seen in school. They found thousands of dead people. The television showed the bodies in green bags lined up as far and as wide as you could see. There had been too many to bury. They were burning them, thousands at once, using napalm dropped from planes. In the beginning some people had been still alive, buried under collapsed buildings. The television had showed some of them as they were carried to ambulances by the silver-suited men. Timothy had had a very bad thought about these people, a thought he had been ashamed to think: they looked like burned hamburgers, all black and raw red, hamburgers patted into the shapes of arms and legs. Of course no one had found any trace of Grandfather or Father or the American President or the leaders of Russia, or any of the people who had been at Grandfather's conference. On the very first day the man on the television had said that there was nothing left of them.

On the television now were big machines, backhoes, clearing the streets of rubble. Cascades of debris fell from their jaws into trucks. Timothy saw bones falling, vertebrae, ribs, skulls burned clean . . . and clouds of gray dust. Father and Grandfather. Mother covered his eyes. He tore her hands away and ran out of the room, out of the house, and he kept on running, his tears streaming from his eyes. He had to keep running. He would run until he could no longer hear Mother cry, until he could no longer feel Grandmother sickening and dying next to him, until what had been on the television was erased from his mind . . .

His foot struck a rock and he fell down hard. Thorns scratched his face as it smashed into the ground. He lay in the warm dirt and panted and felt his cheeks and chin first grow numb and then begin to sting. The pain made him cry more. He got to his feet and wiped dirt and blood from his face and tears from his eyes. He tried to stop crying, but he couldn't. Whenever he tried he thought of Grandfather and Father, and all the green bags going up in flames, and the people burned like black hamburgers, and the bones falling, and the silent people in Paris whom the cloud had killed when *he* had been saved. He should have shouted something from the car. He could have given them a chance . . .

He got to his feet and stumbled on, trying to get away from the house and the television. He didn't know where he was exactly; he was pushing through the weeds of a dead garden behind the house. Just ahead of him in the middle of the garden was a tree, a very old tree with big curving branches. Timothy climbed up into the tree and sat staring out over the ocean toward Europe, his home, where so many people had died. They had died and he was alive. He didn't want to be alive. He wondered how many more bombs would explode and how many more cities would disappear and how many thousands more people would die. Perhaps someday everyone on earth would be dead, if enough bombs went off. Then his tears came in torrents, and his breath in heaving sobs, until he had cried all that he could. Then he grew quiet, almost numb, in the arms of the tree, and thought of nothing for a very long time.

Suddenly he realized that it was almost dark. The evening sky was a horrible red. He had better get back to the house, or Mother would worry. He slid down the tree trunk to the ground and took half a dozen steps through the garden, then stopped. *Look at the tree.*

He turned around. Against the flaming sky of twilight the ancient oak spread out its branches in silhouette, impenetrably black, twisted with years, opening like compassionate arms to the sorrowful boy. A small center of calmness began to glow in Timothy. He gazed up at the tree and felt a healing power spread in him. And he saw . . . He blinked, wiped the tears from his eyes, and looked again. At the top of the tree was an old treehouse, just a rickety platform with half its boards gone. There was . . . A moment ago there had been no one there, and now — now there was. Someone was standing in the treehouse. A tall black silhouette, like the tree.

Timothy's throat got very dry. He came closer. Whoever it was did not move. Timothy came closer. He saw the face. The face was smiling at him, a kindly smile, and its blue eyes twinkled. Under the whispering leaves, in the immortal arms of the Tree, Timothy breathed the name.

Grandfather . . .

TIMOTHY

ACTA GALACTICA

PLANETARY SYSTEM: G1 DWARF
SECTION: LIFE-SUPPORTING PLANETS
PLANET 7-4-687

7-4-687 is one of two planets in the G1 system that supports life. Unlike the other life-supporting planet, 5-3-365, however, 7-4-687 has never evolved a life form more complex than a few varieties of lichen. The highly advanced, polygalactically adapted civilization that now inhabits 7-4-687 did not evolve under local planetary conditions.

The civilization of Planet 7-4-687 is in fact a foreign colony, an evolutionary offshoot of civilization on 5-3-365, founded by a small group from that planet who, after risking the great perils of space travel in the clumsy, primitive vehicles of their day, succeeded in arriving on 7-4-687 not long after their home planet had passed from its Planetary Adaptation phase into the more advanced phase of Galactic Adaptation. The convulsive nature of that transition, brought about by direct intervention of the Galactic Consciousness and necessitated by the wildly disoriented and dangerous course that evolution on 5-3-365 had taken (see entry for that planet), resulted in a period of complete stasis in that planet's affairs. During that time the mutant dominant institutions of the old planetary civilization destroyed their huge stockpiles of fusion weapons and subsequently were themselves destroyed by neglect, through the sheer indifference of their own populations. The people of 5-3-365 had already formulated new institutions more suitable to their new Galactic Adaptation (see

5–3–365, under Religion). Ultimately, evolution on 5–3–365 branched into two divergent paths, one remaining on the home planet, the other emigrating to 7–4–687.

The latter branch, eventually evolving for itself the name *Physian* (see under Science), chose its new home for its nearness, a moderate daytime temperature, and the presence of water. Faced with the serious problems of 7–4–687's inadequate atmosphere and the deep cold of its nights, however, Physians constructed large geodesic domes and filled them with the oxygen-rich atmosphere of their home planet. They continue to live inside these domes, and will do so until the surface of 7–4–687, which they organically seeded upon their arrival, can enrich its atmosphere with a level of oxygen sufficient for the peculiar gas-exchange process that keeps the organisms of Planet 5–3–365 alive. At that time they will dismantle their protective domes and take full possession of their adopted planet.

In the past, scholars in other systems who study the planets of the G1 Dwarf System engaged in a lively debate about which of the two branches of complex life — the aboriginal species inhabiting planet 5–3–365, or the colonizers of planet 7–4–687 — represent the "true" path of evolution in that system. There is now little doubt that those who left their original home are the ones who have continued to bring their system's evolution forward. Under their leaders, two members of the family unit used by the Galaxy in correcting the evolutionary errors of 5–3–365 (see 5–3–365, biographical entries, under Devlin), these colonizers have succeeded in passing rapidly from Galactic to Polygalactic Adaptation, attaining Unified Knowledge of the Field with remarkable speed, as well as the nonverbal, mathematical/musical descriptive language that this final phase of evolution requires. By contrast, those who remained on Planet 5–3–365 have rejected progress toward Polygalactic Adaptation in favor of maintaining their civilization at the less advanced Galactic phase (see 5–3–365, under Religion, subheading Schism).

The Galactic Consciousness therefore considers the evolution of life in the G1 Dwarf System not yet stabilized. Although the Galaxy's extreme measures appear to have corrected the dangerously deviant course of previous evolution on Planet 5–3–365, the unresolved and unstable relations between that planet's Galactic civilization and its superior Polygalactic neighbors remain a divisive weakness in the Field. It is apparent that the archaic Free Will element, long ago discarded as primitive by the other evolving systems of the Galaxy, continues to be dominant on planets of the G1 Dwarf. Therefore, the solution to the crisis — if a solution exists — will ultimately be found in this element, more than in anything more the Galaxy can do; for the laws of galactic evolution, contained in the infinity of the Field, hold that within any system's deepest flaw lies the key to its survival.

IT'S BEEN A VERY LONG TIME since I have seen that look. This morning, at the port, the First Master didn't recognize me. How could he? Long ago I gave my original body to the fusion torches to break down for reuse. But when I told him my name his serene composure vanished, though only for an instant. In that instant I saw the look, the stare of hate, that had followed me when I left the Earth and that now was welcoming me back.

It's my own fault, I suppose. Perhaps I should not have come at all. On one's own world it is easy to be idealistic. One forgets that here on Earth they are slow to forget and slower still to change. I blame myself now for not making an effort to cushion the shock of my return. I shouldn't have come in the form I occupy at home. But the female body lasts longer and wears better over time; it need not be exchanged as often. Nevertheless, I can see now that by returning as a woman I have doubled the First Master's surprise, and his anger as well. He was only a boy when I left, a junior acolyte, and I was already a young man. Now he is very old; by Terrestrial standards I cannot possibly be still alive.

Why do they sit in silence?

The question bursts into my mind and startles me, as though the two great doors I am facing, the doors of the Old Cathedral, had suddenly blown open. I am still not used to receiving mind-speech. Nor to answering it. Let me try. Who spoke? Yes. The legate from the Sigma Draconis System, on my right.

Friend, your question is a perceptive one. As you know, Physians and humans share the same religion, but we interpret our religion in very different ways. We Physians keep to an ancient belief that the understanding of a thing follows from the naming of it. Our Terrestrial relatives hold the equally ancient belief that the understanding of a thing vanishes when it is named. If in any of the solar systems represented in our delegation one of these contradictory beliefs has been proven wholly true and the other wholly false, I should like to know about it. In Terrestrial evolution it has never happened.

So you don't believe your own position?

In my opinion the Terrestrial position was a stronger one in the past, when word-speech was still the most advanced method of communication on Earth. I understand that humans don't use it very much anymore, since generations of meditative introversion have enhanced their intuitive powers to the point of mass telepathy and thus verbal communication is frequently unnecessary. Luckily for us, they have not quite developed mind-speech, which would require something absolutely taboo for them, a technological boost of intuition similar to the computer carapaces we Physians can now implant in our brains. I hope to explain the carapaces to them too, if they don't cover their ears at such blasphemies. You know what I mean, Sigma Draconis. Obstinacy is intergalactic. Didn't you tell me that some delegates from your system once had a similar problem on another planet?

I sincerely hope our problems are not similar. The delegates you are referring to were eaten.

Mind-speech is still odd to me; mind-laughter, especially the awful sounds that Sigma Draconis calls laughter, brings me near to vertigo. Hold on.

Don't worry, friend: my human cousins are only technologically primitive. In any case, you are protected culturally. Even before the Schism, Terrestrial courtesy forbade the eating of a guest. Among humans you are also protected by your appearance, which, I assure you, they find most unappetizing.

Originally everyone on Earth, Physians included, commemorated our Day of Light with silence. In our history, every religious ritual has been a moment out of Time, a transportation back to the original sacred event in which the annual ritual is founded. The religion of the Terrestrial Covenant, whose holiest day is the

Day of Light, is founded in the event called the Silence. The Silence was perhaps the profoundest moment in Terrestrial evolution, certainly as significant as other great evolutionary leaps, such as development of the human brain and human civilization. As you know from the galactic histories, before the Silence the human species, the advance guard of all Terrestrial evolution, was moving in a maladaptive direction. After the Silence, its evolutionary direction fundamentally changed.

I was a young boy then, in my first body, and I still remember it. After the fusion explosion, activity everywhere on the planet ground to a halt. For a little while the stillness was absolute. Humans everywhere were struck dumb with awe and fear. They gathered together and with their haunted eyes acknowledged the terrible and profound thing that had happened. No one spoke. Eventually, when we did speak again, we had become a species with a different evolutionary adaptation.

The old power hierarchies destroyed all of their fusion weapons, agreed not to produce any more, and then tried to continue with their old way of doing things, as if everything was the same again. But no one paid any attention to them. During the Silence we had made a decision, collectively, without speaking. In the Silence we had agreed to find a new adaptation, one that would no longer alienate us from our planet or our Galaxy. The Terrestrial Covenant is the articulation of that silent agreement.

And this Day of Light is what we are witnessing here today?

Correct. Since the Covenant, every year on this day, humans have assembled here in the Old Cathedral. When my grandfather was alive there was a very large city, a sizable concentration of humanity, in this place, where now there is only the cathedral and its sacred precinct. On the first Day of Light, nearly the entire population — including my grandfather and my father, who had unwittingly helped him — disappeared in the tremendous flash of the uncontrolled fusion reaction my grandfather had set off. So it is here and nowhere else that humans come to celebrate the beginning of their liberation from generations of blindness and error (as they see it).

Every year they arrange themselves just as you see them now, in great circles grouped like the petals of a flower around the central circle of the Masters, whom you see sitting a little above the others on the low dais. When all is quiet the First Master strikes a little bell, as you saw him do this morning, and the Commemoration begins. You are looking at it now; it continues before your eyes. Each Terrestrial you see has entered deep into his mind in search of the crystalline, irreducible essence of "all that he knows and all that is" — if a heretic may quote the old Covenant — and he will stay in his own mind, deeply silent, unaware of anything outside, until he finds it. Since this is a completely individual experience, it should not surprise you that among the Terrestrials the Day of Light often turns into Days of Light, perhaps even a Week of Light. Some of those you see assembled before you will be here all night, perhaps longer, oblivious of passing time. They won't even hear me later today when I recite our Physian narrative, which as overseer of the Physian Covenant I am required to do each year on the Day of Light, no matter what other business I have or where I happen to be. On that point, at least, Terrestrials and Physians would agree. However it is commemorated, the Day of Light must *be* commemorated. Commemoration is the First Principle of the Covenant, and on the Covenant all else depends. If we forget the Covenant we are lost, humans and Physians alike. We shall fall again into the old time of error, into the cycles, and be destroyed.

At the end of this silent day the First Master shall rise and strike his little bell again, a signal that the Day of Light has been commemorated, and all who wish to may disperse. Those who have not yet attained their commemorative realizations are free to stay until they do. It is a requirement of the orthodox faith that no time limit be set on the celebration of the holy day, no matter how impractical that may be. This provision is sacred indeed, for it derives from the Second Principle of the Covenant: that nowhere in the Galaxy can anything be known with certainty. Even the current practice of striking the bell and bringing Commemoration to a formal beginning and end is a late development, a concession to the practical need for schedules.

My uncle once told me that in the days before the Schism, when he was part of negotiations between Physians and Terrestrials, meetings were constantly interrupted as orthodox delegates dropped off into meditation without any warning, to seek tranquility and clarification at the peak of an emotional debate. My rather cynical uncle used to say that these unpredictable retreats into Mind seemed to occur at precisely the moment his side seemed about to carry its point and win a concession from the more liberal Terrestrials. Of course the meeting would be brought to a halt; when it resumed, the Physian argument would have lost its punch and the humans would have had time to regroup. But I have never begrudged them that. Despite everything, I have always had a certain weakness for the old orthodoxy. I like it when the sacred imposes itself upon the secular at the most inconvenient moment possible. It has always seemed to me that only the orthodox truly appreciate the meaning of the Covenant's Third Principle: that everywhere in the Galaxy, under any circumstances, the spiritual shall have primacy over the material. So I have tried never to disdain the pure Terrestrial religion, no matter how maddeningly impractical it is. In such impracticality the Covenant will be preserved, beyond what any Physian can do.

Look at them out there, still as stones. I think that when the First Master strikes the bell tonight, not many will leave. Most of them will still be struggling to reach the depth of meditation required for a Terrestrial Commemoration. Even for humans there have been too many distractions on the Day of Light.

Naturally you are referring to us.

The legate from Tau Ceti System is perceptive. Naturally I am. Before today no life from any other galaxy has visited the Earth, and now a Physian arch-heretic appears on the Day of Light with an intergalactic delegation at his side. And — pardon me, friends, but I must be frank — by Terrestrial standards you are most unusual-looking. For example, you, Tau Ceti, would in the system of Terrestrial taxonomy be classified as an insect, despite your size. Although, of course, Terrestrial taxonomy really has no classification at all for a form of life based on the silicon atom. On Earth silicon is used to make a utilitarian substance called glass. Also, remember that my presence on this planet is illegal. They have been gracious, yes. Humans are nothing if not gracious. But understand that it means nothing; their etiquette is a mask, an elaborate self-discipline that helps them concentrate their powers when threatened. It's a plumage display, an exquisite show of anxiety and alarm.

So you can imagine the number of questions our friends are

struggling to keep out of their minds during Commemoration. Of course they will not ask anything directly. A Terrestrial would rather die than ask a frank question, especially of a guest. Nor would any of them recover from the shame if they gave way to crude impulse and openly gaped at you, as I'm sure they desperately wish to do. Among them such a thing would be the height of bad manners. Do you remember what happened right after Contact, when your Tau Cetian delegation first visited our planet? My fellow Physians swarmed over you with cameras and calipers as soon as you appeared. Today your reception has been at the opposite extreme. What a difference a few generations of the Schism have made! It's hard to believe that humans and Physians were once a single civilization.

Harder for them than for you, I think.

Right again, Tau Ceti. Intergalactic visitors are not the only things distracting them today. You can see for yourselves the difference a lighter gravity has made to my body structure. Gravity plus reproductive isolation is already making Physians and humans into separate species. We are diverging, and today is the first hint they have had of it. Humans are not sophisticated in interplanetary matters. As a matter of orthodox principle they never travel beyond the atmosphere of their Earth. They are inward, nurturing, conservative creatures, suspicious of anything alien to their Terrestrial biosphere, and so their science is a science of organism and of mind, nothing else. There is probably nothing about carbon-based life — about themselves, that is — that Terrestrials do not know. The old man, the First Master, is perfect proof of their knowledge. I said he was a young man, an acolyte, when the Schism began. In the old system of Terrestrial reckoning, that was one hundred and twenty years ago, so the First Master is today nearly one hundred and fifty years old. When I was a child living on Earth before the Covenant, scarcely a member of our species survived past his eightieth year, and those who did were in a state of decrepitude that cannot be imagined today. But Terrestrial science, like everything else on Earth, is bounded by orthodoxy. There are limits beyond which it must not go. A human will never extend his life beyond its natural limit; his regimen of meditation and nutrition unifies his organism so completely that he lives two or three times longer than his alienated, overstressed forebears, but when his organism wears out — and most humans are so well attuned to their own inner processes that they know of this far in advance — he simply surrenders his life, quite gracefully, I must say, and piously returns his atoms to evolution's mill.

As you know, our science is very different. Our name, Physian, comes from one branch of the old Terrestrial word-speech; it means "the essence of a thing." In the days before the Covenant it was the name of a branch of Terrestrial science, the most important science of the old civilization, a science that probed beyond the Earth's biosphere into the fundamental nature of existence and tried to make it intelligible to the senses and thus to consciousness. Nothing could be more impious to a Terrestrial today! But the old civilization devoted its best minds and huge amounts of its resources to this effort. In fact, by the time I had my first birth, humanity was already approaching the crude beginnings of a Physian culture, but with that huge maladaptive flaw which was not corrected until the terrible suffering of the Day of Light.

O my friends, you who are so highly evolved, understand how astonished we were! After the Day of Light, when the species at last showed signs of desiring to get its evolution back on track, the Galaxy decided we had passed our test, and opened the minds of many to limited contact. What had formally come only to the chosen few now came to consciousness in the minds of millions. All over the world people began to have ideas, insights, sudden inspirations. They became aware of their own existence and the existence of everything around them in a deeper, subtler way. They began to understand that a Galactic Consciousness existed and presided over their destiny. Now we take all this for granted, as you have for so long, but then it was nothing less than miraculous.

My uncle Steven, who was one of the founders of our religion, used to insist that the species was experiencing the fulfillment of an old Terrestrial scripture. I remember him invoking the Council of the Covenant with it:

> And in the last days it shall be . . .
> That I will pour out my Spirit upon all flesh,
> And your sons and your daughters shall prophesy,
> And your young men shall see visions,
> And your old men shall dream dreams . . .

Later he made this the preamble to the Covenant. He said that in the Covenant what had been predicted had come to pass. In fact, what the old scripture had predicted *did* come to pass, over time, after the Covenant. The mind of the human species seemed to take an evolutionary leap forward. What had formally been divided into "consciousness" and "unconsciousness" and pursued separately as "science" and "religion" merged into a single greater awareness that transcended the old divisions.

The human and Physian civilizations of today owe themselves to the expanded capacities of this new mind. The Covenant that guides us both is a compact that acknowledges our containment in the greater intelligence of the Galaxy. The humans have developed their biospheric sciences and deep meditative faculties to the extent that they have now achieved a kind of contact with the other species who inhabit the Earth. The best of them can meditate themselves past the barriers of physical law into the consciousness of a dolphin or a flower, and hold telepathic conversation with it. And we Physians were able to solve a number of difficult problems in our science with unprecedented speed, at a time when our very survival depended on it.

More mind-speech. The Alpha Centauri legate wants to know how I became a Physian. He detects a certain ambivalence in my account of the Schism.

True enough. I was not always allied as I am now; in fact, early in my first life I was one of the leading opponents of the Physians.

What?

Sigma Draconis, Tau Ceti, and Alpha Centauri assault me at once. Luckily, the question is the same.

Please, don't shout, friends, inside a novice mind. Yes, it is true. What was revealed momentarily at the port this morning was not the simple hostility one feels in the presence of an enemy. It was the deeper hatred one feels toward a traitorous friend. And it's true; I did betray them. For years no one was a greater foe of the Physians than I. You must understand that I had seen my own father and grandfather die on the first Day of Light, and at that time the reason for my grandfather's action was completely unknown. All that was clear to me, and to everyone else, was that the two of them were completely responsible for a hideous tragedy. My guilt of course made me a fanatic; I felt an overwhelming need to make amends for what my father and grandfather had done.

I was also deeply influenced by my mother. Everything that you shall witness on this visit — the civilization that now prevails on this planet — owes its character in large measure to her. Yuzawa, the man who now is revered as the first Terrestrial Master, founded our religion on meditation and the rejection of word-speech; but it was my mother, Diana, who pushed harder than anyone for the formulation of an orthodox creed. Of course, in doing so she flagrantly violated the Covenant's Second Principle, a contradiction that, as I recall, never once troubled her. That she too was driven by guilt seems obvious to me now, but at the time she never spoke of guilt, and I, a son who worshiped her, never dared to ask.

Diana was truly formidable in those days. When the Silence was finished and people began to meet to talk over what had happened and why my grandfather had done such a terrible thing, she seemed to be at every meeting simultaneously, driving home again and again her conviction that the meaning of her father's act was to be found in certain things he had said in his final speech. Somehow she had gotten hold of one of the few videotape recordings of the speech, and she played it over and over for thousands of people. I used to run the machine for her, and she always made me stop the tape and rerun it at exactly the same spot, on the same phrase: *Our technology will destroy us.* My grandfather, she said, had done what he had done in order to discredit Physian science and to awaken a deluded humanity once and for all to the arrogance of Physian endeavors and the threat they posed to the continuation of Terrestrial evolution. My grandfather had intended, Diana said, for us as a species to heed his warning and cease from seeking to control the universe. He wanted us to make our science what it ought to be, the sustaining activity of our own evolution, which was our duty to the Galaxy. This was the choice my grandfather had pleaded with us to make before it was too late and Physian hubris brought annihilation.

When people learned who my mother was, that she was the daughter and the wife of the men who had exploded the fusion weapon, and that she was a qualified scientist as well, they began to listen to her. By the time of the first Commemoration, when the Council that promulgated the Covenant met on the site of the explosion, she had an enormous following.

At the council she sparked a fierce debate after the adoption of the Covenant's Fourth Principle, which pledges that the human species will never again interfere with Terrestrial evolution. She claimed that the Covenant outlawed any human endeavor beyond self-preservation and self-knowledge, and called on the Council to condemn Physian science officially.

The Physian delegates, who were rather an unworldly lot, were no match for her. I remember my poor uncle David arguing valiantly, running his own tape of my grandfather's speech past the technology-damning phrase that had by now become the watchword of a whole movement. He pointed out that what my grandfather had really said was that the path back to our true evolutionary course lay precisely through Physian science, properly pursued.

But for all their intellectual brilliance, my uncle and his colleagues were not capable of seeing that simple, observable facts count for very little in times of great suffering and fear. My mother understood what the species really felt. Not that she was cynically manipulating people — in fact, her power derived from exactly the opposite of a cynic's detachment: her deep, strong intuition of human realities. The currents surging through the world, supercharged with the anguish and terror of a billion hearts, flowed through her, and powered her. She became their engine, a device for transforming them into action, *any* action necessary to prevent Terrestrial life from ever being threatened again. And this life-preserving force that drove her was of course unstoppable.

Her final stroke was to place her most devoted follower — myself — in front of the Council to speak on her behalf. I was only eleven years old, and spoke with the simple straightforwardness of one my age. My words seemed to galvanize the feeling of the still ambivalent adults. The Council condemned Physian science as incompatible with the Principles of the Covenant and declared it a threat to Terrestrial evolution. The old man Yuzawa was appointed to oversee the Covenant and celebrate the Commemorations, and my mother was asked to head a commission to reform human science by merging its goals with the spirit of the Covenant. My other uncle, Steven, who was one of the authors of the Covenant and who had arduously opposed the movement to condemn the Physians, resigned from the Council in despair and died not long afterward, though he was still a relatively young man, even by the standards of those days. My uncle David never spoke to my mother again.

Was it so wrenching, Tau Ceti, so tragic and divisive, when your species came to the stage of Galactic Consciousness? No, I suppose not. The nuclear family seems to be a rather rare trait. As you know, we Physians have abandoned it. Yes, yes, Sigma Draconis, I agree: whether the emotions of those otherwise bonded run any less deep is indeed another story. But to get back to the present one . . .

After their condemnation by the Council, the Physians were forced into a rather shadowy existence. The practice of their science was not illegal, but that was irrelevant; after the Day of Light no one paid much attention to the old civilization's laws. No one disobeyed them, but no one obeyed them, either. They just didn't matter anymore, because the institutions that had made them didn't matter. What did matter was the Covenant. The Covenant was all humanity had in those days, and once the Physians had been judged to be in violation of it, they were nothing less than a threat to humanity's very survival. Mass public disapproval effectively prevented them from pursuing their science.

Meanwhile the human species gradually began to build a new civilization based on the Principles of the Covenant. The site of the bomb explosion was declared to be sacred and the cathedral was built on it. Master Yuzawa, who lived to an exceptionally advanced age and earned the reverence of all, took up residence there and established the Commemorations of Awakening and Light. He taught that the tragic evolutionary errors of our species were the result (as my grandfather had declared in his final speech) of a false perception of divisions between our minds and our bodies and between ourselves and the universe. He taught the disciplines of meditation and silence as a liturgical path to overcoming these divisions. Unity, he said over and over again, was the true essence of the Covenant, beyond any of its words.

My mother's commission issued the Declaration of the Goals of Science, which limited research to understanding the Terrestrial biosphere and improving human and all planetary life. And I grew to manhood, serving as an acolyte at the cathedral and zealously ferreting out the underground Physians. By the time I was twenty-one years old — shortly before the twentieth cycle ended and the twenty-first cycle began — the old nations and their institutions had completely disappeared. People had gathered into smaller, more manageable city-states, each with a code of ethics based on the Covenant and on economic pursuits that suited the shared inclinations of its citizens. In most of these city-states Physian science had been legally outlawed, and only in a few of the most liberal places could Physians work; even there they were merely tolerated, not encouraged. But of course there were Physians working everywhere in secret, and I, fervently committed to the Covenant, made it my business to find them and bring them to the attention of the civil authorities. I organized a planetwide network of earnest young people who felt as I did — spies, in a word — and together we vowed to eradicate the Physian threat once and for all from the Earth.

I was a real hothead, let me tell you. I was sure that the guardianship of the Covenant was in my hands, and that I alone was keeping our new civilization from falling back into the evolutionary errors of the cycles. It bothered me a little that Master Yuzawa never once thanked me or praised my work, or even acknowledged it. "Unity is everything, or the Covenant is nothing" was all he would say, looking past me, whenever I mentioned what I was doing. But my mother was very proud of me, and to me it was her opinion, and not Yuzawa's, that mattered.

My group and I did our work well. We exposed dozens of Physians and their clandestine laboratories. The councils of the city-states destroyed their research and put them to work on projects in nutrition or psychology or neonatology, or any of the other approved, biospheric sciences. But then one day, when I was about to leave with my cohorts to visit one of the notoriously tolerant city-states and convince the citizens there to outlaw the Physians, something very unusual happened to me.

It happened at almost the exact spot where we are now standing. I was in the cathedral, in the evening. I had paused on my way out to ponder the quotations from the Covenant that you can still see inscribed above us, along the walls. I had just read the one you see in the center, below the large representation of the symbol of the Covenant: *Split a piece of wood, and I am there. Lift up a stone, and you will find me there.* Master Yuzawa had had those words inserted in the Covenant and inscribed on the cathedral, and he must have repeated them a thousand times to his classes of acolytes. They have an interesting history, by the way: they come from the writings of a very ancient sect called the gnostics, or "those who know," who existed on Earth over twenty cycles ago. The writings of the gnostics were banned by the religion of the old civilization, just as the science of the Physians was banned by the religion of the new one, and were hidden away in a desert region of our planet and forgotten. They were rediscovered only a few months after the second of our uncontrolled nuclear reactions destroyed the ancient city of Hiroshima — a timing that was not a coincidence to Master Yuzawa, who never tired of saying that if any words could express the essence of the Covenant, they were the words of the gnostics.

At any rate, my mother also revered that quotation, and had made her interpretation of it the guiding criterion for all future science, which had to learn to nurture even the humblest particles of the biosphere as sacred entities, not manipulate and exploit them as the Physians had done. Between Yuzawa and my mother I had heard the words so many times that I used to recite them over and over again in my mind, like a prayer, while dwelling on their profoundly beautiful meaning. So I was doing that evening, while pondering the inscription, when suddenly I realized that the voice reciting inside my mind was not my own.

I tried to stop reciting and think of something else, but I couldn't — or rather, *I* could, but the voice persisted in the recitation, quite independently of me. I can still remember the moment of sheer panic I felt before I got control of myself and listened to the voice. It was an old man's voice, creaking and quiet, and not at all frightening, but quite kind. Nonetheless, you can appreciate that it was quite unnerving for me — having then no capacity whatsoever for mind-speech — to experience a completely independent presence inside my own mind.

After some frozen moments I got up the courage to think a responding thought: *Who are you?*

Grandfather, said the voice, and my heart nearly stopped, because I had recognized it. It was the old voice on the videotapes, played over and over again in my boyhood.

Do you remember the Tree, Timothy? the voice said, and now I was sure. Not long after the first Day of Light, when I was still very frightened and upset, I had climbed an old tree at my grandfather's house and thought for a strange moment that I had actually seen his spirit in the treetop, smiling down at me. I had long since put the moment out of my mind, as a childish fantasy brought on by grief. But I had also been careful never to tell anyone about it. No one could have known.

Grandfather, I thought nervously, *let me see you.*

I am everything you see and cannot see, said the voice. *I am Unity. You are persecuting the ones who will fulfill the Covenant.*

I was stunned; I didn't know what he meant.

Grandfather, I pleaded, *let me see you again.*

You shall not see me, said the voice, *until you have become what you hate.* Then it was gone; there was nothing in my mind except my own frightened thoughts.

A moment before I had been on my way home to pack for my Physian-hunting trip. Now, instead, I sat down on the cathedral floor and was quiet, as Master Yuzawa had taught me to be. When you must confront a problem, he used to say, be silent until you are unified, and there will be no more problem to confront — by which he meant that when it is unified, the human organism finds the solution. Well, I knew perfectly well what the solution was: my grandfather's voice had commanded me to become a Physian, one of the people he had sacrificed himself — and so many others — to save us from. How was it possible? I had the impulse to run to my mother and tell her what had happened, as I always had done when troubled; but I couldn't bring myself to confess to her that I had even imagined such a thought. In fact, the idea of becoming a Physian was so obscenely impious to me that it couldn't have come from my own imagination. Which meant that Grandfather . . .

I sat miserably for a while in silence, trying quite unsuccessfully to become unified, my head buzzing with frantic denials. Looking back now, I think I was like a man who sees a tidal wave coming and tries to build a brick wall in time to stave it off. Then, suddenly, in a moment as startling and overwhelming as the explosion on the first Day of Light, the wave arrived, and all my denials were swept away. I knew in an instant, beyond any doubt, that the years of my anti-Physian fervor had been one long falsehood.

Whether the voice I had heard had been Grandfather's or my own, it had spoken the truth. The wave washed over me; at the center of the cathedral, at the place of unity and serenity, I fell apart, and burst into tears.

The next day I left on my trip as scheduled. But as soon as I arrived at my destination I slipped away from my comrades and went to the Physians.

You can imagine the reception they gave me. When they found out that their arch-persecutor had had a sudden change of heart and wanted to learn their science, they were more than skeptical, and hardly disposed to listen to my pleas. I tried to explain the reason for my sudden conversion, but somehow it came out all wrong, as if I were just making up some preposterous story about a voice. The leading Physians met and decided that I was simply trying to win their confidence in order to spy on them. They told me to go away.

But fortunately for me, the Physians were not vindictive by nature. My uncle David, whom I hadn't seen since the Council of the Covenant ten years before, was one of the Physians living in that city. After I had been officially spurned by the Physian community he invited me to his house. He had never forgotten my speech before the Council, he told me, but he had forgiven it, in consideration of my age and the enormous influence my mother had had over me. He had known me as a child and had always believed that my true nature was not the one I had always displayed. But if I wanted Physians to trust me, I had to prove my commitment to them — if I had the courage to do so.

"I would do anything," I said.

"Then go back to your friends," my uncle said. "Make your speeches against us. Make them good ones. In a week's time come again to my house. Tell no one."

Completely baffled by this strange way of proving myself, I nevertheless obeyed. I made rousing anti-Physian speeches, which I saw had good effect; the tolerant citizenry seemed noticeably less so by the time we left. When I returned to the cathedral my mother gave me a hero's welcome. I kissed her and tried not to look her in the eyes. A few days later I packed some things and waited for nightfall so that I could leave my quarters and sneak back to the airport.

When the moment arrived I opened my door — and found myself staring at Master Yuzawa, who had been waiting for me just outside. Master Yuzawa was nearly ninety years old and his eyesight was failing, but he missed nothing that went on around him. Somehow I had let slip some hint of my secret intentions, and he had picked it up and come to stop me.

I dropped my bag and began to stammer lies. Master Yuzawa bent his frail old body, picked up my bag, and gave it back to me. Then he said to me for the hundredth time, "Unity is everything, or the Covenant is nothing." But this time he looked right at me when he said it, and smiled. By the time I could comprehend that he really *did* know my intentions and had come to give me his blessing, he had vanished.

I arrived at my uncle's house just before dawn. When he opened the door and saw me he smiled and shook my hand, and explained nothing. The others, the men and women who a week before had rejected me, were gathered in his home. They all had suitcases. When they saw me they smiled too, and nodded to my uncle. No one said a word to me. They left the house and took me with them. It was like falling into a river of black night and riding the current. I was carried through the darkness to a field, then into a helicopter. The helicopter took off. Still no one spoke. We flew east, into the dawn light, and in a little while I could look down and orient myself. We were passing over flat, swampy ground, then water, then more swamp. Then over old cracked concrete, choked with weeds. We were landing.

I got out with the rest and was pushed forward as everyone started to run, their suitcases awkwardly cradled in their arms. I ran too. Then I saw what we were running toward, and I stopped. It was a rocket, obviously big enough to clear the Earth's gravity, with a large capsule on top.

You must understand how shocked I was. The Council of the Covenant, at my mother's instigation, had specifically condemned Physian efforts to perfect space travel as a threat to evolution, second only to the perfection of fusion and fission weapons. It was clear to me now that we had landed at one of the old Physian space-research centers, theoretically shut down and abandoned since the Council of the Covenant. They must have been out there secretly all the time, preparing their rocket.

My uncle turned around and saw me staring and finally spoke: "For years we have been working toward this day." Then he grabbed my arm and brought me along to keep up with the others. We had to stay together, because the Physians' secret had leaked out and an enormous crowd of very angry people had gathered around the rocket. I saw at once that the departure had been arranged in advance with the local council (which was doubtless glad to be rid of any Physians in its jurisdiction); security forces were present, and the crowd would not be allowed to attack us. But they hurled rocks at us — one cut my uncle badly on the head — and shook their fists and screamed abuse, straining the barricades to get at us as we passed through. There were many who recognized me, for I had been making anti-Physian speeches to them only a week before. When they saw me they fell silent in surprise, until they understood what had happened. Then their cries of "Traitor!" and "Counter-evolutionary!" (which is what we called Physian heretics then) rang in my ears.

I helped my uncle onto the rusting gantry elevator, and its doors shut. With a jerk we started upward.

"Where are we going?" I asked my uncle.

"To Mars," he whispered, holding his bleeding head.

Beneath us the angry crowds had finally pushed past the barricades and were surging around the gantry. I looked down at their faces, the last thing I would remember of the Earth, and I saw in them a look of pure hatred, a look I did not see again until today . . .

What are they doing now?

It's extraordinary, Tau Ceti. The First Master has struck the bell. For the first time ever they have cut short the Commemoration. They have given up. We're too much of a distraction, even for them . . .

The Masters are coming forward. It appears that something even more extraordinary is about to happen. I think they are about to set aside the elaborate strictures of their etiquette in order to ask me, plainly and directly, the question that has destroyed even their monumental concentration: *Why have you come back?*

This is just what I had hoped for. If they ask me, I can answer them. I can tell them what we have achieved on Mars, and offer them what they have always sought. I offer them the Unity — not the pious ideal of it, the *fact* of it.

On Mars we were free to work on everything the Terrestrial Covenant had condemned, free to worship the entire Galaxy, as we believed my grandfather had intended. And at the very end of his life my uncle presented us with the ultimate achievement of all Physian science, which was also, we now know, the fulfillment of my grandfather's plan. He gave us the Unity, the Field. Now we know that final truth which all of you have known so long: that everything, reality, is one great Field of Forces, infinite and eternal, outside of Time, underlying space and all things known and unknown.

In the Field I have been one with all the Forces. I have seen my mind's dreams become gravity and my thoughts pass into electricity; I have felt the bonding force of atoms. I have stood outside of Time and seen in an instant the completeness of all reality. I have understood what my grandfather was, and his grandfather before him, and all the others who came before. I saw you, Tau Ceti, and Sigma Draconis, and Alpha Centauri, and knew that in the Field we existed as one; and I made the first Contact. And I have seen that which above all else I have come back to tell them — I have seen that the great symbol of the Covenant, the one you see above you now, dominating the Old Cathedral, is a Force also. The great four-armed spiral called swastika, which for generations has been worshiped by the whole Terrestrial population, is the Force of our Galaxy itself.

Terrestrial orthodoxy has always interpreted each swastika arm as a symbol of each of the Covenant's Four Principles. But in the Field I saw that the swastika has an infinite number of arms, as our Galaxy has, spiraling out its life. Our consciousness, Cain's divided mind, can see only four, as it can see only a fraction of light on an infinite spectrum. But the swastika is the dim image of a memory in our deepest Mind, the oldest memory we have — the memory of how we began, and where we shall end. It is the energy of one infinity, dispersed into galaxies when the universe expanded so long ago, remembering itself as it wanders in its dark prison of Matter, struggling to come home.

It is this that I bring to the people of Earth: the knowledge of what all evolution is and has been and will be — the struggle of energy striving to be free of an exile of countless forms, to gather itself together, to reunify, to be again One. With this knowledge we are ready to evolve as Grandfather intended us to evolve after the first Day of Light. There shall be no more Schism, because all schisms are false. All Terrestrials, all Physians, and all else that exists are quanta of energy, seeking the Field. When we have joined together again we shall find it, and come home. We shall know the last days of our long exile in Time. In the field we shall Be; we shall sing forever our long strange story to the Galaxy, for its pleasure; our voices shall blend with yours, dear friends, into eternity. For the galaxies love good stories, and that is what we are: stories spun by vast intelligences spiraling through space. Clever riddles they have made from Matter, to pass the long night of their exile. Random thoughts scratched on the walls of a prison of gas and dust, some cherished, others erased. Tiny engrams encoded in one ultimate Mind. In the Field, after so long, we shall remember what we really are. It is what I have come back to tell them. Abel has returned.